To the
Opera Ball

Books by *Sarah Gainham*

TO THE OPERA BALL

MACULAN'S DAUGHTER

TAKEOVER BID

PRIVATE WORLDS

A PLACE IN THE COUNTRY

NIGHT FALLS ON THE CITY

SILENT HOSTAGE

STONE ROSES

APPOINTMENT IN VIENNA

COLD DARK NIGHT

TIME RIGHT DEADLY

To the
Opera Ball

SARAH GAINHAM

DOUBLEDAY & COMPANY, INC.

GARDEN CITY, NEW YORK

1977

Library of Congress Cataloging in Publication Data

Gainham, Sarah.
   To the opera ball.

   I. Title.
PZ4.G1425To4   [PR6057.A34]   823'.9'14

ISBN: 0-385-12133-4
Library of Congress Catalog Card Number: 76-2773

This book is for
DOREEN MARSTON
who first thought of it

This book is fiction and the persons in it never existed. However, the fact that I have allowed myself one or two minor liberties with the organization of real institutions such as the Opera Ball Committee should not be taken as evidence that historical facts have been altered or that anything that happens in this book was impossible or even unlikely in its time and place in the real world.

S.G.

Act One

FATHER AND DAUGHTER

CHAPTER 1

The aircraft landed punctually in the early afternoon at Vienna, but there being no direct flight that day, the journey had been a quite complicated one and Mme. Chavanges was tired. A headache remained from Zurich where the company employee delegated to supervise their onward passage turned out to be inexperienced and talkative, a combination of faults inconvenient when traveling. Instead of the unnoticeable transfer which usually took place on the rare occasions when the president of the company's wife journeyed alone, there was a confused bustle and somehow they were caught up in the machinery intended for unprivileged passengers. The international transit arrangements at Zurich airport, although notably efficient of their kind, are complicated for those unused to managing their own tickets, passports, and luggage, and can produce a sensation of nervousness amounting almost to panic when compounded by irritation at the incompetence of others. This nervousness becomes humiliating when nobody else in the whole crowded scene seems to share it but, on the contrary, all are calmly concentrated on their own affairs and oblivious of others. They may well feel nervous, those others, but they certainly do not look it; they look competent, practical, as if they know what they are doing and where they should be doing it. Above all they are so equal as between each other that those few who rarely notice their own exclusiveness may receive a disproportionate shock from being for an hour simply citizens like any others.

However, the chauffeur who met them at the end of the journey was both familiar and efficient and the airport being a small one, the process of being put on land was fast, quiet and not at all crowded. If it had not been for the way the official stared at Leona neither immigration nor customs would have been noticed, and as for baggage they did not this time even need to ask about it and still less to handle any of it.

It was on entering the hotel at last that Leona's mother felt again that day, and with great force, the difference made by the two years her daughter had been away from home. A group of men standing discussing something in the inner hall of the hotel all turned, one after the other, to stare at the girl. The woman from whom Leona inherited many of her physical characteristics might not have been present; and since she was barely thirty-eight years old herself and until a week before looked upon her only child as just that, a child, this was startling, almost unnerving. It had come so suddenly that she could not take it in and the repeated signs of the change struck her as insulting. Leona was grown up and grown too into a flowering of looks so entirely in harmony with the contemporary notion of feminine beauty that she might have been standing as model for a conceptual Girl. To describe Leona would be to conjure up the tall, perfectly healthy, open freshness of a wonderfully cultivated and trained human animal. She might just have changed her clothes after coming off a ski slope, but not one of the nursery kind. In fact only a week before this they were at Mégève where Leona won the amateur ladies slalom with that same ease and grace with which she had come first, with just enough points against her performance to make it endearing, in the Strasbourg horse show dressage competition last autumn. But then Leona went back to school and even last week the shock did not quite take place. Not so near home, where

4

Leona's parents were treated with the deference due to riches and where Leona was treated as their daughter; that is, as not a real person.

But now, with superb unconsciousness, Leona walked into the oval hall not in the least as if she were following her mother but with a confident expectation of enjoyment that was all her own. The effect was created simply by her arrival, without her doing anything or knowing there was anything she might have done to enhance it, such as throwing back her hair, or speaking clearly or laughing aloud; she became unquestionably the one who entered and her mother was in a moment reduced to the lady-in-waiting who enters first to prepare the way.

The disorientation was the greater because Leona's mother had married so young that she never went through the period when she might have been a beauty for herself or anyone else. Before she was aware of being a girl she was engaged, out of the running. And that by the agreed action of her elders. She never discovered herself as a person separate from her father and mother before an engagement long planned was followed at once by marriage so that her own will was not involved in decision. Then and later her wishes, hardly known as such, did not operate beyond the details of minor tastes and occasional caprices.

Meanwhile the two ladies crossed the lavishly carpeted, furnished, and flower-decked space, preceded by a bowing servant and followed by a spreading silence deeper than the seemly quiet of a well-run establishment. This silence acquired the quality of that soundless sigh in a theater as the curtains open on a luxurious stage set where the unquestioned center of the play is already standing, doing something by herself as if the audience were not there at all.

The group of men in the hall were all of a certain age, all garbed in dark clothes, all of that dominating calm of manner that belongs to men who manage large affairs. Their speech, the American of the eastern seaboard and the German of Frankfurt, did not cease abruptly but seemed to die away and banking was for a long moment forgotten.

The women reached the lifts before Leona spoke.

"It seems quite strange to be here again, doesn't it? And in a hotel?"

"And cold! I'd forgotten. That sky! I really do feel that the Ambassador might have asked us to stay with them."

"Protocol, Daddy said."

"They always do say that. You want to go straight up?"

"Oh, you think not?"

"We might have some tea down here. But no, perhaps not. We'll unpack first."

"We must take the dress-frames up with us. Do you think they're all right?"

"They are just coming, Madame," said the lift operator. "That is why we wait for a little minute. Here is the page now."

A half-grown boy in livery came across the hall. In each hand, extended upward to the full length of his arm, he carried by the hook a plastic dress cover with a metal frame, inside which shimmered the costly promise of silks, on the left all of white and on the right of a soft and brilliant pink.

"Good," said the lift man with satisfaction. "But take them up in the other passenger lift. I have no room here."

The doors closed on their figures and the two lifts rose silently.

"French," said one of the group left below in the hall.

"Come for the Opera Ball."

"What an absolute corker, the girl."

The other men seemed half to frown at this. She was too absolute to be called by any slang name. And the man who said it with a slightly intimidated bravado appeared himself to feel that his comment was in poor taste. He cleared his throat and took out his cigarette lighter, only noticing when he had flicked it into flame that there was no cigarette to be lighted.

"A heap of money there," murmured one of the German bankers with a brisk little sideways nod of certainty.

"You know them?"

"No, but the look, the aura of wealth. Don't you find? That is always unmistakable."

They had moved over to the porter's lodge and that dignitary now answered a question.

"The lady is Madame Chavanges de Faulemont, gentlemen. He was in the Embassy here until a few years ago, when his father died. Then he resigned to take over the management of the family businesses."

"Ah. And the young lady?"

"I do not recall the young lady. But clearly, the daughter of Madame, there is such a strong resemblance."

None of the group had noticed the resemblance because nobody had looked at the mother; she was only a figure accompanying the girl.

"I feel awfully tired suddenly. I shall have a bath and sleep for a while." The two women were moving to and fro between their rooms, carrying various garments and toiletries with the help of a maid from the hotel. "We should have brought somebody with us. I said so all the time."

"Well, Mamma, it would look . . ."

"Yes, nowadays one has to be ashamed of such things. I find it all very inconvenient."

"What time will Papa be in?"

"About seven, he said. What shall you do?"

"I'll go to the rehearsal, I think. You know, we decided I'd better."

"Oh yes, I think you'd better, certainly. You may have forgotten the rites and formalities in the two years since you were here. And of course, they may have changed something, too."

"You sound as if it's all rather silly, now we're here," Leona replied equably to her mother's sarcasm. "Yet you looked forward to coming."

"No, no, darling. I'm just a little tired, that's all. Of course I wanted to come and to bring you. It seems so suitable for you to come out here too, since we know so many people here and everything."

"And they do have these marvelous presentation balls here! I've been looking forward to it for simply years."

"If only one did not need to fly. So rough, it was. I have a headache."

"Have a little snooze, then. I shall draw your curtains and I'll tell them as I go out not to disturb you. Pity you so hate flying. I just love it. I mean to ask Papa again if I can learn to fly. He's so fussy about me."

"It's dangerous." The explanation had the perfunctory sound of quoted words.

"I know, that's what he says. But not more than skiing. Or hunting if he knew, only he never saw, because it was in England."

"You're further from the ground, you see."

"True. That's what I like about it. Do you want anything, dearest? Coffee, a drink?"

"No, nothing. Ah, that's better. I shall relax for an hour. But you promise to be back well before seven?"

"Yes, of course I will be. You can rest without worrying."

Leona closed the door quietly for she was a considerate child, and within two minutes shed her conventional traveling clothes and slid into the uniform of the young. In black, close-fitting trousers and a many-colored sweater her looks were even more strikingly splendid than when equipped as the well-brought-up daughter of rich and careful parents. Now she could have passed as one of the groups of students just then leaving the University and drifting about their various occasions in the inner city, to the places where they always did go. She could see among the press of traffic

and of other people who did not count because they were already
grown up, groups and couples of young people who looked like
herself, and she knew where they came from and where they were
going. But she was not going to study. That was already decided
upon and she felt a strong envy that amounted to rebelliousness.
She looked now just like the others; her beauty was not lost but
neutralized by her uniform. But although she wore tight pants on
her incredibly long, lean legs, and although her hair was now as
loose and untidy as any other eighteen-year-old's and although she
wore a fur-lined "Bomber" just as they did, she was not one of
them as she longed to be. She could have mingled with them,
gone where they went, for the youth international does not invent
barriers and she spoke their language like her own and with their
own drawling accent. She did not, for with a prudence beyond her
years she knew that such a mingling would certainly be interrupted and then she would feel her isolation even more. Papa
would not like it. Sometimes she said Daddy, being so freely
many-tongued, but the purport was always of some scarcely operated and never explained restraint. So she envied them, focusing
her jealousy on their dirty sheepskins which she did not wear; so
far from any superiority attaching to her denim "Bomber" lined
with fox skins, she would gladly have changed it for one of those
greasy wide jackets with embroidery on the outside and the shaggy
fur inside. But even if her mother did not notice and joke about
it, her father would and then he would frown and she would be
quietly stopped from her new friendships in which the exchange
of jackets held no undertones of bargaining but was simply a matter of which one preferred at the moment. So easier not enter
these possible unities. It had been better in England, where Papa's
voice hardly reached. But school was over. And University would
not begin. Oh stop it, she said in her self-dialogue, you can't
change things. Anyway it will be nice here for a few days where
nobody takes any notice.

At this point Leona fled across a narrow street and into a still narrower one and was engulfed in a flood of her contemporaries who were all trying to get through a dark and narrow door at the same time. Now she felt herself to belong, a temporary belonging for this particular purpose only, but still, better than nothing.

It was the same dancing school she went to during two periods of her changeable schooldays, first as a small girl still at the elementary stage, then after a gap of some years, at the French Lycée in the old Clam Gallas palace. And like all her schools, it was wonderfully mixed, forming a cross section of families devoted to tradition or ambition; the retention of social graces or their acquiring. The children of scrap-dealers and barterers of the postwar period who had made fortunes mingled with sons of old bourgeois professional families, with the offspring of politicians, of foreign diplomatic representatives and the servants of multinational companies and with young people, some of them very poor, who carried historic and ancient titles. The secret of the continuing success of this place which survived almost intact from the old monarchy into the world of two generations after its disappearance was that without its imprint it was impossible to be included in the opening ceremonies of one or other of the great assemblies of the winter season and thus emerge into the adult world with the guarantee of acceptance. One might take part in the cotillion of the Philharmonic or the Opera Ball or of others in a descending scale of magnificence only through the narrow door behind which an extraordinary survival of another world insisted on formal manners, stylized movements, precise etiquette, at least for the hours spent under the tutelage of a frowning little elderly gentleman and his serious assistants.

It goes without saying that almost everyone concerned made fun of the principal of this school, and especially his pupils affected at least unconcern if not scorn or a show of rebellion at parental orders. That was part of the process, but they took it seriously enough when under the old man's faded but attentive eye and in many cases not only to please their mothers and to gain access to the presentation formalities. The long shadow of an ancient prestige, the chill of the crypt of the Past where power and fame and the history of half Europe lay buried, continued here in trivialities the forms that once ruled many millions. It would be a bold eighteen-year-old who could stand in front of the Crown of that empire upon which "the sun never set" long before the English borrowed the proud phrase, and not feel a touch of secret awe. With white cotton gloves and pointed toe the old dancing master indicated distantly that Crown for which their fathers for nearly a thousand years lived and died. It was a joke all right, but a joke at which the laugher looked over his shoulder in case he should be overheard by tremendous ghosts.

A flurry of recognitions and greetings was interrupted by a thin, insistent voice. Lists were consulted in the cramped and dusty office and Leona's participation confirmed with much headshaking at her having missed the preparations and having certainly forgotten everything. Moreover her appointed partner was not present. Leona would have to be paired at the rehearsal with a stranger whose own young lady was also not there that day. For the hundredth time the young ladies and gentlemen were reminded not to address each other familiarly or with pet names as if they were still children. The incongruously dressed, and that was most of those present, were once more frowned upon, but at last with much fussing and trimming of lines the rehearsal of the cotillion could begin. The pianist in her old brown stuff dress, with a dim cameo so high up on her shriveled throat that it scratched her chin if she looked down, struck a chord. The anthem of the republic rang tinny on the ear for the piano was a wretched old thing, and everyone stood still trying not to look rigid, while the dancing master mimed the entrance of the presidential party into their box. With held breath, remembering not to catch their underlips in their teeth as they concentrated, careful to hold the retired foot so that it would not catch in the hem of the still unworn gown, the girls sank down somewhat raggedly in deep curtseys.

"Oh no," wailed the dancing master. "Oh no, this will never, never do. This won't do at all. It is scandalously bad. You look like a gaggle of market women. You are simply terrible. I cannot take the responsibility for such a confusion."

He leaned his forehead on his white cotton glove. Just like the White Rabbit, thought Leona, with an instant's vision of the English part of her education.

"Please," he begged, "I implore you, ladies, relax your shoulders, breathe evenly, count slowly. Heads up, but not stiffly, eyes forward but don't *glare* like that. Now, let us go back for a moment to what you should not need any longer: that is, to counting aloud. Now. One, two, three . . ."

The clear young voices counted, the lithe young bodies bent their knees, the heads of the young men bowed forward, the hands of the partners just touched. With tremors and jerks rippling the lines and eyes rolling sideways like half-trained ponies to judge the distances, they tried again.

"You must not look sideways. How often do I have to say that? Your hands tell you that you have enough space. The young lady in the third row who persists in moving forward a whole step—a whole step—will oblige me to hobble her ankles like a trotting pony if she cannot control herself. Now. Again. Good heavens above, now she is lurching sideways. Stop. Drop your heads, pull on the back muscles. Breathe deeply. Now, hands out. Think what you are doing. Count slowly, don't move your lips when counting. One, two, three . . ."

They were still practicing when the Ball Committee arrived. Anyone whose dress or evening suit was not already in the dancer's possession was singled out, telephone numbers were written down for checks to be made. Those not present were noted, whereby a list was consulted of participants whose absence was accounted for and who were pledged to be in the opera house at the appointed time on the following evening and these were ticked off. The others would all be followed up. Among those accounted for was Leona's partner.

His sonorous title was pronounced and the secretary of the august lady who headed the Ball Committee assured Leona that Kari Lensky's absence from the rehearsal was caused by his being on duty.

"He telephoned me himself this very morning," she said impressively.

"I think Kari might have called me or left a message at the hotel," said Leona discontentedly when their elders had left. "He was supposed to come to the Strasbourg horse show last September and didn't turn up."

"Oh, Kari, he's been a bit odd lately," said a rangy girl as tall as Leona with a flood of black hair and wide, dark eyes.

"He's all right. Just doesn't like doing his military service."

"He did get called up, then? I didn't even know that."

"Of course, after he flunked out of the University. What an idiot!"

"One way and another, he was lucky to get commissioned," offered a blond boy, creasing up his round face in an image of dubiety.

"But why?" asked Leona. "What's he been doing?"

"Nothing really. Just a bit crazy. You know how he is."

"All the Lenskys are wild in youth," said the blond boy sententiously, quoting his father.

"You coming on to the movies, Leona? The new Buñuel's at the Burg Kino. I hear it's super dirty."

"Can't. My father will be back about seven and I haven't seen him for a week."

"What's he doing here?"

"Something with east–west trade. He's concentrating on that at the moment."

"Who isn't? It's the commandment of the hour. Dreary, I call it."

"Those things like knucklebones you use for electricity. What d'you call them, Toni?"

"How would I know?" asked Toni grandly. "I'm doing art history."

"I can't remember what they're called."

"Anyway, they are for Russia, about two million of them."

"What are you doing next week? I say, Leo, come to St. Anton with us. We're all going. The snow's a dream, my brother says. We could have a ball."

"I'll see what they say. When?"

"Next Tuesday we're off."

"Tuesday. Yes, it might work. I'll let you know."

"Tomorrow then. I have to tell my gran we'll be one more. It's their house so I have to sort of let them know."

"Of course. I'll tackle them tonight."

"I say, it would be dreamy!"

"I'm panting to. I'll fix them."

Without anyone suggesting it, they moved in a body to a tiny café farther down the narrow lane between high, age-blackened houses which shut out the daylight even in summer. It was now quite dark. The cold was the deep chill of frozen, invisible snow and the sky that leaned in the afternoon a leaden purple on the city was now a low bowl enclosing it, to be seen only as the dispersed reflection of light thrown upward. It was hot in the low, vaulted room, a heat that struck solidly on entering. They shed their jackets one after the other, seeming to tumble about in the small space like a litter of puppies. They drank Coca-Cola and syrupy fruit juices with soda water and prattled like children all together in voices that swung from adult speech to youthful singsong and back again, sometimes in the same sentence.

"I shall stick to the ski tour. One can be all by oneself. I mean, just the group."

"Absolutely. What with waiting for lifts and the terrible people après, you might as well be in a supermarket as at one of the big places nowadays."

"You'd much better come with us on the tour, Leo. Anton will be full of swank and broken ankles."

"I'd like to, but my father would never agree. But Anton will be fun, as long as you have a house, somewhere private. It's only the hotels."

"Your father seems to have got frightfully possessive."

"It's awful. Being an only child, you know?"

"I'm all right, one of six," the black-haired girl laughed excitedly. "I think sometimes they don't know one of us from the other. Specially since Hansi grew his hair."

"Yes, but listen, let's plan the ski tour for next weekend."

"Nothing to plan. We take the train to Zwettl and off we go, swoopdy-doop across the Waldviertel."

"If the snow holds."

"'Course it'll hold. Why shouldn't it?"

"I say, the film starts in a few minutes! Come on!"

They tore off, running as if their lives were measured in seconds. In the Heldenplatz, under the rearing statues of Prince Eugene, the snow was thick and they stopped to pelt each other. It was snowing again. When they reached the Ring they all ran across the motor road, not noticing that Leona stayed on the near side and ran off by herself. At least she could ask about the week at St. Anton. Someone's grandfather's house, that might sound all right.

CHAPTER 2

"No message for me?" Leona asked the hall porter.

"No, mademoiselle," answered the man, smiling involuntarily and not needing to look.

I suppose Kari is sulking at having had to go into the Army, she thought vaguely. He's a funny-tempered boy. Must be a bore, though, to have to go off alone when the others can put it off for years. Wonder why he got thrown out of the University. What can he have got up to?

Still, under the reasonableness, she was a little cast down. Army service seemed a depressing idea, whether taken after or before the end of the educational process. But it's only for a few months, not like at home, nearly two years. What will he do then? He must have been sacked almost right away, perhaps in the first semester. But perhaps he can go back, after? She was puzzled and dissatisfied by the whole situation. It would have been nicer to be partnered with one of the others, not with Kari whom she had not seen since high school, or junior school almost and who now was, it was undefinedly suggested, different. That made her own differentness more marked to herself, and perhaps to the others. Did she really feel that the ski tour would be much more fun than St. Anton, just because it was out of her reach? No, it would really be nicer up there on the wild heathland plateau, primitive and empty and with at best a small inn to sleep in and probably only a hut. It was unattainable and almost infinitely preferable. In comparison, St. Anton was almost a boring prospect. She walked up the stairs, trailing a hand along the ornamented brass rail, dawdling out the transfer from her own life to the return to convention and the brooding concentration of her father upon her. In her imagination, more than half real, was the open upland, black and white and rolling into the distance where little swinging figures moved in steady rhythm all together.

And in fact, out there under the grape-purple sky of winter night, figures did move all together, in camouflage battle dress of white while over their heads a night fighter wheeled away. A training exercise, winter reconnaissance of Alpine troops with aircraft liaison, drew to its planned conclusion. The file below, balancing on their skis, stared up at the lighted aircraft which rolled its wings in salute, lifted away with a howl of power, and swept out of sight to land. With a wide swing of the arm the leader of the expedition gave his order and the men bent forward and dug in their sticks to gather speed for the downward run back into camp.

Their eyes stung in the stuffy warmth of the debriefing room, their faces burned and they kept yawning, feeling themselves half-stifled by the change from the wide space, the great sky, the brisk movement in cold air; more than anything from the change from speechlessness, isolation, to sociability, communication by words which they all took to be normality. The flyers felt the physical change just as sharply, although not in the sensation of enclosure since their bodies were shielded from sky and air out of doors by glass and metal. But they all shared the same sensation of being abruptly translated back into the commonplace, the meaningless, from somewhere, somewhere else. Prosaically they measured, compared logs, timed their movements, added to reports. But without thinking about it they all moved and spoke with the boredom of anti-climax. What they now did was agreed to be their real purpose, it was the reason for their day's activity. But for them all it was wordlessly secondary, incidental to hours of transcendent reality, to an experience shared but not spoken of, not even thought of.

"Pretty good terrain," said the captain of the visiting Alpine troop, who came from the Tyrol. "Not the Alps, of course, but not bad."

They pretended to take this sole observation as a piece of local patriotism on his part and laughed lazily at him.

"We got the border neatly this time, I think."

"Wouldn't mind going out off duty this weekend. If the snow holds."

"It will," said Rolf. "Why don't we take a tour on Saturday and Sunday? Outside the training compound, I mean. There's plenty of room without getting too far north."

"Would we need leave passes? I'm only due for a weekend."

"That's all right. We can get overnight passes, easily."

"Fine. Let's do that, then."

"If you've quite finished with your private arrangements, perhaps we could get back to business," suggested the debriefing officer dryly, and his junior, who was even more tired and irritable than those who had been exposed to the bitter wind all day, added, "We shall be here all night at this rate."

"Yes, let's get on with it," agreed someone from the back of the room. "Personally, I'm starving."

The debriefing officer yawned too, catching it from the others, and his junior, sitting beside him half asleep and trying to concentrate on taking notes, did the same but with real weariness.

"All?" asked somebody at last. They clattered about in the bare room, collecting equipment, and plunged out into the still, bitter night.

"Rolf! Hey, come down with me. I want to talk to you."

"Okay, Kari, take it easy. You go on. I just have to dump my kit."

The officer from the Tyrol muttered something uncomplimentary about chair-warmers as Kari disappeared. Outside the sergeant snapped instructions, grumbling from habit, and like his fellows, from the need to hide what he really felt about their day on the open heath.

By "down" Kari meant the hamlet nearby and its tavern. There was already a glass before him on the table when Rolf joined him. He looked up as the door crashed shut, and smiled as Rolf seated himself by stepping over the back of the rough chair. He slipped down with a sigh of well-being and stretched out his legs.

"Foul stink this back room always has. Like salted herrings, can't imagine why."

"Horrible. But we do have it to ourselves," replied Kari lazily. "The peasants smell even worse in the public bar and make a noise too."

"Oh nuts. You're in one of your moods."

"Cigarette?"

"You know I don't. Good evening, Herr Pacher. Glass of wine with soda, please, may I?"

"Are you eating tonight, sir?"

"If you've got some of that ham?"

"The wild boar? Sure. You too, sir?" His tone changed, he did not look directly at Kari.

"I suppose so."

"Dark bread, please," shouted Rolf as the man was half out of the door.

He put his head back round the unpainted board. "Horseradish?"

"Oh, please!"

Kari pushed an official sheet across the table, crumpling the faded cloth. "I got you a leave pass."

"What for? I'm going to ski up here."

"You're not, y'know."

"Look, you were there yourself when I said I'd go with them. You know perfectly well . . ."

"You can call off. I'd have interrupted then, but didn't want to talk in front of the others. You're going into Vienna, to the Opera Ball."

"I'm going where? What is this, a change of identity? *You* are going to the Opera Ball, remember?"

"No. You're going. I'm doing something quite different and you are going to the Ball instead of me."

"What is all this? What would I do at a Ball, and the Opera Ball at that!"

"Dance, of course. You dance better than I do by a long shot."

"But, Kari, I don't want to go dancing. What *are* you talking about? I'm going on a long-run ski with the chaps from Spittal and basta."

"Basta nothing. Wait, I'll explain."

Rolf waited while the innkeeper set down a tray and began to lay their table with a clean cloth and set out knives and forks.

"Two other gentlemen coming at eight," he mentioned. "So you won't have to sit here alone much longer." He surveyed the table. "There. Anything more?"

"I'll have another applejack and a beer, same as before."

Rolf made to say something and changed his mind.

"Large," added Kari and smiled at his friend. His eyes lingered over Rolf's disapproval. "I'm not a flying man, you know, dear boy."

"Very funny. And you wouldn't be, for long, if you drank spirits."

"I thought we'd agreed not to discuss my vices."

"Sorry."

"Your expression, Rolf! You're a nice boy and disgustingly good-looking, but sometimes you're a bit of a prig."

"I know. Just try to put up with it, hey?"

"Now listen, now that fool's finished. I want to get this fixed before these other men arrive. I've got to go somewhere tomorrow. Never mind where, but I've got to. I didn't mean this to happen.

It's not a deep-laid plot as you obviously think. It's just come up the way it has. I cannot, just cannot go to this abysmal crush and if you don't show up there for me I'll be in double trouble. The trouble I'm in anyway, and a row at home as well."

"Well, call off your other date, then."

"You haven't got it yet. I *have* to go, I have no *choice*. If I don't turn up somebody will go to my father. Then I shall be cashiered."

"Go to your father! Kari, you aren't playing with those nuts who got you thrown out of the University, are you? Those weirdos who were always demonstrating?"

"No, no. Of course not. You think I'm crazy?"

"But we could never get away with it! Won't your people be at the Ball? Didn't you say your sister's coming out?"

"Yes, but my father won't be there because fortunately he's got an attack of gout. My uncle is taking my mother and sister. Yes, I know what you're going to say. Of course, they will recognize you just as much as he would. But they won't make a fuss and they won't tell the old man. They're on my side."

"But . . ."

"That is, if they see you and they probably won't in that mob."

"But of course Theres' will see me, she'll be in the cotillion. And anyway, your mother will be looking for you."

"I've sort of warned Mother. And Tesi won't bat an eyelid. She's a good kid and anyway she knows a bit. Not much, but enough to guess."

"But the cotillion! I've never done it. It's impossible."

"It's the easiest thing in the world. You just hold hands and bow and step round your partners. And you have done it, at dancing school."

"But that was six—no, seven—years ago," protested Rolf thinking of another obstacle. "But if not Tesi, I shall be asked by someone else. What am I to say about you?"

"Say I've pulled a tendon or something."

"But that's not true. They'd know."

"You'll just have to lie for once. I know you blush like a baby, but the girls will find that sweet."

"Oh stop that, Kari, you know I hate it."

"But why? You are rather sweet sometimes."

"If you carry on like this, I'll hit you. Hard. I mean it. Stop it."

"All right, I won't tease you any more."

"But listen, Kari, it's insane. I haven't a dress uniform to wear, and even if I could get one in the time, I can't afford it. You know that."

"But we've got to find a way . . . I just can't call off. Wait, you have got a parade uniform. You get my new one, I've never had it on. We're just the same height. It will be a tiny bit loose on you but that's a fault on the right side."

"A tiny bit loose! The way you talk sometimes! You do it on purpose, it's a sort of disguise. And I can't borrow your brand-new uniform, anyway. Why, I bet you haven't even paid for it yet."

"Disguise," said Kari, with a startled look at this perception. "And what's the bill got to do with it? Mother will pay that for me. And you're not borrowing it, it's yours. It's your payoff for helping me. I know you can't afford one yourself and you need one, don't you? Just so you do this dismal chore for me."

"You really are an insulting bastard sometimes, Kari. How can you say such things?"

"Hell, I'm beside myself. I didn't mean to taunt you with being poor, you know that. Rolf, you've got to do this for me. Can't you see I'm . . ."

"I didn't mean only about me being penniless. I don't give a damn about that. It's the way you . . . Even your mother, how can you say oh, she'll pay, as if it didn't matter?"

"Yes, I know. I'm sorry. But Rolf, please . . ."

"I wish I knew . . . Kari, can't you tell me?"

"No. You're about the last person in the world I could tell."

"But the girl!"

"What girl?"

"Don't yell like that. They'll hear you. I mean your partner."

"Oh, she'll probably have a fit, but who cares? She can't do anything with the President and the Ball Chairman and about two thousand guests there watching."

"But I don't even know her name."

"It's Leona. Leona Hélène Chavanges. They're French but they were here for ages and she speaks German like us. We were at school once together and her stupid parents are as rich as Croesus and want us to get married."

"That's all I needed. A rich spoiled infant. And what's she like? I wouldn't recognize her."

"When I last saw her, that's two years ago, she was tall, thin, not pretty, rather big features. Lot of very blond hair, straight. Leonine. Her name suits her."

"That sounds like a description of half the girls in Vienna, except some would be dark."

"Well, it's two years. You could get somebody to point her out."

Rolf looked at his friend. Unbelievingly he shook his head and pressed his mouth shut. "You are the most incredibly . . ."

"I know. I know. But it doesn't matter to this girl, Rolf. One man will be the same to her as another, so long as she isn't made to look a fool by being left without a partner. Listen, say you'll do it for me. I swear it won't happen again, or anything like it. I'll pull myself together. If I can get out of this mess this time, I'll try to behave. If you'll just do it for me this once."

"But you've said that before. I'm afraid you'll get caught."

"I know, and I know you disapprove. Oh yes, you do, no need to scowl like that. I'm not ribbing you now. God, if you knew how I loathe myself for begging like this. You of all people. But you're the only man I can trust to behave himself and not to let me down. That's the one thing my mother would *not* forgive, any sort of public scandal, or fuss even."

"But I don't see how I can get away with it. How do I tell them I'm standing in for you?"

"I don't see why you have to tell anybody anything. Officially, as it were. You just turn up and if anybody asks you outright, you say you're standing in for me. They will be grateful to you, if anything, for filling the gap."

"I should think quite the contrary. They'll all treat me like a confidence trickster, I should think."

"Well, but you don't know how these people care for outward appearances. You were brought up not to think of such things, but they think and care for nothing else. They will just be glad not to have this wretched kid standing there without a partner."

"Poor brat. I feel quite sorry for her."

"Then you'll do it? You will, for me, won't you?" Kari put out a hand with bitten nails that trembled a little, and gripped Rolf's knee.

"But what I'm worrying about, really, is you," said Rolf, constrained. "I don't want to keep on, but if I thought you really meant to pull yourself together, and go on meaning it, not just saying it at this minute—then I'd have a shot at it."

"I do mean it. I will try. If only because I'm scared. I'll cut this stuff out, honest. And there's no danger. For you, I mean. It's not as if it were a service thing. Even if it were noticed, and it won't be, you're not the one who is behaving badly. You're just trying to save the situation. You see?"

Until Kari said this Rolf had not thought of any disciplinary aspect to this escapade. Strictly speaking, there was no disciplinary aspect. He was entitled to a long weekend off-duty and he could see that his pass was properly made out and signed and stamped by the adjutant's office. He was not due to fly until Monday morning and only then if the weather held. Like any junior officer who wished to do so, he was encouraged to avail himself of the old tradition that serving officers were welcome at any but the most formal state occasions, as escorts, as partners, as guests. It was a custom that went back to the eighteenth-century Enlightenment and many a career had been built on its discreet use. Rolf had never yet taken advantage of it but he knew he could do so without question.

Yet some anxiety under Kari's offhand, half-serious exaggerations worried him. Supposing Kari got up to one of his pranks, got into a brawl? Kari drank sometimes and then he would do things; nothing really bad but some devil inspired him to mock people. Once when Rolf was with him he went up to a stranger in the theater and murmured words into the man's ear and then stood back, turning away so that the outraged protest caught not the jester but an innocent bystander who just happened to be close by and to have his head bent toward the victim. What did Kari say then to that bald, elderly man who looked like a civil servant which so enraged him that he spluttered threats of the police? Kari had never seen the man before, so he said. A flutter of nervousness touched Rolf which he did not in the least understand. And the time Kari flirted with a silly, middle-aged woman in bright satin at a public dance in provincial Horn; when he was so persistent that the woman, at first foolishly flattered, afterward burst into tears and was removed almost bodily by a thunderous fat husband. There was something hateful and cruel in Kari's smile and voice then. He changed, he was another person, and he seemed himself not to know when the change would come over him. Rolf bent his head, biting his lip. He felt ashamed of his half-formed fears; they were cowardly.

"All right," he said. "I'll do it. Where's your ticket?"

"Here," said Kari and at once produced a small envelope in which was the printed pasteboard giving entry for one person to the Opera Ball on Thursday, 17 February 1970, to be opened by the President of the Republic at ten-thirty in the evening. With the card was a slip of paper showing the time and place at which 2nd Lieutenant Count Karl Henri Rilla-Lensky should present himself for the opening cotillion.

"Your father's name is Henri, too, isn't it?" Rolf said, having to say something. "Do you all have French names?"

"Always. We came from Lorraine or some idiotic thing."

"I don't see anything idiotic about it."

"You would if you'd had it dinned into you daily for twenty-two years."

"I dare say I should, at that. Come on, time to go. I don't want to get involved with these other people and stay up late."

"Oh, don't go yet. We can relax now."

"I'm dropping. Too much fresh air. I'll be off."

They both stood and Rolf reached for his cap.

"Rolf?"

"Mm?"

"Thank you." Rolf looked down at Kari's outstretched hand and then up into his friend's face. Kari's eyes watched him with a cautious and questioning look and he did not smile. Rolf touched the hand and then punched Kari lightly on the shoulder.

"Just take it easy," he said. "And keep your fingers crossed tomorrow night."

"Too late for that. Oh, you mean for you. You bet I will."

Kari watched Rolf as he went out and in his eyes was envy. Then he shoved his hands into his trousers pockets and hunched his shoulders as he strolled to the window to watch his friend walk down the path to the roadway with his rapid, springing step. Behind him several junior officers entered the room and he turned to greet them with a look of brilliant gaiety.

Rolf ran a few steps and kicked at the snow. I must have a word with the ground crew first thing in the morning, he reminded himself and was filled with a sudden flood of energy and pleasure so that he gave a loud crow of joy and jumped over the bush at the corner to his quarters, scattering brilliant frost from it which glittered in the light from the door.

CHAPTER 3

The doors were still swinging on the last of the Tuesday evening audience when, without a moment lost, an army of workmen swarmed into the opera house. Just as a couple of plumbers will install themselves and take over for a time the life of a family household, so this horde of irreverent and indispensable journeymen took over the huge auditorium. The galleries, the corridors, the rehearsal rooms, the dressing rooms, the offices, the electrical circuits, the storage spaces, the cellars and the scenery lofts. Whether some part of the complex building was closed to them or not, they entered everywhere and mysteriously made it their own. Locked doors seemed to unlock of themselves and apprentices lounged for a short rest and ate their thick sandwiches on managerial carpets—for young workmen seem always to sit on the floor to eat—and combed their long hair in front of mirrors that usually reflected Turandot or Isolde. Engineers consulted their blueprints leaning over the tables where new set designs more often lay open for consideration and an uncounted number of beer bottles appeared from nowhere and were left in the most unlikely places.

It was theirs in a more real sense than that their taxes paid for it. Where tenors tore the heartstrings of middle-class matrons they called and caroled, any shout amplified by the perfect acoustics, any casual swearing voice echoing up and down the hollows of the lifting shafts. The musical instruments, which had impregnated the very upholstery of the seats with melody so that a dropped hammer might be expected to sound a Wagnerian chord, were overcome by a tornado of clattering and banging. The rat-a-tat and slamming mingled with yells and thumps as if electronically recorded *musique concrète* were being performed from every loudspeaker turned up to its ultimate decibel. Even in that shrine of noise disciplined to Art there never was such a volume of meaningful sound.

They worked in shifts through Wednesday and on during that night into Thursday morning. They laid a vast shining expanse of parquet over the stalls and parterre straight through to the back of the immense stage. They built, in a night, not only a presidential box as big as a drill hall with balustrades and stairs and retiring rooms like a palace, but set up a dozen restaurants, bars, grills, cafés, a wine garden, a beer hall, a nightclub, and a gypsy encampment. Before they were half-finished with any construction, in ran art students and stage designers to disguise it with such exuberant wealth of fantasy that people who normally worked every day and night on that spot were unable to recognize their whereabouts. Every aspect, angle, and space was changed by commando assault into an entirely different purpose and appearance. It was a siege, a battle, a mass attack on time and the intractability of inanimate objects. Hardly a moment, and certainly not an hour, of two nights and a day passed without a crisis. The only characteristics of war that did not appear were destruction and death. And as the battle ebbed and the troops gradually, regiment by regiment, staff by staff, retired, so the women who belong to armies appeared. A mob of camp followers with cotton scarves tied over their hair advanced with cleaning machines, routed the last lingering stragglers and mopped up all resistance.

In the dark of the early morning flowers arrived in hundreds of flat baskets, which as they were opened released the dews of southern Italy imprisoned in millions of living blooms as paradisial scents into the now dustless air of deep winter. It was no battle any longer but rather the devoted and serious skills of dedicated attendants. It was by now almost quiet in the great cool hollow of the unheated auditorium, the chatter and calling of hundreds of florists sinking like rain onto the receptive calm of lake waters. From the railings of the topmost galleries under the domed roof down to the lowest tier of boxes now level with the dancing floor was fabricated a unique hanging garden of living flowers. If all the famous gardens of the world were blooming at one time and in the same place they could hardly show a more marvelous ecstasy of light and color wreathed and hung in stunning extravagance by artful care allied with nature in ravishing profusion of shade and scent. To come up the grand staircase, still chilled from the outer frost, and in itself a woodland glade of trees, palms and blossoming bushes, into the opera interior was to receive a shock of beauty and grace that might take the breath away from the most hardened utilitarian.

"This is what the hanging gardens of Babylon must have looked like."

"*Now* I know what that quotation about 'even Solomon in all his glory' was all about."

"We shall be doing this next year for Yves, I suppose." The First Secretary leaned over his wife's shoulder, putting out a hand on the velvet-edged balustrade to take in the scene.

"We shall indeed," his wife raised her eyebrows ruefully at Chavanges. "So you see, we sincerely feel for you. Not like the Leclercs, they are too young, they can only pretend sympathy. The threat of middle age is still too far off for them to understand."

"What was that, Marie, about a threat?" Mme. Chavanges came from the arch out into the box, shimmering from exposed shoulders to the carpet in rosy spangles like a blond mermaid.

"Any such threat could only be instantly exorcised by your appearance," said the diplomat, bowing exaggeratedly to disguise his very real admiration.

"Stunning!" cried Angela Leclerc, her merry, round face expressing the word with its wide-opened eyes.

"And here is the Ambassador," Marie turned her back to the dancing floor. She and her husband were only waiting to greet the Ambassadress before going to their own invited places and there now ensued a bustle of embraces and compliments which filled the enclosed space with billows of moving silks and scented arms and the sharp glitter of jewels.

"Bring Chavanges along to us as soon as you reasonably can," said the older man to Leclerc as he made to slip away.

"I recognize Chavanges," said their host when further greetings were over in the other box. "But which is Madame?"

"Pink paillettes."

"Most striking." The tone of his hostess seemed to doubt whether the effect were not perhaps almost too great. She herself was attired in silvery velvet and was already a good deal too warm. "Tell me about them."

"Madame is the older side of the alliance. Her family, I mean of course, she is years younger than her husband. A small company but an old one and of high reputation. I've heard even that they were brought from Holland as long ago as Louis XIV, but I don't know whether that's true. He, or rather his father, acquired the much larger affair which was formerly German. Reparations, you know?" He cocked a non-committal eyebrow at his Austrian host. "Then they bought up still another factory in 1922, or was it '23? Anyway, during the great inflation. When the German part of the district went back to the Reich the whole undertaking was re-erected on the French side of the border and Chavanges told me they built an entire housing estate for the skilled men they took with them."

"Trade followed the flag, then?"

"Some might say war booty," said Marie.

"I can't judge really, but even as a Frenchman I must admit that the ethnic frontier there is blurred. I've never been there but I gather that the local dialect is a most peculiar mixture of the two tongues."

"Interesting. He was rather lordly with me the other day. So his air of not wishing to be as grand as he might be is a bit overdone?"

Circumspectly the diplomat moved his head and smiled for answer. He wished to flatter his host, who had business plans with the Chavanges undertakings large enough to be an affair of state; but he did not mean to do so in a way that could be quoted if those plans should go awry. He himself and his wife too had been Gaullistes when that attachment was by no means universally approved in France; so he found the magniloquent air adopted by some Frenchmen, including Chavanges, in imitation of their national hero twenty-five years later, somewhat comical.

In the other box, the guests spoke again of the flowers.

"They're incredible. An orgy of glorious uselessness."

"What an essay in frivolity! It's taken to the point of genius almost."

"But under the frivolity there is a certain rigor," objected the Ambassador. "I took your view myself the first time I saw it. But after a couple of years here one sees, somehow, a tremendous sense of form. I mean, form as the English use the word."

"One might expect it to have been lost."

"Ah, you connect it then with the old monarchy?"

"Somehow, yes, with imperial duties. A Roman thought lingering."

"Yes, duties. A corporate feeling for outward presence. And it *is* corporate."

"Strange survival. I don't doubt you, but it's strange. It's over fifty years since the disappearance of any real handhold to—to what? A right to grandeur?"

"There's an astounding confidence there somewhere, goes deep."

"Confidence? In what?"

"That's it. What? But they do take something for granted, something that lies behind formalities and really does exist for its own sake."

"But what? Simply 'form'? If so, then form largely without style. Most of the people here are as provincial as can be, copying what they see in the glossies."

"It may be form without style," said Mme. Chavanges, "but I have to admit that the setting, the decorations . . . those flowers! I've never seen anything in Paris to touch it."

"Yet you have been present at magnificent occasions in Paris. I've seen you."

"Yes, charity balls given by Greek shipping millionaires who are the objects of scorn to their guests. You say form without style, which I don't pretend to understand. But where is the style in a gathering of international spivs who accept the invitation because the cameras are there and they get into V*ogue* with Monsieur le Duc de Somewhere. I could point out to you here at this moment people whose landholdings were old in the Crusades and they still live on them. If one cares for style, I'll take them."

"But either way, Paris or here, it is all unreal. It says nothing in the modern world."

"Are you so sure of that?"

"But surely? Nothing but a dead survival."

"It seems to me that any institution that can survive this century is not, cannot be, merely a dead survival. There must be vitality in it."

"I grant you that, it's empirically clear. And, after all, why do we discuss it if it has no meaning for which we search?"

"If it has meaning we shan't find it in any institution. They certainly no longer exist."

"Then, if the form survives when the institutions have long

disappeared, the more vitality it must have, the more it must fill some real purpose."

"But what purpose can it possibly have?"

"It doesn't fill any purpose. It's simply the inertia of history—custom."

"Continuity, then?"

"Continuity? That could perhaps be the purpose?"

"We speak of purpose, history. Those are large words. Isn't all this simply a tourist attraction? The local form of the rout given in Paris by some oil per center, whose contempt for his guests, by the way, is at least as great as theirs for him?"

"Oh no. Where are the *Paris-Match* photographers? Where's the team from *Stern?* From *Oggi?*"

"They are here. But here they are discreet. They must observe the form, here."

"I doubt if they are even here. They think of it—their editors, I mean—as provincial."

"And it is, and that is its secret. The tone is given here by people who simply don't care whether *Paris-Match* is looking or not."

"Is there such a person?"

"A provincial remark if ever I heard one," observed Mme. Chavanges aside.

Her husband drew her to the back of the box. "Do control yourself," he said quietly. "What is the matter with you?"

"Me control myself? How can I? I have always been controlled by others. *You* must control me, surely?"

"I simply don't recognize you. What has got into you?"

"How would you recognize me? You never knew me," she said under her breath.

"At any rate, don't make any more speeches. That one was quite enough."

Leona's mother moved forward and turned her head away as if simply to look at the files of dancers assembling for the opening cotillion, than which nothing could have been more natural. But something in the lift of her head and the turn of her smooth naked shoulders expressed defiance and a sullenness that did not quite reach anger. Then her pose became a real attention as she saw something unexpected out on the floor.

"Who is that?" she asked, and as soon as the words were out she frowned sharply, caught her underlip with an indrawn breath and looked quickly away to the full boxes opposite.

"Who is who?" asked someone, searching the buzzing and shifting expanse with an opera glass.

"No, nothing. I thought it was someone else." He will see, soon enough, she thought, and then I shall be blamed as usual.

A number of official guests and their wives were already moving about in the presidential box. They bowed to each other and to acquaintances in the nearby private boxes. One or two of them directed liveried attendants in the arranging of chairs.

Mme. Chavanges shifted round a seat and leaned over to see the mass of flowers covering the proscenium arch and as soon as her face was safely averted, still apparently inspecting carnations and mimosa, she focused her little glass minutely on the young man now touching her daughter's outstretched fingers with his own. It was certainly not Charles Henri Lensky. Then who was it? Not anyone known to her. A stranger. His only resemblance to Leona's correct partner was that he wore uniform instead of evening clothes. He was dark, tall, his head narrow, the hair looked black, it gleamed with brushing and the general coloring was almost swarthy. Leona's hand could be seen to be pushing his so that he shot a momentary glance sideways and then moved a little in response to the signal. The turn of his head, hardly to be detected, was nervous but he moved with neat, supple grace. Obviously he has not rehearsed, thought Leona's mother; there will be an awkwardness. She did not look at her husband, who had moved to the far side of the box and leaned against the arch to the anteroom speaking to Angela Leclerc. He kept shooting glances toward the lines of assembled young people but had not yet found Leona among them.

The Chief of Protocol was now entering the President's box with his wife. Then came the Chairman of the Ball Committee, that countess referred to with sarcasm by Kari Lensky, with her husband. In their own box the Ambassadress, who was seated, took the jeweled handbag lying on her knee into her hand and with the other hand pushed at the fluted folds of her stiff satin skirts, freeing them for rising to her feet. Everywhere in the great concourse of guests women made similar movements, and through the dispersed murmuring of two thousand voices silence gradually penetrated.

The conductor of the Philharmonic Orchestra lifted his baton and a moment later, to the sedate pacing gaiety of Haydn's music a white-haired old man entered from the back at the center of the box. He was followed by his portly wife and their suite. Everyone rose with a long susurration. He moved slowly, with an air of benign simplicity right down to the balustrade where he could bend forward and muster the ranks of breathless young people before him and he looked them all over with indulgent kindness before straightening his shoulders again rather heavily. This was the moment for which the old dancing master had expended so much nervous energy. Counting silently with an intensity that could be felt, the young girls sank down and the young men bent their heads with almost perfect unanimity. When they stood erect again the old man bowed slowly to them, turned to the left and then to the right to bow to the guests and then, with a gesture of his hands, stepped back one pace level with his wife. Dead silence fell. The entire company stood still as statues for the music of Mozart and the national anthem. Then with a long murmur of movement the crowd sank into chairs, the young people stared with tense concentration at the figure of their trainer poised immediately before them to pass on the conductor's signal, the orchestra took a deep breath and with the first notes of the "Emperor Waltz" the black and white files began to move.

"There's something almost funny about their solemnity," said Leclerc.

"But touching, too."

"You're being very superior," murmured Angela, so that her husband's seniors should not hear. "But you all take your own ceremonial duties every bit as seriously."

"Oh, but surely . . . ?"

Mme. Chavanges laughed softly, and her husband glanced at her warningly.

"The thing that strikes me," Leclerc changed the subject, "really, is how much healthier and better-looking the young are than their elders."

"True. I remember a May Day parade here, years ago, on our first tour. When Leona was at the nursery-school stage. The older men and women were about half the size of their children, and a good many had some physical deformation, undernourishment, industrial accidents, war wounds from the first war . . ."

"How—from the first war? Not the second?" interrupted Angela.

"No, these were old men. They had been both starved and neglected. You didn't see anything like that after the second war, the Nazi generation were in much better shape."

"And this one even more so. Like young Greeks."

"A different race, I agree," Leclerc nodded.

"Yes. We forget that wonderful health and vitality when we curse the modern world."

"From envy, perhaps?"

"You are philosophical this evening." The Ambassadress teased him.

"They make me feel old."

"Leona looks splendid," said a newcomer.

"Yes, she's a handsome child," agreed her father, his face changing.

"Hm. Child?"

The man who said this at once turned to pay a compliment to the mother of another girl who was dancing.

"Well, she's only just eighteen," protested Chavanges and then saw that his companion was already speaking to someone else. He saw too, from the smile of the woman beside him, that his remark conveyed a different meaning from the one he intended. An obscure and puzzled resentment stirred in him and he frowned.

"Child, as one says," said the other man, now safely out of earshot in the chatter and music. "Strikes me as anything but. I wouldn't mind being snowed up for a week with such a child."

"Well, don't say so to her father. He's as jealous of her as if . . . Ah, perhaps better not."

"You are serious?"

"He is. I'm not."

"Poor Madame, then."

"But why? She is herself extremely pretty. No doubt life offers compensations."

"Let's hope so. A pity to waste that figure."

"My dear fellow, then don't let it waste. There is the moral, quite clearly."

"They are talking about Leona," said Angela softly.

"How do you know? I can't hear a word."

"By their faces. Look at them."

"Oh. Yes. How wise the Spaniards are to watch their daughters."

"Chavanges watches her, all right."

"Yes. He obviously knows what men are like."

"Why wouldn't he? His own feelings are a little intense, I rather feel."

"When we were in Rome we knew some people involved in a more than spectacular scandal. He reminds me of them."

"What kind of scandal?"

"The kind we are thinking of. Or aren't we?"

"Ah, then you must mean the Leonvallis?"

"You know them?"

"I know of them. But this won't end like that. Much too controlled."

"Not with such *éclat*, perhaps. But he will marry her to a null. You'll see."

"You seem to know them well."

"Of course. He and I were at school together, and I've known her from childhood, too."

"He may have a surprise coming to him. Leona doesn't look to me as biddable as her mother."

"You forget, she is *used* to that huge fortune. She will do as she's told."

"He would never use that weapon?"

"Consciously, no, of course not. But money . . ."

"I suppose money has immense power. I've never had any so I don't really understand it. But to have built such an empire and kept it. There must be a granite hardness there."

"And in our times! And without calling on American capital! Yes, the family and its possessions are everything."

"He's a slave of duty, you mean?"

"Of what he takes to be duty, anyway. He certainly did not want to resign from the diplomatic service, but there was no hesitation."

"Ah well, where would the world be if we all neglected our duty?"

"Just where it is! But they, the Chavanges, the largest of the large bourgeoisie, *they* keep their eyes on reality."

"A good thing somebody does, you must admit."

"Oh certainly. There's something in him of what we were talking of before. Something like the dour, unimaginative sticking to the point of the Habsburgs. You know?"

"The sense of form?"

"Something of the sort, yes."

"Let us hope then, for his sake, that the girl's sense of form is the same as her family's."

"She will conform."

"She looks to me, on a slight acquaintance I admit, as if she might conform to her own sense of form. And you know, the young have changed in this generation."

"That is said every twenty years."

"And sometimes it's true."

"Yes, it is true, you are right. Their world is much more fluid than ours. And our generation is paying for its hypocritical self-righteousness after the war. All those too-public lectures meant for the Japs and the Germans, about freedom, the dignity of man, social justice, what you will. Our own young people have taken them as legal tender—for ourselves. I say to my boy, Ravensbrück, and he says Hiroshima!"

"You think that's what makes them so censorious? Really, you could be right. You should hear the girls on Vietnam! You'd think I did it personally. And as for the war, I daren't mention it. They burst out laughing."

"Well, there you are. Why should Leona Chavanges be any different?"

"With luck she may like the bridegroom her father picks for her. In fact, has already picked, if what I hear is so."

"Possibly. Perhaps she will, if that's the one she's dancing with. He's certainly handsome enough for any girl."

"I expect it is the one. He's young Lensky, I believe, and they are certainly the modern kind of aristocratic family. Lensky père is Chairman of the Industrial Association here. As well as having an ancient title, which may influence Chavanges as well."

"Lensky? Sounds Russian."

"It's Rilla-Lensky. The Rilla came from Lorraine with—ah, what was his name? The husband of their Maria Theresia. They acquired land by marriage, luckily for them in Styria and not in Bohemia. The Lensky side was marriage again, some refugee who married the heiress after some upset in Russia. I think the Decembrists."

"Surprising they would agree to the little Chavanges, if they are so very grand."

"I tell you, they are the modern kind."

"You are talking of Lensky?" the First Secretary's wife joined them. "He's a charmer. The father I mean, I don't know the son. We were thinking of going to dance. The other music will begin in a minute and there's some pop group downstairs."

"Look, there they are, now. You can see Leona quite clearly, and the young man. He waltzes well."

"He's not a bit like his father if that's young Lensky. They are all Nordic blonds."

"She is magnificent, the girl."

"It must be Lensky. They always waltz this first set with their opening partners."

"There was something about him, I don't recall what . . ."

"But wait, that's not young Lensky!"

Chavanges had heard now. He stared at the speakers, then turned and came to the edge of the box to look for Leona. The woman to whom he had been speaking, left alone, emphasized her abandonment by raising her eyebrows and standing quite still, her lips parted for the next word, which would never now be spoken. The man at whom her assumed astonishment was directed was, however, the only occupant of the box who took no notice of it. Chavanges was a big, bulky man with imposing shoulders and a massive head and he leaned right out of the enclosure, blocking the view of those behind him, who exchanged smiles. He, unconscious of them all, frowned with irritable concentration as if it were somebody's fault that he could not at once see his daughter. His big hands clenched on the velvet rim to correct his balance; he might almost have been about to jump over the balustrade.

"What can have happened?" asked Angela Leclerc with interest.

"Perhaps they've changed partners already?"

"Impossible. They go straight into the first waltz from the cotillion, they can't change."

"If that isn't young Lensky, then where is he?"

"Or even more important, my dear chap, if that isn't young Lensky, then *who* is he?"

"Georges is wondering what Lensky has got up to this time!"

"I've never seen that man before," said Chavanges with astounded outrage.

"And one wouldn't forget," said Angela, leaning past the heavy shoulder to see. "He's like a film star. One of the new French ones, for preference."

"Is he French? Could be."

"He can't be, he's in uniform."

Someone passed an opera glass into Angela's hand and she trained it on the circling couple, following them round as they swung. "Whoever he is, he's a captain," she reported, "and a pilot. He's wearing wings." She sounded amused and laughed as she turned to Chavanges to offer him the glass, but he did not see her. She caught an impression of a broad, dark glower so concentrated that the slight figure upon which it was bent might well have been made uneasy by its penetration of the populous intervening space.

She caught, too, a mutter. "She won't look at me." And Chavanges straightened up so suddenly and clumsily that he almost knocked the glass from Angela's hand.

"Why wasn't I told that the arrangements had been changed?" he demanded. "Solange?"

"Really, what is all the fuss about?" The woman so unceremoniously left alone by Chavanges reached forward and took the glass from Angela. "May I?" After a moment's search she found the couple. "He *is* a most personable young man," she pronounced with malice. "But not a bit like a film star. A real man, but one touched, perhaps, by Apollo's finger."

The Ambassadress gave her a little shake of the head which was meant to be reproving but in fact conveyed her own enjoyment of the joke.

"These children!" she said to Chavanges. "Clearly they changed partners without telling anyone, don't you think?"

At this he turned back into the box at last, but still without changing the bullish, hard-jawed expression of his face, of which he was obviously unconscious.

"Let us go and dance," suggested Angela slyly, "then we can see properly."

"What? Oh yes. Yes, of course. Let's go down." He was blundering as if he could not collect his wits and Angela took his arm.

"Come!" he said impatiently.

"Angie!" someone called as they emerged into the sweep of the wide corridor circling the boxes. "Angie! Don't forget you promised to come down to the pop room later. Can I come up for you in half an hour?"

"Oh lovely, you haven't forgotten. Yes, come to the box, will you?" Turning to see the man who called, Angela saw Solange. "There's your wife. You wanted to speak to her, didn't you?"

"That doesn't matter now. Come along." Then, making an obvious effort to keep to the casual tone, "Your English is perfect."

"Naturally," she laughed at him. "I am English."

"That accounts for the odd name, then."

"You mean Angie? Yes, everyone calls me that."

"Darling Angie," said a tall, gray-haired man as they went down the steps to the floor. "Do keep some time for me, later." And he kissed her swiftly on the cheek without any of them pausing.

"You seem to know the entire world," he said perfunctorily, while his eyes searched over Angela's shoulder.

"We've been here four years, you know."

"I was here three years the first time, and two the second, but I don't know half the people you do."

"Two years is an odd time to be in a post."

"My father died and I had to resign and go home."

"Of course. Georges did tell me, but I'd forgotten. And now you live in Sarrebourg or somewhere there?"

"Near there. Ah, there is Leona."

Chavanges steered his partner with decision for a moment but Leona seemed to have slipped away again, and he slumped back into what was almost a walk, without rhythm, so that Angela was left with all the work. He could hardly be said to be dancing at all, and neither did he attempt to disguise his lack of interest. If Angela had been consulting her own wishes, she would have left this rich boor to take care of himself; but there were influential people here whom he should meet and it was the duty of the Leclercs to see that he met them.

"Look," she said presently. "That's Roder in the end box. The Trades Union boss you were speaking of at dinner yesterday. D'you want to come over? I know his wife quite well, we're on the Children's Homes Committee together. Come, let's slide round this way." And she led him firmly toward the other side of the floor where she could call a greeting and be invited into the Roders' box.

"It's a battlefield," she said, sighing a little as they arrived at their destination. She did not mean the dance floor, but life in general, but Chavanges in any case did not hear her remark.

CHAPTER 4

Most of them chattered a good deal to cover nervousness, adjusted clothes and gloves, even hair, in ways they were constantly reminded not to do. Amid these greetings, sortings out, alterations of detail, the time passed so swiftly that it seemed to be from one carefree moment to the next sinking second of disbelief that Leona saw among the now partnered crowd that Kari simply was not there. She was the only girl left in the anteroom who was not paired and she knew with certainty that he was not coming.

Such a mistrust of herself and of arrangements made for her by others was unknown to her so that she had not looked at her tiny watch set with brilliants, a coming-out present from her father. Then she was afraid to draw attention to her misfortune by doing so, but seeing all those appallingly clearly defined couples she did at last consult its blank little face, so small that her frightened eyes could not decipher the message. She guessed rather than read that it was after ten o'clock, well after, and as she took that solid fact in, a voice nearby, trying to sound flippant but rising so high with foreboding that it cracked, said it looked as if Kari had mistaken the evening.

The anger which is fear, the painful fear of the very young of making fools of themselves, seized Leona with panic force. A vertiginous instability shook her ordered world with the threat of disorder, disgrace, so that she would have fled at a further word. She turned quickly in a trap, the hard lights overhead dazed instead of illuminating and she could see nothing through a shifting blaze of black and white in which an unseen, mythic blow unbalanced her so that her head swam.

At this instant of dismay and unbelief she herself seemed unreal to Leona, she was not there or was disintegrating, flowing away from her core in all directions. This happens often to young girls who are brought up to be artificial and then blamed for living in fantasies, when, since they still know nothing except the falsehoods they have been educated in, they could exist in nothing else. At this exact moment a man entered the anteroom wearing uniform; that is he was different from the general, clear-cut black and white. It was only an impression of contrast and Leona did not see him properly for he went to his nearest group of partners and was merged with them; Rolf had worked out in advance how the matter of identifying Leona was to be managed.

"Where's Leona?" he said, sounding easy although he felt a certain abrasion of the nerves. "I'm so late, she'll be furious."

"But where is . . . ?"

Rolf cut the boy short.

"I was on duty until two hours ago," he said, taking something for granted so that the others were no longer able to question him; his remark made his presence somehow official. "I just don't see her."

"Well, you must be blind. She's hardly to be missed. Look—over there."

She was, of course, the only girl left alone and he did not at once take in that there was another reason why she could hardly be missed.

"Ah," Rolf agreed calmly and left the group to accost Leona with what looked to everyone present to be a hard and adult, a smiling, certainty.

"I'm frightfully sorry to be so late," he said to her, challenging her to doubt that all was in order, and he looked about him again with that smiling coolness. Leona could hardly see him through the mist of threatening unreality and he took in her wide gaze as bemused. "I'm your partner. I hope you don't mind?"

"But . . . !" was all she could say, staring at an apparition that definitely was not Kari. He could have been produced by a conjurer's trick as the exact opposite to what she awaited. He was slender, taller than herself, his movements co-ordinated, under the control of well-trained nerves and muscles, where Kari was, or had been, loosely built and his movements somewhat wide and vague. He was too, startlingly dark, where Kari was blond as a Scandinavian with eyes of that shade sometimes called speedwell blue, an almost chalky undifferentiated light pupil. This man's voice was deeper, too, and he spoke with a crispness, a definition not at all like Kari's tentative, unfinished accents. The face fixed itself against the still swimming background as narrow rather than having the broadness of Kari's; the bones that formed it under the olive skin seemed thin and long instead of thick and squarish. The eyes that fixed hers were dark enough to seem black, with thick lashes that shadowed them further but with glittering, quick sharp glances. She took in the eyes once for all as a focus upon which all her efforts to show no lack of command depended. Large and shining with bluish-whites, the centers were streaked with differing rays from tawny to black that gave them depth like a cave full of shadows shot through with a shaft of sun.

He said something she did not hear so she moved her eyes to his mouth and found him smiling in a confiding, including way as if they shared, or might be about to share, some laughing purpose known only to themselves.

"I'm afraid I've startled you," he said and again she received the impression of calm as if for him everything were exactly as it should be. Was that what he said, before? She had no time to remember. "You see, Kari couldn't come. And we thought it better for you to have a partner of some sort. Even if only a substitute. So I came."

We thought it better. A substitute. So that was it. It had been decided without her knowledge. No need to ask her opinion. It had simply been done. Together with relief she felt outrage and showed it. He thought it was disappointment, offense at the absence of a particular person whom she had, perhaps with impatience, awaited. The thought aroused a competitive impulse in Rolf.

"It must sound awful to you, I know. But he simply had to be on duty tonight. One of those military muddles. He sent his deepest apologies and regrets. And, of course, me, so that disaster should not be total. You see?"

He meant reassurance: you see, he did think of you and is terribly upset not to be here. Such consideration was not what Leona remembered of the absent Kari. She took it in as Rolf's idea, which indeed it was, and was now sharply pleased that this stranger should trouble to placate her. A small pride emerged through the other sensations, replacing the frightened humiliation, the uncertainty. This was not at all like the longed-for being taken for granted of her dancing-school companions. It was something much more pointed and personal, focused on her, Leona. His eyes watched her to see whether he were accepted so that she could see that her agreement mattered to him; this in itself was something quite new. Consultation of her wishes by adults was usually perfunctory, a matter of politeness, and did not affect what they did at all. It did not, of course, occur to Leona that Rolf's pride too was involved. Not only were there elements of humiliation for him in his acceptance of Kari's unwanted obligations and in his putting on for those obligations Kari's expensive handmade uniform which he could not afford for himself. He was anxious too that the substitution should actually please her and not simply be grasped at as a way out of her partnerless state; he was up to that moment assuming a possible disappointment at the loss

47

of Kari as a person. But he could see that she was not thinking of Kari at all; now as the shock receded she appeared intrigued rather with a wide-eyed expectation of something exciting about to happen. It seemed to both of them to have been a long pause since his apologies, and even now Leona did not answer him but smiled and then laughed a little as if at a successful trick, and Rolf laughed too.

"I hope I can remember what to do, that's all I do hope."

"It's easy. You have done it, once?"

"Yes, but ages ago. You'll have to help me."

The conjuring up of a long time ago established Rolf as quite a few years older than herself and several years older than Kari. This at once removed acquaintance with him from the still juvenile figure of a possible future fiancé—the concept had not grown into anything as definite as the word husband would imply—into the adult world. Kari receded into the shadows of the schoolroom of which Leona was already scornful, into the fantasy realm where past imaginings languished; a permanent attachment to him became as unreal as an eleven-year-old desire for the religious life, or the ambition of fourteen to be a games instructress like the springy and confident young woman at school whom all Leona's age-group adored that year.

Not only the unexpectedness of Rolf's appearance, his changeling role, were stimulating. It was not a boy who had claimed her, it was a man. This was no half-formed stripling to whom still clung the hermaphrodite quality of childhood playmates; there was nothing about him of the pretense of being grown up that stamped every other partner in the anteroom. This was an adult male with the authority and self-reliance of his sex complete; he was in charge.

The fear of being left alone and the small shock of Rolf's not being Kari became in a moment a sharp inward excitement, an expectation of ascendancy in him, as Leona, her sight clearing in a little physical blaze, saw that he was not only a man, new and unexpected, but a man with laughing eyes and dark good looks, a man of trim and graceful form who moved with confidence and elegance. His plea for her help delighted her with its absurdity, its flattery, for his innate competence assured her that he did know what to do or would copy the others so quickly that it would be the same as if he knew.

Now that their conspiracy was decided upon Rolf could take a view of the girl before him. Kari had been right, the name suited her. Only more a leopard than a lion. But as to looks Kari was quite wrong; either she had changed or Kari had never looked at her. She did not have "rather big features." She had evenly matched features harmoniously spaced by a wide and calm brow, everything belonged together and could not have been any different. The "lot of blond hair" was of silvery pallor, it gleamed softly and was drawn up in a swooping line, in one line, into a twist at exactly the logical point of her cranium and was crowned by the rather touchingly absurd little coronet that all the girls wore. Only hers looked much harder and more glittering than those of the others which he saw to be tinselly so that he deduced correctly that Leona's was the real thing. It was also set slightly forward in front of the thick twist of shining hair and this gave her head the aspect of forethought and design. It was the look of a first-class hairdresser just as her dress stated the master dressmaker in its almost straight flow with no cross lines and no decoration. She stood quietly; knowing her clothes to be exactly fitted to their purpose and to her person, she did not need to trouble with them and she held her thin arms and narrow hands, gloved to the elbow, quite still. She was slight as a reed and could have swayed, so he imagined, like a reed; there was just nothing of her but an attenuated smooth line. Yet she was clearly not delicate but as lean and tough as a boy. She contained a vibrant vitality instantly to be felt and now that he actually saw her, he was overcome not by her beauty but by a claim to allegiance. They were to be allies for more than this moment; he was to support her in some high enterprise which was his own. And this was instantaneously decided.

But for all that there was now no time. The inchoate groups were being sorted into their proper places and directed into the public gaze of a thousand pairs of eyes, a thousand dazzling lights that swam and jittered in an unbelievable expanse of height and breadth lined, hung and trailed with living flowers, banked by a multitude of unseen people. Nothing could be made out distinctly. All was a vast blaze of light, color and scent in which the senses swam.

Nothing familiar was to be identified. Instead of curved blocks of seats, a great wide expanse of empty floor into which the stage itself had disappeared far back behind them, at once lost and much bigger than it is ever seen by any audience. The entire company of the Philharmonic orchestra was dwarfed into a little block of black and white in the shimmering mass of colors, and the young dancers, even to themselves, seemed like a group of black and white marionettes in the vast expanse of parquet. The transformation was dominated more than by the expansive atmosphere of ceremonious festivity, by the living presence of those myriad flowers, as much alive as the great concourse of brilliantly attired guests. It was impossible not to catch the breath, difficult not to feel a momentary sting of tears at the beauty of the scene in its strange and happy mingling of an exquisite artificiality with the simplicity of a pervasive acceptance of it as ordained.

CHAPTER 5

To his own surprise Rolf found that he could easily follow the quite simple pattern of movement, whether from memory or from the habit of fitting himself into a trained group so that he could pick up their actions and rhythms by his own sense of order. He did not think about this, but he was conscious that his own self-respect required him to get through this task with propriety; that he owed to himself and not to Kari or even to the girl.

The blinding and dizzying light and music shut them all out from reality and made what he was doing seem, if not natural, at least no less natural than some of the military routines he constantly carried out in his own certainty that they were entirely pointless and absurd, but which he submitted to in order to earn the right to do what he really did want to do, and do well. As he often said, laughing, there were much worse things one might be asked to do for a reward like flying. This ridiculous and childish show he was being drawn through came into that category of mechanical repetitions needed for a serious purpose but in themselves meaningless.

Only at the moment when the patterns dissolved into couples in the opening waltz and spread out to circle independently of each other did he for a moment falter in doubt as to what to do. He shot a look sideways at the man next to him, took in what was happening an instant late and felt the thump of a lost heartbeat. His hesitation was long enough to unsettle Leona's rhythm and they both missed a step, she with her hands reaching toward him and he arrested in a broken movement. He took in with some apprehension of her that was not sight a sensation of her imploring him not to let her down, collected his wits and slid his left arm behind her back above the waist, the hand turned formally outward, and laid his right hand under hers extended to him. Her left hand settled lightly and gratefully onto his shoulder. As they waited tensely for the beat of the music her wide eyes stared into his so that he received the full shock of her dependence on his resolution and they both parted their lips with an unheard gasp of nervousness. The first beat of the next bar drew them with it and they turned into the revolving dance like fish in a warm pool. The relief of assurance for each of them that the other really could waltz lifted into euphoria. This relief was so strong that Rolf did not at once become aware of the extraordinary urge to possession which immediately afterward took hold of him, as he held Leona, in its enclosed embrace.

His arm could now feel through the fine cloth of his sleeve the firm muscle of her long back and as other dancers joined the original couples on the floor they were obliged to move closer together and felt the vivid reality of their bodies in every nerve as an expression of animal pleasure contained in extreme formality. There was a moment at which they might, without breaking any rule, have ceased waltzing together but neither of them even noticed it and they continued as if joined together, unaware of anything but themselves and their rhythm, circling sedately in disciplined freedom. When a break came in the music so that the Philharmonic could give place to a professional dance band the stop affected them both with a distinct displeasure. Quickly, before any other claim could be made on her, Leona spoke for the first time since that unheard gasp of fright.

"Let's go and see the pop room," she said, urgent to get away from a possible approaching invitation from her father. Her hand was still half in Rolf's, she pulled like an impatient child and he moved at once in the direction she indicated. "I've never heard them. They're supposed to be absolutely super."

"They're from London, aren't they?"

"Of course. All the best beat groups are. I think, this way?"

They wandered down many stairs, along corridors, bewildered by the size and complexity, by the bursts of music, the lavish variety of brilliant colors where whole crowds of gaily dressed women struck the eyes like a shimmering abstract painting which has no form but only color and shifting line. Every space and perspective was populated by this shifting mass of color, noise, warmth, outlined against the ritual black and white of the men so that it all swam into a blur like a dream in which people are no longer separate individuals. It was a maze and they were lost in it for some time underground until they penetrated a corridor that looked familiar except that down its length they heard the rhapsodic, repetitive wail of tribal music pulling them toward its insistent message.

"Isn't it marvelous?" she cried. "Oh, bliss!"

She turned to face him, not touching, and every line of her body seemed to soften and change into a slack suppleness as if her limbs were not built on rigid bone but on some kind of hawser, a series of sinuous ropes. Rolf had never before danced to this kind of music but the communication of its meaning was instant and he slid into the postures and fluid moves of it effortlessly, never touching the girl but joined to her by their movements and the sound.

Leona did not hear the voice of a short boy with comically heavy eyebrows when he called to her that her father was looking for her. Rolf heard the voice and understood the words but they made no connection in his mind to anything that concerned himself and Leona and were forgotten in a moment in the pounding noise and movement.

"Where can she be?" asked Chavanges fretfully for the third time and pulled out his thin gold watch once more.

"Does it matter?" answered his wife with boredom. "Nothing can happen to her here. She is enjoying herself, no doubt."

"But it's past one o'clock."

"Oh, they will dance until three or four at least and *then* go on to breakfast," said Angela, still patiently taking care of her husband's charges. "Everybody does the first time, at their first ball, I mean. It all seems like magic the first time."

"Breakfast? But where can you eat in Vienna at that time?"

"Some of the big cafés stay open, and you can go to one of the main stations. Didn't you do that when you were young? But for you it would have been les Halles, I suppose."

He was intensely irritated by her frivolity.

"For me it was the war," he said bluntly.

Angela stared. That was a forbidden subject with Frenchmen and she happened to know that Chavanges remained in Paris throughout the war, so that the time was perilous ground for him too. But she did not show her feelings after that one look; she turned smiling to Leona's mother.

"Shall I ask Georges to go and look for her?"

"Of course not!" cried Mme. Chavanges and to her husband, "You hear, they will be dancing for hours yet. So why don't we go quietly home, or rather to the hotel, and go peacefully to sleep like proper, middle-aged parents."

It was not a question; she was taunting him. Angie stifled a sigh at the awkwardness of these people, and was at that moment luckily rescued by the entry of an Italian journalist whom she particularly liked, and who came to claim her for a dance.

"You really are behaving abominably tonight," said Chavanges when they were left alone in the box. "I don't know what has got into you."

"You don't?" She looked at him directly and it struck him that she did not often do that. "This is a bad moment for me. My daughter has grown up. You didn't know that? No, of course you didn't. You know nothing. But for once you will have to put up with it. Unless, of course, you want a scene, here?"

He made some rejoinder in a harsh tone but she did not hear it. She heard instead the thick, vulgar voice of the customs official the day before as she made to offer him her handbag for inspection. With a wave of his hand he refused it.

"Madame, you could have a bomb in there and I wouldn't mind," he said in the half-understood language.

And he never took his eyes off Leona, not as they approached him, not as he spoke to Mme. Chavanges and not, for she looked back, as they moved away and the automatic doors cut them off from his lustful gaze. Foul pig, she thought with a shudder. And then those men in the hotel hall.

Some obduracy in her look warned him that she really would make a scene, and he tried to conciliate her.

"But you're never like this," he said plaintively. "Usually you like to dance and you must admit this is a magnificent party. Come, have some more champagne and cheer up a bit."

"Leave me alone," she said loudly, savagely. "For once. This afternoon was enough for one day."

She was, he could not know it, inside an instantaneous vision, almost as real as the reality, of herself asleep in the hotel bed and her husband entering, banging the outer doors, loudly dismissing the porter, putting his head round the bedroom door and then coming in. I've had too much wine, she thought, but the self-reproach did not drive away the vision. She saw him pulling off his clothes with that brisk masculine assumption of right, saw from outside herself her curled-up body as he exposed her with one sweep, and his crowing laugh as he said "I see you were expecting me" because she was naked. And she saw herself slavishly opening up for him, taking his weight, pretending to want him and seeing for an instant his narrowed, expectant eyes in slanting perspective behind the erect, dark-colored member before he settled himself comfortably between her thighs with the help of her spreading movement, to get it over quickly. But then, humiliatingly, she did want it and worked so that all hope of pleasure fled and she hated him and herself for his release as he reared up, taking the weight of his heavy shoulders off her lungs for a moment, and exploded with a thick, long groan, just like the voice of the customs man. Yes, she loathed him and herself and she wanted something, not anything she knew of, that she would ever have, but something quite unknown. I could have an affair, she thought, but she knew she would not again take that path with no outlet. I could leave him and his childish, masterful ways. I am a substitute, I might be a prostitute. A substitute for what?

"Stop looking at your watch," she said viciously, not keeping her voice down. "She's out of your grasp for an hour or so. Leave her alone. You can't have her. She's for someone else. Perhaps for lots of others. Think of that! But not for you. Another man will enjoy *her*. You'll have to put up with *me* since you're too busy to waste time finding a mistress. Or have you found another since the last one married and left the office? No, or you wouldn't always be pestering me as you do lately."

Spittle sprang from her lips in her bitterness, which instantly increased as she gave way to it. He loves his only daughter. Strange phrase. It could mean many things, including the unspeakable act, the thought of which tormented him. She knew that. But was he aware of his longing, of that need she so often saw in his eyes? This she did not know.

His eyes were starting out of his head at her words, he was speechless with horror. She felt triumph.

"I think you must have gone out of your mind," he said at last, his voice strangled and thick in his throat. He pulled at his white tie with a sweating hand that shook visibly.

"No," she replied, now very quiet, resigned. "No, I've gone into it, not out of it." And deliberately relaxing her rigid muscles, she rose to leave the box. Through the arch, she leaned for a moment against the damask-covered wall. I have done something final, she thought blankly. Today was the last time I shall ever go to bed with him, or rather, he with me. She felt weak with the finality of it. She caught her chinchilla wrap off its hook, slung it over her arm and went away.

Behind her her husband sat alone, slumped down on the silly little gilt chair. He looked impassive, but a great wound was torn in his mind. A self-deception that was absolutely needed had been slashed out of him. He was not even angry; the power to transfer the blow to Solange for having exposed his most precious and unknown secret was not in him. He was totally disarmed by the savage suddenness of the attack; unwarned, he had been unable to prepare any defense against the truth. He too lived in an instant through the hot moments of the afternoon, and for the first time recognized the identity of that vision so often conjured up in such moments, that form seen a thousand times in the mind's eye down a long perspective, with which he transformed a simple thrust of habit into a burst of erotic joy.

"It can't be true," he groaned aloud. But it was true. Hearing the sounds of someone entering the outer room of the box, he forced himself upright and turned to hide by facing the neutrality of the public view. Automatically, he looked once more at his watch and catching himself at it, now undeceived, he felt the last absurd humiliation of tears welling into his throat and eyes.

"Now I just wonder where I left my gloves," said Leona, and Rolf looked about him, pretending to search.

"You shed them somewhere, evidently." He touched her naked, thin little hand, which was quite different from holding her for dancing. "Why don't you shed that funny little crown as well? It's slipped crooked."

"Oh no, I'd have to go back to the box to leave it with Mother!"

"I'm hungry. Let's go and find a sausage, or some goulash or something."

"What a good idea. I'm hungry as a wolf."

"Leopard," he said. "Hunting animal, but not a wolf."

"Hunting all right. What have you got against wolves? But we must track down the scent of goulash. Come on."

"No, not there," said Rolf at the door of an imitated Bavarian beer hall. "That's too big."

"It's an absolute warren, this place. There seems to be no end to the odd places we could go."

They wandered off again to the far side of the building and found in a side room off the main promenade a cozy little, shut-away place with dim red lights where a large woman in traditional costume wielded a long ham knife.

"Ham on the bone," said Rolf, "that's more like it. Look, there's room over there in the corner. I'll get the ham, you take the places."

She watched him as he slid between others toward the fat carver and saw as he moved in front of other people waiting that they did not mind but smiled at him equally as if he carried some privilege.

"Come on, sweetie, cut it nice and thick," he said and the big woman grinned and shook her fist at him, glancing sideways to include the others in the joke.

"I suppose you think you're clever, just because you're young and handsome," she said and everyone standing there laughed with Rolf.

"There you are then, nice and thick, just how you like it, eh?" There was something in her tone that made everyone nearby laugh again in a different way.

"Ah," Rolf leaned confidentially over her counter, "you wouldn't have an evening free next week, would you?"

"For you?" She rolled her eyes. "Any time, lovely boy, any time."

He took the round wooden platter off her and squeezed her hand, greasy with the soft fat. As he went to the cash desk she looked after him, shaking her head and smiling.

"These kids," said a man waiting.

"You're only young once," she replied, and her round face became serious.

"What were you two saying?" asked Leona and it struck her oddly that she heard something in her voice that recalled her father.

"Just flirting."

"Flirting! Do you know her, then?"

"No, never seen her before. Do you have to know people before you flirt with them?"

"I don't know," she felt small. "But she's old and fat."

"That's why I flirted with her."

She glanced sideways at him over her raised fork, trying to understand this new concept.

"This ham is good," she said and he laughed. "Why do you laugh?"

"No reason. Yes, it was the funny way you changed the subject."

"I didn't change the subject. Why should I?"

"Of course you did. Why shouldn't you?"

"This is a silly conversation."

"You think so? I thought it was nice. You want to dance again, then?"

"Not yet. Are you in the Army for the same reason as Kari?"

"I don't know," he sounded cautious now. "Why is Kari in the Army? Anyway, I'm not quite in the Army."

She looked attentively for the first time at the details of his badges.

"Oh. Of course. Pilot."

"That's why I'm in the service. Kari just had to do national service. I'm in for several years."

"But why on earth did you do that?"

"I told you. To fly."

"But you could fly without joining up for years! I want to learn, but my father is awkward."

"The only way you can fly properly, professionally I mean, is in the Air Force."

"Yes, I see what you mean. Will you stay in? Make it your career?"

"I don't know yet. Might do worse."

"It seems such an odd choice."

"It's not odd if you want to fly."

"That makes it sound simple."

"It is simple. It's what I want, to fly professionally."

"And your family approves? Is your family military?"

"I don't know that my mother *quite* approves. At least, she didn't at first. I think she thought I might be taking up a cause, you know what I mean?"

"No, what do you mean? And why your mother? You mean your father *does* approve?"

"I haven't any father, to approve or disapprove. He died the day I was born. My mother too, for that matter."

"But you just said . . . ?"

"She is really my adopted mother, you see."

"Oh dear, how awful. What happened?"

"The war," he said, surprised.

"Oh. That. You mean—I say, I'm being dreadfully rude, you don't mind? You mean, your parents were killed and you're an orphan and your mother adopted you?"

"Worse even than that. I don't even know who they were, not even where I was actually born. I'm registered in Ischl, because they had to put something on the registration forms so that I could be properly christened and adopted. But it all happened on the trek and even my mother, who carried me all the way with my grandmother, doesn't know exactly where it was or what they were called."

"But how absolutely . . . !"

"Is it so very bad? I'm me, after all."

"Oh, I didn't mean *bad*. I think it's marvelous just to be you and not a bit of other people."

"I don't know. You see, I don't know how that would be. Anyway, I am part of my mother, and I was part of my grandmother."

"Oh, she's dead? And didn't she ever explain? What an exciting mystery!"

"She wasn't my real grandmother, she was adopted like Mother. But it's not so unusual. Lots of people lost their whole families in the war."

"Well, I know that, of course. But they usually know who they are, just the same. But you—you're so free!"

"No I'm not. I'm bound by all sorts of rules and regulations. In the service to start with, let alone lots of other ways."

"The service, yes, but you chose that so it's freedom in a way."

"I see what you mean. But aren't you free too, in another way?"

"Me? Free? Oh, you don't know! If only *my* parents had died!"

"You don't mean that."

"Well, I suppose not quite. Perhaps not. Perhaps I'd settle for them just being different."

"It seems to me to be freedom to have money, as your family obviously has."

"Well it isn't. There you're absolutely wrong. I can't explain really, but you belong to the money, not the money to you."

"That's what Kari says."

"Anyway, it isn't having money in any exciting way, like having a heap of gold in the cellar and going down to get a handful when you want it. You never see money, or even earn it. You pretend it isn't there, somehow. But I can't explain it."

"But you have the things it buys. That would be something, I rather think."

"I don't have them. I don't have anything. *They* have them."

"Well, you're not quite grown up yet, are you?"

"But my mother is, and she doesn't have anything either, not really. Although half the property comes from her family, it's not hers. And it will be just the same with me. I'm not even allowed to go to the University."

"Have you asked to go?"

"Of course. Dozens of times. When I was at school in England my headmistress even wrote and asked for me! There was a blood row about that! Daddy said I'd put her up to it."

"But why shouldn't you have?"

"Why indeed, you may well ask. But I didn't even know until I got home for the holidays. He saved the row up until I got there."

"If you really wanted to study, you'd just go and do it. Have you got your Abitur?"

"Of course, a whole year early. That's why she wrote to Papa."

"Then why don't you just register at the nearest university?"

"Oh, you don't understand! He'd make the most awful fuss. He'd turn up and talk to everybody, threaten them and bribe them and spoil everything. Until I gave up. So why start when I know I can't?"

"You make him sound pretty much an ogre, you know."

"No, he isn't ogreish. He's sweet. But he gets all sort of sad and gloomy."

"Oh Lord, even worse! Come along, let's go and dance."

"Oh, very well, if you don't want to talk any more."

"Hey, hey, not that complaining tone, if you please! I like to talk all right, but I'm bored with the subject of your family."

"That makes two of us. Let's talk about flying instead."

It was these two sentences that Chavanges heard as he came up to their corner and stood looking down at the two heads, the fair and the dark, bent close together.

"I thought you might come and dance," he said to Leona, trying to sound light. They both started. He shifted his look to the young man and saw puzzled embarrassment in dark eyes raised to his. He gained a general impression of pleasingness which was far from pleasing to himself, and was forced to go on speaking. "I'm sure you have had quite enough of this unwelcome duty, so I'll relieve you of it now."

"No duty, sir, and far from unwelcome," said the young man, rising. "I'm Rolf . . ."

"Yes," Chavanges cut him languidly off. "I gather you were good enough to stand in for Rilla-Lensky. Very kind, very. Might have been better, perhaps, if someone had let us know, but most kind of you in any case."

"There was no time, I'm afraid, sir, to let you know . . ."

"Well, anyway. I'll take her off your hands now. Come along, Leona."

Rolf was not used to this particular kind of rudeness. In his experience the desire to hurt was expressed with more crudeness. But he recognized it in this new guise for what it was and an unaccustomed anger lent him cunning.

"Shall I pick you up in your box, then?" he said to Leona. "About half an hour? We've promised to go to the Lenskys," he added, smiling at Chavanges. It was quite untrue and Rolf was himself surprised both at his invention and the ease of pronouncing a lie with which Chavanges could hardly quarrel.

"All right," agreed Leona with a calm equal to Rolf's. "Half an hour, then?"

"That was awfully clever of you," she said later. "I'd have been stuck with duty dances for the rest of the night if you hadn't thought of that."

"When I'd said it, I was dead scared, in case they'd left already and he might know."

"I didn't give him time to think. I just chattered on."

"Was he mad, really, or only with me?"

"Mad. But I thought you were bored with my family?"

"Well, I was . . . But, which one of the ladies in the box was

63

your mother? I didn't take in what was being said properly. My French is not all that hot."

"Neither, she wasn't there."

"The older one, she said something about Kari . . ."

"That's the Ambassadress. She only meant, there's some kind of joke about Kari. Do you know what it's about? Was it some punishment, will he be on duty all night, or only for the evening?"

"He's not on duty at all . . . Oh Lord, you see how bad I usually am at lying!"

"You mean he wasn't on duty at all?"

"I'm afraid not. You see . . ."

"He just didn't want to come to the Ball? Or was it that he didn't want to be my partner?"

"I don't know. Honestly. He just couldn't come. You know how it is, one can't quite ask."

"They've probably been nagging him endlessly to propose to me. That's enough to put anyone off."

They were on the edge of one of the dance floors and stopped now, the better to talk.

"Not if he'd seen you lately, it wouldn't be. Will you marry him? If he does ask you?"

"No! Well, I don't know. It depends. Listen, why did you come instead of him, tonight?"

"He would be in trouble if he just didn't turn up, you see. I'm sorry, Leona, it's stupid of me just to let it come out like this. I'm not frightfully clever about such things."

"Not as clever as Kari, you mean? Well, don't look like that. You can't expect me to like it, can you?"

"I didn't look at it from your point of view, you see, but if I had I still think it's better not to have left you just standing. Imagine!"

"Why would Kari be in trouble?"

"With his family, he said. I suppose they would try to find out why he didn't turn up, if there were any sort of obvious fuss. Or perhaps the Ball Committee, or whatever it is, would complain. Then he'd have trouble with the Colonel, d'you see?"

"So you came for him."

"Well, of course. I'd never seen you, then."

"I see." She turned her head away and her expression of glowering insult showed a likeness to her father. Rolf saw that the breadth of her forehead was what her face inherited from him, otherwise she was unlike, both in coloring and feature. There was a sweetness, a hint of laughter, in the set of the pale, full lips, even when she scowled.

"So where is he?" she insisted.

"That's just what I don't know." He took her hand and shook it a little. "Look here, Leona. Does it matter where Kari is?"

The question surprised her out of her sulks and she considered it. They looked at each other directly and they were very serious. Then she shook her head and said quietly, as if it were a matter of importance, "No."

"And do you mind me being here instead of him?"

"No. No. Do you mind?"

"I didn't want to come. But now I'm glad. In fact, the thought that I might not have come simply horrifies me."

"Oh. Does it? Because of the Ball, I suppose." Her gaze wandered.

"Not because of the Ball."

"Then why?"

"You know. Don't you?" She looked at him now and saw how his eyes expanded and lightened with sudden laughter and she gave a little gasp, but not this time of nervousness.

"Yes, but tell me."

"You're marvelously beautiful."

"Oh, is that all!" she said, disappointed. "Anyway, I'm not. Everyone says I'm too tall."

"You thought there was something else? Something more?"

"Well . . . I don't know."

"I . . . Hell, there are those people who were in your box, they're coming straight for us. Come, quickly. Talk, say something."

"This way. Let's talk about flying. About flying Saabs."

"They're not as fast as Mirages. But a good aircraft for our purposes. Are they out of sight?"

"Yes, they saw we didn't want to be bothered with them."

"Good. How I wish I'd never said I would meet that crowd tomorrow and finish the tour with them!"

"Meet who? What tour?"

"Some men we were doing an exercise with, last week. They are going on an overland ski run. In fact, they've already gone and I said I'd meet them halfway. But I wish I hadn't, now. We could have talked all the weekend."

"An overland run!"

"It's pretty good, up there. Wild, you know."

"It must be splendid. I was talking to the others about it, yesterday. They're going off, too, a place called Zwettl."

"If you know somebody who's going, why don't you go too?"

"They'd never let me. I think myself lucky I can go to St. Anton for ten days. Papa did agree to that because the house is somebody's grandfather's."

"Well, you'll enjoy that. Anton is fine."

"Dreary old *pistes!* I want to go on a long run. I've never been on one."

"I suppose it's not really a thing for girls. But it would be fun, wouldn't it?"

"Why isn't it a thing for girls? Other girls do."

"Well, yes, it depends how well you ski and whether you're in form."

"We were in Mégève only a few days ago. I won the amateur slalom. That's the second year."

"Oh, then you must be quite good."

"I bet I'm as good as you are!"

"I expect you are," he agreed. "I'm not all that good. When are you going to Anton?"

"Tuesday," she said rather sulkily. "But I've a good mind not to go at all."

"Why not? You'll love it when you're there."

"It's dull. You know what I mean."

"Most people don't think so. Unless, of course, you can get to St. Moritz."

"St. Moritz! That's even worse!" She turned so quickly that her twist of raised hair slipped its fastening and descended like a blond snake, uncurling itself over one shoulder. "Merde to St. Moritz!"

"Good God," he cried, horrified, "you mustn't say things like that!"

He found that his eyes were fixed as if they could not move away from the loosening twist of hair which made him conscious in a quite new way of her thin, bare shoulders, pale in contrast to her throat and face, which were sunbrowned.

"Your hair's fallen down," he said and his mouth was dry.

"I know. Does it matter?"

"Of course it matters." He put up his hand and touched the silky hair. "It's quite straight, isn't it?"

"It was taking off that stupid coronet did it, when I went to the box."

"I think we'd better go and dance," he said uneasily.

"So you won't take me on a ski tour?" she said, as if that were the subject of their conversation. "I can't dance any more with you. They'll notice, they have already. I've hardly danced all night with anybody but you."

"I haven't danced with anybody else at all."

"No, you haven't, have you?"

There was a silence between them, filled with laughter and chatter from outside.

"Shall I go and dance with somebody else?" he asked.

She gave him a sly little glance and they both laughed for sheer happiness.

"You won't, will you?" she said.

"Not if you don't want me to."

"Will you do everything I want?"

"Of course."

"Then take me on your ski tour!"

"You know I can't do that."

"But why not?"

"There will be other men there. And anyway, you said yourself you'd never get permission."

"But next weekend I could, because I'll be away then, anyhow."

"But in St. Anton."

"I could come back. I wouldn't even have to lie. I could just tell them in Anton that I have to go back—say on Friday night. Then you could pick me up on Saturday."

"Your people would make an unholy to-do."

"They wouldn't know." She gazed dreamily before her. "Nobody need know. It would be a secret!"

"It's a lovely idea," he said indulgently, for it was, of course, only a fantasy. "I must take you back, it's after three. Your father said you must be back by then."

"Yes. Even you are beginning to do as he says, I notice."

"Don't be cross. We've had a marvelous time. And you know I can't help it. He'd never let me see you again if I didn't."

"He won't anyway. I saw that in his eye. It's such a shame to stop now."

"We'll arrange, somehow."

"Listen, Rolf! I've just thought, they've got a dinner party tomorrow. We could meet then?"

"Where?" he said, the ski tour instantly forgotten.

"Do you know a place called Riedl?"

"What, that dirty old wine shop in Margareten? But I can't take you there."

"That's just what you can do. Nobody will possibly see us there, don't you see?"

"Yes, but—it's hardly the place for you. I'm amazed you've even heard of it."

"But there's nothing wrong with it! It's just a sort of working-class place, isn't it?"

"How *did* you hear of it?"

"From the others. All the art students go there. It's the done thing. Didn't you know that?"

"Now, how would I know about art students!"

"No, of course, that's all nonsense, I know that. It's not real life. But—it's agreed, then? I'll be there at seven-thirty. Is that all right?"

"You mean it? You're sure? Seven-thirty. I'll be there before you."

"And you won't say anything. Not to a soul. It's just our secret?"

"Not a soul!" he laughed at her. But he too felt the excitement of the clandestine without quite believing in any need for it.

When he took Leona into the box he bowed and exchanged civil farewells with three or four people and afterward could not recall what they had looked like. But as he drove to the little flat belonging to Kari Lensky, where he was going to spend what was left of the night, the dreamlike sense of Leona was troubled by an undertone of restraint, almost of gloom in the few moments spent with Leona's father and those other people. The little car bumped noisily over the cobbles in front of Augarten, giving physical sensation to an oppression of memory which gradually took on the broad and dark aspect of Chavanges, implacably attached—somehow clutching or taking over, he could not get hold of the thought—and shouldering away with his big, solid presence, Rolf from the company, from the girl.

And in fact Chavanges did plant himself with massive authority in the center of the group, separating Rolf and the Leclercs—the rest of the party were long since gone—from himself and his daughter, so that the Leclercs were obliged to retire as if to see the younger man out of the box, off the premises as it were.

"You look worn out," he said, concerned.

"I'm exhausted," she agreed, and she was suddenly very tired. "Where is Mamma?"

"She went to bed ages ago," said Angela, hesitantly. "It's a pity about the flowers, all fading. But a wonderful ball, wasn't it? Did you have a good time?"

"Marvelous. It was wonderful," Leona's voice fell away.

"Have you had something to eat?" suggested Georges, feeling the need to intervene. "There's some of the supper left on the trays. Come and look. Yes, the lobster is all gone, I fear, but there's some chicken salad."

"We did have some delicious ham, but I'm starving again." Rescued, Leona was already picking out the best leavings from the two silver trays sent in by a caterer for the party's supper.

"It's a delightful mixture, don't you agree?" Georges leaned against the arch to watch her eat. "The Ball, I mean. Formality mixed with unpretentiousness. Full of fat, rich people, but lots of handsome young ones too. I quite envy you your first Ball. And the thing doesn't degenerate into a rabble, either. I really enjoyed it." He took the last cigarette from the box on the supper table. "And how was your substitute young man?"

Leona glanced over his lounging shoulder and saw that Angela was firmly in charge of her father.

"He was rather nice," she said with her mouth full. "Good-looking too. Kari did rather well to be on duty, that's my view."

"On duty, was he?" Georges looked a little sly as he said this, but Leona's defiance kept up. She could feel that Georges was on her side, and smiled at him with a little jerk of her shoulders that denied any knowledge.

"I see you're not saying! He probably committed some military crime and got extra duty. That was always happening to me in the Army."

"I should think Kari's a rather unsoldierly type, wouldn't you?" agreed Leona.

"Exceedingly, I should say. However, all's well that ends well. Who *was* your partner, by the way?"

"A pilot. He flies Saabs but says they are not as fast as Mirages."

"His name, I mean," insisted Georges indulgently.

"Rolf Almeric Forstmann. But he isn't *anybody*. He was adopted by someone who picked him up at the end of the war. His real parents were killed the day he was born."

"You've made that up!"

"Oh no. That's just what he told me. And he went into the Air Force because it's the only way you can fly. Properly, that is."

"I must say, young Kari has quite a nerve," Georges smoked musingly.

"It's all right to do that here, it's an old military tradition. Junior officers are accepted everywhere."

"Did he tell you that, too?"

"No, I knew that before."

"Still, a man without even a name. One can't help wondering what your Fa— your parents will say to that."

"I don't see what they could say. It wasn't our fault. Except, perhaps, to thank him."

"And it's not as if the matter will go any further."

"Further?" she said blankly.

In the car, Georges Leclerc considered the evening to have been well spent. Chavanges would certainly now place the subcontract with the Austrian company; whatever his private reservations about young Lensky's conduct, they had not prevented his business plans from prospering.

He said this to Angela. "He's quite different when he's talking business and much nicer. Like he used to be. He was a splendid

all-rounder, before he left the foreign service. Attractive chap, too.
I wonder what happened, there?"

"You know, I think it's the girl growing up. The parents are
going through a phase, like we say about the children."

"You were there when he talked to Roder. He says they got on
well, did you think so?"

"Well, Roder's very easy to get on with. For a trades union
boss, surprisingly so. Yes, they got on like a house afire, I'd say."

"So he said himself. I shall tell the commercial people tomorrow that they can pretty well count on it."

"Why was it important he should like Roder? You didn't have
time to explain to me."

"If the unions didn't want the contract he'd have gone elsewhere. In fact, of course, there is no industrial problem here, but
Chavanges naturally thinks in terms of French labor attitudes;
and it never does any harm to have the boys on your side. They
are very powerful."

"Some say too powerful."

"Well, there's no doubt, there will be a sort of corporative state
here in a generation. And not only here. It's the trend of the
times. Either you take the reasonable men into your confidence
and make their interests the same as your own or you have trouble
with the extremists. It's happening everywhere and I think it's
rather civilized, too. It's the outcome poor old Marx never
thought of."

"Oh, Marx!"

"Angie, do you think we shall get like the Chavanges when the
children grow up? Grim and possessive and hating each other?"

"Of course not. We've got three. Anyway, I think it all depends
on whether you were in love when you married. They weren't and
they both feel there is something they missed, something they will
never have now."

"You don't think they have affairs?"

"Even if they do, it's never the same. People who were married

72

by their families always feel cheated. It's incredible that arranged marriages can still happen."

"You're thinking of Leona? Something tells me that plan will not come off. But I suppose it may. Certainly arranged marriages do still happen, far more than one thinks. Like the other family sin, you just don't know about it."

"What other sin?"

"Incest, of course."

"Incest! Georges, you don't mean that?"

"I do, though. I think lots of men have distinctly odd feelings about their daughters. I dare say mothers do about their sons, too. Not to mention sisters and brothers."

"But you're a sink of iniquity! I never heard of such a thing in my life. Literally. Neither have you, not in real life."

"People wouldn't talk about it to you, you're so innocent. But even where nothing happens, the feelings are there, quite often. Like all those ancient Greeks. Archetypal situations, all those myths."

"I don't know what archetypal means."

"Just as well. Come on, I'll leave the car here for tonight and hope not to get a ticket."

"Archetypal," said Angela, yawning as they trailed up the wide stairs to the first floor. "What next!"

CHAPTER 6

"Why do you gloom into the middle distance like that?" Leona slid into a chair and shuffled her heavy coat off her arms so that it settled over the back of the seat. "No, leave it there. It's all right. You looked quite different from over there, out of uniform."

Arrested in the movement of rising to hang up her coat, Rolf slid back on to the bench.

"Do I? You look rather different in a pullover, from last night, too. I didn't see you come in."

"No. I watched you for a long time. What were you thinking about?"

"Well, as a matter of fact—Kari," he said with a quick grin in anticipation of her reaction to this. She made a face, but only for form's sake because he clearly expected it. "But I'm sorry you find me different."

"Don't be," she said, "close up you're the same. It was only from across the room."

"Of course, we'd only seen each other close up . . ."

At first sight he did appear different in the dark jacket with green revers but now that she looked closely into his face, she was mysteriously stirred by the recognition that in these so changed surroundings he was exactly *so*, just as he had been the night before. When he smiled his eyes slanted a little, outward, altering the whole expression of his features and the narrow and very slightly aquiline nose pulled against his upper lip so that faintly sarcastic—or were they challenging—lines were drawn. There it was, the indescribable differentness of Rolf's face from any other face, its absoluteness, its "onlyness" as it seemed to Leona. He was, just as he was, precisely the same. The alteration that takes place on a second meeting with some new friend and which was already familiar to Leona, and usually as disappointment, did not take place. With a shock of pleasure that gathered into excited expectation she took in as actuality that he was here and real and she was here, that this was not the daydream of light, color, music and scent which slipped unnoticed into fairy-tale unreality and into the past. Here, now, in an ordinariness that bordered on the sordid, among things and people in workaday forms, they were at once magically alone and included in the world of every day.

"You ought to be sitting here and me there. Somebody will bump you there."

"I could sit on the bench beside you?"

He moved over a little and she slid sideways onto the wall seat so that they were almost touching, their eyes very close so that they both felt they could not disentangle their looks. He felt an impulse almost uncontrollably powerful, a physical tug, that he must kiss her just parted lips and the impulse communicated itself so that she drew in her breath, awaiting something unknown but delightful.

"You did manage to get away, then."

"Of course; did you think I wouldn't?"

"I wasn't sure."

He glanced quickly away.

"I was sure," she said proudly. "Tell me, what were you thinking about Kari?"

His eyes came back to her face, with that quick expansion and lightening of laughter. "Not what you think. He wanted to come with me."

"Gracious, what for? But you didn't let him?" Her voice lifted with triumph.

"It's not really funny. Your father has been telephoning the Colonel. Well, not him directly, but he got somebody from the Embassy to ring up and find out why Kari sent me to the Ball instead of keeping his appointment himself."

"Oh no!" she cried and put up a hand to her mouth. "You see? I *told* you."

"Told me?"

"How he was. What happened?"

"To me? Nothing. It's Kari. He can't explain, or he won't. Neither of us thought of that. That he might be asked to explain afterward."

"Oh, why didn't I think of that! I could see he was terrified of you, you being so handsome, and so much older, so that he knew he couldn't get at you with bullying. Why didn't I think of it in time!"

"What could you have done? It's Kari, refusing to explain."

"I could have asked Mamma, she would have insisted on his keeping quiet for once. She's furious with him at the moment about something or other and when she is in a temper—she isn't very often—she can be a real Tartar. Then he does as she says to keep her quiet."

"What a picture of family life!"

"Is it unusual? I don't think it is."

"I don't know, as a matter of fact. But depressing."

"But listen, can they do anything to you? Or Kari?"

"The trouble is, you see, where was Kari last night? If he'd stayed on the station he'd have been all right. He could have said he felt rotten. But he just cleared off as if he really was going to the Ball. Now he won't say, so somebody or other is bound to want to know just where he was."

"Well, where was he, then?" she asked, her voice hesitating with a not understood intimidation.

"That's just what I've no idea of. And, of course, I can't ask because he evidently wouldn't tell even me, since he kept it so quiet in the first place. And that means . . ."

"That he was somewhere he ought not to have been?"

"You think it's obvious too, then?"

"Yes, obvious. But I don't see . . ."

"What?"

"Why it worries you so much. Won't he just tell a lie?"

"He may not get away with that, now. An inquiry from a foreign Embassy, I should think it will have to be reported. Officially, you know. And, you see, there's the business of him being sent down from the University and his father refusing to protect him from being called up. I mean, that's all known. And I'm not too keen on being involved. Of course, Kari is my friend, but I don't want to get any bad reports that might interfere with me flying. If I'm asked, and I may be, I not only don't know the answer, but I couldn't tell even if I did. I mean, he relies on me."

"You evidently suspect something really awful . . . Not just . . . But are you not assuming that he simply had another date? I was taking that for granted."

Rolf did not at once answer. He was frowning before him with the look Leona had commented upon. It was penetrating as a fact into his mind: not for a moment had it occurred to him that Kari's reason for missing the Opera Ball was a girl.

"What am I going to answer if I'm asked? About why I agreed to stand in for Kari last night?"

"That's easy," she replied at once. "You wanted to go and took the chance when it was offered. That commits you to nothing as far as Kari is concerned. And it doesn't commit Kari either."

"Can I get away with that?"

"Why not? As long as that's *all* you say, that's all there was, you just jumped at the chance."

It did sound convincingly lighthearted as Leona said it. He looked at her directly now and began to laugh again. "And it's true! Now I did want to go, now I'm glad. Imagine if I'd missed you!"

"Impossible!"

"You're clever. Fancy you seeing that so quickly. I bet you can cook, too."

She groaned. "What a primitive thing to say."

"I think I am fairly crude. Can you?"

"Cook? No, I can't. Is that bad?"

"Well, you must admit it makes a difference."

"Not to me. If *you* can't cook, I mean."

"Nor to me. I can always eat in Mess, after all."

"This is a silly conversation."

"No, it's a nice conversation. We've said that before. It's better than what we were talking about before. And, you know, I can see me in your eyes. Your eyes are a strange color, gray and blue together. I noticed that, last night."

"I've never seen eyes as dark as yours, all different dark colors. But I can't see me in your eyes."

"The light's in the wrong direction. I have the advantage. Is it all right to kiss you?"

"You taste nice."

"Not half as nice as you. You taste sort of scented."

"Have you had lots of girls?"

"Not many. A few. Do you mind? None that I liked much. Have you?"

"Boys? Oh, lots."

"No, I mean really."

"No."

"Really not?"

"I'm afraid not."

"How old are you?"

"Eighteen. Just."

"I'm nearly twenty-five."

"That's what I guessed. When's your birthday?"

"You know, I told you I don't know. We reckon Easter, it was sometime in the first half of April. That makes me awfully responsible. Being so much older."

"Yes, I see that. But that's a good thing."

"It isn't at all good."

"But why not?"

"It makes everything impossible. It will be years before I can be responsible for anybody."

"Oh. You mean in that way. I rather meant . . . But why do you think like that, straightaway?"

"It just seemed to come up, quite naturally, that I'd be in charge."

"Yes, that's what I meant."

"But it makes it impossible. Because I can't be."

"Would it be different if I earned my own living?"

"Of course. But you don't."

"I could."

"You don't mean that. And if you did, it would be years."

"I might mean it. I could just get a job. Any job."

"That would be a waste. You have to learn something, do something seriously, something for you."

"If I told them straight out that I mean to study, would that make a difference?"

"Yes, naturally. But you won't. Not seriously."

"I might. I think they'd know if I really meant it. I mean Daddy, I think Mamma would be glad, anyway."

"You'll forget all this by the day after tomorrow. When you're in St. Anton."

"So will you when you're flying."

"No, I think I shall remember you more than ever when I'm flying. And if we don't?"

"Forget? By next weekend, you mean?"

"I suppose that is what I meant."

"We could leave a message somewhere. If I haven't forgotten, I could telephone and if you haven't forgotten you could call back and then we could meet."

"Listen, you could telephone from St. Anton on Friday and say you were catching the night train. I'd meet you at the West Station on Saturday morning."

"You mean it, really? Where shall I telephone?"

He wrote the numbers down for her on a used cash slip that lay on the next table.

"It's the little pub in the village near the squadron. They are used to taking messages for us. Just say to tell Forstmann you'll be on the train."

Leona folded the scrap of paper and put it carefully away.

"Will you mind if I do telephone?" she asked. "I mean, I can see . . ."

"If I remember, then it'll be because I want you to have telephoned. That makes it sort of inevitable. Doesn't it?"

"Yes, that leaves us both free to forget or remember."

"I see what you mean about this place," he said after a moment. "There are quite a lot of students. But it's mostly just people resting after the day's work."

"People who are not being anything or anybody, like everybody I know. I get so sick of people who feel that they have to be something else. I mean, at school, everywhere, we talk about 'the people' and imitate dialect, but really everybody, the 'people' too, are being something they aren't. But you can see here that there *are* people who are just carpenters."

"You're not like that, though. You are just what you are and let them be what they are. I mean, you can't be a pseudo-workman who is really an art student or a writer. That would be condescending to people who *are* carpenters."

"A writer—do you think I should be a writer? Would you feel I was working then?"

"I don't see how you could be a writer, just like that. What would you write about? You haven't done anything yet that you could tell other people about."

"Can't one be a writer, just as you're a flyer?"

"Now, Leona, that's silly. Flying is a skill that you learn. Well, I suppose writing is too. But words have to mean something. There's no point in them except communication. You can't write for its own sake; it's for talking to people. Telling them something."

"Even poetry?"

"Surely, especially poetry? If it isn't true then it's nothing, it seems to me. I should think it must be the hardest thing in the world to be, a poet, even for somebody with a lot of talent. To say exactly what you see, feel, mean."

"And say it beautifully as well. But somehow I don't imagine you thinking about poetry. Do you think about a lot of things like that?"

"Well, you see, it's so hard to say anything about flying, or skiing or anything real, that matters. About people, too. How would I say anything about you to somebody who had never seen you, so that he would know how you are?"

"Yes, it's true. How could one tell about horses . . . how beautiful they are, how sort of loving and innocent and happy. How they want to do what you want, how they love showing off. I suppose that's what you mean about flying. Full of something, something you know and want to express and don't know how to. One can't say even the easiest things, like the difference between skiing at ski resorts and skiing as it really is, like it is itself without the lifts and runs and fancy clothes. And without the competitions that are all about money and winning and not about doing it."

"Perhaps it's better just to do things and not talk about them. Let other people tear everything to pieces with words?"

"That's what Kari said; he wrote me a letter months ago, the only one so I didn't forget about it. He was supposed to come in September and he didn't turn up. He wrote and said there was too much to do to waste time playing, the world was all mad and must be changed."

"But that's the opposite of what we're talking about. Kari loves to talk about doing things, changing the world, but he doesn't—just as well—actually do more than talk. The trouble with Kari is too much money. I didn't mean we should do the sort of things Kari thinks about. Just nice, ordinary things, I meant."

"You're not ambitious, then? And you don't want to have a revolution?"

"I guess I'm ambitious, yes," he smiled, unconcernedly paying lip service to what is expected of young men; the rest of her question he took to be a reflection of current fashion, not requiring an answer.

"What I really should like is to grow things," she said, gazing vaguely in front of her. "Like the gardener's family at home. How I envied them when I was small!"

"My mother's mad about gardens. She says when she retires she's going to find a little house with a kitchen garden in a forest and grow potatoes and beans."

"Perhaps your mother played with the gardener's children when she was a child."

"I doubt if her family had a garden, let alone a gardener. They were townspeople and not a bit well off, I think."

Leona said gloomily, "We've got whole squads of gardeners, not only one. I'm hardly allowed to look at things, and certainly not to do anything. It was only when I was very small . . ."

"Well, when she gets it, you can share the garden in the woods with Mother. I'm sure she'll let you do anything you want to."

"Do you think she'll like me?"

"Of course," he said.

They were silent for a time, enclosed in their corner while the big, half-dark room with its bare wooden floor and paneling became more and more noisy with the clatter of many eaters and drinkers and talkers. It was as if there were a glass bell over the two of them, an invisible bubble of privacy where they were alone together.

"It's a long time to next Saturday morning," Rolf said at last. "But it will go quickly. Won't it?"

"I'll tell you when it's gone. It doesn't feel like it now, but it may do."

CHAPTER 7

They parted in the tram and he felt a sharp qualm of uncertainty as the thin, swift figure disappeared into the black night, made darker by the stabbing of streaked wet lights. It was a long time, she would forget to telephone, he did not know at what time the night train arrived, or even what train it was. But Saturday morning remained a fixed point; he took it for granted under the doubts. It was all quite definite and arranged; she had begun, mysteriously, to live inside his mind as soon as she disappeared. It was not like remembering; she was there and every detail of sight, sound and movement was crucially sharpened because everything was related to her. As far as the outer doors of the hotel, which he thought of as huge although it was not large as luxury hotels go, he could see her passage. She ran down the stairway of the star-shaped underpass, ran—he saw her run—across the center always called the rondel, rose again skipping impatiently up the moving staircase and then merged into some confused light bustle that he could not envisage because he had never been inside the hotel. She returned at that point to him in the tram as it trundled and swung along, screeching on a curve, stopping with a double jerk, on its way to the place where his little car waited.

Some passenger had left the evening paper lying on the opposite seat; he picked it up, explaining to Leona inside himself that he had not seen a paper for days. As he idly glanced at the news on the page at which the *Kurier* was folded, it was she who needed to be told what was going on at some interminable international meeting. He refolded the sheets to the front page. More snow coming. The United Nations was holding its General Assembly. In Luxembourg the European Coal and Steel Community . . . New Soviet cruiser said to be patrolling in the Mediterranean. Two daring raids, one on a training unit of the border police from whose barracks several machine pistols had been stolen; the other on an outlying storehouse of the Alpina Mining Company from where a quantity of explosives was missing. The spokesman for the police said not enough care was taken to guard mining explosives and the rules should be tightened up. In answer to a question the official replied that there might well be some connection between the two raids; that was the line the police were working on but they had little as yet to go upon. Rolf had too little experience to divine that the reporter's question must have been an inspired one, planted to get just that answer. But he did wonder how the police could know in less than twenty-four hours that the two robberies had something in common. Leona, what was that you said about wanting a revolution . . . something to do with a letter from Kari, wasn't it? You don't think he could have meant it, do you? Rolf raised his head, laid aside the paper and stared out of the tram window. Next stop, he noted from the street scene. Of course it couldn't be, but odd how the idea had just popped into his head.

The glass door swung almost invisibly away in front of Leona and from the gripping chill outside, the heat of the hotel hall hit her in the face. The keys were upstairs, said the hall porter. So they were back from their dinner party. A familiar knell of warning clanged in Leona's ears as she imitated her father and checked her watch to confirm that it was rather early for them to have left.

She slipped as quietly as possible into her room. The connecting door to the sitting room was not quite closed so rather than draw attention to herself by shutting it, she tiptoed across to her bathroom to hide in there, when she heard her mother's voice speaking of her.

"I can't think why you should assume that Leona is meeting *this* boy. She knows dozens of young people here."

What her father replied came through as a mutter. He was, although Leona could not see him, on the far side of the room staring out of the windows from which he had drawn back the heavy damask curtains. Impatiently, as if interrupting, her mother spoke again.

"In any case, to forbid her to go to St. Anton would be the stupidest thing you could do, if you really think she will see him again, this what-was-his-name." Leona was aware that her mother was only pretending to have forgotten Rolf's name in order to make her husband's concern seem more foolish. "It's a good long way away and she'll be with a whole group of children of her own age. If she stays in Vienna the whole week she can see him at any time."

"I shall send Leona home," he said. His voice sounded strange, thick and painful.

"You can't do that! How will you explain to the Rilla-Lenskys? There'd be a scandal—you know how people talk."

"I don't have to explain anything to the Lenskys. On the contrary, they have some explaining to do to me at luncheon tomorrow."

"But you're making far too much of it! You must have been mad to get Georges Leclerc to ring up the Air Station like that. Whatever Kari Lensky's antics may be, you can't treat him like a naughty child. And you've not only got the poor boy into trouble, but involved Leona as well."

"I admit, it was hasty of me. But what was I to do?"

"You just don't stop to think when you get into a rage. You wanted to damage this perfectly inoffensive young man who was simply standing in for his friend. If you had thanked him civilly that would have been the end of it. Now you've got poor Kari into no end of trouble and made a public scene over Leona. What I'm amazed at is that Georges did as you said. I should have thought he had more sense!"

Without knowing she was going to do it, Leona found herself moving into the half-open door and as her mother saw her with a start of surprise, she spoke, still without knowing what was going to come of it.

"I'm not going to marry Kari, so there. I'm not going to marry anybody. I'm going to the University and if you don't let me go to Paris, I shall stay here." Even as she said it Leona felt that she did not really want to study; she repeated a formula to hide her real wishes.

Her father swung round from the dark square of the window. His whole face was distorted with terrible feeling so that Leona was frightened. He looked ashamed, enraged, fierce and brokenhearted. He flung out one hand toward her mother.

"There! You see? That's what we've come to!"

Leona's mother fixed her daughter with a look of such intense warning that it was a threat. It was the warning already felt downstairs in the hall.

"Let's not lose our heads," she said rapidly. "Let's try to talk calmly."

"Calm! After the things you said to me last night? Today?"

"I am only trying to get you to recognize that this is now a crisis. All families come to it and we have to face it. The child is grown up and she wants to be herself. We can't live her life for her."

"Grown up? She's an infant. She'll make a complete mess of everything, and that's what you want I dare say."

"You see. You instantly say something that makes it impossible to discuss the real matter."

"The real matter being whatever you want it to be, and changing from one minute to the next!"

87

Leona's mother admitted the grain of truth in this by bending her head with a sigh.

"That's often true. When we have arguments I can never say just what I mean." This astonished Leona, who had thought that only she was affected by this powerful and not understood taboo on expressing herself to her father. "The conversation always seems to get into the wrong shape for me to keep hold of it. At this moment I can see in your face that you simply think I am defying you to annoy you. You can't imagine that anything a woman says, let alone me, can be useful, that I may know things about this that you can't know."

"I don't know what you're talking about. As usual, you have at once gone off into a different subject—yourself. I am talking about Leona."

"So am I. And I know what is happening to Leona because it happened to me. Only I was brought up to be stupid and I didn't know it at the time. She has been properly educated so she is conscious of herself. But her way of looking at things is just as valid as yours. Every law says it isn't. But it is, and that is why families quarrel because men can never agree—they don't even know—that women have an entirely different approach. No, it's much more than an . . ."

"God, as if I didn't know that! You instantly, all women instantly, become hysterical, emotional, and talk about something else."

"But can't you see that it is you and not me who continually tries to change the subject . . . ?"

She would have continued to stammer out what flooded through her whirling mind when she shifted her gaze and caught from Leona a breathless, imploring, helpless glare. The bewildered child was literally hanging on her mother's next words, she could feel it like a physical clutching as if Leona felt herself slipping down a slope of dependence from which she would never again be able to struggle back. This image of a helpless slide toward a precipice fixed itself and cleared her mind for the moment of her own complex angers. This time, at least, she would not be deflected into a quarrel without an outcome.

"I will explain. And in words of one syllable. Leona is as much my child as yours. I disagree with your methods of handling her, even with the whole idea of 'handling' her at all. She is not going to be 'given in marriage' as I was, she is not yours to give away. It doesn't matter for Leona what the Lensky family say about the Opera Ball, what their son intends. She has to make up her own mind and she has made it up. You can't say that wasn't clearly expressed. She has just told you that she doesn't want to marry Lensky."

"Of course she has to make up her own mind. Can you possibly be saying that I have ever dreamed of marrying her against her will? That's a monstrous idea, typical of you. You hate me and you'd say anything—in front of the child, too—to put me in the wrong."

"Yes. You have dreamed of marrying her against her will. For over a year you have put every kind of moral and emotional pressure on her to agree that the Lensky boy is her predestined husband. How can she withstand your wishes? She adores you, you have always spoiled her, given her everything before she even felt she wanted something. She can't formulate it, I'm amazed she feels it, that there is a fundamental difference, basic, absolute, between your buying her a new pony and your buying her a husband. Her wanting to study is her way of saying she doesn't want to be managed, it's the first thing she's ever wanted that you didn't suggest, arrange for. That's why you stubbornly refuse to consider it. Because then she would see, talk, experience, without your supervision, she would get a *means of comparison*."

"Now I am blamed for taking care of my only child! Was it wrong to spoil her, as you call it? Wrong now to want her safety, stability?"

"You are talking in rhetoric. Oh yes, I know what rhetoric is!

89

To marry her before she knows what she's doing is not wanting her safety. It's wanting your own safety, the safety of your possession."

"Even you will hardly deny that possessions need to be protected. In our mad world? Think what you are saying for once, Solange!"

"I'm not talking about . . . No. I won't go off on that tack. There's no reason for all this fuss. No reason to do anything at all. Let her go to St. Anton to ski, where she's chaperoned by a whole mob of young people and won't be alone for a single waking moment."

"I'm going anyway," said Leona, feeling herself almost forgotten as the object of her parents' argument. She was jostled and hemmed in by the shadowy and formless bulks of a dozen different meanings in which the only factor clear to her was that her mother was, for whatever reason, doing what she, Leona, wanted. That was clear, and something else was taking shape; in the welter of old animosities and conflicts between her mother and father, the figure of Rolf was disappearing. She must not say anything to cause his reappearance.

They were still arguing but Leona did not hear what they said next; she was thinking about her mother's words, about emotional pressure, which comforted her in her feeling that she was devious and dishonest with her father. She had felt as a burden for years the unspoken, unthought even, threat somewhere that she could hurt him; she felt it obscurely as a weighty dark presence having something to do with the lack of love between her parents, a factor she was aware of, it being contrary to the whole body of implicit and explicit statements forming the contemporary atmosphere. Her mother's words suggested that for Leona to hide herself, and in this moment to hide Rolf too, from her father was not so unnatural as his constant demand for total subjection in return for his total love always made it seem.

"Papa, do let me go," she implored him plaintively as they

paused in their angry battering. "I can't call it off now! And what would I do here all next week when you'll be busy all the time?"

She moved toward him, intending the physical plea of an embrace, but to her surprise and dismay her father withdrew sharply, giving her the impression that he really was angry with her.

"But I haven't done anything," she complained. "It wasn't my fault last night. Why should I be punished?"

"You are quite right there," he muttered, agreeing to be manipulated. She saw that he capitulated and was now quite unable to follow what was happening, so abruptly was his displeasure altered into a familiar, half-sullen complaisance. She glanced at her mother for advice and was startled by a look of disgust and contempt which she hid from herself by throwing her arms round her father's neck with exaggerated childishness and rubbing her pale head against his already rough and dark chin. The mingled odors of brandy and tobacco and toilet waters and the sensation of his solidity which were always at once comforting and exciting reached her for the first time as strange, even unpleasant. There was an inner flash of recall, the taste of Rolf's mouth, and Leona felt a bewildered consciousness of doing something wrong. She connected this, not with its unknown real cause, the use of physical love for something not itself, but with her mother's scornful look, and she moved away from her father with a hoydenish jump as he patted her shoulder not at all in his usual manner.

"Then I can go?" she cried. "Oh, you are a darling!" She whirled on her heel with joy and relief, to pay his fee of pleasure at giving her her wish. "Gracious, look at the time. I must go to bed."

It was a double door between the rooms and Leona closed both, shutting off all sound from the sitting room. Not that there was anything much more to hear. The words that hung in the air between the man and the woman remained unspoken. You have robbed me of my daughter with your filthy, degenerate suspicions, made it impossible to give her even a good-night kiss. Her mother ignored him, sinking down into a chair to examine a sudden perception which amounted to certainty, that Leona really had been in touch with "what-was-his-name" and that something much more than a breach in her own passivity over Leona had occurred. Where did she get that idea; it just was there and she knew it was more than an idea. What shall I do if it does go further? But it won't; he is bound by his military duties and she is going away and will forget it all.

For a few moments she was unconscious of the man lowering in his defeat and his inability to understand it; then he roused her by speaking aloud.

"I have to get out of this room for half an hour. I'm going downstairs."

"I'll come too," she answered, from the habit of agreeing with what he decided.

"Must you? Well, I can't stop you. But open the windows."

Reminded of their changed relationship, she looked up quickly and caught such a stare of his black anger and hatred, a mutilated look she senselessly thought it, that she was almost afraid of him. Her apprehension affected him powerfully with the knowledge of his superior height and weight so that he lifted his clenched fist as if to strike her. She flinched and withdrew sharply, her elbow catching the rested receiver of the telephone that stood on the table by her chair. This instrument of the public world gave out a small pinging sound. His suffused eyes shifted involuntarily to it and its presence restrained his primitive urge to repay her for breaking the first law of civilization; that the truth is too powerful to be spoken aloud.

He went out by the door direct into the corridor, leaving it swinging. His wife went to the windows, where the curtains were open, and unfastened the quite heavy inner ones which fitted so closely that they resisted at first and then gave way, letting in a chill that became a blast of bitter and damp wind as she opened the outer frames as well. The door slammed, the window on one side was sucked back into place with a thump hurting her wrist. She pulled impatiently at it again, it moved easily now that there was no counterdraft, and the silken room was full of icy movement so that everything loose in it shifted and rustled as if alive. She shivered and a sob of weariness and disgust caught in her throat. It was immediately cold inside the room and she went into the bedroom to escape the wind. But the two beds standing primly together, covers neatly turned down, with their nightclothes draped across the corners were too much for her. She fled, waiting only to pick up her evening bag, but when she reached the warm little bar, empty for it was after eleven o'clock on the evening after the Opera Ball, there was nobody there but the barman. She sat down in the corner by the silent grand piano. The man came over but she could not think what to order, and when she glanced up, lost for words, she was frightened by an expression of sudden caution in his inclined polite face.

"Whisky and soda, please," she stammered. "No ice. And can I have some cigarettes?" She never drank whisky; she had simply repeated words frequently used by her husband.

"Which cigarettes would Madame prefer?" he asked.

"I—I don't know the brands here. Any mild ones will do."

He brought her the drink and a packet of Kent, which he opened and offered so that she took one and he lit it for her. She had never in her life been in a bar by herself before, but she was so dismayed by her own strange appearance reflected in the barman's look, and by the absence of her husband, that she did not notice that. He must have gone out, without a coat, without anything. The man had spoken to her in English and she had replied in that language. Now she forgot and asked him in French if it were snowing.

"I believe it is," he replied in the same language, "or it was, half an hour ago."

"It is terribly cold here in Vienna."

"It is always colder in winter than in Paris," he agreed. "And this has been a winter! It started snowing in the first week of November and hasn't stopped since."

She considered offering him a drink, but was not sure whether that was a possible thing to do, so she said no more. What can he be doing, where can he have gone? He'll catch his death of cold and then he'll have bronchitis again.

Like many big, solidly built men, Chavanges was not as robust as he seemed. In spite of regular injections every autumn he never passed a winter without some ailment, while his wife and daughter, who both looked as fragile as water sprites, did not so much as sneeze. If he does get ill, we have no doctor here. But of course, the hotel will know of one. And the Embassy. What am I worrying about? There was something absurd about her wifely concern and the faint humor of this thought cheered her up, or perhaps it was the whisky which she found she rather liked, for the first time. The flavor which had always seemed coarse was now aromatic and comforting. Two men came in and ordered "Scotch" but since they were Americans they found nothing odd in a beautiful woman in evening dress taking a nightcap alone and did not stare as Europeans would have done. She sat there for some time, but her husband did not appear.

She did not know what time he came in, although he woke her. It must have been very late, or early, for after spending hours half-sleeping and confusedly dreaming of unrecalled but unpleasant flights and pursuits she had fallen deeply asleep. She murmured a question which he did not answer and a moment later was floating away again.

For the next two days they were, fortunately, fully occupied and on Monday evening Leona left on the train for St. Anton. Her father took her to the sleeping car and heavily tipped its attendant; she was met at the other end by her host and fellow guest after a long telephone call between Chavanges and the grandfather of one of her friends who owned the mountain cottage. None of these precautions was of the slightest avail. Before she even left the railway station Leona found a telephone box and dialed the numbers given her by Rolf. The scrap of paper was hidden, not in her passport which one of her parents might conceivably look at, but in the little colored purse inside her shoulder bag in which Leona kept a rarely used lipstick and eyeshadow. Nobody was likely to look there. She had been well trained, the well-brought-up young girl, to deceive; it was her only means of defense.

The deep, slurring voice of the man at the other end was difficult to understand; she made him repeat back her message and write it down to pass on to Rolf that evening. She thought of him as an old man with a rough head who held her message in a big, coarse hand used to farming implements, who wrote slowly on a slip of paper such as she held in her own hand, and tucked it away in a tobacco-smelling pocket of his waistcoat until Rolf should arrive. She imagined all this as if it were true, even the beery taproom where the telephone hung on the wall was not in reality unlike her picture; indeed she did not need to invent much for she had seen many such rooms in a country where coffee and soft drinks are not divided by law from beer and wines. She had been to such places with her school friends formerly, because most of them had little money.

Such simple, undecorated places of refreshment were unknown in the place she was actually in; there everything was carefully arranged with a clever use of Alpine folk art, half-original and half-imitated and all designed for the enjoyment of strangers. It was just what Leona needed at that moment to add to the excitement of her small, still childish and only half-serious plot; it showed her what her whole future life was to be, a pretty, posed and carefully planned unreality. With the secrecy of first love she put Rolf out of her mind. He did not belong in this interim and could be damaged for her by its artificiality; she hid him as the charming *kitsch* of St. Anton hid the reality of the mountains and the harsh, stubborn and xenophobic nature of their people. This was tourist Aus-

tria which did not exist unless the holidaymakers were looking at
it.

Asleep she dreamed a great deal, dreams in which Rolf always
appeared and was always different. The differentness was important, *he* did not change but represented differentness and liberty.
Leona even recognized with some clarity that Rolf had inherited
the aura of the sole moments of liberty she knew; the later years
at the French Lycée in Vienna when in company with her fellow
pupils she went to school and back, to tennis or skating, to music
practice and dancing class on the trams and buses without adult
supervision. Children in that old, urbane and well-ordered city
need no protection and are much freer among their equals than in
a boarding school or in places where pupils are delivered at school
by automobile and collected again, like privileged prisoners. And
Leona's night dreams reflected these memories; in them she constantly wandered about parks and gardens, and Rolf was constantly just about to meet her in a magic transformation scene
that might well have been the Opera Ball held in high summer in
the Belvedere Gardens.

On Friday afternoon she returned early to the house and telephoned Vienna so that she could pretend a recall from there. In
the snow-streaked and light-splashed evening she climbed aboard
the night train and so completely was she lost in her masquerade
that she half believed herself to be obeying a summons from her
parents.

The end of such an adventure might have been the blank
loneliness and uncertainty of no greeting among the crowd of ski-
carrying travelers on the platform who menaced each other's eyes
with every swing of their dangerous toys. The hazards of the appointment were great enough to daunt anyone with enough experience to count them over. Rolf might mistake the train, he
might be delayed on his way to the city if he ever started for he
might be recalled to duty, he might quite simply have forgotten,
Leona might have become an unattainable ghost from a world

he did not know and could not enter, or he might have met another girl who was present and real; he might even be ill or even have crashed an aircraft. But he did not oversleep, nothing at all intervened. He rolled out of bed at five-thirty in the black and drove his rattling little Fiat over the snow-scoured and slippery roads, over the wide Danube bridge dwarfed by the huge blocks of flats in the new northern suburbs and across the city to the West Station where the train was late, held up by driving snow, as the chalked notice informed him.

It was bitter cold with a Siberian wind on the exposed platform; Rolf was given time to consider what he was doing, time for prudence to begin whispering. By the time the train slid quietly in he was convinced that he was about to explain to Leona how impossible was their undertaking, about to drive her, whether she liked it or not, to the hotel where her parents still slept. The long strip, almost empty a moment before, was immediately populated by a noisy and multicolored mob; he could distinguish no single figure. Then he saw her because she was the only one there who was standing still, waiting to be found. There was no shock of excitement, but recognition of something already decided, a reliving of what had happened a hundred times in his mind. So he spoke as he came up with her, carrying on with a conversation begun nine days ago with the same words. But this time Leona spoke those words.

"I'm awfully sorry to be so late."

"Watch it with those things. You'll brain somebody," he said simultaneously. And he grasped her black and yellow skis, swaying over her own and other heads as a horde of schoolchildren, similarly equipped, rammed her from the side. "Hang on to me. What a crowd."

"I was lucky to get a sleeper," she gasped, jostled and shoved, deafened by shrill shouts and the shriller whistles of the exhausted schoolteachers trying to collect their unruly charges. "The train was crammed to busting. But somebody canceled."

"Aren't stations awful in the early morning?" he said. "This way. D'you want breakfast?"

"Yes, please. Starving, I am."

They struggled through to the comparative space and calm of the railway hall bathed in the cruel and jaded light of the previous night's sleeplessness.

"Not here, though. The station place will be full of over-nighters. Let's get to the car and we'll stop at the first coffeehouse we can see open."

"What a darling little car! Can you manage my skis? Here, I'll hold them steady while you do up the straps. Don't they look funny! About twice the length of the car!"

"You leave my car alone," he said. "It's a very respectable car, I'll have you know. I'm its jubilee owner."

"Twenty-fifth or fiftieth? All right, all right. I take it back. Yes. That bag is all my luggage. Will it go in?"

"It'll have to." He shoved it sideways on the back seat beside his own. "Good thing you didn't bring a big case, though."

They forced themselves in, made bulky by ski suits and boots, folding up their knees, his discarded leather coat on top of the luggage almost touching the roof behind them. All the windows at once steamed up.

"Come on, let's get going," she urged, "let's eat quickly and get out of the town."

"I can't drive any faster. Two pairs of skis make it unwieldy. We'd fly at more than fifty."

"Here's a place open, here on the right. I can see a waiter polishing tables."

CHAPTER 8

•

The wind was too steady to batter and pull at the little car as long as they drove directly northward, but when past Horn the exposed road bent to the northwest, its driving force could be felt pushing from the northeast with slanting, stubborn energy. It was not really weather for driving a motor intended for use as a town runabout over the open swell of the Waldviertel plateau. The snow flew across their path, almost horizontal in the gale, piling up against ledges and windows on the passenger side so that presently they were enclosed in the strange, pale gloom of it as it clung half-frozen to their moving box. The blizzard alienated the countryside; field boundaries and low dwellings were half obliterated and many of the villages being well off the road, they passed invisible, hidden by the whirl of gray-white obscurity. Forest loomed black on westward faces, streaked white and black to the east so that it appeared as great solid masses, rock outcrops perhaps, rather than trees. Buildings tall enough to be recognized as such wheeled jerkily and mysteriously by, silos like fortress towers, once or twice a big house on an eminence. It was silent, unpeopled, a land abandoned, left to the wild. All its activity, sparser and slower in any case than in any other part of the country, was stilled, held up until the weather should change, and what was to be seen might have been one great open heathland without human habitation.

There was not only no traffic so that another vehicle approaching or overtaking could be seen for miles on the curving and sweeping road, there was none of the advertising near buildings that they were used to, filling stations were few and far between, and only once did they cross a railway track. •

"Why is it so empty?" she asked, after a long silence.

"It's only fifteen years, less, since the Treaty," he said. "We're always getting it in citizenship lectures. Of course, I was a boy then. Anyway I wasn't brought up here. But nothing much was done during the First Republic, the frontier being so abruptly cut off there." He vaguely waved a hand past Leona. "And then, you can imagine, the Russians for ten years. Even now it's harder to get any kind of investment for this area than anywhere else. I suppose it's just terribly poor, really."

"Of course, anywhere would look empty in this weather."

"It is pretty lonely here, always. Does it . . ." He looked sideways to judge. "Does it—intimidate you?"

"No. It's wonderful. Don't *you* think so?"

"I do, yes. I just wondered."

"It's even more special than I expected. Like a lost, dreaming, deserted wasteland."

"Most people don't like it. Strangers, I mean."

"Good. Let them stay away."

"A startling contrast to the Opera Ball, isn't it, though?"

She thought about this.

"Not really," she said at last. "Now that I see it, it feels like what ought to have been outside, in the night, the night of the Ball."

"I don't understand that."

"No. I can't say it like it feels. Listen, the Ball reminds me. I meant to ask you. Why is your second name Almeric? I've never heard of anybody being called that before."

"He was a Frankish knight, who went to the Crusades. Abandoned home and family to fight in a cause. He helped to found the Lusitanian kingdom, you've heard of that?"

"Vaguely. Was he in a poem?"

"I believe he was. Some troubadour thing, perhaps."

"But why, then?"

"Why me, you mean? Ah, that I don't really know about. My mother has a prejudice about people who take up causes, I think she was making some point."

"How interesting. When I know her I shall ask her."

He laughed at that. "She won't tell you much. She's a tough old silent bird. She never really tells anything, you won't get much out of her."

"Tough?"

"Not rough and tough. Quiet and logical tough."

"And very old?"

"Well, she must be. She was a trained operation sister during the last war, so she must be over fifty, I think fifty-two or so."

"I don't think that's so very old. My father is almost fifty but he doesn't like to be thought even middle-aged. But don't you know? Don't you celebrate birthdays?"

"Never. Name days. Not birthdays. But perhaps she just seems older. She's so—um—detached from everything."

"Including you?"

"In a way. She always made me think for myself, starting when I first went to school. She would never tell me what to wear, for instance. I had to decide and I remember, one of those things you remember very clearly, wanting to wear a new pullover without a coat, because it was new. It was absolutely freezing. She didn't comment, just let me learn for myself. I always had to clean my own room and as I got bigger take my turn shopping and cooking with them. They never told me, it was all example. I was just expected to."

He stopped and considered.

"It was good practice for flying. Perhaps that's why I'm a good flying instructor now. You have to make people think for themselves, you see. It's so much easier to do everything yourself, or drum it into other men by rote, repetition. But that's no good for flying. They have to learn why they must do things, what it all means. I didn't know until I began teaching myself, how much quiet patience has to go into it, how much she must have thought it out when I was small."

"Are you a flying instructor all the time?" she asked, disappointed by the idea.

"I've only done one tour of teaching so far, but it will come round again. I rather enjoyed it, at any rate as a change from operational courses and all that. But really there's nothing like flying alone. That's the best. Especially at night."

"It must be," she said dreamily, enviously.

"But everybody has to do everything in our air force, in turn. There aren't enough of us to waste anything."

"Doesn't your mother mind you having taken up a cause?"

"But I haven't. I told you, it was the only way to fly. Anyway, if it turns into a cause, it will be defense. The cause would be survival and nobody could quarrel with that. If it ever became necessary."

"I'm going to learn to fly."

"Yes, you have to, or you'll never understand."

"You think I'll be able to?"

"Of course. Why not? You can do anything. You just have to concentrate and learn. Afterward it's splendid, when you know how."

"Well, I don't know about *anything*. I haven't got much brains."

"It's not a matter of brains, and you don't know. You haven't really tried at anything yet."

"No, I haven't, not yet." She pursued a line of thinking that was not clear to herself yet. "I told them, though. That I'm not going to marry. That I'm going to study. Only I'm not sure that I want, really, to go to the University."

"You *told* them! Leona, did you really?"

"Yes, truly, I did." She did not resent being thought a liar; although, the accusation being true, for she constantly lied to her parents, she might well have felt anger. "And not hinting— straight out. They were discussing me and I interrupted. I said I was not going to get married and I meant to study and if they would not let me go to the Sorbonne, I should stay in Vienna."

Leona was obliged to admit to herself that this factual statement did not sound at all convincing; it was more or less true when she said it to her father and mother but it had, in the meantime, become untrue; the mention of Paris established definitely in her own mind that she had not the slightest intention of going to any university and certainly not to the Sorbonne. And she felt with astonishment that she could stick to this decision and that she knew where—she felt it as coming from outside herself—it came from.

"But you can't stay here unless your father agrees. You wouldn't have any money."

"That's just it. I have a bit. Not much. My grandmother left it to me direct. Mamma and Uncle Alain are the trustees, but it's mine after my eighteenth birthday although naturally I've never had anything to do with it."

"And you really mean to do something about it?"

"I already have. I wrote to Uncle Alain from St. Anton."

"Good God. You show signs of real determination."

"Well, I told you."

"There will be a blazing row when your father hears."

"I suppose there will. But he'll be back home by then, with all his businesses to take care of."

"That sounds as if you mean to stay here now, not go back home at all. But things couldn't possibly be arranged as quickly as that. And anyway, this Uncle Alain will at once get in touch with your father."

"Oh no. I said to write to me direct."

"Who is he? Is he a lawyer?"

"Yes, of course. He's the chief legal eagle of, what's it called, the holdings company."

"Then of course he will tell your father immediately. Even if you were of age, he'd do that I should think. It's the first thing any lawyer would do."

"But why? He's supposed to be *my* trustee. I've seen the will where it says so, they showed it to me after I was eighteen, in January."

"The will may say so. But that's what he'll do, go straight to your father. You being a girl and all that."

"You really think so?" She was much cast down by this thought. "Yes, I suppose you're right."

"Well, it's obvious. He's in charge so he'll get in touch with your parents at once. He would have to, I think, if as you say, your mother is the other trustee."

"I hadn't thought of that." Leona thought this over, but the crucial fact of her position was so much taken for granted by her that she never even thought of mentioning to Rolf that she was the only child of her parents and therefore the heiress to all their property. That all-important detail remained unknown to him.

"It's unfair," she burst out, almost in tears of dismay.

"Well, let's not think about it now," he said hastily. "It will probably never happen."

And while she was still examining the thought that Rolf did not quite believe her and clearly did not take her action seriously, they reached a crossroads and he stopped the car to read the half-obscured sign.

"Yes, this way," he said. "There's a nice pub in the village. It's not far now."

"I'm hungry again."

"So am I. It's nearly twelve o'clock. It will be boiled bacon and dumplings, I bet. I hope you don't mind?"

"I don't mind. I'm sick of foody food."

It was an aggressively square house, recently rebuilt and full of modern plastic in bright colors with correspondingly stark neon lighting in the taproom, where there proudly stood an automatic music box. Next to the counter with the beer pulls was a large table for regular customers, surrounded by a group of elderly villagers in a fog of harsh tobacco smoke who stared covertly at the tall young strangers making their way toward the table at the far end of the room. All the tables were enclosed by low-backed benches of highly varnished, light-colored wood. The floor was of red tiles, gleaming and clean; everything was almost painfully clean. Except for the local men and themselves, the room was empty. The two looked at each other and Leona made a slight grimace at the fortunately silent music box.

"Don't say anything," he cautioned her in an undertone, laughing a little, "they are terribly proud of their newness."

Without warning, the smile, the warmth of a guiding hand on her forearm, the inclusion in some exclusive duality, sent a jolt of brilliant intense sensation through Leona such as she had never before felt so that she paused for a second in her movement and a tiny gasp of wonder escaped her. She was no more ignorant than any other girl, and like other girls not entirely physically innocent either; but that instantaneous pang, carrying a quality of terror as well as joy, left her quite weak as if her knees must give way. A brawny girl with brilliantly dyed hair greeted Rolf as an acquaintance and nodded at Leona, in whose cheeks a bright color had come up.

"It's lovely and warm in here," she said quickly, to cover that, and smiled dazedly.

Rolf was right. They had cooked bacon and dumplings for their midday dinner. Yes, certainly there was plenty. Yes, they had no other guests. All the five rooms were free.

"Even our usual salesmen haven't got this far this week," said the girl cheerfully. "Usually we have one or two of them but the weather is just too bad. So you mean to try your luck, do you? They say it will stop in the next hour or so."

To indicate the source of this weather news she tipped her piled hair in the direction of the table surrounded by local men.

"Even at the weekend you have salesmen staying?" asked Leona in order to be included in the conversation.

"Oh sure, sometimes. They do half their business private, you know."

"What does she mean?" whispered Leona when the waitress went away.

"Commercial salesmen. Travelers. They always go to the same hotels, wherever they are on their rounds." He frowned at her, curious. "Don't you know how farmers are supplied with seeds, fertilizers, machines? Shops, too, for that matter?"

She shook her head.

"Perhaps they do it differently in France?"

"I don't know. You know—I've never thought about it."

"I believe it is going to stop," said Rolf, pushing the curtain back to see out of the half-obscured window.

"It's letting up," said the waitress, seeing his gesture as she came back with their pale, foaming beer. "They said it would. Food's just coming."

"I won't be a minute," said Rolf, catching sight of the figure of the landlord at the half-open door to the kitchen.

The man had magnificent moustaches and these were emphasized by his short stature and thick shoulders. He hardly came up to Rolf's chin as he turned to welcome the guest.

Rolf greeted him and his wife who was doing the cooking. "It smells good in here." To the man, he said, "Have you a room and somewhere to put the car in case it starts snowing hard again? We want to make a short tour this afternoon and won't be back until dark. Then we can do Long Back tomorrow if the snow holds off."

"You know the district well, then?" the man put his question in a way that could not offend a guest.

"Oh yes. I'm stationed near here. And I have a compass. You won't have to get out the rescue people."

"You'll be wanting supper, then?" his wife intervened.

They were slightly uneasy and the man glanced past Rolf's arm toward the corner table, but an air of unquestioning naturalness which was not quite authority in Rolf's manner made it impossible to ask direct questions, although the first thing the waitress had noticed and reported on was Leona's unringed hand.

"And a bathroom if you have hot water."

"Of course we have hot water," said the man. "You can have the corner room next to the bath."

"It'll be private. There's nobody else likely to come today. I'm surprised to see you as it is."

Rolf smiled at the woman gratefully. She was ladling soup into their plates and putting them carefully onto the waitress's tray.

"You're at the tank school, then?" queried the landlord.

"No, the air base. I'll sign the form now if you've got it."

The girl hearing, she pulled out a block of registration forms from under the counter and gave Rolf one before picking up the tray. He scrawled on it, his head still half turned to the innkeeper.

"Then you know about going too close to the border?"

"Yes, I know," said Rolf nodding. They grinned at each other, something having been decided between them, and the slight alteration in their manner was reflected by the two women at once. This happened before the man read the information on the form, which in districts near the Czech border still had to be correctly filled in, a regulation long fallen into disuse in most places.

"He's all right," said the landlord as Rolf went back to the table.

"Handsome, isn't he?"

"Yes, he's a right fellow," agreed the man.

"Pity about beer," said Leona. "It looks so much nicer than it tastes."

"You should have said. I didn't think. You could have had wine and soda if you'd rather."

"What was all that conversation?"

He looked straight at her, direct into her wide-set gray eyes.

"I was arranging the room," he said, quietly but very clearly. "But it doesn't have to be a decision, not yet. It's absolutely whatever you say."

She looked away. "I don't know," she said uneasily. "You're very definite about it, suddenly."

"It's just, while I was talking to them, I felt how important this is. I felt like you do when somebody taps you on the shoulder and says, 'Hey, what are you doing?' You know how I mean?"

"Oh dear," she said. She was frightened by his directness and his level look, but not in the way that she expected and wanted to be frightened. To temporize she piled food on her plate and began to eat.

They put the car into the big outhouse of corrugated metal, glowing fantastically with orange-colored anti-rust paint. It was, apart from their own persons, the only splash of brightness. All else was composed of infinite graduations between black and white. The wind had dropped a little, the gusts still buffeting but less constantly and they were no longer obliged to lean into the strong pressure of the air. The man stood at the sliding door of the new barn and showed them where the lane dipped away into fields obliterated by the infinite blankness.

In less than five minutes they were entirely alone, isolated in a great sighing emptiness of snow slopes. Human dwellings with their claims were smoothed off into humps and as they moved away from a long tongue of woodland even the wind lost its moan and rustle against barriers and swept with a hushing blast over the upland so that it seemed like silence in the sustained bleakness. For a long time they moved upward, the roll of the land providing long swoops between stretches across which they must almost plod forward and up. After half an hour Leona was tired but then without any noticeable change she felt the different rhythm that was needed and adopted a quite new style and drive. It was now much colder and the wintry afternoon was drenched through and through with a steely blue chill light that produced no radiance and was almost palpably weighty. It was a dream world of white and cold emptiness but without the least threat or fear in it. It was pure escape.

Not a word was spoken and speech would have been impossible, until they reached the upper surface of a long swell from where, on the southern side, could be seen a higher spur, not all open but patchworked with forest. They halted in unspoken agreement.

"That's where we shall go tomorrow," said Rolf, his voice sounding unreal from inside his closed helmet to Leona strapped inside her own padded headgear. She pushed up her goggles and the blue dark glare that was not light blinded her so that her face was blank to him.

"Snow princess," he said. "This is the country of the Ice Maiden."

She leaned against his long flank, their padded suits were like the furs of animals, but being artificial they divided so that the vulnerable bodies inside could be felt to each as cut off from the other.

"Not ice," she said. "I can feel everything gathering itself to grow again. And all the little animals cuddled down in their burrows but sort of dreaming the freezing weather up here, feeling how warm they are, lovely smelly little coziness."

"They come out sometimes when the sun shines. Then they make the neatest little tracks in the snow."

"I don't want them to venture out. Better stay where they are and be safe."

"Anyway there won't be any sun tomorrow, I think." He lifted his cheek in a sideways gesture to take the wind. "It may even snow again."

"But we'll go out anyway, won't we? Up there?"

"Oh sure. It doesn't really make much difference so long as you have a compass and know the district."

The entire landscape, all over, was silently and evenly darkening. It was not dusk; the steel deepened and hardened into gunmetal.

"The wind has dropped."

"It's freezing hard now."

"We shan't feel it going back at all. It will push us on." He shifted his arm to stab one stick down firmly into the snow so that he could put a free arm around her narrow shoulders. He kissed her cold, colorless mouth, exposed between the chin-guard and the forehead of her black helm, the dark glasses glinted above her eyes like the false eyes of cats. "Good thing you've got that spacesuit thing on," he said prosaically.

She twitched her goggles back over her eyes with a mittened fist and then clutched swiftly at her stick before it could fall.

"Let's get back," she said.

It was hot inside the house. The bedroom had two beds close together with fat feather quilts in starched white covers, beside each bed a rag mat. The ceiling lamp was uncompromisingly bright. Her undersuit was of red and white lateral stripes, which made him laugh.

"Like a convict," he said.

"Shall we bathe now?"

"Better. The water may be hot now. It certainly won't be after supper."

"I'm starving."

"I've never known anybody as hungry as you are. Except perhaps me."

They could not stop yawning while they ate and at every yawn Leona could feel the skin of her face stretching. She sat this time on the other side of their table and could see the large table where the regulars sat, a group of elderly men as at midday. They looked to her like the same men but were probably others. She felt clumsy leaving the taproom, and surfaces seemed to shift under her eyes, still dazzled from the out-of-doors. Their muscles were pleasantly strained and there was a sensation of a translucent membraneous barrier between themselves and their surroundings, inside which they moved with a pleasant ache. And all the time, beyond the warm house they sensed the great lonely lift of the uplands, swept by a steady wind.

Rolf padded across the room upstairs, silently for they both wore knitted houseboots with soft chamois leather soles. That soundless step too added to the unreality of everything around them. Only they were real. In the shadow of his own head he tried to examine the weather through the window. He could determine nothing and his gaze shifted to the starry patterns framing each pane of outside glass. He was almost unnerved by an awe that seemed to have nothing to do with himself, as if there were another being in the room with them, perhaps some emanation of the snow-obliterated frontier to the north which was actual and constantly present to him but not to Leona; a barrier unseen past which lay territory indistinguishable from the landscape they crossed that afternoon and yet mysteriously different, hostile and only to be expressed in a foreign tongue. He was obscurely aware that he was confusing this man-made line as one might do in dreams, with another boundary guarded, he now perceived for the first time, by antique sanctions.

"I wish I'd never had anybody else," he said aloud, not knowing he was going to speak.

"It doesn't matter."

"It does to me."

"No. It's unhappened."

"You can't be sure of that, if I'm not sure."

"Are you not sure?"

"I don't mean in that way. I mean, I don't want to bring anything else with me into this."

"That's the only thing I don't understand. Why do you bring some—something else into it?"

"You wouldn't want me to lie to you, would you?"

"N-no. No. But do we have to speak of it? Of them?"

"It would be a lie if I didn't. You see, you don't know, it's clear you don't know. Things are all right as they are. As long as you remain a stranger I can . . . what do I mean? Maintain things as they are. We could go on like this for months. Or even part. But it's like an unknown door. Once we go through that door everything will be different. And that is what you don't know."

"So they meant something to you, or you wouldn't know that . . . what you say, that things are different."

"They didn't mean a thing to me. 'It' meant something at the time. They didn't. That's what makes it so awful I mean . . . *Because* it wasn't anything before, I know now that it *is*."

"It's just a bogeyman. You're trying to frighten me." Even as she said them she knew the words were not true. "But I'm not frightened."

"No. I am, though. It's like making up your mind to cross that frontier there a few miles away from this house, where you know it's another country."

She raised herself on one elbow.

"Oh!" she said, startled. "You mean like the Rhine? Now I get what you mean. So you see, it's all right. You don't have to stand at the window like that, talking as if we were two separate people."

He turned, trying to see her face. When he moved from the window, from where his shadow had been a strange pale sheen that might, on a less overcast night, have been moonlight, flooded into the room. In that dim snow reflection they could now almost see each other.

CHAPTER 9

M. and Mme. Chavanges sat as widely separated as the spacious room allowed and in complete silence as they waited for the person referred to by the servant who showed them in as "Madam Administrator." The reserved and neutral greeting accorded them, quite normal when dealing with unexpected strangers in a private hospital, seemed to both of them to have expressed a calculated coldness. And now the rather severe symmetry, a restrained neatness in the well-appointed, palely shaded apartment which combined sitting room with study, induced a hint of nervousness at any rate in Mme. Chavanges. She found the place intimidating for some reason with its white-curtained wide window showing the wintry garden outside as being almost in the house, which was Edwardian in style and imposing in extent; a rich man's villa become a clinic. There were pictures on the walls, clearly a set but neither of the visitors examined them; they saw only a repetition of plain frames emphasizing the angled arrangement of the furniture of light woods and fawn upholstery. In the square bay of the window a varied collection of plants and ferns provided freshness. The only brilliance came from a massive azalea smothered in dark red blossoms which stood imposingly in an ornamental urn on a satinwood table almost too fragile for its weight.

Chavanges sat forward in his chair, elbows on knees, and continually clasped and unclasped his hands in front of his lowered face. He was clearly only just in control of his anxiety, and his unease was painfully increased by a heavy cold which caused him to cough and blow his nose several times, each time frowning in embarrassment or humiliation at this undignified ailment.

It was only a few minutes, but the quiet of discipline and decorum made it seem longer. Then the white door opened and without rattle of doorknob or click of footsteps, a woman entered. There was nothing in her slight figure to account for the involuntary jerk with which both waiting persons moved in their chairs. She wished them good afternoon in the subdued but clear tone of one who constantly speaks to the very ill, and as she did so she went automatically to the azalea and tested the moisture of its earth with one finger. Then she crossed to the large, flat writing table that seemed to fill one side of the room and touched a bell-push. Immediately came a tap at the door and the servant entered.

"It needs water again," said the slight woman in German. "I do believe it takes a liter a day when it's in bloom." The maid nodded slightly and disappeared without speaking.

A severe gray, close-fitting garment with something of uniform about it gave her the appearance of a deaconess. It was closely buttoned from the trim waistline to a high collar with a frosty white lining. The narrow sleeves came down over pale, dry, thin hands. A nurse's starched cap covered a small head with close-lying short gray hair. The nearly colorless, calm face showed the ageless neatness of feature which is associated with the epithet Dresden. Altogether she did have something about her of a porcelain figure, of that kind which is not by chance connected with the first European chinamakers, for the women of that part of Saxony do, in fact, tend to have those well-assembled and small features.

"Please forgive me, Madame, Monsieur, for keeping you waiting.

My name is Forstmann. I understand you wish to see me on some matter that concerns my adopted son?"

They were not surprised that she spoke French with clipped competence. Anything she did would be done competently; that was at once clear.

Chavanges remained standing now and felt his own solid, masculine bulk as too big and too dark for the essentially nunlike woman and her room. His solidly well-formed person and clothes made the only large, dynamic and swarthy bulk present among all the pale and rather delicate furnishings and drapery. He was clumsy and out of place and the total lack of "manner" in the woman somehow emphasized this quality of inappropriateness. She reduced his accustomed authority by her neutrality although he was, of course, aware that this deliberate impersonality was part of her professional skill, which was evidently of a high order.

She went now behind the wide desk and picked up from it a large bunch of keys which she put into the right-hand drawer. The metal keys made a loud clang, startling in the quiet, and she closed the drawer which shut with a brisk click as the automatic lock caught. She then moved away to a different chair, evidently so that she should not sit officially behind the desk.

"Please be seated, Monsieur," she said with an air of slight surprise.

He looked about him, struck by the fact that neither he nor his wife had spoken after the murmured greeting.

"I had better stand," he said. His wife frowned nervously at this indication of something uncompromisingly unfriendly to come.

"I understand the Embassy has been in touch with you already, Madame Forstmann? You know why we are here, I believe?"

"Madame Perriot, whom I know quite well, telephoned me. I gather you wish to find your daughter, who has gone skiing with my son. And, I take it, with others as well."

"No!" he now sounded explosive. "Not with others. They are alone, I don't know where."

"It might be preferable not to mention their aloneness, don't you agree? That was really what I meant."

"I regret to say that the matter has gone too far for that."

"You yourself have pushed it too far for it to be hidden," said Mme. Chavanges in a suppressed undertone. "Madame is quite right; it would have been better to have kept silent as far as possible."

"Yes, the cant of the modern world. Everything is to be open and everything permitted. But I prefer to state clearly that my daughter has been abducted."

His wife closed her eyes for a moment but said nothing. At this moment, after a discreet scratch at the door, the servant entered, this time carrying a watering can from which she liberally damped the azalea. In dead silence she again left the room.

"Well, now," said Mme. Forstmann as the door closed behind the maid. "It may be best if you tell me exactly what has happened."

"They met at the Opera Ball. This . . . your son stood in for Leona's partner. My daughter is an extremely handsome girl and it was clear at once that he . . ."

"Recognized that fact?"

"One could put it like that. She then went to St. Anton with a group of friends, to ski. My wife insisted that she would be safe there. From there she wrote to an old friend of mine, a family friend and business associate. He is in fact the chief lawyer of my companies and I have no doubt Leona also thinks of him as her trustee. At least, he says she wrote to him in that sense."

"He is in fact her trustee, for a small inheritance from my mother," said Mme. Chavanges.

"Please allow me to continue. My daughter's letter wanted information as to how much money she could expect and when she could have it. Naturally my friend telephoned me at once on receipt of this letter."

"I gather that your daughter is not yet of age, then?"

"She is not. She is just a few weeks over her eighteenth birthday. But even if she were of age, I should hope he would have informed me of her—her—I don't know what to call it!"

"Of her wishes?"

Chavanges glared at this assistance and from the way Mme. Forstmann dropped her eyes so as not to take his anger, it was plain that, with whatever feelings she had entered the room she now viewed Chavanges with at least wariness.

"To continue this wretched story," he went on more loudly, "I at once called the house at St. Anton where my daughter was staying. As I supposed, staying. To my horror, her host with great surprise told me that Leona returned to Vienna last Friday night. She told *him* that we had recalled her. But we did nothing of the kind. Where she then went I do not know. But I gather from a fellow officer of his that she went with your son who has gone on a ski tour near the Czech frontier. That is all I know; though I got the impression that Rilla-Lensky knew more than he would say. He was, by the way, extremely flippant, almost insolent, about the whole thing."

"Rilla-Lensky!" she showed surprise.

"You know him?"

"I know his mother, well. She is on the board of directors of this clinic."

"Her younger son, Charles Henri, was the partner who ought to have been with my daughter at the Opera Ball. But he evidently thought the appointment of no importance. Not enough to let me know he did not intend to keep it, or even to apologize afterward. And now my daughter . . ."

A violent sneeze overtook poor Chavanges and he sat down suddenly and heavily and began to blow his nose.

"Let me get this clear, Monsieur. Several days after the Opera

Ball at which she danced with Rolf, your daughter—Leona, did you call her?—went skiing at Anton. From there she took a train without telling anyone where she was going. That was three days ago and you have not seen or heard from her since. Is that correct?"

"Yes," said Mme. Chavanges. "You can imagine that we are naturally worried. If you have any idea of where . . ."

Mme. Forstmann shook her head slowly. "I evidently know less than you do, since young Kari has said that Rolf is skiing in the north. But what I do not understand is why you connect your daughter's disappearance with my son?"

"But of course, it's perfectly obvious!" Chavanges almost shouted, and was stopped by a cough.

"It doesn't seem at all obvious to me."

"At the Ball they were . . ."

"*He* was!" interrupted Chavanges. "He was obviously . . ."

"They danced together almost the whole night. It was difficult to get Leona away from him long enough to dance with the other gentlemen of our party."

"It was a deliberate campaign. He was determined to seduce her, that was clear from the first moment I laid eyes on him." Chavanges put his head in his hands as if trying not to see some dreadful threat. "And now he has abducted her!"

"Are you sure she left St. Anton alone? Perhaps she traveled with some of these friends of hers. If so, we could ask their host, their parents."

"She did not leave with any companion at all. They all remained where they were and believed Leona to have returned to our hotel in Vienna."

"Do you know she returned to Vienna?"

"She took the night train here. Her host saw her off."

"She may have got off the train on the way. Have you thought of that? You see, it is so very unlike Rolf. He has the usual number of girl friends, true. But he is not at all an irresponsible young man. Because he knows, of course, that he can't expect to marry for several years."

"Marry!" said Chavanges thickly, raising his head to stare at the speaker with a baffled, black look of disbelief. "Did you say *marry*?"

"If they are together, if, I say, then it is so unlike Rolf that I'm quite bewildered. In any case, there can be no question of abduction. If your daughter took the train by herself then she did it of her own free will. That is perfectly clear. Nothing could have made her do it if she didn't want to. She had several days to think it over, and plenty of other companions. Isn't that so?"

"I think Leona *is* with your son," said Mme. Chavanges, her husband being apparently unable to speak for the moment. "And Charles Henri Lensky gave that impression too." She shot a cautious glance at her husband's averted head. "He certainly was very offhand about it all, but I got the definite impression that he knew, though he didn't say anything directly, that Rolf and Leona were together."

"I know Kari Lensky. He's quite capable of trying to mislead you. He has a very peculiar sense of humor, has Kari Lensky."

"No," said Mme. Chavanges slowly. "No. I think it—our understanding of what he meant—is correct." Mme. Forstmann gave her a sharp look and was just about to ask a question, when Chavanges rose abruptly to his feet and swung round as if he could not see properly.

"You mentioned marriage," he said thickly, breathing heavily through his mouth. "And I see now what this is all about. It is just as well that you should know, without any doubt, and should tell your fine son. I will never consent to my daughter marrying a penniless and nameless junior officer. Never. Never. I would rather disinherit her. No matter what has happened, she shall never marry him. I promise you that!"

Both women stared at him, startled and dismayed by his vehemence.

"In the Army!" he shouted, losing control of himself. "And what an army! Why, it's a joke, the Austrian Army! The French service would be bad enough, but the Austrian . . . !"

"For heaven's sake," begged his wife. "Try to control yourself!"

"Control myself!" he turned on her so that she flinched visibly. "He hasn't even got a name, you heard it from Leclerc. Who knows where he came from, what he is? He could be a Russian, a Pole, anything! The only sure thing is that he's a beggarly adventurer, a fortune hunter!"

"He is certainly titleless," said Mme. Forstmann quietly. "But I assure you that my adopted son is worthy of any princess."

"You see, you say it yourself! Adopted. He is nameless, he doesn't exist. He doesn't know who he is himself, and neither do you. Thrown up out of the millions of refugees roaming Europe at the end of the war—a Jew, a gypsy, God only knows what. He's dark enough to be anything!"

At this Mme. Chavanges drew a sharp breath and put up a quivering hand to her cheek. There was silence while both women gazed widely at Chavanges, who stood still, his shoulders bent forward like a wounded animal, and groaned aloud.

"I don't recognize myself," he muttered at last. "Please forgive me. You can have no idea of what I am going through."

"But yes, I have a very good idea. I deal here with suffering all the time. And I myself have suffered enough to know real pain when I see it. If you could only bring yourself to believe it, you are among friends."

"No," he cried. "No. I must find her. I must rescue her."

"Oh God," whispered his wife. "I can't stand much more of this." She supported herself against the arm of her chair, for they were by now all three standing.

"You can't stand it," he shouted, the tears starting from his eyes. "*You!* The whole thing is your fault, with your cynical indifference to the child! If you had not . . . If you had never said . . ." He stopped and swung his head, not able to express himself.

The two women stood still and silent, awaiting some further outbreak, which was already to be felt in the room.

"I have to get outside in the air. Just for a moment. I must try to calm myself. Excuse me. I will walk about for a few minutes, if I may."

And he blundered out of the room, hardly able to see where he was going. His wife faltered a step or two after him but the other woman put out a hand and stopped her.

"Let him be," she said. "He will come back. His instinct is right. It is better for him to walk off his fury than to break down completely in front of us."

"Break down?" whispered Mme. Chavanges.

"Don't you see? He is on the verge of a weeping fit."

"I have never seen him weep," she protested indignantly. "How can you know such a thing? And it is bitter cold outside."

"I have seen many people in his state. Let me tell you something, Madame. Your husband is on the verge of a complete breakdown. You must take what I say seriously, I know what I am talking about."

The wife stared at her companion; she seemed hardly to be taking in the reality of what was happening and the professional could see that her nerves too were holding only by a thread to something masquerading as normality.

"I am becoming very worried by all this," said Anna Forstmann. "I don't want Rolf's life to be ruined by some quite unnecessary scandal. You look surprised, Madame? But surely you understand that I am as much concerned for Rolf as you for Leona?"

She went to the wide window and scanned the parklike gardens shrouded in snow, looking for Chavanges; but he was not to be seen.

"What did he mean, when he spoke of something you had said? It sounded, his voice when he said that, quite different. As if the real point of this outburst might be something *you* said."

"When he said . . . Oh, I see. But you heard, he was quite disconnected. He didn't know what he was saying."

"I am aware of that. But what did he refer to?"

"What? I don't know, how can I . . ." The lack of any reply forced her to go on speaking. "I—very well, I'll tell you. At the Ball he was making such a fuss about Leona dancing with your—with Rolf. He kept on so that everybody in our box was laughing at him. He couldn't even see it, although normally he's quick enough to protect his dignity. He was beside himself with jealousy. At last—I admit I should not have done it—I lost my temper. He—I—we are not well suited to each other. I said he was in love with her, with Leona. I wasn't the only person present to think so. Another guest joked about incest, he thought I didn't hear, but I did. It was in the air, you could feel it, you know how I mean? I was so upset, I can't explain, it was . . ." Mme. Chavanges began to cry. She sank into her chair but then sprang up again. "My God! You don't think . . . he won't do anything?"

"I doubt it. Certainly not until he knows where Leona is. But tell me, have you any reason to suppose, suspect, that anything ever—you know what I am talking about?"

"Good God, no," she stammered huskily. "No, it was all, is all, in his mind. There couldn't be, there never was, anything."

"Forgive my questions. I am trying to understand. Will you tell me, was your marriage a family affair? What used to be called an arranged marriage?"

"Yes. Yes, it was. He never loved me, and I never loved him. I don't even like him. I'm only sorry for him."

"Well, well. But you live together, in the usual sense?"

"Oh yes, up to now. Yes. Too damned much," answered Mme. Chavanges without hesitation as if her questioner were entitled to ask her such things.

"Yes, I see. Love has to break out somewhere. Your husband's store of love has all been piled on the child, it seems." She searched the white gardens once more with her eyes. "And it may have been a terrible shock when you spoke as you say to him. It may have been the first time it ever struck him as unnatural, his love. Which it must be, you see, or it couldn't have so horrified him. You can understand that?"

"Ah," said Mme. Chavanges with a deep resigned sigh of bitterness. "I dare say it was. I gave him a shock, poor sensitive creature. And me, for twenty years? What about me?"

"Don't imagine that I do not see your side of the story, Madame. I see it very clearly. But for the moment you are more stable, more in command of yourself, than he is. It is with him that we must concern ourselves if this escapade of our children is not to end in disaster for one or other of them."

"Escapade!"

"If it is even that. It may all be a mistake. Your daughter may be somewhere else, with somebody else."

"Oh no. She's with him. I'm sure of that."

"You sound very sure. Have you any evidence?"

"No, I'm not hiding anything—from my husband, I mean. It's just . . . When he threatened Leona that he would send her home, or keep her in Vienna, that she couldn't go to St. Anton, I just knew somehow that she was in touch with this boy. Rolf, I mean. I knew there was something going on."

"But how? And then, why did you insist that Leona should go to St. Anton?"

"There was something in her manner. She was not lying exactly, but being devious, seeming to say one thing and meaning another. As to why I thought she should go to St. Anton, obviously she was safer there. I couldn't know she and Rolf had already made their plans. I assumed anything serious would take much longer to mature than it did, in fact."

"Yes. They did move with extraordinary speed, I must say. A pity you didn't decide to have it out with Leona, when you felt her disingenuousness. Or was it a pity? Really, nothing more likely, unfortunately, in a girl with a doting and domineering fa-

123

ther, than that she should be devious. But is it all such a tragedy? Do you yourself feel that some irreparable harm has been done, if what you think is really the case? I must say, for myself, I really rather envy the girl Rolf has fallen in love with. They are young, innocent, apparently equally beautiful. They evidently fell in love at first sight at the Opera Ball and they are living the wonderful idyll of love."

"You think then Rolf must be really in love? Seriously?"

"Oh but obviously! I know Rolf. He would not take such risks for a slight fancy. He is much too sensible."

"But if they really are in love, that's terrible! He will never consent! Never! You probably think he is frantic now but will come round, but you don't know his stubbornness as I do. He is so used to getting his own way . . ."

"He may not have much choice. Have you thought of that?"

"But she's under age, and you know the law in France . . . Of course, I know things are not done like that any more, but I can just see him . . . !"

"I seem to recall that young people do not always find marriage indispensable. Until it becomes imperative."

"You can't wish that they should live together! I assure you, he will ruin the boy, ruin him. The very least would be that Rolf would have to resign his commission. You saw how he is. The telephone calls to Rolf's commandant, this coming to see you—they are only the beginning!"

"Wish it? No. But they are not doing what any of *us* wish. Ah! There he is. He is coming back."

Mme. Chavanges clasped her hands together and began to weep again, helplessly, as she saw through the window the figure of Chavanges, bulky and black against the snow-fronded trees of the drive, hurrying with stumbling strides back to the clinic.

"Poor fellow, he's beside himself with misery and wounded pride. You ought to have stood up to him years ago! What a mess you've made of your lives between you!"

A moment later Chavanges almost fell into the room, followed closely by a young nurse and the elderly parlormaid, both protesting and arguing.

"It's all right. Please leave us alone," said the administrator and fixed them both with such a disciplinary look that the two women retired as hastily as they had entered, muttering sulkily to each other.

"Solange! Come along, get your coat on. We're doing no good here. I have decided to go to the police in Vienna."

"No, don't do that!" cried Mme. Forstmann sharply. "Do you want your daughter dragged through the courts? Now, listen to me, just for a moment. Sit down and listen, please."

He stared at her without taking in what she said. He was shaking, his eyes were bloodshot; he was almost unhinged. Somehow he seemed to have fallen into a snowdrift for he was soaking wet and his handmade shoes shed damp clumps of snow and mud on the pale carpet where he stood. He swayed, choked and could not speak.

"Sit down, I said." She spoke crisply, without raising her voice. After a moment he sank down into the nearest chair, gave her a baffled look and leaned forward, dropping his head in his hands.

"Don't go to the police, you can't do that. Give me twenty-four hours to find out what I can. You are unjust to me. I would tell you if I knew anything. But you forget, a man of twenty-five does not come to his mother with his love affair. Rolf is a grown man, not a child. But I can discover what is going on without creating a scandal, if you will only promise me to be reasonable. Just one day. Until tomorrow evening. Come now, agree with me that it will be best?"

"Please," begged his wife, with tears. "Please. Let her try. Please promise."

He lifted his head and fixed one of them after the other with his reddened eyes. "All right," he groaned, "all right. I just can't take any more. If only I didn't know she had lied to me. It tortures me. How long has she been lying to me? It's like a poisoned arrow, the thought of it."

Chavanges made a clutch at the breast of his white shirt as if some lethal dart were in fact sticking in his flesh, more real and painful to him than the room he was in or the two women.

"The picture tortures me," he cried loudly. Once again he could not, dared not say what he really meant. "It's a nightmare. I'm dreaming and she will be there when we get back. Come along, why do you sit here chattering when Leona may need you? She may be waiting, frightened, hurt, ill . . . who knows what!"

"Yes, we must go," stammered his wife.

"Let us go. But you have only one day. You understand? I can't stand it any longer." He wheeled blindly around to find Mme. Forstmann and found himself glaring out at the trees and bushes through the window, draped in festal white, trailing patterns like lace. "Like a wedding," he muttered under his breath, and he shuddered deeply. Then, raising his voice, "If you don't find Leona by tomorrow at this time, I go to the police. You understand?"

"I understand," she said, behind him.

"But no matter what has happened, I shall never allow her to marry this penniless . . . Never. I know what he's after but he shan't get it. Never. He's nameless, no family, no country, nothing. He doesn't exist, he isn't anybody. I'd rather she was abandoned, in this terrible weather, in this primitive backwoods place —Waldviertel! What a name!"

He swung his big body around again, lowering his head menacingly.

"Never!" he shouted, flinging out a shaking hand. He almost lost his balance, his bulk swayed and he fell sideways into a chair. "Where is the car? We must go, we've been away far too long. She may be there, we must get back."

Mme. Chavanges was horror-struck at the repetition of a pattern; it was exactly as on the evening when he agreed suddenly after long argument that Leona should after all go to St. Anton. The abrupt capitulation, the urgent need to get away. He is mentally ill, she thought with real fear. I must do something or he will collapse. She turned about to seek help and her terrified eyes met the straight, considering look of the older woman, who seemed to know what she was thinking.

"It is not so bad as it looks. He has a temperature, he is ill but above all he needs to sleep. I will give you something." Even as she spoke in an undertone she moved over to a side door and disappeared for a moment, coming back with a small plastic tube in her hand.

"Give him one when you get back and one late this evening."

"He won't take them."

"Of course he will take them, if you give him them as a matter of course."

"Well, I'll try. But . . ."

"I will ring for your coats, your car. You have a driver, I hope?"

"Oh yes, thank God. I couldn't manage alone. If he gets worse . . ." Mme. Chavanges caught a trembling gasp of breath, trying to control herself, "I am so terribly sorry about . . ."

"Please! I shall telephone tomorrow afternoon. Yes, I know where to reach you. Madame Perriot told me. Get him back and keep him warm, put him to bed. If his temperature rises or he breathes harshly, send for a doctor. This *grippe* may turn to pneumonia if he stays long in those wet clothes."

It was incredibly prosaic, unreal. The lights of the borrowed car flashed over the window in the deepening dusk as it turned at the door.

"I can see why he thinks you must know something. You seem to know everything."

"Here are your coats. What magnificent furs. Yes, I will telephone without fail tomorrow afternoon."

Somehow they were gone and the young nurse was standing in the doorway.

"Bring me coffee, please. Strong coffee."

"At once, *gnädige Frau.*"

She stared after the tail lights of the big car as it slipped away. People always think it is some kind of magic, knowing what is in their minds, she thought. And naturally, one can't tell them how stereotyped such scenes are, no matter what the causes; how often one has witnessed them. For them, each one of them, it is the crisis of a life. For me it has been gone through a thousand times. What a situation! And he is almost conscious of it, and was, before his girl met Rolf. Otherwise he would not have chosen a husband for her, so young. So that *this* could not happen! Kari Lensky, who neither could nor would wish ever to be a rival to him. Solange, he called her. A pretty name. Old-fashioned, but pretty. I wonder what his name is.

"You are tired I am afraid," said the nurse's voice, behind her, and set down a tray with a slight clink of china.

"That was very quick. Thank you. Yes, I am tired. Very tired." She turned and putting her hands on her slight waist, she pushed downward in the habitual settling gesture of nurses who are always adjusting their tight belts. It was many years since she wore that starched waistband but she still retained the habit.

When she was alone she allowed the armor of long training to slip from her features as she gazed blankly out at the twilight, her aspect no longer expressionless. Her eyes reflected an old suffering and the memory of horror that, if an onlooker had been there to see it, would have shown Chavanges and his pain as almost histrionic. Names, she thought. Nameless. No, I cannot allow this to happen. So for a long time the middle-aged Anna gazed stoically out at the lacy, soft-piled snow masses, underfoot forming pillows and overhead traceries on branches curving down under the embroidered weight.

Winter. The word appeared in her mind. Not as it was now, a fructifying sleep with spring and summer pregnantly buried inside it. She felt it as it was then, twenty-five years ago, a limbo of negation, unreality, death, disaster; winter as a gloomy and chaotic hell which is always cold and gray, unlighted. Now the snow was in itself safe and impermanent, not threatening to remain forever in refrigerated timelessness but a resting interval, giving life and spring time for rebirth. The time has come; it is time to resurrect it. Already, conjured up by the need to set the present to rights by the past, the young Anna stood before her successor. She had been shut out for many years in her hell and it was not memory that saw her bowed form, but revision.

CHAPTER 10

"We've been lucky," said Rolf at the window, through which in the whirling black, nothing but snow streaks could be seen. "It held off the whole weekend, just until we have to go back. Now it will snow for days, weeks perhaps."

"Perhaps we won't be able to get back, tomorrow morning?"

He turned to smile at her, shaking his head. "Don't hope for that, little one. Whether we can or not, I have to report for duty."

"There won't be any flying. You could telephone, say you're snowed in?"

He did not reply to this, so completely was the fantasy dismissed, but Leona saw from his indulgent mouth that she had said something childishly absurd. She watched closely his dark, vivid eyes, waiting for some sign of approaching laughter. Instead of a joke to deny reality, she saw his puzzled distress. The proposal hidden behind her make-believe grew up into seriousness for she could see they thought the same thought, faced the same prospect.

"But we can't separate." It burst out in protest.

He came and sat on the edge of the bed beside her and their hands gripped each other's. He put his head against hers so that their tears would remain unseen.

"What are we going to do?"

"I shall stay here. No, not here in this house. Nearby. Near you."

"Sweetie, you don't understand. This is real."

"I know that, now. Wait, Rolf, I could stay with friends. I have some where there are six, not counting parents. They won't even notice I'm there."

"Yes, that . . . No, that's just what you—we—can't do. They would be involved, if there really is trouble. With your father. And from what my mother said on the phone, there will be."

"How did she find you?"

"She just asked where I'd been skiing before, with other friends, and then called one place after another until she got me."

"But so easy! He could find us just as easily."

"Oh no. They wouldn't tell a stranger. But they all know her, you see."

"Couldn't I go to friends if I told them?"

"Then they'd be bound to feel that you are too young to know, to make up your mind. They would get in touch with your parents. Like your Uncle Alain did."

"What it amounts to is that I have to face my father, isn't it?"

"Could you?"

She thought, and did not answer.

"What about your mother?" he insisted.

"She's as bad as I am. If I couldn't stand up to him, she'd be even worse, she'd back down and leave me to it."

"But you said she was on your side."

"Yes, she was. But that was about going to St. Anton. In a way, you see, that was getting rid of the problem, getting out of the disturbance. Inviting the storm would be something quite different."

"Of course."

"What about me going to *your* mother?"

"That's an idea! No. No, that's no good either. She thinks of my future, and you only in relation to that. From what she said he's in a terrible state, and she is worrying about the outside world, the service, the public scandal."

"That isn't quite how you've made her sound."

"Well, if he went to the police as he threatened? She'd do anything for me, to fix it, if she could. But she wouldn't defy your parents' rights, the law, not even convention in a way. She is trying to arrange matters, but she won't fly in the face of the world, as the saying is, to hide you, because of the danger to me. If I asked her to take you in she would say, she almost did on the telephone, that we have to face things as they are. You see, I've never known anyone before who would just go straight ahead and force the issue. I suppose we tend to arrange things always, go roundabout, if we can."

"And she feels she can't arrange things with my father. No, nobody could." There was silence for a long time. Then Leona said quietly, in a different voice, "I can't go back. I can't. Even if you don't want me . . ."

"Don't talk like that. You *know*. It's not a question of what we are going to do, only of how. And what we really need is time, time to think."

"Time. We must think of a way to stop him from forcing the issue, as you say. Stop him going to the police, or—or something diplomatic. He might go to—who? The Foreign Office or something like that."

"Mother said somebody called Leclerc—were they at the Ball? —promised her to stall on any suggestion like that. At least for a day or so."

"She knows the Leclercs, too? She seems to know everybody."

"Oh, she does. She's already talked to Countess Lensky, as well. Lensky! Wait a minute. That's the one person who is absolutely bound to help us!"

"Countess Lensky?"

"No, idiot. Kari. Kari can't refuse and he doesn't give a damn for anything. He's got a flat in Vienna, his hideout he calls it. I've stayed there often. And it's on this side of the town, in the second District."

"What a queer place for him to choose."

"That's why he chose it, no doubt. Nobody he knows ever goes there."

"But what does he do there?"

Rolf smiled and raised his eyebrows, the first sign of gaiety since he turned from the window. "That, I sometimes wonder," he said. "But it's a godsend for us. I'm going down now to call the station and find Kari."

"I'll come too and we can have supper afterward."

As if all their questions had been answered, they laughed and ran out, their arms around each other, jumping down the stairs so that the waitress watching from the hall below laughed with them at their happiness.

A somewhat sulky Kari, for whom the results of his own demands now appeared as an imposition on his good nature, gave them the required promise. They had found a hiding place and that was what was important for them. They would not be parted for more than a day or so at a time. Their real problem dwindled to a distant point of which they need take no notice now.

"He said he would have to stay away from there for a few days in any case," said Rolf as they took their usual places. "I wonder what he meant?"

"What are you thinking about?" he asked a moment later, and touched the veil of pale hair that fell forward when she bent her head.

"The flowers. In the Opera, the flowers, you remember?"

"In the middle of winter."

"Like us."

"Like you anyway. Winter rose, blooming in the snow. It'll be a long time before we see anything like that again."

"Probably never, don't you think? I don't feel that we'll ever go again to the Opera Ball, do you?"

"We don't need to. It's still there."

"Oh, you feel that too? I might have known. I meant to tell you, I woke up in the night, I think I must have been dreaming. Everything was all white in the dark, from outside."

"What was the dream?"

"I don't know. I just woke and heard a bit of poetry. Pity you weren't at school in England. Poetry is about all I learned there, except the right slang."

"Tell me. Perhaps I'll understand it."

" 'I saw Eternity the other night, like a great ring of pure and endless light.' "

"Mm. Again?"

" 'I saw Eternity the other night, like a great ring of pure and endless light.' "

"I saw Eternity once, flying in the mountains. It has nothing to do with time."

"Yes, we try to think of it quite the wrong way, I think. It's not time extended forever. It's not time at all."

"In the last few days, since that moment in the Opera, I've had a feeling over and over again. Nothing to do with us, not really. But I wonder whether we don't think about a lot of things in quite the wrong way. I mean, we try to define things but we can't because we're using the wrong faculty."

"What moment in the Opera?"

"We stopped dancing and moved to the edge of the floor to talk. I leaned back against the wall and smelled, I think, carnations and syringa. No, it can't have been syringa, can it. But some piercing flower scent."

"I expect you mean freesias. There were a lot of them just there."

"Anyway, piercing. I don't know what we said, I can't remember. But that was the moment when it was decided. Only I don't know how. Certainly not with words."

"I wonder what we did say."

"The odd thing is, I didn't notice the smell of flowers then, only now. Has anyone said that, that poetry, in German?"

"Must have done, somewhere. I should think Rilke said it in other words."

"Or Hölderlin. Translate it."

"Just a minute . . ."

"I think I got it but I can't be sure."

"*Ich sah die Ewigkeit, ja gestern Nacht; ein hehre Ring, reines, endloses Licht.*"

"Who wrote it?"

"A chap called Vaughan, a long time ago."

"And it's all right now about tomorrow?"

"Yes, I'm not scared any more. Only there's Kari—you don't think his mother will get at him, to tell where we are?"

"Why should she? I mean, she can't know he knows anything."

"I think somebody will think of it. Of anything and everything."

"Probably. But what matters is we have a space of peace and quiet to work things out. But, speaking of mothers, there is one thing. If my mother actually asks me where you are, I can't lie to her."

"But she didn't ask, straight out."

"No, because of that. But if she did, if she insisted, I couldn't say I didn't know."

"If she did," Leona worked it out slowly, "it would mean he means to do something really awful, as you said, like go to the police?"

"Or the commandant."

"There's one thing I could do. I could talk to *my* mother. I could ring up the hotel and ask her to come downstairs, not put the call through upstairs. I could say I'm all right and I will keep in touch with them. Yes, listen. I could say, if Papa does anything that gets us—you—into real trouble I'll never come back, never see him again."

"That sounds dreadfully cruel."

"Well, I suppose it is. But perhaps it's better to be definite, to stop him in his tracks, before he does anything fatal. Don't you think? Then he won't do something without really thinking it over. Perhaps he wouldn't believe it, but he would stop to think."

"But from what Mother said on the telephone, he might go berserk, get out of control."

"I just can't imagine it. You know, when he fusses, he always knows really what he is doing. It's the way grown-ups get their own way, making scenes."

"Yes, but . . . I can see he would be, sort of, helpless, where you're concerned. I mean, to restrain himself . . ."

"Well, it was his idea that I should marry quite soon anyway; that was *his* plan. Why should he mind, if he stops to think it over, that it's a different person?"

"Yes, that's been puzzling me too. You may be right. Of course, I don't know him."

"Look, I think I'll do it. Shall I?"

"It might work. Can you manage it?"

"As long as I don't have to talk to him, I think I can. Shall I?"

"If you're going to, do it now. Get it over."

She stared at him over the shiny table, somewhat frightened. Then she caught her underlip between her teeth and her eyes dilated as the reality struck her. She pushed a small fist against the midriff of her red pullover.

"I feel funny here," she said, breathlessly. Another moment and the effort would have been too much. But just then one of the men at the club table came clattering over the tiled floor and began to read over the titles in the music box, holding a coin ready in his hand. Rolf and Leona both looked across at his back. She rose, bending between the table and the bench, and slipped out of the narrow space. She went very quickly but not running toward the hall where the telephone box stood.

If chance arranged it so that she got through the first time, or at the second try, she would be able to carry the plan through, she thought, as she looked for the numbers. If a third attempt proved necessary, she would give up. If it comes out right, that means all will be well. There was a small pad of message paper, scrawled upon, dog-eared, and a tethered pencil. She sought out the numbers and wrote them down. There was a cold draft here in the hall, which went through past the staircase to the back of the house. She hesitated then, a superstitious qualm stilling her hand as it reached for the instrument; but she thought of facing Rolf with her failure of courage and picked it up. She was frightened when the dialing resulted, not in the half-willed engaged tone but in the staccato interrupted buzz; it rang several times and Leona was just about to put back with a craven relief the sinister black instrument, when the hotel operator announced herself. There was only one more chance, but she was not to be saved; not only was Mme. Chavanges in the hotel, but the operator seemed to take it quite for granted that Madame should be asked to come down to the hall to take a message. Leona had clung to the hope that a complicated argument might be needed which would give her the excuse she required. She was tempted again to break the connection while the page went up to fetch her mother; it was the thought of getting her mother all the way downstairs for nothing that stopped her from doing that. She wished, though, that Rolf would come out to hold her hand. Brought up to a self-reliance that he expected to find in others, he did not do that. Her mother's voice, not in the least puzzled, not dim with distance. Leona found that she ought to have rehearsed what she would say. She stammered, repeated herself, could hardly answer her mother's quick questions; she was rationally nervous now, of saying more about her whereabouts than she meant to in the reassertion of habit, of being a child who must account for herself.

"How did you know that you should not telephone our rooms?" asked her mother's voice. "Did Madame Forstmann tell you?"

"Tell me? No, I just didn't want to talk to Papa. I thought I couldn't . . ."

"Then you don't know?"

"Know?" She quailed. What could have happened?

"Your father is ill. He caught cold and then went out in the snow, it has turned to a congestion of the lungs. He has a high fever and is a little delirious, so I told them not to ring any bells, so as not to disturb him. They are going to put in a telephone in the corridor tomorrow, so that I don't need to go down every time. I thought you already knew."

So that was why nobody thought it odd when Leona asked for her mother to be fetched. That accounted, too, for the quiet way her mother accepted what she said. She might have known. He was bound to do something. That was Leona's thought: he was bound to do something. Her mother was speaking again.

"Sorry, Mummy, I didn't hear."

"I said, are you all right for money? I suppose you will need some, cash, I mean."

Leona had not yet thought of this. She had not been in the position of actually paying for her own necessities with bank notes; money was pocket money.

"I suppose I shall."

"Alain and a secretary are arriving tomorrow, early. I will ask them to send you some money for the moment. Where should they send it? No, no, I see you don't want to tell me where you are. Though there is no need for you to fear anything for a day or so. I mean, which bank?"

Leona thought quickly; what had she heard schoolfellows say about money?

"Oh, the post office," she stammered hastily. "Wait, I can't think. Yes, the main post office, it's in the Fleischmarkt. I'll pick it up there. Is that all right?"

"Fleischmarkt? Funny name for a street. I've written it down but it looks wrong, I must have misspelled it. Doesn't matter. Listen, Leona, don't be scared. Don't disappear again, will you. I mean, not from me? It's very upsetting, you know. I won't . . . Uncle Alain won't . . . You wouldn't like to see him, I suppose? Anyway, you know, you are quite safe for the moment, because Papa can't—can't do anything."

"Is he very ill?" asked Leona, intimidated. "Oh dear, I would love to see you. I feel suddenly so lonely."

"You're not alone? Not on your own?" cried her mother's voice, for the first time sounding alarmed.

"No, oh no. Rolf is here."

"I thought he might have had to go back."

"Tomorrow morning he has to be back."

"Will you telephone me tomorrow? I promise I won't say a word. But I don't want to lose touch again."

Her mother's voice broke slightly and Leona gulped, blinking away tears.

"I'll call in the evening," she said quickly.

"Promise?"

"Promise."

"Look, I must go back. The woman they have lent us is having her supper, and he's alone. He may need something. They'll decide tomorrow whether he had better be moved to a clinic, when the specialist comes. But I shall be here for certain in the evening. You won't forget?"

"No, of course I shan't forget. Till then?"

Leona leaned against the chilly metal of the telephone booth, both frightened and comforted by her mother's voice. On the way back into the taproom, it occurred to her that she had left no message for her father, hardly even asked after him.

"He's ill," she announced abruptly. "I *knew* he'd do something to make me feel awful!"

"Very ill?"

"I don't think so. But he can't do anything at all for a few days. He's in bed, with a temperature, somebody has to be with him. A specialist is coming in the morning, and so is Uncle Alain and some secretary."

"What can he need a secretary for, when he's ill?"

"Oh, there are always messages, orders. He never goes away for more than two days without a secretary at least. Even on the beach or anywhere, there's always somebody rushing around with telex papers."

Rolf was looking very puzzled; the constant attendance of secretaries, one evidently of several, was something quite out of his experience. Some instinct told Leona that the extent of her father's business affairs was a subject of dangerous import; and she quickly changed it.

They talked of skiing, and of future plans for more skiing; of horses, of flying. Leona's family formed no part of their converse, and neither did the nature of their relationship. The name by which their state is known never passed between them; any words they might have used were for them so entirely worn out, so meaningless, that they did not even think of them. Such labels could be and were attached to clothes, food, to dance tunes. They did not love, they did not adore, they did not desire each other; the "sex" Leona only a few days before felt such a curiosity about did not exist for them. They were in a new country; like the landscape outside in the obliterating snow, their here and now was a land without signposts, where every newcomer must find his own way. Since neither of them was in the least "intellectual" they did not miss phrases.

CHAPTER 11

Leona's mother came out of the telephone cell behind the porter's lodge so completely sunk in her own thoughts that she stood still by the archway into the inner hall, frowning in concentration, seeing and hearing nothing. Until the doctor retained by the hotel for its guests had twice spoken to her, she did not even hear her own name.

"I was just about to come up to you," he said, when she gave him an abstracted, meaningless smile of polite greeting. "If you can spare the time. I am a little puzzled by your husband's state," he went on as they slowly mounted the stairs side by side. "I'm not sure whether you understand, but there is really nothing in his physical condition to account for what seems to be a general collapse. There is some congestion, yes, but the temperature is higher than I would normally expect, the degree of—er—confusion, or delirium, greater. I have almost the impression . . ."

"Yes," she interrupted him, too used to the implication of her being an idiot to take offense. "It is just as Madame Forstmann said it might be. She told me he was on the verge of a nervous breakdown."

"You know Anna Forstmann?" He raised his thick gray eyebrows.

"We were out at the clinic, yesterday."

"Really? To see the Professor? I am glad you told me that. I will telephone the clinic in the morning and consult Professor Smolka."

"No, not to see the Professor. To see Madame Forstmann on a personal matter."

"Oh, I thought perhaps to get advice. Your husband's nervous state?"

"No. We had private business to discuss with Madame herself. It was my husband's manner then—he really behaved very oddly—that made her warn me." She considered for a moment, her hand on the door handle to their rooms. "It seems she was right."

"She would tend to be right. Indeed, it is her fixed habit to be right," agreed the doctor, sedately amused. "She and the Professor have built up his clinic out there in the little spa more on Frau Forstmann's being right than on the Professor's considerable reputation."

"I can well believe it."

"It was derelict twenty years ago, and the whole place, the baths, the waters, everything, unused. And today it is one of the most renowned private hospitals in Europe. I am a great admirer of Anna Forstmann."

He shed his heavy overcoat and hat and followed Mme. Chavanges into the sitting room from which the door into the right-hand bedroom stood open.

"Ah! Alain! Already! I am so glad you have arrived," she said on a rising note of relief. "And Monsieur Yves too. Did you have an easy journey?"

"Considering we were driven at breakneck speed half across Europe in the middle of winter, surprisingly so," said the elderly man addressed as Alain as he kissed her cheek.

"We knew, of course, that you would need the car, Madame, if you are staying on for a week or so," said the young secretary primly, "and since the flights are all over the place with all this snow, it was better for us to come with the Rolls."

Mme. Chavanges perceived a reproach in this speech and smiled to cover her ignoring of it as she gave the younger man her hand. "Much nicer than flying in this awful weather," she said as if agreeing with him.

"This is Dr. Berthold," she went on, "Monsieur Schneider. Monsieur Filemond. Have you seen him, Alain?"

"I went in for a moment. He doesn't really look very ill. But . . ."

"Exactly. But," said the doctor.

"How odd that I didn't see you arrive, Alain."

"Oh, we went to our rooms first. We've been here over half an hour. I told them not to bother you until we had cleaned up. I know how you hate a fuss."

"And then I was downstairs . . ." She remembered what she had been doing in the hall and broke off with a glance at the secretary. That would all have to come later.

"There are several matters that need decisions," the secretary indicated a flat briefcase near him on a table. "Monsieur Chavanges said they don't matter. But . . ."

"I will deal with them. I told you," said Alain gently.

"But there are some technical things, Monsieur."

"The world won't stop in two days, Yves," Mme. Chavanges warded him off with a delicate hand laid on his sleeve and he colored a little at her touch.

"It's so unlike him," he said fretfully.

She moved to the bedroom door so that she could look in at the patient. "He's awake, isn't he, Doctor? Strange, he seems to be thinking, I mean he looks as if he were."

"Just what I thought!" said Alain, frowning quickly. "Certainly he is not interested in us."

The doctor went past them with a little bow and went up to the bed, where he lifted the strong wrist with its black hairs to take the pulse. The man lying in the bed ignored them. The broad head, more saturnine than usual against the brilliant white linen, lay unmoving, eyes half closed. The thick hair that grew solidly, flecked at the sides with gray, was not disordered but the jaw and cheeks were dark with yesterday's unshaved beard. He did not look particularly ill, in fact the slight flush gave him rather a healthy than a hectic aspect; but his breathing was heavy and rough with congestion. Yes, he looked as if he considered something important that the others could not understand.

There was a slight tap at the inner door and a woman entered. She wore the black dress and white apron of the hotel servants with a small white cap on coarse and frizzy hair that was obviously dyed to its rich brown color.

"If you please, Madame, I moved your things into the second bedroom as you asked." She indicated with a movement of her chin the smaller room where Leona was supposed to sleep. "The young lady's things I packed."

"Oh, thank you," said Mme. Chavanges absently. Then she thought and repeated the phrase in her awkward German, turning her eyes, still puzzled, to the newcomer as the maid went into the bedroom. She went straight up to the bed, murmuring a greeting to the doctor, and then moved to the far side where a chair stood by the bed, now the only one in the room.

"They took the other bed out, then. I told them we needed more room to move." The doctor raised his eyebrows at this evidence of the woman feeling herself to be in charge in the sickroom.

At the sound of her voice Chavanges opened his eyes and turned his head slowly on the pillows. The expression of indifference to the outside world, of concentration, faded and he now looked anxious, almost dismayed. The woman leaned with one knee against the side of the bed, pushing up the swell of the quilt in its shining white cover so that the bluish shadows rippled and altered. Then she reached down and patted the arm in its blue pajama sleeve. Chavanges stared up at the somewhat gnomic face as dark as his own but thin where he was well-covered, and already wrinkled. She gave him a familiar little grin which he did not return.

"So you are there," he muttered. "I thought I'd dreamed you."

"Yes, I'm here all right," she replied in the near-derisive tone of one who is never ill. "What, yesterday too, you thought you dreamed me?"

The doctor, taking the thermometer from the patient's armpit, looked sharply up at her familiar tone. She said quietly, to the doctor, with perfect propriety, "He's better, isn't he, Doctor? Much better than yesterday."

"He still has a good deal of fever," the doctor said coldly. He was preparing a hypodermic phial now, holding the base of the needle daintily in a square of gauze as he squintingly fitted it to the small container without touching its point.

"Round here," he said, "the pajama cord," and tipped his head toward the door. She went over and pushed it closed. Then she rolled back the cover, pulled the pajama cord neatly, and turned the heavy body skillfully with one hard middle-aged paw against his unresisting shoulder while she twitched down the garment with her free hand. The doctor moved the silk a little farther with his elbow, rubbed one spot with a swab and slipped in the needle, all in an instant.

"To the manner born," he said sarcastically. "Were you a nurse?"

"Me, Doctor? Oh no. But four children—you know?"

He nodded, released the now empty phial and looked for the wastebasket. The woman took the little glass from his hand.

"Have you worked here long?"

"Thirty-four years. On this same corridor."

"Can you manage? It is not easy to get a private nurse without notice, but if . . ."

"I can manage." She was busy making the man in the bed comfortable again. "I can use the overtime money, too. Good evening, Herr Doctor."

145

"She seems quite competent," he said, emerging into the sitting room. "Unless you feel that you must have a nurse, I think she can take care of him." He turned his head back toward the half-closed door and shook it. "Queer little thing."

"I thought she was a nurse," said Mme. Chavanges, surprised.

"Oh no. The temperature is down slightly. He seems to be somewhat easier. Of course, the sedatives do that, too. Give him one as last night, please," he glanced at his watch. "In about an hour's time."

They exchanged civilities as Mme. Chavanges moved with him to the door.

"But keep the sleeping pills yourself, Madame, if you please," he said as an afterthought. "They should not be in unauthorized hands."

"You think she is not reliable?" she asked sharply.

"Yes, as far as one can judge, certainly. But to be on the safe side. Everyone has different tolerances to these drugs and I do not know your husband. I don't know about France, but the law is very strict here." Picking up his hat he added, "Don't worry too much. Your husband is in no danger, you know."

"No," she agreed, smiling faintly, "no." As the door closed she said to Alain, "Odd little woman. Like a monkey."

"Who?" he asked, surprised.

"That little maid woman. I must get those flowers changed. Alain, the doctor seems more worried about his nerves, I feel, than about this pneumonia." She glanced swiftly in the direction of the waiting secretary with his injured and patient manner.

"Perhaps you wouldn't mind seeing that Phillippe has what he needs, on your way down to dinner," Alain said easily. "I'm sure he has, such an independent type, Phillippe, but as well to be sure. A bad-tempered driver would be a hazard in this climate."

The younger man smiled politely and picked up his document case, moving slowly to the door as he made a conventional rejoinder.

"I should leave those papers there." Alain's voice was conciliatory. "Just in case I get the chance to discuss them."

"He's furious at not being in charge," he explained to Solange as the door closed once more. "But I was sure you must have some good reason for wanting me to come too."

"I had indeed. As soon as the waiter has gone, we must talk, Alain."

She turned as the waiter appeared: the guests in this suite never had to wait for an answer to the bell. "Please ask the head waiter in the restaurant to come up, would you? Alain, I'll just make sure he doesn't need anything, then we shan't be disturbed again."

Solange found the woman whom she thought of as being like a monkey finishing some rearrangement of the bed. Her husband lay still, his eyes now quite closed, but he was not asleep. He did not stir at her whispered questions which were answered by his attendant, to whom Solange gave one of the sleeping tablets. As she turned to go, the woman behind her said something with a little chuckle to the patient, but Solange did not understand what she said.

"I wish I understood German better," she said to Alain, but he was busy consulting with the maître d'hôtel as to what they should eat and hardly answered her. Solange went over and poured herself a glass of dry sherry, considered it for a moment and then mixed a strong whisky and soda instead.

"Alain, you can't eat cheese after pheasant," she interrupted their serious discussion. "Leave the sweet to them, that's one thing they know about here. Monsieur, bring us some of those little pancakes that taste of burnt apricots. You know the ones?"

"I know exactly, Madame," agreed the professional. "Now, for the wine?"

Finally, Alain came to claim a drink.

"Now tell me at long last, Solange, what is this all about?"

"It's all about Leona," she said. "I'll begin at the beginning."

147

In the adjoining room, silence reigned. The screen normally in front of the bathroom door stood now across the entrance from the sitting room. The man lay still in the now dimly lighted bed and the gypsy-like woman sat in the chair beside him, leaning forward. As if he knew he would be left in peace at last Chavanges opened his eyes a little, trying to focus so that he could determine whether the bed was really swinging a little or whether this was the result of fever and the various medicaments. No, it was not swinging but neither did it feel like a bed standing on four stable feet; it was rather like a hammock supported in air so that it could sway with any move. The figure seated beside the bed was actual and real, he knew now that he was not dreaming her, which did not mean he had not dreamed the other things in which she had participated. It only meant that the presence yesterday for whom she had been the stand-in was not real. Or did it mean that? He was only sure of one thing, she was not important. This woman here and now meant nothing although he knew she was in fact there beside him. There was a difference of realness in this that he could not quite get hold of in his state of troubled haze. It was very warm under the feather cover, not the floundering sweating suffocation of before, but still warm enough for everything to be damply sticky, even in the fresh pajamas. From somewhere just above and to the left of his head came a very faint rustling sound which was pleasant and musical. It was the tiny bubbles rising in a glass of Gastein water from which she had just given him a mouthful; here again was the difference in realness because he was aware of the sound's identity and yet it was also the sound of something else, he did not know what. Not loud enough to be leaves stirring, they rustled quite loudly he remembered from a long time ago when he had nothing better to do than listen to trees. It could have been gnats in hot summer airs. Or the minute touches of grasses if one were lying out on the hillside in an afternoon drowse.

The covers shifted slightly and he felt a hard small living creature move in toward him; it was a familiar, a pet, and though he knew it was a hand it was not attached to a body but a being on its own. This small living creature moved quietly up over his arm, slipped down his flank and then up to his breast to caress him so that he felt an inward jump and then lost interest again, inert and floating, trying to recall something. Not a boy lying on the slope of heath in hot sunlight, nearer than that, perhaps even inside him. Distantly he heard or remembered a chinking sound and thought of jewelry being taken off and set down on a glass table top; where did that come from? But the notion came back from yesterday or sometime when the danger that his wife might enter at any moment added the pleasure of insulting Solange to an absorbing and ferocious lustfulness. Yes, bemused in the headache burning from a high temperature he recalled himself both yesterday and on other occasions pulsing with urgent fantasy inspired at this swinging moment by that hard little warm creature that scuffled in the warmth so that although real in itself it represented something else that he could not place. It moved in the thick hair, cozily, teasingly before going, just as before, yesterday, to cup and weigh his maleness, squeezing gently and tickling. He was awake but the day before he thought she awakened him from a morbid sleep, or had he attacked her? For an instant it seemed important whether it was a dream or waking but at once again ceased to matter. Had he really invaded her body in a delirious daydream? It would be better, yes, if that were so. Better if it had been the undersized dark woman, although he was now aware that whoever had begun to act she, whoever she was, was the rapist. It was done to him, then, and he was confusedly conscious of the flick of white cloth and a lifting of black which was savagely exciting before he felt her sinewy thin flanks, squeezing, forcing, working in a frenzy of silence at him. And at the same time that every nerve in his so much larger body was concentrated into wild enjoyment, he could still see, or had seen, his own penis outside what was happening, reared up by itself as tall as a pillar and dark

149

with engorged purple force. He must have been, or be, alone because he could see it all the time, only he knew that must be a dream for it was huge and both wonderful and menacing.

She muttered something, the sound floated above, and with a strange inward blow of relief that was black disappointment, the voice was the wrong voice speaking the wrong sounds. And with that piercing knowledge the fantasy was there, taking over, more vivid than any reality. It was a young girl whose thin hard thighs clutched his loins, he could see and feel the pale hair falling forward so that her face remained invisible, was veiled from him. She rode above him as he lay there like a conquered and joyful centaur, slight and taut and almost breastless, and it was she who cried out through clenched teeth at the power of that huge lingam that was outside himself. Outside. Not himself. Another. He groaned aloud, straining for the reality of that girl and the vision vanished as from release everything slid into a falling dizziness, a rosy sway of increasing darkness. The dark enfolded him and he enfolded it in an immense, all-embracing love; in him and he was in it, flowed an intense, longing, adoring love.

He felt himself alone now, and alone he could contemplate his vision, too secret and precious even to be thought about in the presence of any other person. As on the day before but more strongly so that he knew it was a final judgment, in the rapture of his lovingness was its loss. Obscurely through the sinking and fading of consciousness penetrated a knowledge; now that he had recognized that lovely myth it would never return. He possessed only the reality of secret love.

Act Two

FATHER AND SON

CHAPTER 12

Standing by the window on Monday afternoon after M. and Mme. Chavanges left I decided to write the story down because I knew I could not talk about it, let alone recount it by word of mouth. Even if I could they would not listen so long, and where could I have taken them to hear it? But written, they will read it; curiosity is very strong in human nature. There are things here I shall have to face again that were never spoken of even to my companion on that journey. Those things I have never once told; they will be dragged out now from the obscurity of twenty-six years' silence. The narrative, with or without a pattern—for perhaps I only delude myself that there is some faintly discernible symmetry under the outer shell of events—that will hardly develop in a straight line. No doubt I shall recall passages of the story and go back to them out of their time sequence. But I can only write it as I remember it, trying to tell the truth and trying to write clearly so that they can understand how it was. I understand from other people that this is a very difficult thing to do. No doubt I shall now discover what writers have told me, just how difficult it is. To tell the truth about even one moment is hard enough; how often have I listened to the life histories of patients, their confessions or justifications, their apportioning of blame or responsibility for what has happened to them; and afterward listened to the same history from their relatives. Entirely different stories about unrecognizably different people. And this is true too when the speaker, as in the case of M. Chavanges himself, is used to marshaling facts and ideas in a logical sequence; invariably much is taken for granted as known when in fact it is not known. For instance, M. and Mme. Chavanges have both said things intended to explain their own lives. But they both concentrate on the erotic or its absence because for both of them this part of living is, so far from being an active part of their story, just what is lacking to them, just what they cannot take into account. The central fact that dominates their lives is property, and for him everything he touches, including his only child, turns into property; a dreadful Midas fate. This is not perhaps because he so strongly loves property but because he was obliged to give up his own career to conserve a great inheritance and the duty has become an obsession as unwillingly adopted duties tend to do. It cost him so much that it must be of paramount importance and he expects everyone else to admire, respect and defer to his own sacrifice of his chosen life —for he evidently much enjoyed being a diplomat, and was talented—in the name of a family trust that probably could very well have been undertaken by a board of directors. With that example before me, I shall try to include details which to me are repetitiously obvious, because I know that they can't know these things. Not even the plain facts of that time historically are known. They have been only rarely written and even less rarely translated from German into other languages.

I have said already that I shall try to tell the truth. It is my truth only, but it is true. There are two small additions I must make to that claim and in all humility I am aware of its being a tremendous one. One is that by the time the world had reduced itself to dissolution there was no longer any responsibility that could be attached to any single human caught up in the tempest, any more than people flung about in an earthquake can be blamed or praised for the antics of their limbs. The other is that these things and much worse happened then to millions using many different languages and coming from many different places, on all sides of the tempest. I ask my two readers, then, to accept their own ignorance. Finally, I shall give them the real name of the only person in my narrative whose name has been changed, so that they can trace Jean-Martin's family and satisfy themselves as to his identity.

The road went on forever, nearly straight and for long sections at a time, quite straight. Raised somewhat above the fields, it was visible from horizon to horizon, shallow ditches on either hand, bordered in places by ragged tall apple trees which once had been evenly spaced but now had gaps between them. It ran almost exactly from north to south and everything on it or beside it was pointed toward the south in the direction of retreat for armies, refugees and cattle. There were motor vehicles of all kinds as well as handcarts and horse carts, scattered, smashed and overturned. There were trucks, cars, wagons, tanks, troop carriers, motor bicycles, regimental officers' transports with their insignia, dispatch riders and messengers dead and frozen stiff beside their broken wheels, torn metal plates, ripped leather upholstery, shattered glass. The dead were strewn everywhere, scattered across the fields, crouched still in the ditches where shelter had proved too meager to save them, flung in wild contortions, crushed and dismembered on the road's surface. There were cattle dead of thirst, soldiers dead of wounds, women and children and the old also dead of wounds, or simply of exhaustion and hunger. There was no sound, no movement, no smell from any of them. A horse with its belly ripped wide and one haunch torn completely off reeked as little as the three bundled humans flung off the flat cart by the same shell. The explosion point and its radial fragments could be clearly traced. Some of the animals had been cut about after death for food, some not. So there were, at the time, survivors from this minor scuffle.

They all made plenty of shelter for the half kilometer or so that they covered. Then that mauled group, no less silent than the empty road past them, was overtaken and the only shelter for a long stretch was the dry and frozen grass of the ditch and the tattered trees as they loomed up to be leaned upon for a moment and then slowly left behind again. There was no sun. A gray even dim light of midwinter hung in a haze over the blank fields. Frozen stubble, unplanted plowland, alternated with unharvested crops lying flat and black with rot in the deathly flat emptiness. A rutted track led off the right of the road across the exposed ground to a group of trees which probably hid houses or the ruins of houses, but if they existed they were invisible in the mist. Houses were to be avoided but even if they were known to be empty the decision to change course was beyond strength to make.

In a way the landscape was not dead. It was too frozen for anything so much connected with life as death. It was simply empty, rigid and sterile wih silent, colorless, feelingless cold. It bore no relation to anything human or animal or even plant and the remains of life were meaningless as if painted or stuck onto a cardboard relief of land with a raised road running pointlessly over it forever.

Somewhere miles over there to the right, that is to the west, the open land ran into dunes and then into sea as flat, dim, gray and silent as the hard unreal earth. That was a long way off. It formed itself as being there only because months before a possibility suggested itself for a moment, of getting away in that fashion in some then still conceivable boat that would rock and creak on the unfamiliar water. It was no more real now than the gaunt wreckage of buildings which was all that remained many miles behind over the flat horizon, of the town and the hospital left months before, when life still was. And there incredibly it had been warm. Of the intervening time, before the road, there was not even memory. That time was cut off, encapsulated somewhere out of mind, not to be seen or felt or even envisaged as past.

Now, as far as anything as definite as now still existed, there was the road to the edge of which a tiny figure was attached and slowly moving along a vast measureless void, hanging with shapeless and meaningless obstinacy to the one reality which was the road drawing that crawling scrap of matter along it. The point of movement, seen from its outside as if from some other place, the sky or the sea, or perhaps from some other state of being that had once been consciousness, continued to move without will or purpose because it moved and there was nothing left in it to reason that it could stop; not even the certainty, also outside itself, that if it did it would freeze hard and silent like everything else.

The bundle of scarves wound about its upper parts prevented hearing if there were anything to hear, and the figure occasionally turned itself from habit to scan the road behind, the fields on each side, in case anything else moved. Nothing did move.

That scrap of crawling matter on the road was myself and there is a real sense in which the road did go on forever. It goes on unending in me. I do not know where, measured in the real world, I joined the road nor where I left it again. I know where it ran and probably still runs, as an actual *chaussée* in East Prussia then, Russia and Poland now. There are maps and others have mentioned the area occasionally but that is objective evidence of what has for me no relation to time or space, so that it might just as well go on forever or never have existed and of course, it does go on, the plodding mover with it, as long as I live. And yet it never was, it is outside the world in limbo. How long I stumbled over its length, whether I found things to eat or drink, how many milestones, turnings, groups of wreckage I saw, how many vehicles I crouched down motionless to hide from, where or when I slept if I did sleep, are meaningless questions. The road is silent, frozen, empty and I am there for a space of eternity.

I know, for common sense tells me it must be so, that the existence in me of the road comes from the dreams I dreamed of it for years. For the first few years almost every night; later less and less frequently. I can even fix the point in time at which gaps begin in the nights, gaps where the dream did not accompany sleep. There was a period of years when for months at a time I did not dream that nightmare. Naturally, it has again been much more frequent while I have been deliberately remembering. Perhaps when I have written down the story the dream will cease altogether? That would be a reward for telling the truth as far as anyone ever can, an additional payment of interest. And yet I feel that possibility almost as a threat; I fear, apparently, to lose myself by losing that incommunicable horror that stamped millions with its brand. I do not mean the millions of Germans. That needs to be carefully said. I have to remember to say that, for I do not wish to belong to that vast number who have torn that time to shreds with their words for twenty-five years. All those of a dozen nations and of none, of several beliefs and none, who survived mutilated —none who survived was undeformed—who talk and write endlessly in real hatred, rage and self-pity against the particular enemy who damaged them; all those who make propaganda with artificial anger from the agonies of others and all those who have literally cashed in upon the cosmic wreckage. They can easily be identified by this test: according to their particular standpoint they all show one enemy, the others; and one victim, themselves. It is too late now to disentangle truth from the coils of words. The historical lies of the second European war have joined their companion lies of the past and hardly anyone pauses for a rational moment to consider the impossibility that one group, I have even heard it said, one man, could have created that universal chaos. We were all enemies and all victims of each other. Across frontiers and inside them, between families and within families; sometimes, indeed often, inside individuals. That can be said to be a simple truth if ever there was one. In the end we were all victims; of what we were victims we still do not even try to think.

Especially in the vast space without natural barriers that lies roughly between the Elbe, the Baltic Sea, Leningrad, Odessa and the line of the Danube; there none escaped unharmed because in that area geography, climate and the nihilism of this century combined to brew a hell on earth that seeks its equal in vain in human history. Where sufferings have perhaps been sharper they have lasted a shorter time, or they happened in kinder climates or the lack of comprehensive and determined controls allowed some evasion or escape.

Sensation comes back, brings me back by pain from limbo, with a recognition that my body is close up against another mass which has warmth. A long time after I become aware of this warmth I am vaguely staring up into blank grayness and slowly know that this is the sky, or mist. The warmth moves and I feel the bitter loss of it as an icy chill along my side. I roll myself up and the dark returns. From far away a voice murmurs, comes nearer, is actually heard as a voice. It is a voice but I do not know what it says. Either then or later I hear the voice again and this time I recognize words in my own tongue but I cannot or do not answer that, yes, I am awake. I stare up and know that I am looking but it is dark, there is no mist or pale sky over me. The sky has gone. There is a slight glow, reddish, not daylight. My head is raised by some force behind me and a hard and hot pressure pushes at my mouth. It is liquid too, unbearably hot, I choke and feel heat slip over my chin and down into the shawls round my neck. Some liquid goes into my mouth and I swallow painfully on the heat and close my eyes which have filled with water at the agonizing joy of hot wetness. The hard pressure withdraws and comes back, I know now that it is some kind of cup and curl my stiff lip toward it so that more heat drains into me, I can feel it as separate drops of life. I can feel myself trying to move, I am raising my hand but nothing happens. I am sinking again into darkness, not able to keep myself there.

The dim gray is there again. My head is pushed up and something pushes a soft mush into my mouth which I chumble about and find I can swallow. I am rediscovering how to eat and from somewhere I know that the pinkish gray shapes moving in my dazed sight are fingers pushing food into my now open jaws. Into a blank of unknowing this penetrates as evidence that a human being is there and very gradually I feel that I am not out in the open but in some kind of shelter. Most of the time the mass and pressure of that warmth I was at first aware of is close to me and I would cling to it if I could, clutch it to me, but it is formless and I cannot move to grasp it.

Very slowly, with pain that amounts to agony and makes me wish to die, or rather since I do not formulate the wish, to be unconscious and not come back ever, feeling returns with circulation. Now I fear. If I was so frozen, my feet and hands may be damaged and yet I may live; I am being forced into consciousness and feel with the fear a resentment of that. Somewhere a voice is saying in a hushed tone that I must try to move, bend my knees, turn my elbow. I do not try and pressure forces my joints to creak, change position. The pain is so sharp that I begin weakly to whimper and feel tears running backward down my throat. I know that the pain means the circulation is not stopped and gradually that encourages me to try so that I do at last move. At first my head, I can roll it. Then the joints of my shoulders.

This goes on for a long time, the pushing of food into my mouth, the forced movements, I am making a thin sound of protest which turns into a kind of grunting at the effort I am now making. When something forces a circular movement at some distance from me I scream. The voice hushes me and its bulk and warmth are removed, and in spite of my annoyance at being shoved so brutally back into life, I begin to weep again at its loss. But all is well, the bulk and warmth return and bully me further.

When the circular move is made once more I do not scream; not because I am not still being tortured but because I know dimly that I must not make a noise.

So I returned to consciousness with the recognition of a fear outside myself, a threat. This conscious state must not be understood at all as the brilliant, sharp, manifold apprehension of detail, registration of a thousand things at once which is normal consciousness. I was aware of my being in some relation to the surrounding reality of what was outside my body; that was all for the time. I was in something like the state of a fairly primitive animal, I suppose; and this condition lasted, only hesitantly advancing into humanity and then into my former civilized complexity of understanding and skill over a period of months. Probably about a year. For the moment only the animal instincts operated, even after I could again move about.

I grasped that the voice, the bulk and warmth, were another human being bundled into a roll of various garments; and then that it was another woman. Then I took in that we were in a shelter which had once been a small cottage and was now the walls and roof, lacking doors and windows, which had been removed whole with the frames. I recognized this; without examining the memory I was aware that this had been happening since the Russians were there and this brought back the reason for the caution already imposed by animal instinct. The other woman had collected some of the doors—there were several in the original building—which must have been thrown away just outside. She had dragged them into the cottage again and set one of them against the window space to cover it. I was lying on another, to raise me and herself from the brick floor. Sometimes when she was quite sure there was nobody within sight or hearing she pushed the door from the window and I could see the milky mist of frosted emptiness outside. The fog of deep frost was one of the circumstances that saved our lives, for as long as it lasted the smoldering fire which she had somehow made could be kept alive. The trace of smoke did not show in the fog and several trees about the house added to a confusion of any outside view. What really saved us was a nanny goat in milk, incredibly left alive for Ronni to find there. The soldiers who had gone through here were in a hurry and the sacks of grain were still in the cellar, cut open and the contents scattered, but the grain could be gathered together and made into a gruel with water and goat's milk. This was incredible riches. People killed each other at that time for one potato or a chunk of iron-hard bread.

The house we were in was the last outpost of a former village, now razed to the ground by tanks and fire. This one cottage stood well away from the rest, hence its survival. We never knew the name of the place, a hamlet of perhaps forty small buildings. The former inhabitants almost certainly left on the trek just before the troops arrived. That was happening everywhere. Forbidden to leave on pain of death, the intimidated country people, cut off from any news except the radio, would leave in a body by common consent when they heard the guns, or when a group of re-treating German troops roused them to self-preservation by their condition of struggling defeat. Then came the enemy and de-stroyed the hamlet, village or town. Anyone left there was de-stroyed with the place. But here nobody had been left for there was no sign either of corpses, of people, or of cattle except for our goat.

We began to talk, to pool our common stock of knowledge about our situation. Her voice sounded like a normal human voice, mine scraped rustily in my own ears. She spoke German with a soft, southerly accent and some other intonation which I became used to as a mixing of Polish. Without her telling me, al-though she did so, I knew that she must have been married to a Pole and was therefore in the foregoing years an outcast. It was quite impossible at that time to assess anyone's age and she, like myself, must have looked an aged crone. She was about fifty then and her name was Veronika which was at once shortened to

Ronni. My own name was not altered; there is no diminutive for Anna. At least none that she would have used, as I later assumed.

We did not speak of anything but of our present state. That would have been impossible. When living is reduced to its fundamentals and below them, nothing that can weaken is allowed into the mind, or since mind is a false word in that condition, into the soul. First, we had water, nourishment and heat. We were for the moment safe from the elements. We were surrounded by struggling armies at some distance greater than hearing. Where any part of those still battling groups were in relation to ourselves we had no idea. In relation to ourselves meant toward the south, away from the invaders and in the same general direction as their thrusts must be. That these invaders were all around us had been known since before I left the hospital and that was the previous September. I described the encirclement as I had always heard of it, the result of a dastardly betrayal by the commanders of Army Group Center which broke the line of defense and allowed the Red Army into Prussia. She did not argue with this way of putting the matter, but said only with a slow movement of an arm to indicate the country about us that the terrain offered small chance of successful defense. It was unrealistic to expect that any line could be held in such open, wide and level country. The Russians reached the Vistula and the Oder some two months before as far as she could count and since these rivers were no obstacle we could assume that not much less than the Alps would form a barrier to such an onslaught. That was a long way to walk south, as neither of us said aloud, supposing that we evaded capture or death so long.

We no more considered staying where we were than birds do in that country when the first gales of autumn sweep across the plains from the sea. This was not discussed; it was the condition of survival to escape and that condition operated our wills as one from the moment I was able to take in once more the fact of being alive. What we did pool was our combined information of the landscape; where rivers ran and railways; where towns and hills were. All of these must be avoided. What we needed was forest. I had walked from the lake and forest country but I did not say so, so as not to approach anywhere near the lost, forbidden time and place. I said only that there were forests scattered to the east of here, roughly southeast and stretching with gaps to the rising country. I knew that from my holidays from duty in the last three years. On the other hand neither of us knew much about the westward land except that it was flat, as flat as a hand. But, we thought, not wooded or not enough. It would be easier to walk to the southwest but much more dangerous. Especially as we knew from years of hearing the army communiqués that armies always wish to occupy coastlines. They would drive that way, we supposed.

Later Ronni said she knew the southern country to the east. "We once had a summer house," she said, "in the hills the other side of Krakov." We could be wrong about the main drive of the invasion. It could be due south for Warsaw and more or less west for Berlin, covering in effect the entire area. The original attack was circular, the summer offensive that reached Warsaw on the far side of the Vistula, but consolidation might dictate that supporting columns should move due south or nearly so. I moved hastily to stop her speaking when she mentioned Berlin, for that was absolutely a forbidden subject. What she said next I missed for I was occupied with the sensation of astonishment and light-headedness that filled me like drunkenness at the idea of it no longer mattering if one spoke aloud of the possibility of Berlin falling. The suppressed certainty that this would happen, there since the previous summer, was no longer a deadly secret. Berlin at that moment was surrounded, but that is an interpolated footnote of hindsight. It became clear in this slow conversation of what can have been several days that we must move south and east, missing Warsaw on our right or west and making for somewhere near Krakov, to take the dip in the mountains formed by the Vistula from the north and the March to the south. This last geographical knowledge was Ronni's. I had never been down there. If possible we must join a trek; if not then we would crawl like bugs over the center of Europe alone.

Later we discovered that the idea of sheltering ourselves at least from our terrible isolation by joining another slowly moving group of escapers was quite unreal. The time of treks was over before the spring came, long over. Those who had left it too late, later than the previous autumn, had been overtaken by the thunderous lava of steel, scattered, killed, collected into camps or trundled in long trains of goods wagons to unimaginable places far away in the east.

Our aloneness, and we knew it, was also our safety. This we knew by instinct, the need of animals to hide from the hunter. But the silence and the emptiness all about us was dreadful, a lowering curse on our heads, the lifting of which was longed for as a sign of salvation, forgiveness, the readmittance to the human race. Neither of us had committed a crime but we felt ourselves outcast and accursed, the scapegoats driven out alone into the desert. Every human being was gone from that land, only we were left and the condition of being abandoned was that of felons, simply of itself and not for any reason. Neither the invaders nor the broken remnants of our own troops counted for us as human; they were all alike our hunters and the dead were more related to us than they. In their senseless battles they would kill us without even knowing it, and if they knew they would be totally indifferent. It is a strange state to be the survivor of the end of the world. The human consciousness cannot survive for long in complete isolation, and although we still existed we felt with all our souls the need to rejoin with others in order to become living survivors.

"At least there are two of us."

"Three." Veronika gestured toward my belly.

"It can never be born alive."

"Don't say that."

"I know what I'm talking about. I'm a nurse."

"It's still alive."

"Still."

"What we must do is wash you and clean your clothes."

This was a limited project to occupy our thoughts. We debated the folly or otherwise of visiting the wrecked village in search of water. The barrel half full of ice from rainwater and snow under the roof drain of our cottage was needed for drinking. The danger of being seen on the open path was great, for once or twice an airplane had droned overhead and for quite a distance there was not enough cover for a hare to hide itself. We did not know how thick the covering fog was from above. Then Ronni thought of collecting frozen snow from the side of one of the trees where it had drifted in the last storm some weeks before. Most of the snow was melted into sheets of hard ice from the daytime sun before the fog came down, and we could only get enough to fill our one large vessel, once a metal bin used for cattle mash, by kicking it loose in chunks. This took a long time but the movement was good for me, we thought. Yet I was frightened by the thudding of my heartbeats and Ronni went blue around the mouth. We were weak from months of starvation, in no state to exert ourselves. Each looked covertly at the other, trying to assess her strength. It occurred to me that Ronni's health was not of the best in any case and we were both townswomen. Until last year I had been a vigorous girl, taking with ease a job that uses up great funds of energy and playing games as well. But the deep stamina of country women was lacking in both of us and Ronni was, or had been, of confined life and a sedentary habit. Her work, in the last years, was that of clerking in an office of the civil administration that dealt with the Poles. Even as the most contemptible member of the community, a former German who refused to abandon her Polish family, she was useful for her command of both languages and her local knowledge. But that kind of work on civilian rations was no training for hard physical exertion. It was a sign of my return to something like sense that I now began to worry about her ability to stand our long march when we set out. We had already decided on that moment.

Getting my clothing off me was difficult. Neither of us had shed our coverings for several weeks. Everything was stuck together and Ronni had somewhere picked up a lost sheepskin coat with the inevitable result of lice. Well, that was the least of our worries. In any case there was nothing to kill them with. In my rucksack there was half a piece of soap and that washed the pair of us, a couple of scrawny hags with veins and sinews showing under the gray skin, my six months pregnant stomach matching her dropped abdomen and hanging breasts.

"How many children have you had?"

"Five. You?"

"This is the first."

Neither of us asked after the fathers. She knew I wore no ring, but that meant nothing at that time. It could have been stolen, or bartered for a raw turnip. The questions were of a clinical nature, there was no reminiscence and neither of us—we could see from our eyes—needed even to try to force memory away. There was no room for feeling, there was only necessity. She rubbed carefully over the rounded belly, pressing gently to test the muscular wall and then leaning her head down to hear the inner rapid heartbeat with the side of her head against my body. At that moment the fetus kicked vigorously so that my heart jolted.

"Nothing much wrong with him," she said, grunting with the effort of rising from her knees.

We cleaned each other's feet, paring the nails with the broken half of a knife blade found outside the house. Care of the feet was going to be vital. Last of all we washed our hair and then bit by bit our inner garments, keeping some to cover us from the cold and then changing over.

When we had done we felt purged and renewed as one does when all is washed and scrubbed before Christmas, ready for the feast. Tired, we rested close together, storing our body heat and crowded to the meager smolder of the fire. The smell of drying cloth filled the small space with a steamy haze. In the quiet of sat-isfaction we slowly became aware of a sound in the dusk of the dim daylight. The unearthly silence was pierced by a tiny thread of air piping outside and even the dry rustle of our sheltering tree branches as the twigs brushed together could be heard. That meant the end of the fog, a change in the weather. If it cleared, we must douse the fire. If snow or rain came, we could stay here a little longer.

We did not use the overflowed and frozen earth-closet some steps from the cottage, but went in the shelter of one of the trees and I went outside now. It was already routine to look and listen for any sound before going outside and I tried now as well to test the wind. We knew roughly where north and south were from the main road off which the empty hamlet lay. I judged the air to be moving from the northeast and already drops of half-solid rain were falling. It would turn to snow in the night. The sleet thick-ened in that few moments of dying gray day. I could hear its rustling and then again the thin moan of the wind rising. Stealth-ily, like something living, the snow was creeping back. Winter was not over. Eerie flakes took on visibility, floating in the empty twi-light in slanting fall, whitish against the bulk of the wall, dark in relief upon the livid, flat sky.

As long as it lasted we could continue in our shelter if no one came.

It snowed then for several days, the storm wailing and howling about us like demons in the fast obscure waste that was neither sky nor earth. The hole in the wall that once was a window faced away from the blizzard or we should have been drifted up inside as well as outside. We were, as it was, obliged to get in and out of the window for the door was snowed in up to the low eaves of the peasant dwelling. This was painful for me, I was unsteady and un-wieldy and my feet were bloated well above the ankles. I tried to drink as little as possible, but that meant taking the goat's milk undiluted and what had seemed ambrosia when it brought me back from the dead was sickening now and I had to force it down with nausea into my displaced and resisting stomach. The reek of the poor creature in the dark cellar, our main hold on life, was so disgusting that to go down the uneven steps was a penance.

To occupy the time of inactivity we talked, I of my hospitals and she reciting poetry and stories from her vivid memory of literature which I altogether lacked. Ronni had read everything, it seemed to me, and quoted whole passages from writers whose names I had not heard since I left school and others of whom I had not even heard. Sometimes meaning was beyond me and only the rhythms and cadences were reachable, so that Rilke, for instance, poetry I know now equally by heart thanks to her, was just music. This was wonderful to me and has remained so, a joy and enrichment that I owe entirely to that beautiful and faithful soul. I mean faithful in the sense that lovingness and understanding of human beings never forsook her in even the most terrible and inhuman of moments because it was rooted in her nature as I have never known it in any other woman or man. So that she was filled with faith in a way that was never spoken, a creature of natural grace. I think now that the death within me would have continued for the rest of my life if I had never known this quiet woman, already almost old, whom strangers looked upon and treated as plain, homely and inconsiderable. Compared with Ronni, I was a primitive savage.

But then the poetry and my own anecdotes were equally just a means of passing the time which seemed in the stillness to go on like the road, endlessly, in some dimension that was neither time nor space. Cut off from the immediate past by a black barrier, we seemed, and it was so for both of us and we knew it of each other without explanation, to have lost our hold on ourselves just as we were lost bodily there in the waste of snow and silence. Even when the wind howled that silence was still present, encompassing us both; like time and space it was part of the weird dimension we existed in. The interior silence that symbolized the end of the world.

CHAPTER 13

Yes, the end of the world. But we were not to get away so easily, not from the wreck of the world and not from ourselves. The intruder in my body was there, however unconsciously determined I might be to ignore the source of his presence. I must, it was absolutely necessary for me to ignore that, simply because the fetus was there. If I did not shut its cause out I could no more go on breathing and pumping blood through it than I could transport myself back to the living time before those so simple and self-evident words were spoken which opened up the gulf between what I had understood and what was real. The immensity of that difference broke off my ability to think and feel or to recall, like shearing off a wall as I watched it from my room in the hospital just before I left there. That wall at which I was gazing when the bomb hit it did not explode or disintegrate as walls usually did under bombing. It was cut cleanly, probably by some chance of its construction or its angle, so that in an instant one stretch of wall was still standing and the other part simply was no longer there. No rubble, no jagged edge to be seen, it just no longer was. That was how I was, cut off cleanly from myself and no longer alive. I was not me any more, I had ceased to be, just like the wall. A body existed because of the fetus which I was forced to nourish and if I had been able to think about myself I should have expected to cease to exist when the child inside me reached its time. I did not in fact think of that for there was not enough of me left to think; I was so mutilated that the most I could manage was the primitive practical need of any given moment. Even if Ronni's recitations had all been much simpler than Rilke's sonnets I should still not have grasped their sense. Meaning was not there, any more than it is there for the piece of a worm cut by a scythe. With meaning memory was gone too; I literally had not existed between the moment of deciding to leave the hospital and the moment of Ronni forcing goat's milk and hot water between my rigid jaws. And even before that decision there were patchy gaps that were no longer there. The gaps reached back to the spring; before then I was able to recall everything quite clearly and normally. There were moments, the evening when the wind rose and the snow crept back was one of them, when some dark menace shifted outside but near me. There was enough objective cause for fear to account for the momentary darkening of the mind and it did not come near enough to have to be explained. But at such moments I was afraid with a deep, terrible fear, blacker than any of the various surrounding threats; that was the dread of not being able to maintain my unknowingness. But I did not recognize that then. I just felt the menace outside myself but near, different from any normal fear, which I cannot express except as the gaping mouth of hell.

When I later used that expression in trying to explain to Ronni, she was shocked; she, of course, was not brought up on Luther's Bible, as I was. But that belongs to later.

We have reached a point at which two things happened. The snow stopped as the wind shifted into the west. And we gradually heard a low thudding and booming in the distance. The sound was not of bombing. We both knew that from much experience. It was artillery fire. Artillery is worse than bombing because it means the presence of human beings; from the sky attack is not personal. The shift in the wind made it likely that the guns were firing to the west of us, between the road and the coast. We guessed about fifteen kilometers away, but in that very flat and empty country sounds carry trickily and it is difficult to judge distance and direction. There are wide lakes there, to the north of where we were, and forests to the east, and both these distort sound. Even in normal times, that is in the past, it is one of the sparsest-populated and least-built-over districts in Europe. At that time and for years afterward it was almost entirely deserted. It probably still is but nobody can go there now to make sure. I read in the newspapers a month or so ago that the hospital where I was stationed for three years is now used as a mental home for political cases.

These two changes faced us with our great decision. It was time to leave. Our plan was to cross the exposed road in the murk of dusk and make our way as far as we could during the night toward the forested land. We should take our goat with us and load it and our own backs with as much cooked grain from our dwindling store as we could carry, together with all our rags of covering and the broken knife, an eating vessel which was a small enamel pot much bent and cracked, the remains of the soap, a length of rope and the half-box of precious matches that Ronni hoarded.

Our feeling was partly dread and equally anticipation of a more hopeful kind. Not that we conceived of our project as hopeful; we knew all too well how small our chances were of avoiding becoming embroiled in the chaotic battles, of avoiding capture by the Russians, of withstanding the tremendous exertions of a march in late winter and early spring—it was by now about the middle of March—of what we reckoned was over three hundred kilometers partly through hilly country, of finding enough to eat to keep ourselves alive, of bringing the unborn safely to life. And if we should survive all these hazards, of establishing a claim to stay where some other rule than either the Nazi Party or the Russians was still in existence. The feeling of anticipation that was akin to hope came from doing something, undertaking the enterprise of escape.

If you who have not known such extremities do not understand our drive to move, to get somewhere else, then you understand nothing. It was the drive away from a rigid corpse to something still warm and breathing. So must have the clans of our ancestors been driven afar, without calculation, without thinking anything over, when great droughts in southern central Asia drove them from their ancient pastures toward the temperate regions of middle and west Europe. Instinct made us rest as long as we could, and instinct then made us move without knowing or caring how far we must go to reach any place where we could stay and rest.

All that night we could hear and feel the guns, a shudder coming into our nerves through the iron-hard earth as much as it was hearing their rolling sound. We prepared everything and then slept again.

In the dusk we left our shelter, loaded and leading the loaded goat. We crept to the road and listened, Ronni lying flat with her ear to the ground. There was no sign of anything approaching, so we crossed that first barrier. If the sky had not been closed in with immense palls of cloud there would have been a moon, and this made an eerie diffusion of the night in which we could, after a little while, see enough to recognize any movement, and after an hour or so the thicker darkness of trees. Nothing but ourselves moved, and we could hear and feel the trees long before we came into their chill damp cover. First a tongue of woodland, giving way to open fields again, and then in the middle of the night into the forest itself which we knew stretched for many miles. We moved very slowly, and slower still once in among the trees. Not only to conserve what little strength we had, but out of caution. A fall could be a disaster and outstretched hands were of more use than eyes. Moving one foot before the other with sideways groping steps to test for declivities or half-buried roots, we progressed slowly deeper into the embrace of the forest. I have noticed since then how many people who do not know that country believe that all those forests are of conifers. This is by no means so. New plantations, as elsewhere, were thereabouts mainly of firs. But the old forest, the natural one, is of mixed growth, larches, pines where the soil is sandy, and as well great oaks and chestnuts and all the familiar and half-known woodland inhabitants. Stretches of undergrowth are interspersed with whole glades where nothing grows under the tall trunks, and then alders and willows cluster to mark streams. There are thickets of hazel, saplings and grass, matted old bracken, brambles. Most of the animals were still in their winter sleep but we heard creatures once or twice, which listened to us as we to them. But no humans; we were the only people in that sheltering crowd.

Once started, we could go on for hours, not knowing whether our direction was changing. Not until the sullen sky gradually lightened when by a lucky chance we came to a broad ride and could see on which side the gray was paler and identify east and therefore south. Then we cautiously crossed the open space and crawled into underbrush to rest. There was no snow under the thick twigs and it was not quite freezing, a damp bone-chilling cold. Ronni's sheepskin and the torn blanket I had over my shoulders when she first found me were our shelter and we huddled close to the goat, passing into a state of almost unconsciousness that was not really sleep.

Coming to, we found ourselves bound by stiffness and muscular pains as if with heavy fetters. This was dangerous, for not only could the temperature fall again, without warning, well below freezing point, which could mean our deaths, but once awake, we could hardly move. If we needed to flee or to hide quickly while we were so muscle-bound, we were lost. So from that morning on, we ignored day and night. We struggled for a few hours and then rested and repeated the process, treating night and day alike and taking only the precautions needed to remain invisible and unheard. This entailed one of us always having our head coverings loose enough to hear clearly. This we took in turns. We also saw quite quickly that in spite of our need of her warmth, we must always tether the goat at some distance from our own hiding place for she would now and then give her snorting whinny which would betray her if anyone came near.

There was a period of some years, perhaps lasting roughly for most of the fifth decade, during which the survivors of such journeys, when they met, discussed endlessly their experiences of the trek. There were several details on which everyone I ever talked to agreed. One of these was the curious condition of alienation into which we fell after the first day or so of creeping forward. I mean literally alienation, in that we could apprehend ourselves only as if from away and above, always above, our crawling and suffering bodies. Some described this as being observed by another being, a sensation which sometimes moved over into the certainty that another being was watching one's movements, one's struggles. Mostly, the delusion was of creatures unknown to our normal selves, fabulous or demonic presences in the form of birds hovering, animals stalking or voices whispering from the sky. We did see and hear real birds and real animals, but they were quite separate from these illusory beings. If they are illusory. Perhaps we were able to pierce the bandages of our earthly stupidity during that voyage through the end of the world, and to see and hear spirits always there but unreachable by us in our usual cloddish state. Another aspect of that journey upon which almost every survivor known to me agreed, was the growing reality of the natural world. Trees are living creatures, stones and water contain their own essences as humans do. The soul of a rock becomes sentient and nearly palpable—but not palpable as the rock is palpable—and the rushing little fall of a stream speaks, laughs and chants so that it could be understood if only we knew its language. And as the division between realness and our unknowingness is thinned, so the body that holds us in servitude is felt as more brutish, more dull and unwitting and less to be taken seriously. Instead of being the whole, everything else ignored, the body seems inconsiderable as well as maddeningly weak and cumbersome.

It is felt as a miserable clot of matter. Its bleeding, crushed and swollen feet refuse to carry its weight. Hands get torn and bruised from struggling with natural forms that could easily be managed if they were understood. Eyes see two things instead of one or fail to see what is in front of them. But these disabilities are no longer the objects of constant consideration and self-pity, they become contemptible and irritating in their clumsiness. If only we lived with the world of natural beings instead of despite them, we obscurely feel, our passage through this hell could be transformed into ease and calm, the expansion of light would illumine us instead of our being closed thickly in by the darkness of acquired ignorance. We should be enlightened.

So we felt at the time and so we talked much later, to each other and to those others. We talked to rid ourselves of the memories but only to those who needed no tedious explanation, those who already knew. Those who knew these things identified themselves to us as we did to them, and unless we knew of our common experience we never mentioned such matters. This is the first time I have tried to tell it to unknowing outsiders.

The goat, poor creature, ate anything and everything as goats do. We ate perhaps two handfuls a day—time divisions were not clear—of the stodge of seed-wheat and barley boiled in goat's milk and water with which we were loaded. In that weather this stayed fresh for some time and then gradually went sour. But we continued to eat it, our stomachs getting more and more flatulent and rebellious as it fermented. There was no other food. It was immense, immeasurable, good fortune to have it. Millions then went for days at a time, even weeks, without anything to eat *at all*. We drank from running water when we found it.

During one rest pause, it was black night, the weather froze as the wind shifted capriciously. I was roused from that half-waking sleep by the weak complaint of gasps from our goat. I struggled to all fours and then to my feet, and went to it and put my arms round its stinking, pathetic head so that at least it did not have to die alone. To lose it was a terrible blow, more than the loss of milk and warmth. It brought the threat of death, our own deaths and for the first time I thought of one of us dying and leaving the other alone. It would be a great disloyalty for me to leave Ronni to make her way alone; I knew that without each other neither of us would last for long. Only much later did I think of that moment and recognize that for the first time I felt something, a pain for someone not myself and which was not physical. And Ronni, the only human creature left in this limbo of an ended world, was increasingly frail and slow. About such things I could not deceive myself for they belonged to my profession. I could see that she was constantly in pain, distressed and uncertain of eye and tongue. We labored on with immense exertion, achieving almost no gain from our weary efforts but driven forward by the need to escape. I could see that she watched me as I did her and with the same fears and forebodings. If only we could have stayed back there in the peasant hut until better weather came! But on that great sweep of flat openness, we would have had no more chance of escaping observation than rabbits have of escaping the eye of the hawk that seeks them.

Now and again we came to a country road winding through the woodlands. We would explore and wait and listen before we crossed it or made our way along beside it for a time. We never actually walked on even the merest pathway in case some forester or a straggler from one of the ranging armies should spy us. Several times we came to one of those low timber huts in which foresters stored their gear while felling or planting in the summer. Except for one of them, they were locked by heavy padlocks but one was unlocked and we took the risk of sleeping there for a whole night out of the weather. There was something pathetic and comic about those locks. Of course I know that foresters' huts always are padlocked, but to have worried in the last year about preventing the theft of a little oil stove, a few candles, a bundle of staves or an ax seemed infinitely sad and childish when the entire human race was robbing and murdering itself. But then, I know that perfectly sensible people carefully shuttered and locked their houses when they left on their long journeys from which they knew, in spite of everything they said or that was said to them, there would be no return. It was just habit. The habit of order.

A doctor told me, some years after this journey, in the Allied hospital where I was working, that there are two kinds of human society, those founded on the idea of order and those on the idea of freedom. He was clever and that was a striking thing to say, but it is not true. There are societies which have neither order nor freedom. However, the society I belonged to before that journey and which formed my habits was one of those founded on order, although the order was torn apart long before the whole structure collapsed under the hammer blows of war and chaos. Unlike that doctor I am not clever and I still do not understand how there can be any freedom without order; nothing in my experience has shown me any such possibility. And at that moment the habit of orderliness provided us with a great gift. Whoever last used that hut, he left three tins of meat on a shelf there and four candles.

We debated long as to whether we should eat all the meat, staying there until it was gone, or save some at the risk of having it stolen. In the end frugality won, we ate one tinful and packed the other two, one at the bottom of Ronni's rucksack and one deep down in mine. We decided that it was not theft to take food stores when we were starving.

It may have been two days later that we came to a lake, deeply sunk below steep banks, enclosed by massive trees, the dark waters rippling from underground springs. It was really hauntingly lovely and so we should both have thought it in more ordinary times. We waited for hours before venturing toward the bank, for we could see in the distance several small summer houses with rickety, half-sinking little jetties, scattered along the far side. As we emerged from the sheltering trees we saw too that at one extreme stood a real house, timber like the summer lodges, but stoutly built to withstand the winter and with an upstairs window. Its jetty, too, was stout and large enough for several boats, which, we guessed, were stored in the lean-to beside the house. There was even a glint of light from the upstairs window, giving the place life and therefore danger. Then we saw that the glimmer was from outside, a reflection off the leaden flickering waters in a crooked pane of glass. Still we were cautious, retreating into the woods again and making a detour to survey it from the land side. We came upon a scraggy chicken picking in the carpet of sodden leaves. Then a paling fence, the rustic gate hanging open on its hinges. Inside the enclosure were fruit trees and a garden that had been tilled up to the last few months, for where the remaining snow was patchily melted, raised rows and a crossed pathway could be made out. On this side a sloping gable jutted making a porch big enough to be called a verandah, with a crudely carved rail and steps. All was absolutely still, but intact. It was the first time for months that we had seen glass in windows, or even the frames still in place. Only the house door was ajar. The sturdy stone chimney block was smokeless. Slowly, we stalked the house, watching and listening. And at last, creeping step by step from bush to bush through the fruit patch, came up to the wooden balcony at the back of which the window was shuttered. A skittering and chattering paralyzed us both with terror and we clutched each other and the trunk of a plum tree behind which we were sheltering. Then Ronni nudged me and jerked her chin and I saw more chickens under the raised platform of the porch. They went about their business with perfect unconcern. Nothing else moved. The fisherman and his family must have fled. There was no sign of any menace that could have made them do so. Some fearful news had reached them here. At last I put a foot on the lowest step, resting one hand on the rail. It creaked loudly and we fled to crouch under the boarding with the chickens, who raised their senseless fuss at the disturbance. If there were anyone at all nearby they must have heard us in that stillness. But nothing stirred, no step,

179

no rattle, no slipping sound of something creeping along the wall. We went back at last, and got ourselves up the steps to lean close against the wall by the door to hear again the deep hush. Yet there was something there, we both knew that; the silence itself was evidence, it was thick with meaning and there was a strange, sickening smell. From there the door was clearly visible; I decided that, left on a faulty latch, wind and snow had pushed it slightly open. Very slowly, crouched over and venturing one step at a time, listening in between steps, we entered the house. The entrance went back to a stair, dark in the background. One door was closed to the left and another straight ahead, beside and below the stairway. Ronni pushed the door to the left and disclosed the tidy, clean parlor hardly visible in splinters of light from the closed shutters. A corner bench with cushions, a table covered by a cloth woven in traditional pattern, a glass-fronted cupboard with dim glasses and platters, the glimmer of glazed family photographs against the pinewood walls. On the floor handworked rag rugs. The dark gleam of an old-fashioned tiled woodstove. Nobody there. Ronni closed the door which whined on its hinges so that if anyone were alive in the back or above—we were sure now there was no one although the feeling of the house was intact— they would hear and if anyone opened it we should hear. The other door went, of course, into the kitchen. Here the people of the house could be felt, here they had lived their lives with sturdy much-used pots and pans, the cooking stove with uncleared ashes, plates stacked in the flat stone sink under the window, three pairs of stout boots by the back door and heavy weather-proof cloaks and coats hanging on hooks above them. Even their hats were there, two men's felts and a woman's. Keeping to the wall I advanced to the stove and laid a hand against its iron side. It was cold with the chill of unuse. But in here was a smell stronger than the general house odor of pine resin and floor wax. Rotten green stuff, sour edibles ghosted. A smell like dustbins, rank but subdued. They left everything and simply went, it seemed. Ronni reached my side and whispered, but the first time I did not take in what she said.

"What?"

"The coats," she murmured. "They can't have gone without their coats."

I looked over at the back door again. The boots too, were there. We stared at each other's eyes, taking in the trapped sensation, and then moved by common consent to the outer door which we could see had its key in the lock. But still no sound, no movement except the cackle of a hen just audible from the other side of the house. We ground the key in its lock and pulled on the stiff door which resisted and then came open with a jerk. Like an answer the front door creaked in the draft. Here on the lake side were crates tidily stacked, an old man's bicycle leaning against them, a pile of something protected from the weather by the remains of a worn-out piece of carpet hung over it. Beyond, on its side, a zinc pail and beyond that a hod for wood, also on its side as if flung away hastily. And past that we took in with slow dread and un-surprise what we made out to be a hand. It was clawed over, the dead fingers dark with old blood, clamped into the hard ground in rigid agony of struggle. From the hand the strained muscle of an arm used, like the hand, to constant work ran into a rolled sleeve. It was once a woman, middle-aged, lying spread-eagled past the corner of the house where she had gone, we could see the scat-tered pieces of wood, to fetch firing. There it was, ranked neatly against the house wall as it would be in a place of this sort, enough for the whole winter and half-used by the time of her death. She had worn the full skirts of the old-fashioned country woman, dark-colored. They were bundled up over her head which we could not see. The lower part of her body looked as if she had been ripped to shreds by wild animals and a few rags of her cloth-ing were scattered about her feet, stout elderly feet in woolen stockings knitted by herself which bunched down toward her an-kles and the heavy clogs she still wore. It was obvious that she had suffocated in the folds of her own skirts on which—we knew, we knew—one of the men would have sat to hold her down, pressing her wild howls and strainings into the ground. The other arm was broken before death. There must have been a whole gang of them, there was nothing left recognizable between the waistband of her skirts and the stockings. Just a mess of mud, blood and her own ordure. One or two dried leaves had drifted over the sodden cloth of her skirts where they were wrapped around the identifying head.

How long before our arrival? It was impossible to guess, but from the coagulated odor of the kitchen it might have been a week or so.

We cringed there by the wood stack for a long time. We were trying to work it out. Had the two men whose coats hung inside fled headlong? Or were they, or the attackers, somewhere nearby? We were oppressed by the uncanny absence of signs of the attackers. Except for the pail and hod and a dozen flung wood blocks there was no sign of disorder, and none either of arrival or departure.

"Rats?" whispered Ronni, jerking her chin again at the corpse. "Or foxes?"

"Do foxes eat carrion?"

"I don't know. We can't bury her. It."

I turned my head to stare at this, but she was quite serious. I knew what she meant but the idea was madness.

"We might be able to drag it to the water," I suggested reluctantly.

"It's only a little way and the ground slopes."

"It would be more decent than leaving it like this, to be pecked away by the chickens. Or whatever has been eating it."

We came slowly out from the shelter of the house and approached the body. Neither of us was able to touch it directly, let alone drag it ignominiously along the ground as it was, horribly naked and destroyed.

"The coats," I turned and went back into the kitchen, where I found as well as the two heavy cloth coats—the frieze cloak was a woman's, I saw—a rolled length of string in a drawer. We wrapped the coats about the body as well as we could and tied them fast with the string. Then we could tug it by the feet without that last indignity being visible. Slowly we dragged it toward the water, which was fortunately quite deep just here.

"Won't it float?" Ronni gasped hoarsely with the effort, as we paused to rest. We found some stones and pushed them into the pockets of the shrouding coats.

"It's the best we can do."

"Be careful on the slope here. Don't slide with it or we'll end in the lake ourselves."

Groaning and gasping for breath we got the thing to the edge of the grassy bank. It was incredibly unwieldy and heavy. Then we moved to the land side of it and pushed, but it would not move under our weak shoving. We needed a lever. In the end we used our own feet. At last, it seemed a long time, our combined weight shifted it over the slight barrier of the bank edge, but the upward thrust of our two right feet lifted it so that it turned over and described a complete turn in falling. The arms flung themselves out, the broken arm at a right angle, almost as if the thing tried to save itself. The skirts rolled off the head. Witchlocks of gray hair flew. For an instant I saw clearly the fearful face, jaws wide open, the tongue black and swollen protruding, the eyes glaring red. It was the Medusa itself and I fell forward, transfixed by that look, and hid my face in the sodden chill grass. With no splash but a deep gurgle the corpse instantly sank, still turning. I saw a wash slap over the bank and subside, the deep ripple running in a half circle far out in the lake. When I lifted my head again the following rings of water could still be seen, slipping mysteriously into each other and disappearing in the dark waters. Ronni was kneeling beside me, and the deep retching of my empty stomach clutched right down into my guts. There was a ring of black around her head for a moment, and then the nausea sank and I could see her properly again, as I blinked the tears of sickness away. When I closed my eyes and tried to relax, to still the thick banging of my heart, I could see those blood-filled eyes.

"Let's get away from here," I groaned when I could speak.

"You have to rest for a bit," she answered. She had a hand pressed against my belly, feeling for a contraction of the muscles. She caught my hand as I made a gesture of rejection, and I was too far gone to argue. Supported by Ronni's arms, I got into the house. She forced me through into the parlor, where the wood floor must be warmer than the bricks of the kitchen. She pushed one of the seat cushions from the table corner under my head. We lay quite still for some time, I don't know how long, I was only half-conscious. But I could feel her arms round my body and her head against the soft flank of my stomach, waiting fearfully for any reaction. It did not come. Presently I could raise my head without the retching starting again. She gave me water and when I held it down successfully, she left me for a little while.

In the cellar she found potatoes, already shooting, but that did not matter, and cooked a pot full. In the kitchen food cupboard with its airholes through the outer wall, there was even the remains of pork fat in the usual crock. It was somewhat rancid but by the time I could stand up she had a princely meal ready. It was the first fat we had eaten for many weeks, either of us. We both held our breath in fear I should vomit, but the shock was past; it was going to be all right.

"We are going to stay here tonight," said Ronni with sufficient determination to prevent any protest from me. "We can sleep in a real bed. Think of that."

I did not know until afterward what she had done besides cooking while I was resting. There was a box bed as usual in such houses, in a corner of the kitchen. But upstairs was a proper bedroom with double beds and real bedding, as clean as they could have been in the former world. There was also the remains of an elderly man whose head was shattered by gunshot. Ronni dragged the dead man by means of the bedside rag mat on which he lay through into the tiny boxlike attic room next door. There the rest of this family tragedy was clear. There was another man, this one young enough to be called a boy, still leaning forward propped by the bedhead and the barrel of the shotgun, the mouth of which he had put into his own mouth and pulled the trigger with his big toe. Evidently, after the attack on the woman the father and son had agreed on this act, and the son had shot his father before killing himself. Such things were not unusual. Ronni then locked that door and pushed its key back under the gap into the little room so that I could not open it by chance.

This she told me the next day. By then it was getting dark. We closed the kitchen shutters and locked both house doors, putting metal pots near them so that an intruder would be heard at once. Then we retired upstairs, just as we would in the real world, and went to bed in the unbelievable luxury of a mattress with a sheet over it and a great puffy, down quilt to cover us; there were even pillows for our heads, goose-down pillows into which we sank like princesses. The bliss of that night's sleep remained with us for a long time. In the dawn Ronni searched for and found three chickens' eggs in the shelter under the porch and we ate them before we left.

In a few minutes' walking we discovered the foolhardy risk of our wonderful night. Only a few steps from the garden fence on its far side ran a road, trailing the other bank of the lake where the summer cabins stood. It was as silent and deserted as the whole district now; but clearly to be seen were the tracks of tanks or armored cars, the grinding scars in the surface and here and there broken patches where their weight had sunk through the covering. The mud trails, twigs and scattered grasses showed where the vehicles debouched into the road and we could see through the trees that there was a large clearing to the left where they had obviously camped. The scars were old now, as old as the corpses, and we could reconstruct with fair certainty what had happened. A group of the soldiers must have gone exploring, seen the house, savaged the woman and then been recalled before they could plunder or burn the place. They had then rejoined their comrades and continued their progress in the same direction as our own, as every journeyer of that time. Somewhere in the stretch before us, they still pushed on perhaps.

With renewed caution we followed their passage, keeping well away from the road itself on the lake side, for the whole length of the water. On that side there was plenty of underbrush and bushes where we could hide if we heard them. But we heard nothing. That day it began to rain with stolid monotony.

CHAPTER 14

In spite of the woman's cloak appropriated for me, and in spite of Ronni's sheepskin coat, we gradually became soaked through and remained wet for days on end. Even "days on end" is far too precise; I do not know how long the rain lasted. Ronni was better shod now; the woman's sturdy footwear was only so much too big for her that an extra pair of heavy wool stockings there for the taking in a drawer were needed to make them wearable. My own strong winter boots were still in good order, but the rain, of course, penetrated them and everything else.

In the rainy murk of the dripping forest, in the enclosed rustling and pattering of unending water falling, we could neither see nor hear well. But then, neither could anyone else, so we were no worse off as far as safety went. We squelched and slipped in slippery mud and dead leaves, shaking the streams off our faces now and then, stumbling along with blind obstinacy. With no change of light in the rustling and pattering of unending water falling, we could not know if and in what direction we changed our course.

That country continues flat for a hundred miles or so with no hillock or moorland above five hundred meters. Such rises appeared massively steep to us, needless to say, but we could manage them. It is one of the many circumstances unknown to strangers to that great plain, which is never taken into account in the his-

tory of Germany and Poland. There is nowhere there, from the
Elbe in the south to well into Russia, as our trek proved, that can
form a barrier to the weakest foot traveler; nowhere to draw a
boundary for even the widest river, the Vistula, is passable by
primitive means. I doubt if we could have crossed the Vistula
alone, but we believed it to lie well to our right or west. But we
did ford many small streams and twice with our lives in our hands
we crept over bridges spanning fairish rivers, tributaries of the
larger one. We should have to cross the Vistula somewhere, but if
our luck held, not before it was quite narrow. So we thought, but
our geography was faulty. The Vistula was still before us in its
east-west track before it turns to the south. Had we really been
where we reckoned we were, we should have been on the border
of Russia proper or even over it. Mercifully we were ignorant for a
while longer.

With infinite slowness we emerged from the forests; they gave
way in patches and tongues and then altogether. And not only because of that did we now see people and vehicles with increasing
frequency. Several times we heard artillery, several times we saw in
the distance the lurid flickering glow of burning villages or perhaps they were country houses or storage barns. Several times we
crouched under brambles or in ditches while parties of stragglers
and dazed scarecrows like ourselves crossed our path. At last it
penetrated our dim exhaustion that we must be nearing the outer
orbit of some sizable town. We were, in fact, within forty miles
more or less of Warsaw itself. That is marshy ground and in late
winter, as it was then, it is a slough where the greasy and water-
logged expanses of heavy mud are crossed by roads raised above
their level. Not roads like those we left behind us in Prussia, but
with broken causeways and great frost holes, badly built in the first
place and never repaired except in the last five years where the
Wehrmacht had needed them. The sides of such roads were
crumbled away and undermined by water. When we reached one
of them we must crawl up to it out of the full ditch on our hands

and knees for if we stood erect we were outlined against the endless skyline.

Our progress was now even slower than our trembling exhaustion forced it to be, for more and more we had to wait behind or
under some exiguous cover for our way to be clear of others. This
made us colder than when we moved at a regular pace. To be
soaked to the skin, from our heads to the soles of our worn feet,
was now the condition of being; there was no longer any such
state as dryness and still less warmth. We were also uncertain in
our movements and our sight began to play tricks, objects looming up and then slipping away. Once I turned myself painfully to say something, in the hoarse croak that was all our throats
would produce, to Ronni beside me, and her figure swelled and
swayed like one seen in those distorting mirrors at fairs, and I almost fell down with vertigo. When Ronni clutched at me we
both sank together, face to face, and knelt there, part of the endless stinking clay, clinging to each other and unable to rise.

Ronni was struggling with the bag that held our food, and was
obliged to push her hand right down to its farthest corner before
she could collect about as much of the blackened, stinking mash
as would have filled a serving spoon. As she pushed a little of it
into my mouth before taking any herself, I could feel, emanating
from her as well as myself, a lassitude of resignation, the inky
depths of despair. After a while, when we breathed more steadily,
she spoke.

"We shall have to ask for help. Find somebody."

I shook my head slowly, I could feel the swimming sensation as
if outside me that the movement caused, but I could not speak for
I had to hold the food down against nausea with the last effort
my body would make.

We were in a small thicket of low bushes just then. They had
thin straight red stems, a marsh growth. I have seen them used to
bind thatching in Silesia where straw-roofed houses are sometimes
seen. Such details remain in memory sharply after all these years

when long stretches of country were blank even at the time. Most of the incidents of our journey need to be brought back with a conscious effort, but here and there quite pointless oddments have stuck in a fold of the mind and come back at a great distance but distinct, both waking and in dreams. That cluster of thin, supple red stalks is like the road on which Ronni found me, there forever with the drops of moisture running down them. I connect them with the longed-for and dreaded threat of approach to other people and to this day when I must face strangers in some difficult situation, I feel their clean whippy lines and the red stripes of color with an odor like poplars into which penetrates an acrid and coaly smell carried in the stirring damp.

"There's a railway near here."

"So that's the smell! I couldn't place it."

"That means an embankment."

A little after that we could hear the rattling and rumbling of a train, trundling slowly and unevenly so that the muffled clanking of its bumpers reached us above the languid chuffing of the engine.

"If we could only get onto a train."

That was a dream thought from another world, not a suggestion. What mattered was the embankment that would need to be climbed. And when the long habit of moving dragged us out of our thicket, we could see it, a ridge as high as a mountain a long way off across the fields. Long before we reached it we knew we could not cross that barrier by ourselves. It was too steep and too bare. To our left stood a high block and presently we recognized that. It was one of those dwelling houses built in the last century all over Europe during the railway age, four stories of smoky blackish brick containing perhaps a dozen small proletarian homes of railway employees. It seemed to be undamaged and we could see too the square patch of divided gardens that were always part of the perquisites of railwaymen and their families.

"Working people," said Ronni. "If they are still there we might get help from them."

"Not if they know I am German."

"They need not know. I will talk. You are too exhausted to talk. You just remain silent. You know a few words, enough to pass muster."

I should do as Ronni said. Already an absolute trust combined with the unthinking bleak obstinacy of our condition. She would do what she could. I knew that.

A greeting, the words for please and thank you, those I could manage, for the cleaning and stretcher-bearing staff of the hospital at Insterburg were always partly Polish and though as theater sister I did not deal with them much, I could understand simple directions and some of their daily speech. But for a while I slumped there in silence, struggling with an oppression deeper even than fear and weakness, that overcame me for a moment. Even as rage against the rearing obstacle of the railway embankment filled my throat with sour resistance I was obscurely cringing toward that obvious reason rather than away from it; I welcomed a cause for fear to replace its deeper cause.

We were still silently debating the first initiative of our journey that would involve others, the risking of our escape among human beings who were, our every instinctive move had proved it, felt to be our greatest enemies.

"You can manage a word or two of Polish? Anna, are you all right? I shall say you are from Ruthenia. That will explain mistakes or accent."

Her anxious questions were reassuring, for somewhere in another place and time, far away, it was not the Polish language I feared to hear spoken, to be obliged to speak. We approached very slowly, trying from habit to hide ourselves. We were at the back of the house and we circled it at the distance of its aged and broken wooden fence where the pocked and sodden growth of chrysanthemum plants still leaned from the previous autumn.

They grew at the edge of every garden of that kind, all over the center of Europe; the scrap of sour earth was just the same for them no matter what its nationality. Here and there dotted in the allotments were tiny sheds made of boards, flattened tins and the like and we moved up behind one of these to watch again. It was not at that moment raining. It must have been the middle of the afternoon for there were no children or men about. Neither wars, revolutions nor invasions make much difference to railwaymen. They are always necessary and keep always to their shift times.

As we watched, a woman emerged from a cellar door sunk through a sloping entry on this back side of the block. She glanced about her in the lightless afternoon and the wind lifted her grayish apron. She smoothed it back, a gesture as automatic as her look around the enclosure, and then raised the same hand, the back of her wrist, to stroke away the hair whipped across her face by the dank air. She stretched her shoulders wearily and dragged on a sack of some kind, its mouth in her other hand, the bulk of it on the brick pathway. Then, without having seen us crouching behind the little lean-to, she plodded off around the house. We followed, stopping at the corners, until we saw the entrance in the middle of the front, facing diagonally to the railway embankment about forty meters away. Between the path on this side and the sudden rise was nothing but a tangle of dead couch grass and swampy plants. If they had been Germans the patch would have been drained and cultivated. It was by such differences that we long since knew we were in a Polish district.

That does not mean any criticism; I have grown used to pre-empting accusations of German arrogance or nationalism. But there, where borders have been arbitrary since there were any frontiers between the tribes, only such signs could indicate boundaries at that time when any and every formal line was invalid.

We slipped around the corner and edged along the front wall toward the door that stood open. There were bound to be patrols or even stationary guards up on the line and they would be Russians. We went into a grimy, narrow entry. On one side hung the board with official notices and the list of tenants. These were still those of the German occupation administration although the district was evacuated months before. There were some new notices caught by the same pins as the old ones, on scraps of torn paper and handwritten. To the left was nailed on the frame a proclamation in smudged heavy type with many emphases, in Cyrillic, with the unfamiliar seal of the new occupiers. The boards of the floor and a wide space of the walls were splashed and daubed thick with wet mud and so were the narrow stairs ahead. On the house door the lock was broken off and one hinge was loose. The passage went back from door and stairs into an obscure corner but there were no rooms down here for like most such houses the dwellings began a little way above ground level, up the first flight of stairs.

We moved quietly back into the murky corner, to think over what we were doing. The woman had gone up the stairs and we could hear her moving about somewhere not far above. Ronni held my wrist and nodded upward and I agreed.

Once we went up the stairs we were trapped. But the railway trapped us too. There was, either way, no help for it now. From outside came the murmur of wind and from a long way off a clinking as if there were a forge or workshop downwind. No voices, no steps on the brick path. We bundled ourselves up the first steps as well as we could, hanging onto the rickety handrail to help ourselves. Even ten steps made us breathless as if we had run a mile. The tiny window was unbroken but its single glass had not been washed since the house was built and in the gloom we saw only that there were two doors on this side of the landing, one closed tightly, the other slightly ajar. In there was the woman.

She may have heard our harsh breathing; it was loud enough, no doubt. Or we may have thumped on the hollow stair. I leaned forward over the well trying to make sure no one had followed us and when I turned myself clumsily around, there she was, staring at us with her mouth slightly open.

Half-dead creatures like us were not rare at that time, far from it. If we had not both been almost done for we would have noticed her amazement. We ought to have known, too, from the wholeness of the building. I think now, from this distance, that the effort of approaching any human being was so great that it blunted our growing faculty of awareness; that is, we assumed that our unease was simply the fear of humans. It is difficult to express this in a way that can be understood by those who have not experienced such extremity. But it is truly the case that together with the weakening and becoming clumsy of the five senses under such immense physical efforts in a cruel climate and without shelter, some other faculty comes alive which I have tried to express as the inanimate world acquiring its own being. Or human beings becoming capable of sensing the realness of the natural world. But there, at that moment, our increasingly acute antennae failed us, or our exhaustion was such that the hazard of any human contact at all overtaxed our warning systems. For the house was full of Russians. The woman then facing us and her husband were the only Poles left there.

We were right when we assumed that the railwaymen's tenement would be occupied by rail workers; but they were occupation troops who were operating the vital line.

"You are Polish, aren't you?" asked Ronni, to make sure that she was not German; for to ask help of another outlaw would have been worse than useless.

"Of course. But are you looking for somebody? Because they've all been cleared out. Gone to the town, I think."

"You are the only ones here?" This was good news.

"My man is the only one that understands the signals up the line. We had to stay."

"We have to cross the line."

"They won't allow that. Nobody can."

"Isn't there a bridge over?"

"They're all smashed. Like the signals. This is the only signal left between here and Warsaw, they say."

"Then the river . . . ?"

"Over there." The woman described an arc with her arm, vaguely indicating some unknown area past the rail line.

"We have to get south, to Krakov. My son is there. And, you see . . ." Ronni indicated me and I needed no further explanation.

"You can't." She shook her head, wondering perhaps at our ignorance. "They don't let anybody over. Why, even the man, he can't cross to the other side of the line."

From a distance, from the direction of the clinking noise, now came a cracked hooting sound, it broke off and began again. Damaged like everything else.

"Shift time," said the woman. She looked in at her own door as if to check something and then, with an arrested movement of the head, toward the door down the stairs. "You'd better come in here."

She pushed the door half shut after us and we stood in the bare little room helplessly.

"We're filthy," protested Ronni, faintly apologizing. The woman gave a slow forward shrug, jerking her chin out resignedly. It said clearer than words how little a few more clods of mud could affect matters. And the floor in there, though much less plastered than the entry, was indeed too dirty for our state to make much difference.

This room faced away from the line, but we heard the sounds of several people approaching and I turned toward the door, shrinking my body into a protective curve as pregnant women do.

"They don't come in here," the woman assured me. "Because of the man, you see, the signals, they don't touch me."

Then we knew, even before we heard the voices.

195

The woman closed the door of the room, gently and slowly so that her movement would not be noticed from outside.

"They always sleep when they come off work," she said in a hushed undertone. "But don't speak loudly. Here, you'd better sit down." She took my hand and pulled me to the only chair in the room, standing by the rough table in the middle. "When is it?"

"About two months," Ronni answered for me. "Breathe deeply," she said to me. I did as I was told, bending my head down until the forehead was resting on the edge of the wood. The woman pushed sticks into the grate of the cooking stove and I heard through the roaring in my ears the metal scrape of the water jug against a pot rim.

"We get rations," she said to Ronni in that cautious mutter, "so I've got tea. There's a bit of kasha too, but she'd better not eat anything yet."

The sticks began to sputter and then to crackle. Presently I could smell water boiling in an open pan and there was the slight hiss of the tea leaves being thrown in and the sound of the saucepan dragged off the fire. But even the scent of tea could not make me lift my head; I was slain by the quiet blow of fate. It was inevitable, it was bound to be so, all our efforts were only the struggling of dumb creatures already in a trap up to now invisible until the barrier of the railway showed its limit.

"Come, Anna, drink the tea." Ronni lifted my head and pushed me back against the chair, holding my shoulder to keep me there. I knew quite well what she said and the woman, too. Even where the words in the other language were new to me I understood them, or the sense of them. Accustomed as I was by now to doing what Ronni told me to do, I sipped at the tea, first from a tin spoon and then from the mug. The woman drank from a handleless cup, shaded upward from white at the base to deep pink at the rim and on one side was a picture of a rose half washed off with long use. The mug we drank from was a tin one, such as workmen take with them with their bread and dripping when they go off in the dark of the morning. As my head cleared and my sight too I could see that the rain fell again, clouding the curtainless window on its outside panes. In the comparative warmth our soaked clothing was beginning to steam and smell; the warmth came in from our outer covers while next to our skins the damp stayed cold. Our own stink we did not notice, of course, but the woman was almost as unwashed as ourselves. The wet clothing added to the sourish odor of a small single room in which people ate and slept and which was not aired during the winter.

They were talking quietly together. The man would be back in about two hours and then we must be gone. Without saying a word directly about it the woman made it clear by her own acceptance of the fact that her husband would at once tell the occupiers if he found us here. The cellar from which we had first seen her emerge was no use as a shelter, for the fuel was kept down there and the men went to fetch it for their fires. There was an attic, yes, but to reach it we must not only make our way up the public stairs but after that mount a ladder and then keep perfectly quiet. None of the one-room dwellings in the house was safe, although one or two of them were not in use. People came and went, as we ourselves proved, and the number of Russians belonging to the rail company varied. Whatever their system of army administration might be, it was incomprehensible to any non-Russian and appeared to the Polish woman to be non-existent. But as she said, after five years of "German orderliness" she would have found even a return to Polish methods slack. She spoke of the former occupiers in a tone I recognized. A curious mixture of grudging respect for their efficiency and a kind of contempt which I have noticed at other times among people whose social forms do not seem to need the regulated structure required by the Germans for their comfort.

With an abject dull patience I waited for their talk to lead them to the thought of the little huts among the allotments. It was as if I knew I did not need to suggest it myself; they would hit upon the idea themselves. I knew too, that we would hide in one of those huts—not the one belonging to the woman's husband —and that we would be discovered there. In some as yet unknown dimension of time that had already happened.

"There's the gardening sheds," said the woman at last and a smile for the first time moved under the stolid patience of her features. The two exchanged looks and it was settled. She went down to the front door and after a while signaled to us to come down. The dangerous moment was when we left the shelter of the house wall at the back and crossed the uncleared vegetable beds still tangled with the rubbish of last year's cabbages. Then we could be seen from the windows if anyone were watching. There were no locks on the shed doors, for the first law of Russian occupation was in force. It was forbidden on pain of instant shooting to lock anything against the invaders.

After the warmth of the inner room it was bitter cold in the hut, but it was more or less weather-proof and there was space for us to squat on the hardened mud floor. It was lightless, too, and drafty, but we hardly noticed the wind, deeply grateful as we were to be sheltered and to keep still.

When it was quite dark the woman brought us cold kasha and a bottle of tea; a feast.

"On their radio, they say, the order of the day is that Danzig and Stettin are surrounded. And in the south they're on the Oder, I think that's near Berlin. The war will soon be over. I'll come out in the morning when it's safe."

The murmur in the blackness ceased and we felt rather than saw the board door open and close as she went.

CHAPTER 15

The first news and the first shelter for many days and nights. Very slowly, torturing us with rheumatic pains, our clothing dried out on us. Three days and nights we crouched in our narrow housing. Our protectress brought us food and news. More precious than war news, she found a reason for going to the neighbors to ask what means there were of crossing the railway. Nothing under civilized rule works so quickly as the underground that forms against total control; the harsher the discipline, the more comprehensive the network of evasion. A matted undergrowth of disobedience and secret understanding of which I had been aware for five years was now turned against the Russians. But for the time it was largely ineffective; not because the Russians were less corruptible or the population less sullenly determined, but because the entire surrounding situation was in a condition of indeterminate confusion. The structure of living, from sewage and food distribution to laws and police, was in dissolution and nobody knew from one hour to the next what even the next village was doing or was like. It was impossible to say that a certain span of road or rail was passable even if it was known to have been so an hour before. Troops moved continuously and even such service units as communications and transport were transferred farther along a series of moving fronts—fronts unknown to any but the staffs concerned and often not to them—at frequent but irregular intervals. One man or even a party would cross a major road safely while the guards were drunk or asleep; the next attempt ended in a burst of machine-pistol fire, screams and the reeling forms of the dying, the shouts of angry commands.

So the only answer our friend could bring back from her foray was that there was no way of knowing. Chance was the only law.

"The only thing is," she added, "you're worse off here than almost anywhere along this stretch of line. There's the signals box just round the curve from us where you can't see it from here. And being the only one still working, they guard it with special care. It's the only switching gear for the south-north traffic until they get some repairs done."

"We'd better move south then, as soon as the rain lets up?"

"Well, away from Warsaw," she agreed, moving her hand to indicate in which direction the city lay. North and south were simply railway terms to her and produced no directional pattern; they were attributes of the line beside which she had spent her life.

"They say the line is being ripped up, one line, the up-line."

"But you said they were going to make repairs!"

"So the man said. Just the same, the line's being taken up, that I've seen myself, German prisoners working on it. He says it's being sent to Moscow as reparations." "He" of course was her husband whom we never saw.

"But this is Poland?"

She shrugged, her forward jerk of shoulders. "Who knows?" she said helplessly. "I must go back."

It was only a little while after that conversation that we heard shouts and laughter. We clutched each other and stopped our discussion of the news, such as it was, keeping quite still. They were on this side of the house. There were more shouts, a breaking sound of wood and a burst of raucous laughter. Cries of encouragement and another crash, then a confused discussion of which we could make out nothing. Now the voices seemed farther away, but then there was a stumbling rush of heavy boots grinding and slithering on the stony, muddy path and the thump of a massive body falling quite near by. This caused a roar of enjoyment. An instant later something was flung at the boards of our shelter, shaking it crazily. Then the boots pounded away and the cries and laughter receded.

"They've gone."

"Hush."

Whoever had fallen on the pathway now groaned loudly, theatrically, and we could hear his boots scraping as he scrambled slowly and uncertainly to his feet. The planks creaked as he leaned against the hut. He snorted and muttered discontentedly. Never in a life not lacking in fear have I felt such a suffocating physical dread, sheer paralyzed bodily terror, worse than air raids by far. As he stumbled against the loose door my heart jolted with a frantic leap as if it would jump out of its rib cage, and then seemed to stop. The terrible oppression of asphyxiation squeezed my inner organs into an agonizing clutch, pain spread a shroud from inward out. Immediately, from an eternity of plunging threat all was uproar, flailing limbs, a startled shout, the crash of the large bulk as he fell into the shed, yells from the others as they rushed up to pull him out or to enjoy his discomfiture once more.

Not human and certainly not animal, for no animal could ever be so mad with lust and malice, they dragged us out with whoops and howls of drunken frenzy into the weeping day. A swinging foot tripped me and I fell full length with a shriek heard as if from far off that tore through me like a knife. A great weight flung itself over me and rolled off again and then a boot caught my shoulder with terrific force. They were as blind and helpless with vodka as we with weakness and fought in a tumble of legs and arms over their booty, dragging us to and fro in the mud and cabbage stalks, one trying to pull us by an arm away from the mob and another hauling on a foot to regain possession. I heard not only their shouts and howls but screams that must have split heaven if heaven existed in that wild horror, and the cracking of sinews, the straining and thumping and devilish wailing, the unknown curses which yet could be nothing else. I was rolled over and my face went into the mud so that I was blinded but at that moment the ground gave way and I slid down, coming to rest on one side in a—I discovered afterward—a little trench where a former railwayman once grew leeks. This was a miracle and undoubtedly saved the child's life and probably mine. Not only was I suddenly removed from the grasp of the man who had succeeded in hauling me away from the others far enough to have leisure to get a grip on my clothes, but I was lying on my side and could breathe. My conqueror had lost his hold on me and in his stupefied state must have crawled out of the shallow ditch and sought his mysteriously disappeared spoils on the path.

Just on the end of this path straggled a few of the dead chrysanthemums, and the smashed stalks, strewn by the struggle, fell over the ditch, hiding me. I was half unconscious from the kick in my shoulder and from the slamming of my head to and fro on the small stones of the pathway as the men fought over me. The noise receded and I floated away to lie, as it seemed, behind the timber house by the lake in the forest. Only it was not that house but another one, smaller, darker, warmer, and we were inside the house and arms held me in a warm bed and a voice murmured endearments in French so that I swam away into a dream of bliss where in the half dark, brilliant black eyes sparkled near mine and skillful hands gave me remembered pleasure that was at once ravishingly intense but had at the same time the quality of perfect calm.

Somewhere distant from this dream I heard two shots, and shouts of an entirely different quality from the hellish uproar of the drunken gang. A word like one I knew in Polish echoed, and drained off into the voice of a nurse I worked with for several years saying it was time to go on duty, but she said it in Polish or something like it. This translated itself again into a man's voice shouting unmistakably military orders although I was stupidly unable to understand them. The problem of why I did not understand dimly worried me; he might be giving *me* orders; perhaps there was another air raid but I heard no whistle and crash of bombs, no slamming of anti-aircraft guns. The noise had quite faded now and after a while the doctor's voice told me I was pregnant and then said that he would give me a leave-certificate and I could feel him and see him staring hard at me, frowning, to tell me something he was not going to say in words. He spoke German. Him I could understand, and was filled with the happy conviction that I was to be allowed to go away to the little house in the woods with Jean-Martin. And even as I heard the doctor's impersonal voice I was aware that this was not quite a dream but a memory, and an appalling wave of misery rose up in blackness and overcame me. From that memory and that anguish I sank with the vagrant sensation that I did it on purpose, into unconsciousness.

It was miserably uncomfortable, the crisscross of the wire mattress cut into my back.

Somewhere in the warm and dry darkness there was a moaning sound. It was not myself. My left shoulder was a mass of swollen and stiff pain and the same kind of bruising pain was echoing in a number of other muscles. But I was not enough hurt to be moaning aloud. Though my head ached drearily.

There was a rough cloth over me and the same prickling feeling under me, too. I was wrapped in a blanket and lying on a cot mattress. The last thing I remembered was a voice shouting with authority and an extraordinary smell mingled of chrysanthemums and rotting onions, no, leeks.

I moved an arm, it hurt and the unmistakable creak of an iron spring accompanied the hurt.

"Anna," whispered a wavering, thin sound. "Anna. Are you there?"

I came awake.

"I'm here. Ronni, where are you? Ronni!"

"Here," the faint voice was hardly hers but enough like it to convince me and fill me with dread. I rolled, felt about me, sat up with a gasp of pain from the wrenched shoulder, sought with an agonizingly stiff foot for the floor and got onto my feet. The rough covering slipped and I caught it with my good hand. Underneath it I was undressed. Every bone in my body ached. My stomach was a burden that weighed me forward. There was another voice that groaned, muttering a phrase I was awake enough now to know was Polish, over and over again. It must be a prayer.

Without having to recall or to think, I knew what must have happened. The Polish woman and Ronni had been savaged by the mob. I had been spared. Tears of guilt and pain squeezed from my closed eyes. My searching hands found the edge of another bed frame. I reached over and touched another blanket but the shape inside it which cried out at my touch was not Ronni. I could see somewhat now in the dark. I felt my way past the bed nearest to me and over to another that filled up the wall space. There was hardly room to move between them. I could spare no time for anyone else, I must find Ronni, make sure she was alive, touch her, comfort her. She was huddled on the third cot, wrapped in a blanket like mine. I sank down beside the cold metal and put out my hands, not feeling the bruising any longer, and touched her poor head. She moaned aloud and moved her head so that her lips came against my hand. I clutched my harsh woolen cover about me and slid onto the bed so that I could gather her to me and hold her in my arms. That was better, that was much better. I could weep now, with her, and beg her to forgive me for not having been raped, implore her to tell me she was all right. We slept then, I knowing that a black injustice had seen to it that I could not repay my debt to her. She saved my life on the road and fed and succored me and the unborn child in the peasant's ruined hut and journeyed with me day after bitter day, never faltering. But when I could have helped her, I lay in a ditch, unconscious.

Irrational, the thoughts of such moments. It would not have helped Veronika or the Polish woman who had been so good to us for me to share their horrible fate. But I felt then and still feel now that I escaped at their expense. Naturally I have known for many years now that neither of us would have survived if it were not for the presence of the child and the instinct to protect it and bring it to birth. But that has nothing to do with what I felt then.

It was the inclusion of the wife of an essential worker in the weekend sport of soldiers who somewhere had found vodka which angered the new authorities. The men, we heard later, were ferociously disciplined once they slept off the aftereffects of what I suspect was wood alcohol, or at the best the raw product of a potato mash fermented by themselves. Some said they were sent to a labor battalion from their privileged technical company; others were sure they had all been shot. But that may have been one of the many rumors of the time; it was always said after anything went wrong that the culprits were shot out of hand by their officers. And it is the case, as on that day, that it was sometimes the only method of controlling the men for the officers to threaten them with their service revolvers and even to fire shots over their heads. No doubt such disciplinary means were the source of the execution rumors. At any rate on the next day the whole rail company was moved out of their quarters and others came to take their places, this time accompanied by a special "polit-commissar" or military official of the political police. A doctor came to examine the injuries of the victims and was followed on the next day by a woman in Russian uniform. The first to come may well have been a doctor. His subordinate certainly was not.

She came slouching in with a cigarette hanging out of one corner of her mouth, hands in jacket pockets and her uniform cap pushed back on a head of unruly black hair. I was the first object

of her attentions and she leaned over me and belched the powerful breath of cabbage into my face. With her left hand she pulled
off my covering and as she drew her right out of her pocket I saw
not only the state of her hands but the hypodermic as well.

"I am all right," I stammered. "The others need your help
more." This was carefully rehearsed and I said it slowly. I need
not have worried for she clearly spoke less Polish than I did. She
turned her tousled head toward the door, where a tidily dressed
officer watched her, frowning and earnest. What she said I do not
know, but it may have been some coarse joke about my condition
for the officer answered her with growling disapproval and she
stood upright again with a shrug of bravado, pulled the blanket
back over my nakedness with a scornful twitch and turned to her
next patient. Iva, for that was the name of the railwayman's wife,
tried to shrink away but she was too helpless to defend herself.
The amazon heaved the inert body over with one powerful shove
and drove the needle of the big syringe into the scratched and
bruised buttock. About half the dose of whatever was in the hypodermic was saved for the other patient, with whom the procedure
was then repeated.

The watching officer showed no sign of any prurient interest in
this scene, so I said in my stammering Polish that if I could have
some hot water and rags I would wash the two battered bodies.
He frowned at this and shook his head, but he looked both
puzzled and embarrassed and did not ask the "doctor" for enlightenment.

He muttered something in his own language, and then could be
seen to think of a way out.

"Do you by any chance speak German?" he asked me in my
own language.

The question frightened me and I stared at him in silence.

"I mean—you might have been conscripted to work for them,"
he explained, but the trap in this suggestion was hardly likely to
encourage me.

"I don't speak any Polish, you see," he continued. "I was trained for German re-education."

I shook my head cautiously, but I knew from his voice that he was an educated man and could certainly tell from my expression that I understood him. It took me a little while to think over the new situation. The gap between the concept of taking care of the helpless and that of restraining them is, for Russians, very narrow. Twenty years of Stalin had in the main cured them of humaneness out of dread of making mistakes for which they could expect no mercy and I was already aware that whether we were considered patients or prisoners was in effect a difference of words only. This man was obviously responsible for us to his superiors and we were therefore in his hands. His whole training must dispose him to consider us as enemies of the state simply from the fact of our being in his charge, quite apart from our foreignness. And he may well have orders to make sure that we could not spread abroad the story of what the soldiers had done to us. On the other hand it was well known that for short periods the troops were allowed to run amok as a reward for their valor and I did not know at that point that the men who attacked us were to be punished. In any case, consideration for a signalman, even one who knew the only signals between there and Warsaw, would not reach to any great concessions. They could always compel him to do his work.

A weary sigh from Ronni penetrated my slow brain, and stimulated my conscience.

My wretched physical condition made my voice slow enough to convey uncertainty, but I thought fast enough to leave out the connecting words which show proficiency of language.

"Hot water," I stammered, gesturing to the women. "I could clean them."

His face cleared at this and he spoke at once to the "doctor," who answered in a sarcastic tone, but he insisted evidently, for she now went away with a bad grace and I could hear her yelling at someone. Her orders echoed and I was confirmed in my guess that we were on one of the upper floors of the railway tenement. After a long wait two Polish women appeared, carrying between them an old enamel bath such as is used for bathing babies. It steamed invitingly. The odor of hot water was almost unbearably sweet, and when one of the women came back after a few minutes with a handful of cleanish rags and, incredibly, a small piece of coarse washing soap, my joy knew no bounds.

At first I thought the officer intended to stay and watch the cleaning-up process, but when he had satisfied himself that I really meant to bathe his charges and not to commit some strange necromancy with the bathful of water, he went away. What he might have suspected me of I could not even guess, but in spite of my relief at something I could do for my friends I still puzzled over this for in this strange world every nuance of understanding might spell the difference between good and evil.

It would be unpardonable here to go into much detail; except for medical purposes any description could only arouse either disgust and shame or a lewd interest masquerading under some more permissible emotion. I shall go only so far as to say that my poor Ronni was more badly injured than Iva, who was knocked unconscious at her first appearance in the garden when she ran out to discover what the noise was about and was instantly seized upon by the attackers. Veronika remained conscious the entire time and therefore struggled. So apart from multiple lacerations and contusions, they had almost dislocated her left hip and the major muscles of thigh, pelvis and abdomen were seriously wrenched and torn. Fortunately the real doctor who first arrived wrenched the dislocation back into place with agonizing but merciful brutality before it could stiffen into a crippling injury, but naturally Ronni was lamed as well as horribly and indescribably ripped about. Other constant dangers of such attacks, septicemia and venereal disease, were, we thought at the time, disposed of with the injections given by the woman who reappeared on the following days to continue the treatment. It was only later that we knew the worst. Whatever had been ordered for the patients, it was almost certainly water in the hypodermic syringe and the drugs went, as was frequently the case, to others who were prepared to bribe her for them. But this I discovered only months later when the unmistakable signs of syphilis were well advanced and could no longer be hidden from me by Ronni's old-fashioned shame.

On the second day after our visit from the police officer Ronni could speak coherently to me. Her first questions were for the welfare of the child, whispered not only from weakness but so that Iva should not recognize the language. Satisfied at last that I was not lying in my assurances of having escaped, Ronni then called feebly across to Iva, who lay on her back, staring at the dirty ceiling. There was no reply. I edged between the beds and leaned over her.

She lay quite still, and gave no sign of hearing or seeing us. With her work-worn hands slackly at her sides, she stared up at nothing. She might have been lying in her coffin. I leaned farther over so that my face was directly in line with her eyes, but her eyelids did not flutter, she did not blink nor did the still gaze of her colorless irises change. I felt for the hand nearest me and held it, pressing it and shaking the wrist a little. As it was released the hand fell back to the blanket lifelessly. Yet the pulse, though slow, was thinly beating in her arm. I put out my own hand and stroked the dry, brittle hair back from her forehead, feeling the furrows in the brow, which was slightly damp. Then I slid my arm under the nape of her neck and lifted her a little. Her head lay heavily, inertly, and with dreadful calm the eyes now stared at the wall instead of the ceiling.

I tried to recall when she stopped moaning her repeated prayer, but could not fix the moment of her silence.

"Ronni, talk to her," I demanded, forgetting to be cautious about the language. "There's something wrong. We must try to rouse her."

She was not, by the standards of the time, badly hurt. On the first part of my long walk I had seen women much more damaged in the villages beside the road. There were some terrible sights, more frightening even than the dead woman by the lake, for the victims were still alive and suffering. But until the forester's old wife who died of suffocation the only death from rape I had seen was that of a young girl hardly in her teens who was literally torn to pieces, but even she went on screaming although her jaw was broken and one eye lay out on her cheek. She screamed until she died. And later, when they were all gone and the fires were burnt out and I crept out of hiding, the last to venture out, what was left of her lay there, and the snow drifted over her. The pool of her blood was frozen, it did not stain the falling snow.

It was after that day that I began to avoid houses and stuck to the edge of the main road. Being raised above the fields I could see and hear from there.

And I thought, as I bent over to hold up Iva's slack neck that it was after that day that I withdrew some part of my mind from the disintegration of the world about me, from the iron cold and the hunger, the human wolves who disgraced the name of men as of wolves, the wreckage of cities, machines, people. Understandable that Iva retreated from such a world; only one quite lacking in knowledge would call her alienation madness. On the contrary it was the last sign of sanity to reject the hell we struggled in.

There was somebody coming up the stairs, so I laid Iva down and retreated behind the door until I could see who it was. A stranger shoved open the door which was not closed and without a word threw in a bundle of clothing, left the door as it was and slouched off again down the stairs. It was the return of our "clothes" from the steam disinfection. Most of our stuff was there, stiffened and shrunken, but there. Everything was now of a uniform darkish gray color as if the mud now impregnated the fibers of the various cloths and garments instead of only clinging to their surfaces. The armful gave off a reek of some harsh disinfectant almost as foul as the former filth, but we could consider ourselves highly fortunate to get back more or less what had been sent, and to be rid of lice for the moment.

Except for the visits of the pseudo-doctor, who may once have been a ward servant in a hospital, and the twice daily arrival of a pail of soup for the three of us, we were left in peace for days. The soup was princely; cabbage and potatoes with kasha and even some pieces of meat. But I could not induce Iva to eat. It was necessary to feed her; she would swallow when the big spoon was pushed into her mouth and that was all. The delicious odor of the food had no effect on her at all; my mouth watered as soon as I heard the clang of the pail's handle but she lay supine with her eyes wide open, her breath not even moving the blanket it was so shallow. During the second night I think it may have been, I thought I heard some movement and got up to lean over her. She was staring still. Not really staring; simply her eyes were open blankly toward the ceiling. I knew then that she would die and tried to pray, but no words came, not even "Our Father." I had seen soldiers lie and gaze blankly like that when they were apparently recovering from their wounds and they invariably died. It is not the injuries; they die as Iva was going to, from broken hearts.

One thing I did not understand was that Iva's husband never once came to visit her, and if I had dared I should have asked the policeman about that when he reappeared.

That was three days later. He came just after the rations arrived and asked civilly if we were getting enough to eat.

"Was her hand injured?" he asked, for I was feeding Iva.

"No." I did not look at him.

"Then what's the matter with her?"

He came right into the room and inspected Iva's face. His eyes showed the same puzzled, anxious, almost embarrassed expression of the first time I saw him, when I suggested washing the patients.

"She's given up," I used an idiom and Ronni gave a murmur of warning. But he took no notice of that phrase, so commonplace that no foreigner could use it unless he had lived for years among German-speakers. He glanced sideways at Veronika, making comparisons, for she clearly was not giving up.

"Probably the shock," I suggested. "She thought she was safe."

"Maybe."

"Can you get the doctor for her? The man who first came?"

"He's gone," he said absently. Then he looked at me, saw what I meant and nodded. "Yes, *she's* not much use," he added almost humorously.

He turned away and then looked frowning back at me.

"She'll pull through in a few days."

"I don't think so."

"What d'you mean? How would you know?"

"I've seen this before. She'll die."

"But that's ridiculous!"

He muttered something under his breath.

"You got your clothes back, I see," he said aloud.

"Yes, and clean. Thank you very much indeed."

He came and leaned over Iva on the other side of the iron cot. "Stinks," he said. "I thought you cleaned them."

"She is incontinent. I tell you, she's given up."

"But we've done everything we could!"

"Yes. But you can't make it unhappen."

"I didn't make the world! Why should *she* . . . !"

"Who knows? You can never tell, with people. She might have given up anyway."

"You can never tell with people," he repeated. "You can't indeed. You Poles. I always heard you were cantankerous!"

The temptation to comment on this view of rape was almost too much for me. But of course I said nothing. At least he took me for a Pole and that was a great deal. I did not know then that military newspapers and broadcasts were officially encouraging the savage mishandling of the civil populations as the Russian armies moved forward, so I did not know either that a tug of war must be going on in the mind of every cultured Russian between the doctrine fed to him by authority and his private conscience. Either for that personal reason or because it was daily more obvious what effect such behavior was having on the people the Red Army was supposed to be liberating. Years later I actually heard a lecture by a famous Russian writer who wrote among many other things a book describing the end of Stalin's influence which gave this phenomenon its international name. At the time I am now writing of, that writer was broadcasting every day, inciting the troops in the name of liberty and the brotherhood of man with all the eloquence of his great talent, to torture and murder every German woman they got their hands on. Since the words for foreigner and for German are almost interchangeable in the Russian language, and in any case the ordinary soldiers could not distinguish between Poles and Germans or any other people, the effects of this deliberate policy were as long-lasting as they were terrible. Very well. I know that you for whom I write do not and can not believe me. But I tell you what is true and what you can prove for yourself by reading the texts of those official broadcasts and army newspapers. And before the reply of German atrocities is cited in mitigation of these crimes I will add that no German, criminal or innocent, was likely to be cured of his wrongdoing by such methods. Nor were millions of the victims Germans. This was recognized quite quickly and efforts were made to prevent the spread of barbarism, but it was much too late to do more than deny officially what millions knew, thus adding cynical unbelief to the fear and horror felt universally everywhere the Russians went. Such things change the consciousness of whole peoples and are not forgotten for generations.

Something of this went incoherently through my mind, overlaid by my fear of the man, who might at any moment decide on a simple way of resolving the problem of three unwanted pieces of rubbish left over from the wreckage. He could shoot us out of hand or he could get rid of us just as effectively and more tidily by declaring us arrested and dispatching us to the nearest collection point for undesirables of the bourgeois world.

He did not, however, do either of these things although his uniform with its blue insignia made some such solution more than likely. Instead, he simply went away. And I continued to feed Iva, holding one of the washing rags under her chin to collect her dribbling. After a few spoonfuls of soup she stopped swallowing and would take no more. I talked to her, trying to entice her as one does a difficult child, although I was well aware that endearments in my language were not likely to reassure her.

Suddenly something about this business of language struck me painfully with its insoluble stupidity and I sat down on the side of her cot, the spoon still in my hand, and sank my head in unspeakable weariness, closing my eyes. After some while I brushed away the tears and blew my nose on the scrap of rag. Ronni was sleeping the uneasy sleep of pain. I would not wake her to tend her injuries. Let her sleep.

Wincing from bruises and stiffness, I maneuvered my unwieldy shape to the window past Iva's bed. It was raining again, it would never stop. Yet the silvery, rain-swathed fields, horizonless with mist, made our shelter more desirable. All was perhaps not yet lost.

A solitary figure walked one of the allotment paths, hands clasped behind its back, head bent forward and but for the peaked cap unprotected from the rain. Unreasonably, I felt sorry for him too. It is one of the many things women are never able to explain to men; the sad accepting sympathy that lives underneath frustration and resentment, even in happier circumstances than those.

Less than a year before that day I was a girl still, skilled in my own work, experienced in human nature as any nurse is and by no means inexperienced in more personal ways than the relation of nurse to patients. Life with my father by itself would have provided an education. Looking drearily out of that dirty window I measured without examining it the eons of brutal apprenticeship I had been subjected to in a few months which turned me, still in my twenties, into a middle-aged woman. All the drive and passion of life was behind me; I could look back on myself and out on to others like a fifty-year-old. I recall the feeling of oldness as I stood there in the tenement room, dreaming as I would have said, out of the window. And I recall, too, swimming up out of that sensation of all being past for me, the sharp, agonizing warning to myself not to examine the pastness of the past.

Yes, I can relive that; unlike poor Iva I was not going to give up and die of my broken heart. But somewhere in my soul—what word is one then to use?—I was at that moment aware that there was something I must not recall about my education in living if I was to go on breathing. Who knows what long suffering had worn down Iva's spirit? The very knowledge in me that she could not so suddenly have resigned herself to death, no matter how shocking the fresh blow, unless some other grief already weighed on her, was a sign that I was unknowingly but deliberately shutting out my own recognition. The difference was that Iva had no child to care for. I was forced to live; she was not.

I was aware of something about Iva that I could not have known if that time I refused to remember had never been. But all I allowed into my mind was the sad peace that came from the accepted, irrecoverable ending of passion. Neither love nor hatred was ever going to be real for me again.

CHAPTER 16

In my reverie I still gazed out of the window, forgetting the man below, until he lifted his head and stood still, facing the house and looking upward. I moved to one side so that he should not notice me and continued to watch him. He watched the window, and I watched him. At last something attracted his attention and he lowered his head and hunched his shoulders as he walked back toward the house. Behind me, Ronni awoke and stirred, and I went to do my nurse's duty.

She never wept or complained. She bit her lip until it bled rather than upset me by crying out when I dressed her lacerations; that is, I washed them and laid more or less clean rags over them. Now that I could get about and had my clothes back I could go out to the common water tap on the landing to fetch clean water in a bucket which I heated over the fire in the little cooking stove. Once a day a soldier brought up wood for the fire.

"It's as good as a hotel," I said to Ronni.

"Better. No bill."

I forced a laugh at the little joke.

"Listen, love, if you hold me up I can sit on the edge of the bed."

"Not yet. Another day or so."

"But I must move or I shall seize up altogether."

"Another day or so, I said. This is where you do what I say. This is my job, remember."

I was afraid of the moment when she would try to walk. It was by no means certain that she would be able to. I could not tell how badly the sinews and nerves were torn. I wished then that I had specialized in rehabilitation therapies and massage instead of becoming a surgical nurse. Still, I found I remembered a good deal of the midwifery course that belonged to my training years and that helped. It was part of the insanity of the time that I, within two months of giving birth, should be using half-forgotten skills of obstetrics to patch up the abused body of a woman past childbearing. That outrage was one thing we did not need to worry about. Fortunately, for it was then a capital offense to frustrate the final humiliation of rape.

"How long do you think we can stay here?"

"He hasn't said anything, the officer, I mean."

"Do you . . ."

"What? Say it."

"D'you think he'll let us go?"

"Perhaps. We're not locked in so we aren't prisoners."

"Dare we ask him?"

"Better not. We don't know what his orders are."

"He isn't hostile, not *himself*, wouldn't you say?"

"No. *He* isn't hostile. And so far he believes we're Polish."

I put a hand on her shoulder to warn her, thinking I heard steps outside. It was one of the new company coming off duty. We were not afraid of the new arrivals, knowing that they would have heard about the punishment of their predecessors. Only if another changeover was made should we need to be wary again. Indeed for the moment we were safer than anyone else in the district. But it was of the utmost importance that nobody should overhear us talking in our own language together. All Germans without exception were outlaws, fair game for anything. That fact was one of the very few to be absolutely counted upon at that time. I continued in silence to rub Ronni's legs and back and to move her joints as gently and rhythmically as I could. Weeks before she did it for me and now I did it for her. The rags used as bandages which were in the water pail on the fire began to boil and I moved the pail aside a little. They gave off a sour reek but would presently be sterilized.

Veronika was already mending. Iva's condition remained the same. But evidently a report had been made somewhere for ten days later two men in uniform appeared and inspected her as she lay there. They were not doctors, for they attempted no examination. They just came in, without knocking as usual, and stood looking down at the still and silent shape on the iron cot. Then, without looking directly at either of us, one of the men spoke.

"She's been like this for two weeks, is that right?"

Ronni answered in Polish.

"Don't you speak German? I thought you did."

"Yes, but I'd rather not."

"Just the same. Is it two weeks?"

"Almost."

"But you two are all right? Recovering from the accident?"

"Yes. We are almost well." This was an exaggeration, but Veronika was much better.

"I see you limp badly."

"I have limped for years," she lied.

They seemed mildly pleased at that.

They talked in undertones to each other for a few minutes and then left again, leaving the door open. It was several hours later that two men with a stretcher clumped up the echoing stairs and without a word lifted Iva's body onto it and carried her away. They did not reply to our questions, probably because they did not know the answers.

In silence we looked at each other as their hesitant tread receded. We would be next; perhaps our fate was already decided. We had agreed in our whispered discussions that flight was now impossible. Ronni could not walk without pain and only very slowly. Moreover we were now known and almost certainly registered in some official fashion. If we drew attention to ourselves our nationality must at once come out, for among Poles I could not hope to pass for a Polish woman. We sat side by side on Iva's bedstead which reached almost to the little rusty kitchen range that was both cooking and heating in each of the one-room dwellings in the house, and stared at the small fire. It was an invaluable privilege, that fire, and we were well aware of it. If our real identities were to be established by some continuation of the process of tidying up the "accident" in which the three of us had become involved, it might well be the last fire either of us ever saw. On the other hand, for all we knew, no further action was to be taken about us; we might be considered able to fend for ourselves. Simply to stay on seemed foolhardy but we dared not ask what was to become of us for fear of putting ideas into anyone's head. Nor dare we ask to be sent to some town farther south on the pretext Ronni had used once already, that we were going to her family. Incredible though it may seem, I did not then or ever ask Ronni if her son really lived in Krakov. Mention of her children or husband, as of the father of my child, was tacitly but absolutely banned.

Presently we heard several people come into the quiet house and braced ourselves to face them. But no one came near us; it was a shift change evidently. There was not much regularity in the railway shifts, no rhythm of work could be established. There was the clatter of a pail or metal pan and the sound of running water. A man's voice said something impatiently; by now, Ronni and even I did recognize one or two words that were often repeated and were roughly similar to Polish words. Another of the strange voices answered and the first man then said in effect that it was too bloody far to walk.

"He must mean the canteen," whispered Ronni.

This gave me an idea. The men seemed often to get their own

food and cursed about it. I said nothing but thought over this idea, trying it out before I shared it with Ronni. The day was drawing in, it must be about five in the evening. No doubt they could get hold of more than their eternal mush of kasha if there were someone to cook it for them.

It may have been an hour after that when the political officer climbed the stairs with the news that we were now considered cured and our hospital rations of the excellent soup would cease on the following day.

"Must we leave here, then?" Ronni asked.

"I have no orders about that," he said uneasily and looked at me with a considering frown. "But this is a railway-company billet, you know."

"If you can get rations issued, we could cook for you," I said without quite knowing I was going to say it.

Having blurted out my idea, it sounded in my own ears as if I wanted simply to ensure our being fed with the men, which of course was the case. But such subtleties were out of place both for us in our situation, and for his accustomed views.

"Why not?" he said after a pause for consideration. His look was a little puzzled, and Ronni said quickly that we would be glad to return his kindness to us by looking after him and the men in his command.

"Why did you say that!" I protested when he disappeared down the stairs. "He must have thought you were being sarcastic."

"I don't think so, my love. You'll see, he took me at my word. I think they believe the stuff they are told. That we're being liberated. Especially if he thinks we are Poles."

"I expect," I said, searching for the obscure thought, "it's like that always with official information. People sort of agree to believe it. It was the same with us, after all. I never heard anybody actually say 'I don't believe that' about the army reports on the radio. Did you? But in the wards, soldiers and even officers made jokes all the time about the news. They took it in and winked at it, as it were, all the time."

"Even more so for them than for us, I think."

"Have you ever been there?"

"No. But I've known people who had. And in Vilna before we left we could hear their broadcasts. I got quite used to hearing hymns of praise for the great Leader and Father of his people when every day in the Polish papers were columns and columns of reports about the hundreds and thousands of Ukrainians being deported. That was a couple of years before the war started, but I don't suppose things have changed much, unless they've got worse."

"You don't think people are still being transported?"

"Sure. Why not? Half Vilna was, for instance, after they occupied the district."

"That was 1939, then? And then you got away to Insterburg?"

"I was allowed into Prussia, you see. And after I was there, we managed."

Such oblique hints were the nearest we came to mention of our families. But I did not need to be told, for I knew perfectly well how valued workers could "fiddle" all kinds of illicit privileges, just as the Polish signalman was privileged by the Russians now, because they needed him. In the hospital, we employed a half-Polish dispenser whose whole family lived with him and the entire medical and surgical staff pretended not to know it. The rows we went through when inspections took place! But we always got away with it because he was such a good chemist. The arguments were about him, of course, the inspectors never knew about his family. *They* went to see friends for a day or so, and came back when the coast was clear. So I knew more or less how Ronni had "managed." Which does not make the necessity to "manage" any less shameful to a civilized people. Men like our dispenser made us think, whether we wanted to or not and like other people we mostly did not want to; and that is so although he was in fact a rather unpleasant little man, I never liked him.

So we became housekeepers for the Russian railway company. The men avoided looking at us, never came nearer to us even than they were obliged to. They referred to us between themselves as the polit-captain's women and it was clear that they all supposed he reserved our more intimate services for himself. In fact, he never touched either of us, which may well have been because we did not attract him, the one of us old and the other about to give birth. Not to mention our tattered and unkempt appearance although that did not put off the soldiers as a rule; every weekend there were incidents among the women in the villages near to us. It was by now taken for granted. We had all gone back to the Dark Ages.

But he did talk to us, quite often. After a few days I realized that he was lonely. He began to sit with us in the room taken over for a kitchen where we spent most of our days. At first he talked only at dinner time, but one day he sat on after eating and smoked, drinking a glass of tea. The next day he brought an oil lamp with fuel for it. The glass chimney was cracked and the top chipped but the lamp itself, an old-fashioned and ornate bulbous affair, was intact.

"I bought it in the market in Warsaw this morning," he said. We did not believe he actually paid for it, but said nothing of that, thanking him with real gratitude.

"If you'd thought to buy some needles and thread we could mend your clothes," suggested Ronni. "Your things are in an awful state. No officer should go about like that."

I was horrified by her frankness, not for the first time. But he seemed to take it as kindness, as indeed it was meant.

"Would you?" he said with that shy and puzzled look. "Would you really? I was going into the city again tomorrow . . ."

"Of course," said Ronni, almost laughing at him. "We'd like

something to occupy our time in the evening, now that we have a beautiful lamp to give us light."

"Soon the electricity will be working again," he said with the formality his voice would take on when he made an official statement. This was one of the things he was required to believe, but neither he nor we did so.

"Certainly," we agreed, no doubt with the same prim tone of voice.

The next day he was away all day and came back with two needles, a spool of dark thread and a thin skein of darning wool. These were riches indeed, even more astonishing than the piece of meat that he laid on the table with great pride.

"Not on the table!" reproved Ronni. "We have a plate for it here."

"You'll be making quite a domestic character of me," he said as I put his glass of tea before him. "I've never had any home life since I was a boy, you know. I've been in the Army since I was fifteen."

"I haven't seen anything like that for the last year or so." Ronni stood admiring the meat, now on an enamel plate. It was half a leg of pork, about two kilos of good meat. I could not help wondering where such large and well-grown pigs were still to be found in this war-devastated countryside. Ronni put the plate with the meat on it out between the two windows to keep cold, the usual larder of poor people.

"Did you have some leave?" I asked our benefactor. "That is two days running that you've gone into the town."

"Yes, I took some time off. An old friend of mine was in Warsaw."

"What luck."

"It's always nice to see old friends," said Ronni, and she pulled a bundle of his underclothing toward her on the table to inspect it for mending. He did not possess much and what there was was of poor quality and worn almost through. Only one garment was of any value, a pullover of high-grade wool in a color later familiar as khaki.

"Lease-lend," he said smiling. I smiled back, but without knowing at what, for this was an expression that my school English did not reach to.

"You speak English, then?" asked Ronni.

"Only a little."

He was then silent for a long time, watching our hands as we worked. The lamp threw its typical circle of yellow light which wavered very slightly. It was warm in the kitchen and the light was kind. On the body of the lamp was an elaborate design of flowers in bright colors picked out with shiny gold; people used to give such lamps as presents to stand on the table in the parlor. I could imagine that one just like it stood once on the dresser of the front room in that little house in the forest where we had thrown the dead woman into the lake. I could just see it there, moved onto the table when guests came to drink coffee and eat home-made cake of a Sunday. Perhaps there actually was such a lamp in that room when we saw it; at the time I was not in much of a state to notice details. Or perhaps it was just the kind of ornamental light one thought of as being in such rooms. With its bulb-shaped vessel for fuel repeating the lower part of the chimney in shape, and its naïve glass pattern it gave off a small innocent homeliness belonging to a world now gone where good deeds and sins, pleasures and sorrows were on a human scale; where cosmic evils were as yet unknown. I doubt if that lamp was much different from an oil lamp from a village in the Dordogne, or one from an isolated crofter's hut in the Outer Isles, or even from a "dirt farmer's" wooden house in Oregon, before the war. And I doubt too whether the talk around that lamp was much different in those places, any more than the people were, who in every country took their modest pride in such respectable little machine-decorated possessions. Only the languages make them seem different. I suppose country people in all those foreign places have electric light, today, but I doubt if the new population has in the district that particular lamp came from. On its base the maker's name could still be fragmentarily seen. *J. Herricht, Wehlau*. That is the name of a smallish provincial town between Königsberg and Insterburg; the place-names like the people who lived there are more dead than Carthage; if towns now exist where those names once had meaning they are quite new places, frontier posts on the new borders of the Russian Empire.

I was startled when the officer got to his feet with a sudden movement. It was easy to frighten me then and I was constantly afraid of this man in spite of his kindness to us; whenever he moved near me or spoke loudly as he did to the soldiers, I flinched. I did so now and Ronni turned her quiet eyes toward me for a second, frowning very slightly and reprovingly. She had far more reason to fear than I but she was not afraid of this man; it seemed almost as if they knew each other. As if she might say of him, "Oh, he's all right, I've known him for ages." Now he followed her glance and watched me for a moment before his eyes went back to Ronni with a question.

"It's the baby," she said calmly, although he had not spoken. He pressed his lips together at the tactful lie and moved the three steps to the dark, uncurtained window evidently needing space and movement. I did not look round but I knew because I should have heard him turn that he was not looking at us; he must be staring out at the night. Ronni turned the greatcoat she was patching, one of the side pockets was torn, and the heavy stuff made a scraping sound on the table with a faint click of a metal button. I could feel her waiting. She knew something was coming, and it was her expectation that told me news was in the air.

His boots crunched as he turned and Ronni turned sideways toward him.

"This place is small. You need the open air, I expect, Captain. You're not used to this office work in confined rooms."

"It's not too bad. Not so bad as . . ."

Her busy hands were still and she seemed to hold her breath.

"Yes, one has been in worse places," she said at last. "After prison, this is a dear little room, like home."

"You have been in prison?"

"Only for eight months, three years ago. But enough to be content now."

"They let you go, then?"

"Yes. They let me go. I even got my job back."

"They needed you, I suppose?" He said this in a tone of inexpressible bitterness.

"Languages, you know. They are always useful."

"You were an interpreter, then?"

"Clerk-interpreter in the local administration. Registration office."

"And why did you land in jail? Or should I not ask?"

"I was suspected of falsifying some registrations."

"And did you?"

"Oh yes. Certainly. Sometimes one did things for friends."

"And they let you go?"

"They couldn't quite prove it."

"Ha!" A sharp sound of scorn or disbelief. "With us you'd have got ten years, at least!"

"With them, there had to be a trial. It's different, I expect."

"And they decided not to try you?"

"That's it. Of course, things might have gone otherwise if my employers had not kept on asking for me back."

"They did? They dared to do that? When you were accused of treason?"

"Well, not treason. I would have had to be a German citizen for that."

He frowned at this, considering it in some puzzlement.

"Did you really keep up the bourgeois forms, even in the Occupation?"

"That wasn't the Occupation. Insterburg is East Prussia."

"Was," he said. "But you, you were a Pole." He considered again and when he spoke again it was with a noticeable hesitation, a nervous tone of taking a risk which I recognized. "You know, it's all right with me, but I would not admit that to everyone if I were you."

Ronni looked up from her needle and smiled at him. "I wouldn't," she reassured him.

The next question was one he felt he could not ask, but Ronni knew what it would have been. One occupation by foreign troops is very much like another, after all. The variation is a matter of gradation, not of kind. She had often been asked and would be again, and so would I, in the future.

"I had other people to take care of," she explained. "I was lucky to have the chance."

He nodded. "Yes. I can understand why you worked for them. But I still wouldn't talk about it. Either of you."

This was, it should be understood, an incredible thing for a man in his position to say. If he were overheard by a fellow officer of his own branch he would quite likely get a ten-year sentence for saying it. Not only for warning us, but for what amounted to a criticism of his own service. To another Russian it would have been treason. And few would hesitate to report him for it; a witness who did not do so was guilty of the same crime.

The whole conversation made me acutely uneasy. I would have been afraid of it before, if he had been a German officer of the security police even though in those days—already at a great distance of time and experience—I was a privileged German nursing sister. And for a Russian the trend of what was being said seemed to me within a hair's breadth of being a provocation. I could not understand why Ronni did not suspect that.

"You are right," said Ronni at last. "Thank you." She was now pulling at one dull metal button on his greatcoat after the other, to test them. Several were loose and she set about resewing them firmly on.

He seated himself again in his place at the table and drank from his glass of tea. Now I could look straight at his face and I saw from his anxious frown that there was more to come. But I dropped my eyes again at once and went on with my darning.

There was a long silence, broken only by an occasional sound from some other room and a murmur of voices upstairs.

Presently he got up, pulled at his heavy leather belt, which was always weighted to the left by the big holster, and went to the door. We could hear him mount the stairs, walk along the narrow landing and return. He pushed the door almost shut but left a narrow gap so that anything moving outside could instantly be heard within. And when he spoke again it was in an undertone.

"I shall be leaving here in two days' time. I got my orders today."

This was news of such import that we both stopped sewing and stared at him.

"Then we must leave too," said Ronni at last.

"For the south?"

"For Krakov," said Ronni firmly. "We have friends there."

He nodded slowly. I could see that he knew perfectly well that if we could we meant to go much farther south than Krakov. It would be a miracle if we got over the railway, let alone over the Vistula. As for Krakov, Ronni might as well have said New York and made a job of it, for all the chance we had.

He was lighting one of his tubed cigarettes and while he was engaged in pressing the little mouthpiece into its proper shape, Ronni gave me another of her looks, a quick little frown with an accompanying head jerk and the encouragement of a smile. Just like a mother with a shy daughter, she was telling me to join in the conversation, to show myself amenable. Not that I was normally shy; I was always a talkative, sociable girl, but the half-comradely, half-flirtatious tone which formerly made me popular seemed to be gone with everything else from the past. I had lost the trick of it. Now that it was impossible to recover that tone I could assess it as if it were the attribute of someone else, aware of its usefulness and its partly assumed quality of a manner put on both to please others and to disguise my inner self from them. All young women do it, of course, especially attractive girls; there is nothing shameful about it but once abandoned, the trick appeared ridiculous and false. I could not be naturally pleasant to this man, neither could I act pleasantness with any ease. I had to think of something to say. No doubt my extreme consciousness was caused even more than fear by the need to speak my own language as if it were foreign to me.

"How is your friend?" I asked him. "Did you see him today again?"

I was looking down at my work but I could feel his movement and that he arrested it, and I could feel him staring at me with the almost paranoic suspicion that is second nature to Russians, a matter of self-preservation. I knew I must look at him with a bland question and I did so. Nothing could have been more milkily placid than my face.

"The friend you spoke of yesterday," I added, thinking he might have forgotten telling us.

"Yes," he said slowly. "I saw him."

I was really now looking at this man for the first time. Obliged by my own question to face him if it were to appear as innocent as it actually was, I took in his features. It was not a very Slav face. Longish and lacking the typical cheekbones, the jaw was narrower than usual and the brow higher and rather bulbous. But the striking features were the eyes. The Russians I had so far seen were all grayish- or brownish-eyed which, with their normal fair hair and comparatively dark or heavy skin color, gave them a somewhat uniform and colorless aspect. This man was slighter of build than any I had yet seen, his bones narrower and his eyes of a dark blue-gray. Depth in the eyes comes from differences in the rays of the iris and his were strongly marked even from the distance of the table's width. They were not those uniformly blue irises which make blue-eyed people sometimes look blank or opaque about the eyes, but deep both in their color and deeply set in markedly hollow pits. Where the expression of eyes comes from is mysterious, at least to me. But his eyes were sad, there was no doubt of that. The questioning, embarrassed frown he often wore must have had something to do with it, but the eyes themselves conveyed a thoughtful, stoical suffering. And although his gaze was fixed on my face he was not looking at me but inward or perhaps back into memory and I felt his whole mind and being concentrated on one single question which tormented him. Why? How? His eyes asked of himself things he could find no answer to. I knew I was not being fanciful.

For a year or so some of the men and women I lived and worked with had been asking themselves and each other those questions of why and how. Why have things come to this pass? How can it have happened? What is really going on? Amid all the noisy, promiscuous intercourse of our leisure and the strict disciplines of work, there was much more real discussion than I ever heard in any other period of my life. We talked incessantly, sometimes in euphemisms or roundabout terms when we were not quite sure of someone present; often with astonishing openness among ourselves. Always with seriousness. It was clear to me then that this stranger, this enemy, this policeman, was hag-ridden by the same questions I had lived with for years in the operating theater of a military hospital which became in the end one question. Why did we all work eighteen hours a day to patch together bone, sinew and nerve in order to send the finished job back to the inferno of pitiless slaughter? For what purpose, to what end did we in the hospital presume to keep the souls in the bodies of men so tortured, so unspeakably weary, so condemned to cruelty and to having cruelty practiced on them, that their humanity was burned down into those questions of how and why until nothing else was left of it? His doubts cannot have been so very different. I had no right to assume that he did not understand at least as well as I did. That he like ourselves was faced by questions, even more serious and poignant ones than of life or death, since death as I well knew was often longed for as a way out of the problems as much as out of the suffering.

What caused the renewal in this man of what must have been old self-interrogation I could not know, but it was clearly something to do with the friend he met unexpectedly in Warsaw. His searching was by no means new for that look in his eyes cannot have appeared suddenly; it could only be the outward expression of years of inward examination. And he, I knew, was much more lonely in his inner discussion than I had been or was. Even by the methods of control practiced on Germans it was not possible to root out the centuries-old confidence of civilized life in ten years. We could and did find friends to talk to now and then, and in the comradeship of a group committed to a common task, such as I was used to, the talk was almost continuous. For him it would be unusual good fortune to know two or three people in the whole of Russia to whom he could speak openly. And they would certainly be physically separated by war. If he possessed somewhere a wife or a friend whom he could trust, it was very sure they were not here in Poland, and unlikely that he had set eyes on them for years. Unless perhaps, in the last two days?

For us there were certainly taboos; in recent months the possibility of Berlin falling was such a taboo and the actual person of the Führer was permanently in that category of forbidden things. But by transferring specific topics into the theoretical, by discussing our contemporary affairs in terms of history, religion, the theater or a book, we talked with freedom while sounding conventional. In the society of Russia where the old, agreed bases of culture had been entirely and deliberately destroyed, this could hardly be possible. Except among the most intimate of friends.

What he had said to Ronni and myself was more daring than anything I have heard then or since from any Russian, especially considering his job. To admit to foreigners that ten-year prison sentences without trial were taken for granted at the mere suspicion of a minor dereliction of duty was unheard of then and now. Up to then it was for me a sign of black barbarism that Ronni could be arrested for a "mistake" in her office records, and I may add that I still do think so. But we live and learn; my notions of barbarism had been radically changed. Ronni spent months in the interrogation cells, but that was nothing to a sentence of ten years' hard labor without trial. By contrast the Gestapo appeared comparatively restricted in its powers; thus do we slide back into the dark ages of the human spirit. I now took things for granted that six months before I could simply not have believed.

Yet this policeman, coming from such a concept of law and incited every day by their official broadcasting—and he and his comrades were all compelled to listen or be classed in the formal records as unreliable—to a view of the populations among which they were now living that would not have been strange to Genghis Khan, this man remained a human being and a civilized man. This is a remarkable fact. So he must have been a remarkable man. I have wondered many times since what became of him.

This glimpse of his reality was all we were destined to know of him. We never even knew his name, but it was probably an assumed one in any case. It was already well known that officers of the N.K.V.D., as it was called at that time, acquired different names on being posted abroad. They were issued together with the new uniforms.

When we saw our friend on the following day, his uniform was new except for his greatcoat which was evidently considered, thanks to Ronni's housewifery, to be in good enough order to do his corps credit. This made us fairly sure that his destination was one of the large German cities which had either already fallen or was about to fall.

Of his own destination he said nothing, naturally. Of ours he spoke.

"There is a truck leaving this afternoon. Not directly to Krakov, unfortunately, but in that direction, to a small town nearby. From there you can get to your friends."

"You mean, we can ride in it?" Unbelieving.

"I've arranged it. One of our drivers has to go there and you can go with him. You will be there tonight some time, because the man and his vehicle must definitely be back with his unit by tomorrow evening."

With this he was telling us that any extended dependence on this transport, or on the driver, was to be neither feared nor hoped for. We knew what that meant. The soldier would expect to be paid off for driving us. But with what? We had nothing.

"I suggest you hide this until you leave the truck."

This was an unlabeled bottle containing a clear white fluid: vodka.

In spite of the tremendous impression made on me by the evening before, I was instantly sure that we were being drawn into a trap. Either we were to be convicted of possessing alcohol and trying to bribe the driver, or he was to be convicted by means of us.

"That would be dangerous," said Ronni, quietly. "Better not."

"You had better take it," he urged. "You must have something."

"We can't hide it. He would take it off us."

"There is always that risk," he admitted and turned his head away. "Just the same, you should take it with you."

"And if we give you away?"

"You won't do that, and it doesn't matter. This man is under observation. He can't do anything to me. That is why I chose him, because there are three trucks going."

"We can never thank you," I stammered, half-convinced and wanting to be convinced. "Are you sure you aren't taking too much of a risk?"

That was tactless of me and I knew it as the words came out, but I was so overcome by this incredible piece of luck that I did not think what I was saying.

"I'm taking no risk at all," he denied it, at once becoming stiff. "Trucks often take people with them."

"We shall pray for you," said Ronni.

"If you want to do anything so pointless, I can't stop you." But he smiled a little at Ronni, the way one smiles at an old friend with whom jokes need no explanations.

"Now," he went on briskly, "the trucks will stop here at the corner where the entry meets the road. I shall be there to give them their passes and lading bills. I will indicate which truck you should climb into. There is a big box to mount by beside the road. Just get up without saying anything to me or anybody else. Take everything for granted. You understand? And don't look at me, don't wave, nothing of that sort."

He was already going out of the kitchen.

"Then we must say goodbye to you now?"

Ronni put out her hand and he took it, shyly. Then he gave me his hand. "Good luck with the baby."

"Good luck to you, too." And at his dismissive shrug, "The war isn't over yet. You may still need luck."

"Superstition," he muttered, shaking his head, and went.

So we made up our bundles once more and pulled on all our outer clothing. Both the sheepskin coat and my cloak were as stiff as boards from the cleaning and the skin coat made cracking sounds as Ronni moved. We stood still at the door of the kitchen, reluctant to leave what was luxury to us.

"We shall remember this room," said Ronni. She crossed herself and bowed her head. Then we went out.

The promised crate was there, by the jagged trunk of a tree smashed by a shell. We huddled by this stump, off the roadway and a couple of meters from the rise of the railway embankment. We waited a long time, several hours. Then, belying our skepticism, three heavy trucks rolled into sight around a bend and drew up where the path to the railway tenement branched off. By a stroke of that good fortune which our protector pretended not to believe in, a long train was rumbling past just then. We waited until the officer got down from the leading lorry, a bundle of papers fluttering in the wind, and came first toward the second truck where he spoke to the driver, who leaned out of his cab to take his documents. They were all three massive American transport trucks, almost new and with wonderful clean olive-green paintwork camouflaged on the upper surfaces and with fat, unused tires and untorn tarpaulins. They were so clean you could see the flecks of mud on them, as neat and polished as ambulances. As our friend left the second truck and came toward us and the third one, he walked along the side of the monster and put out a hand to balance himself on the tussocky edge of the road. He tapped the side and inclined his head in a gesture that would not be noticed by anyone not waiting for it. Then he signaled to the third driver to take the lead, and mounted the runningboard of the cab to speak to him while the man pulled out and moved up past the waiting convoy, taking the officer with him. The train above us was slowing down with a great clatter of chains and bumpers. Ronni pushed over the crate and helped me up onto it. From there I could easily mount under the loosened canopy into the back of our truck. It was piled full of crates with a narrow runway in the center and after helping Ronni up beside me, we both made our way forward into the dark interior. I noticed how much more easily we climbed up now than we had gone up the stairs of the house only a month before. Our strength, or mine at any rate, was restored. And Ronni, although she was in constant pain when moving, was also much recovered.

From outside someone secured the heavy canvas and replaced its seals. With a jerk we started our journey. As soon as we were away Ronni took out the bottle of vodka from under her coat and stuffed it down where we could get at it but where it was not visible. We were now, of course, in the dark. We lowered ourselves on to the floor and crouched there, holding hands.

I think it is about two hundred and fifty kilometers from Warsaw to Krakov, so the distance we were driven was something short of our walk of three or four weeks. The drive took about five hours, and although this is a guess it is probably not far out for one becomes quite accurate at time-measuring when there are no clocks.

CHAPTER 17

The convoy rolled, swayed and jolted over stretches of wrecked road and sped swiftly where the road was unbroken. After a while we fell into that half-slumber we were used to, in which consciousness is never quite lost. Twice we halted for a few minutes while passes were shown to road blocks or inspections, but nobody either got down or climbed up. Whatever the load that was being transported, it was important. There must have been several towns on our way but our route was evidently so planned that we bypassed them, or perhaps the convoy was awaited and the traffic held up where necessary. But at long last our transport began to stop and start and we could hear other traffic. That must have been a considerable town. Once out of it, and the difference was to be felt between driving in streets lined by buildings and the open road, we picked up speed again. Not long after that the hydraulic brakes went on with their hiss and jerk and we slowed down to a stop. The door of the driver's cab slammed twice and at least two men got down and stood talking. Then we heard the boots of one man crunching over a stony path. A moment later there was fumbling with the back cover and a faint lightening of the midnight black told us that wherever we were this was our journey's end.

A voice called to us to hurry up. Ronni went first, with the bottle. She stopped before lowering herself out of the back-board and set down the vodka just inside the truck. The man spoke to her and she answered him. I turned myself and kneeled on the open edge, so that I could slide off as a bather who cannot dive slides into a swimming pool. It was not far. I landed safely and steadied myself. Then the man took hold of me; he could evidently see us a little although we were still not able to see anything in the pitch dark. He said something I did not take in, being too paralyzed by his smell to think, and Ronni answered. I knew she must be telling him that there was a bottle of vodka just inside the truck. He grunted and pushed me roughly and I backed away. He came after me, Ronni pulling at the bulky sleeve of his greatcoat and repeating the same words as before. Now I could feel rather than see that there was a high wall to one side while the other seemed open. From a little way off a man shouted and the man holding my arms shouted back. A reply came and from the tone and a word or two it was clear that our driver was saying he would come in a moment or something to that effect. Though the bulk of the transport was sideways to us I could now see slightly in the faint illumination from the shaded headlights and as his head turned I saw his face set and gloating, and knew instantly that I was not going to get away. Ronni saw him too. I heard a moaning cry from her.

The voice shouted again from a distance and again the man answered, angrily now. But however hurried, he did not mean to be balked. He gave me a strong shove, putting out his foot so that I fell to the ground. I tried to roll over away from him while he grabbed at my clothing and pulled.

"Don't struggle. Let him." Ronni's voice hissed almost unrecognizably into my ear.

He was on me now, panting and muttering to himself as he tore at my rags of underclothes. I knew I must try to relax but every nerve in me resisted and I was rigid with disgust and rejection. My distended belly frustrated his first efforts and he stopped pushing and pulling at me for a moment. Then he hit me on the side of my head with his fist and with a clumsy jerk threw me over on my face. Now he could mount me from behind and grunting with satisfaction he found what he wanted with his hands and entered me, half-kneeling. His excitement was so intense that in a moment, two or three shoves, he relieved himself and lay still. I did not dare move in case he should be stimulated to start again, but before he could do so one of the heavy motors started up over from where the voice had shouted. He raised himself, fumbling at his clothes, and stood up. Instantly I rolled over and over again, pulling up my knees so that I could then rise by pushing up my weight with my hands from the ground. I heard boots running over the gravel and his shout that he was coming. Then Ronni was helping me to my feet and we stumbled away in case they came to find us.

Dimly we could see now. We were on a rough field path. To our right was the high wall. The last of the trucks accelerated its engine to a roar and pulled off around the corner of the wall that towered black against the reflected lightening of the sky which indicated a town. It was very faint since there were hardly any lights, but still visibly there. Wherever we were, and of course we had not the slightest idea, we must go away from the houses.

We moved slowly, holding each other. Veronika wept forlornly as she had not done for her own humiliation. Unlike her, I was not hurt; he had got his "victory" too easily to need to force me. And, most fortunate of all, he was the only one. It was when they fought over the female prey that it got hauled to and fro and the roused rivalry and sadism became savage. I was perfectly clear in my mind the whole time. Usually when some sudden mishap or accident occurs one is so taken by surprise that afterward the details blur in memory, but I had been wide awake to every movement from the act of sliding down from the truck, when the hard edge of the tailgate dragged roughly past my swollen stomach.

And the warning feeling as his bulk approached behind me in the dark before he grabbed me remained sharply menacing.

Afterward, too, is all still clear to this day now that I have allowed the memory to return; this was probably because my health was so much improved by rest and warmth and the good food provided by the Russian "polit-captain." I felt sick, naturally, from the mishandling; I felt quite irrationally dirty too as if I would never be clean again. But what I most felt and what has lasted was anger at my degradation. I can still feel the queasy rage and contempt for creatures that could do such things, could get pleasure or even relief from so meaningless an act. That has left a permanent moral scar of distrust and resentment. Something else I felt then for the first time which returns from time to time, usually without my recognizing its origin; a terror with something of awe in it at my own defenselessness and the vulnerability of women with child, an incredulous recognition that there was nothing and nobody in all that chaos to protect me, and that nothing except civilization in its literal sense can shield the female bearing the future. The awe in that memory comes from the disbelief I felt then. I was confounded by the denial of an absolute claim; no, *the* absolute claim, the foundation of all human communities. The Child is the future, immortality, survival. To protect it, clans and tribes form themselves, loyalties establish themselves, and are worded into concepts. Religions and philosophies build up, peoples become nations and then powers. These superstructures are so vast and their ramifications so almost infinitely varied and complex that the origin of them all gets forgotten by the protectors, whose power came from their ability to defend and who have built that first duty that gave them authority out into monstrous constructions of thought and ambition existing for themselves. Every few hundred years one of these constructions collapses under its own weight and chaos returns for a time; it is only in those historical moments of destruction and disorder that —simply because it has failed in its purpose—the base of the entire structure can be seen anew. That base is the Child who is the future. That most mysterious utterance "in the beginning was the Word" is already an intellectual concept, an Idea, because the real beginning was the Child, who has no known father, whose parentage does not matter, who is ours and not mine or yours or his. The origin of the child is life itself, or God if one can accept the word, and the advent of the unknown baby whose mother is known because the mother must be known but who is a stranger coming from another place and whose father is unknown, is the promise of immortality in the simplest possible form.

The still unborn child protested inside me at the way he was treated but I could not give it any rest; we must get away from that unlucky place. It was Ronni who at last could no longer suppress her panting groans of pain and we were obliged to stop for a moment to look about us. Slowly dawn lightened the clouds like a dirty dishcloth wiped over smeared glass. Our pathway ran over a wide expanse of old plow in which, not far away, we could see the ragged remnants of a haystack. If we could reach it before the day was quite light we could hide there. I dragged Ronni the last few steps. She was bleeding again from a deep gash in her thigh, superficially healed but now opened again by the chafing of harsh cloth. And her hip caused her agony with every crooked step. We got behind the pile of mildewing hay and I managed to pull bundles of the damp, stinking stuff around us both to camouflage us and to keep us warm. She lost consciousness and I huddled beside her. I leaned my head back on the bales of straw and longed for death to release us.

But energy returned after a while. I crept out of the shelter and looked around me. I was hungry but could not eat the bread we had brought with us until Ronni awoke. Some of the piled bales of hay were tumbled and scattered and I cautiously looked around them. Then I saw that the haystack had not been disturbed by weather or a stray shell as I supposed, but by human hands. Someone had pulled part of the hay down to cover a motor vehicle.

Under the shelter, half full of torn hay bales from which ragged straws drifted off in the gusty breeze, stood an army Volkswagen with its plank body and tarpaulin cover. It looked to me to be whole, possibly even in working order. Instantly the idea came into my head. I did not know much about engines and I had no fuel, but if I could get some and the thing would go, I could drive it. Fuel. I might as well have thought of champagne and smoked salmon. But I did think of it. The five-hour truck drive had made me ambitious. And I learned to drive years before, before I went to Insterburg.

Thinking this, I gazed across the fields where a line of cropped willows suggested a stream. When dusk fell, I would go over there and get a precious drink for us. Then it seemed to me, staring half-concentrated on the wild thought of gasoline, that the lumpy profile of some bushes or grasses under the trees was different. Had something moved there? I narrowed my eyes to focus my excellent sight; no, I imagined it. Still, with redoubled caution I pulled in my head and made sure I was not visible. After a long wait I felt sure there was nothing alive over there under the willows. I slipped back, crouched over as far as my misshapen body would let me, to where Ronni lay. Her eyes opened, but without fear for she knew it was me. She smiled her own characteristic smile which crinkled her eyes, full of patient lovingness and the small humor that could so easily have been cynicism but never was. In a rush of love I put my head down against hers and hugged her.

"I've been exploring. There's a car on the other side of the hayrick!"

"And I've been thinking. You must leave me here, Anna. I can get into this town, whatever its name is. I'll find something there, you know that. I can pass as a Pole."

"Don't be absurd. I wouldn't get anywhere without you."

"You won't get anywhere with me. I'm nothing but a burden, now."

"Don't talk like that," I began to cry, seeing that she meant it. "We stay together. Don't talk like that."

"But you see for yourself, I can hardly move! Be reasonable, darling. You saw for yourself last night how it will be. Next time the brute may not be in such a hurry. Then you're in trouble. You have to think of the baby first."

"No! No! Don't! I couldn't live without you! What should I do when it comes? It can't be more than a week or so now."

"If we could only find a shelter!"

"Perhaps we can. There must be an empty shed or even a cottage. When it gets dark I shall go and look beyond those trees."

"Oh God, help me. Help me to convince her."

We were both weeping helplessly and that is why we heard nothing. But I, and I think Ronni too, felt a shift in the bulks of matter about us, a change of density, the addition of a fresh weight. This change penetrated but not at once, and then I looked over my shoulder. Behind us a man was standing, against the light. He stood quite still, watching us.

A jolt of horror stabbed through me that forced a strangled cry out of my throat and I felt the almost-ready child inside me surge as if it struggled. This caused a stabbing pain and I felt a powerful downward and outward pressure so that I clutched at my underbelly and moaned aloud in fear. For a second even the threat of the man retreated in a dark pall and I was conscious only of my own body and that other living creature within it. Then it passed; it was not yet time.

The figure moved and appeared again in front of us. In absolute silence we all three stared at each other, eyes and mouths wide in life-and-death tension. When my sight cleared I could see a small, middle-aged man with several days' beard and a full-grown moustache. There was nothing on his half-bald head, and his hair was graying, straggling. His face was the livid yellow-white of want and about his scrawny neck under the open collar of his tunic was a filthy old bandage.

"What were you doing with my VW?" He whispered in a dry rustle, no doubt the result of a wound of which his bandage was also evidence. We could hear at once that he was a German and from the south. His clothing was the tattered remains of uniform, all badges and other signs having been torn off.

"I only looked at it," I whispered back.

"What are you doing here?"

"You can see for yourself," answered Ronni brutally. She had already seen that he could be bullied. He looked at me and nodded slowly.

"Where are you from?"

"We started from Insterburg," and at his incredulous gape, "oh, weeks ago."

"No you didn't. You came in one of the transports last night."

"Yes, the last stretch. Were you watching?"

"I watch every night," he said cunningly and I saw that he was a little unhinged. "There's a gasoline store in that warehouse where they bring the convoys. If I could only get some I could get away."

"Those big trucks use diesel," I said, "not gasoline."

"I know that! But they have gasoline there too. I've seen the cans when the gates were opened. Piled like this." He raised a shaking hand, dark with dirt, above his head.

"You go up as close as that?"

"They don't look, and their own headlights dazzle them. The local people never go near the place. It's police stores in there."

"But it must be guarded!"

"Of course it's guarded. But you know the Russians."

By this he meant that the sentries periodically got drunk.

"What is the gasoline for? Police cars?"

"Of course. It's collected regularly for the units in the town. Four of them. I've been watching for over two weeks."

"Sit down," said Ronni. He obeyed, first squatting and then sitting.

"Where is it loaded? The gasoline?"

"They bring the cans into the courtyard and they are loaded there."

"Not outside the gates? Pity."

"No. Inside. That's the problem."

"I don't believe you," I said. "You haven't been here two weeks watching anything. Your beard is not old enough."

"I could shave up to a few days ago. It's not my fault I can't keep clean. I had to move in a hurry. They nearly found me. I pushed my kit under a bush and when I went back for it, it was gone."

We frowned at each other, not knowing whether to credit this or not. The area surrounding any police installation would be patrolled, we knew. Or would it? Once again the unfamiliar military organization made any guess useless. As in the railway tenement we could not work out their arrangements from any past experience or observation of our own. A Gestapo store would be guarded round the clock and its surroundings kept under rigid control. But we knew enough by now to know that such facts proved nothing. For instance, any patrol must have stumbled over the little automobile; it had clearly not been disturbed for some time. Or were we just outside the patrolled area? The lack of any means of calculation, any evidence about the occupiers' frame of reference to their own command structure, made our situation doubly nightmarish. We knew the extreme simplicity of the Russians' attitude to us, but to use our wits we needed to know about them.

This man, on the other hand, if one could close one's eyes to his present appearance, was of a familiar type. He probably spent his life since leaving school in one job, some shop or office in a provincial town. The fussy precision with which he formed his words in that rustling voice, his insistence on having kept shaven, the hanging on to a tiny evidence of respectability, placed him. I grew up with people like him. Until he was ordered to register in the auxiliary militia he was certainly enthusiastic about the Führer and the war, keeping minutely all the rationing and air-raid regulations and watching jealously to see that everybody else did too. As every boy in the neighborhood was called up, he would speak of patriotism; before 1941 of the hereditary enemies and after June 1941 of the bulwark against Bolshevism. But when the same boys, turned into men, came home on leave he would comment on their arrogance and indiscipline. Just like my uncle Hermann. The only time he was an individual person would be in the pursuit of his hobby—he certainly had a hobby—and perhaps, but only perhaps, in his intimate personal relationships.

Now, lightheaded with hunger and danger, he was a sad little figure. He might betray us to the Russians to curry favor, or he might be useful.

The news that the very treasure we needed was nearby, which was only an hour before an unattainable fortune, had changed a helpless depth of despair into the euphoria of renewed energy. It was now a question of how to get it. The near impossibility of driving more than a mile without being arrested was a secondary problem. The army Volkswagen was a vehicle of wonderful sturdiness. With its robust flat chassis base, rear drive and high axle it would go almost anywhere a tank would go.

Ronni brought out our precious bread, cut it with the broken old knife in half and divided one half into three. We ate.

"Now," she said, putting the knife away in her clothing, "tell us what you know about this warehouse."

He did not know much, most of it surmise although he was sure it was fact.

"Are there any windows or doors on the other sides?"

"No. Only the main gates. The wall goes blank right around and it's high, the roof starts about five meters up."

"It's not a surrounding wall, then, but part of the buildings?"

"Of course." His tone was the familiar one of condescension toward ignorant women.

"So it's a four-cornered warehouse, everything looking into the courtyard in the middle."

"Right."

"You don't speak Russian? Or Polish?"

"Of course not."

"No need to sound indignant," she said mildly. "It could be a useful accomplishment at the moment."

He stared at this, and grunted sulkily.

"The thing would be to get inside and hide."

"You'd never get out again."

That "you" said everything about him.

What we need is a small boy, I thought to myself. A sharp-witted nipper.

"Do they have any women in there? In the store?"

"*Women?*" Then he saw what she meant. Self-righteous horror spread through his whole person. If he had been wearing skirts, he would have drawn them aside from her.

"Yes, women!" she said sharply. It was the only time I saw Ronni show impatience.

"Not that I've seen," he said sullenly.

"Another thing," I said. "D'you know where we are here? What is the town called?"

"How should I know? All I know is the Czech border is over there."

Borders were effectively non-existent at that time, but it was good news, just the same.

"How far?"

"Through that gap in the hills there. I suppose it's about twenty kilometers."

Even across country, provided there were no unavoidable rivers or sharp inclines, that was no more than an hour away in a car. It was a heady thought. For us afoot those hills were impassable, yet nothing more than hillocks. We knew that, perhaps because of the mountains farther east, Bohemia and Moravia were not in the flood path of the advance into the Reich. The flow, immemorially, and both ways, was over the plains of Poland and Hungary.

I stood up and keeping close to the protecting bulk of the haystack moved to its far side where I could see the nearest houses of the little town. In the distance rose a church tower with its globular base and tall spire. The rest was low houses, mostly of one story, I judged. It was a rather treeless neighborhood and somehow the town looked poor and meager, as if it had been nourished by one or two small local manufactories now closed down. I was quite wrong; it was a minor spa, long out of fashion but fairly prosperous. I have seen it since then and there is a pretty little *Kurhaus* of the early nineteenth century and a number of modest hotels and boardinghouses. I looked at it then not only at the wrong time but from the wrong side, away from the main road and the railway station.

When I returned to Ronni the man was leaving, saying he wanted to have a look around.

"He's not dangerous," she said when he was gone, disappearing suddenly into the willows where I had first seen him move. "Even if he's captured. They won't give him time to talk."

"Probably gone to visit some food he's got over there. These fields look as if they were planted with sugar beets or turnips. There may be a whole row of winter dumps buried over there."

"Yes, he may have food of some sort."

"He would eat our bread but he won't tell us of anything he has."

"That must be quite a dip over there. A stream, d'you think?"

"I think I'll go over. The water may be drinkable." I was dragging the pot out of my bundle as I spoke. "I thought of going into the town, but the trouble is, this is a purely Polish area and I could never get away with it."

"How far is it?"

"The nearest houses must be about a kilometer. No, not as much."

"We could try to get near, tonight."

"You're not up to it."

"Oh yes. If you bind up my leg tightly it won't chafe so much." She rose to her knees and turned. "I don't like you to go across this field. You'll be seen."

"It slopes a little over this way, I'll go the way he did, then I'm cut off from the warehouse or whatever it is." I showed her, stretching out my arm.

"Yes, it does go down a little, but go slowly. We don't know what may be over there beyond the dip. There may be a village, even a main road."

"I'll watch out."

I did watch out but saw nobody, not even the man who walked over here a few minutes before. People did not walk about the fields then. Here the country folk were all Polish and they had not fled in a mass exodus as the Germans in their millions had done, but thousands spent the winter in their cellars, hardly ever going aboveground. And no work was done. The inhabitants of isolated, outlying houses had all gone into the next town, the next village, to shelter with their kind. The countryside was depopulated. It was part of the return to the dark ages; if it went on for more than a year or so all these fields for a hundred miles around would go back into heath land and then into forest and half the people would starve. And I for one did not believe the war was nearly over; it would go on and on for a generation.

We were right about the stream. It chuckled and prattled away in a sloping bed lined with hazel saplings and rushes, the matted dead stalks and leaves of the summer flowers between. A narrow path ran alongside, no doubt into the town. It was obviously unused for under the bank in spots where wind did not stir them, hardened snowdrifts still lay. Evidently over here the long rains did not fall. The snow was white, not gray or yellowish as it is near a used path. Encouraged by this evidence and by the stillness, I washed myself as well as I could in spite of the near-freezing temperature. The need to cleanse myself was brought back with force by the sight of clear water. Then, a little farther up the stream, I filled my pot and drank and refilled it for Ronni.

I set it up as high as I could in a little nook in the bank and gripping a hazel stem, dragged my unwieldy body up. No easy matter. Then I lay down on the ridge and reached down for the pot, lifting it very slowly so as not to tip it over. I was maddeningly awkward, but managed to keep most of the water. Any pressure on my stomach made me feel ill, so I sat still for a few minutes, breathing deeply, to recover. Near me in a tangle of dried willow herb a small bird stirred. Up on the bank the breeze struck cold, but there was a heaviness in the wind, a damp freshness that was less stringent than winter and might have been filled with some fruitful moisture, some softness to impregnate the sleeping earth. It was a false hope, there was more winter to come, icy winds and freezing stillness still lying in wait. But spring would at last come, whether or not we were there to feel its blessing. I looked up and around me and saw starlings wheel and from somewhere a slow comfort came that promised nothing but was simply there.

We huddled in the hay until the sky lightened pale in the east and then I helped Ronni down to the path and we moved very slowly along it as it wound into the outskirts of the town. We took a stout stake from a pile of snow fencing which this year had never been set up, and this gave Ronni some support. As we came near to buildings we stopped frequently to listen and look about us. Presently a wider path sloped up from the bank between cottage gardens, and since the houses seemed to face away from it, we decided to go up that way. Keeping as near to the fences as we could we made our way to where the path joined a rutted side road, unpaved, with scattered suburban dwellings, all closed and shuttered. There were the usual signs of war, a house burned to a black skeleton, smashed glass, broken furniture beside the road, a military car full of rusting bullet holes, its smashed front axle dipping it into the shallow ditch. Just past there we both heard the sudden noise of horses galloping and the rattle and crunch of wheels. There was a gate leaning on one hinge and we bundled ourselves inside and crouched down behind the bushes. The racket came so unexpectedly that we knew some cart had been turned into this road. A moment later it flew past our hiding place, a dark pony at full stretch, its rough coat flecked with foam and a wild eye rolling, pulling a long and narrow cart that jounced emptily. A Russian soldier with his fur hat pulled down, the flaps flipping over his ears and neck, stood up on the driving board using his whip and shouting encouragement to the horse with bursts of laughter. That picture stayed with me, contrasted with the moment the day before in the fields, as if they belonged together.

We waited for some time after that. An old woman went by muttering to herself. Nothing else stirred. What we expected there we did not know, nor what we sought. Perhaps, the habit of solitude having been broken, human instinct had reasserted itself and we were driven to other human beings. In the distance a slight rumble of traffic or perhaps a train could be heard, over in the center of the place. It could only be Russian troops, there was no other traffic possible. At last we emerged and moved a few yards farther, where a side path made us stop again. Here was an empty space of rank and sodden grass with a shell hole from which several long planks reared crookedly and behind that one of those small general shops to be seen on the outer street of every town everywhere, whether small or large. Old advertisements of cracked enamel on metal hung on its wooden walls, and we could see that some of them were old enough still to proclaim extinct goods in the German language that prevailed here up to the end of the first war. Over them clung the tattered remnants of later posters stirring in the cool air. The shutters were closed, the door protected by a scissors grid. Then something moved. From the back of the tiny house of creosoted wood the figure of a woman emerged, creeping almost as cautiously as we ourselves did, and as she came she pushed a small packet into the front of her dark coat and then pulled the kerchief forward farther over her brow. She hesitated when she saw us and searched us with her suspicious look. Then she crossed to the other side of the pathway and went past, turning so that she did not take her eyes off us until she got across the roadway with its deep ruts. She went inside one of the low gates and turned again to watch us before disappearing. The instant her figure was gone we heard the sound of someone else, moving much more quickly. A small boy came out from behind the shop and almost ran up the wide path toward the road, his muffled head turning this way and that, obviously in search of the woman. He was stalking her. Then he saw us at the side of the path in the shelter of an old fruit tree. He looked again after the woman and we heard clearly in the quiet the sound of a door shutting and he made a slight movement of the head, confirmed in his guess as to where his quarry was. He then turned his attention to us and came toward us. Boldly he approached, staring with wary curiosity. He was not frightened but ready for anything. His thin face was grimy with dirt and he looked about twelve years old and yet much older.

He came quite close and we saw a pair of bright round black eyes, full of snapping energy and enterprise, which mustered the chance of our having anything of use to him. Those sharp eyes went over me twice and then he spoke in a hoarse little voice, quick and impudent.

"That must be pretty heavy."

I understood him before I realized that although the other words were Polish, he used the German word for heavy.

"Why do you speak German?" Ronni asked him in a scolding tone like any grandmother.

"Why not? I get mixed up sometimes. Where've you come from?"

"A long way."

"I can see that!" Scornfully.

"Then why ask?"

He stared anew at that, pausing to reflect that here was an antagonist worth taking seriously.

"Are you from here?" continued Ronni.

"No! 'Course not. Just got left here."

"From a trek?"

"Last autumn." He nodded. "You left it a bit late."

"You too," she pointed out. "Why did you stay? You could go on after the others—your family."

"I can eat here. Sometimes. And I've got somewhere to sleep. The soldiers give me food now and then, they like kids."

"From over there? The warehouse over there?"

"Christ no! Nobody goes in there, that's forbidden. In the town."

"Do you know what's inside?"

"It's the police. Just police things." He was vague.

"You don't know. I know one thing that's in there."

"What's that?" He pounced instantly.

"Gasoline."

"Ha, what's the good of that! Can't use that."

"If we could get a can of it *we* could use it. You could come with us."

He came close up, narrowing his brilliant eyes with an extraordinarily adult look, like a sharp merchant with an awkward customer.

"What are you talking about? Out with it, if you've got something!"

Ronni shook her head, bargaining, smiling at him challengingly.

"Oh no. Then you'd be as wise as we are. And where should we be then?"

He looked at her doubtfully.

"Na, you're cracked. There ain't any cars within a million miles except the Russians'."

"Ah well," she said sighing heavily. "I thought I'd just try you out."

He did not like that but was too intelligent to give in to his boy's pride. He moved away as if to go. Then he stopped, back to us, and frowned at the ground, trying to work it out or to make up his mind. At that moment we all heard motor engines.

"In here," he snapped, and before we even moved he was shoving us rudely into the bushes of the hedge. "Keep still. Don't move." He was gone. We pulled our head shawls over our faces so that their pallor would not betray us in the dark wintry shrubs and remained there, rigidly still. It was now as light as it was going to get, at perhaps about seven o'clock in the morning. The sounds of engines increased in waves as one truck after another turned the invisible corner of the road farther up. The first one roared past, lurching over the ruts, then another and another. It was a whole convoy. I counted ten large and heavy transports. Slowly quiet returned.

So did the boy.

"They're for your warehouse," he said, jerking his head toward it. The convoy had come from the town center, probably reloaded from a train. "They'll all be drunk tonight. You'd better watch out."

"Aren't you afraid of them?"

"Yes, everybody is afraid of them. But the others, the soldiers, no, they're all right. For me, that is."

"If they are drunk they'll be careless. It might be our chance."

"Sure, they *are* careless, but they shoot too. Just for fun, y'know?" He turned his sharp, bright eyes on me, standing there in silence. "And, of course, you're women."

"Did you ever see an old man hanging around there, by the warehouse?" asked Ronni.

"I've seen a crazy old geezer. You mean that one?"

"That would be the one. He says he's watched them, knows where they keep the gasoline. But he can't get in, he's old and slow. You might, while they are unloading."

"But they'd catch me! You think I'm nuts too?"

"Not if they were looking somewhere else, they wouldn't." Ronni paused. "And not in the dark, they wouldn't."

"And what would you be doing?"

"Taking care of the fire on the other side of the building."

"Fire?"

She nodded, not taking her eyes from his. "One section of the outer wall, it must have been patched at some time, is tarred timber. You see that pile of rubbish up the street here? Some of that is upholstery. It's been dry here for weeks, so the old man said. It would make a lovely fire, that kapok and horsehair."

"Kapok and horsehair," he repeated thoughtfully, as if the words were a children's rune like the set rhymes of the games we used to play on our way home from school. He thought for some time.

"Yes, but how do I know you really have a car? And if you have, how do we know it will start?"

"I'll show it to you if you're game for a try at it. Anna can drive and she will wait in the car until we get to it. As soon as the up-roar is loud enough, fire-fighting company and all that, we start the engine and drive off. That is, if you get the gasoline."

"It's the wildest caper *I* ever heard of!" He sounded like a man of forty.

"Look," she said patiently, "at least let's try the first stage of it. We all go back up the street now and take armfuls of that wood and rubbish. Nobody is going to take any notice of that. People must always be taking bits of it for a fire, aren't they?"

"Yes, you're right there."

"Well, then. We carry what we can and dump it by the wall on the side away from the road and the entry, where the wooden part of the wall is. Then you go around to the main gates, just as if you were scrounging about, like you were when we first saw you. You might even talk to the men unloading, they won't do you any more harm than a cuff over the head. You can look around you, see where things are. In the meantime we clear off back to where we were hiding. I'll show you where, when we get over there. When you can get away without them taking notice of you— you'll have to be careful of that—you follow us. But indirectly, mind, you must go down here to the stream and walk along the path until you get to a row of stumped willows. You understand?"

He nodded, his eyes never leaving hers. He was heart and soul in the gamble now.

"Then you cut into the field to the haystack. You'll see it from this side when we get back to the warehouse, across the fields. Then we'll show you the car. You'll see it's in working order. The old man looks after it. Then we'll talk again and make a plan."

"What about the old man? Is he in this?"

"We haven't told him yet, but it was he who thought of it, and he who got the car as far as here. If we get a can of gasoline, of course he comes with us."

"He'd be a nuisance. Cussed old fellow and stupid." His eyes fixed on me. I would be an additional hazard, too, his look said.

This whole conversation, of tremendous weight and moment, was only a few minutes in the speaking. Twice we broke off and froze back into our camouflage of bushes behind the fruit tree. There were also local people moving about but we took no notice of them. They moved like us, cautiously, listening and watching, like frightened game in a jungle where great carnivores are at large. There was never more than a single figure to be seen, apart from ourselves. But now and then a face appeared at a doorway or a shutter was opened to spy out the prospect from one or other of the houses. Most of these were one-story affairs, the town cousins of peasant cottages; one or two were of two floors with sharply tilted roofs of more recent build. It could be seen that the town had spread out to here; a generation ago this was an outlying village to which were added suburban dwellings with stucco facings. The road had never been made up, there were no sidewalks, no metaled roadway. An overhead cable brought electricity to the newer houses, but I could see where in the distance it sagged to the ground, broken. I could see, too, away by the church, one house of more ample design with symmetrical side wings of five casements each and an upper story in the middle section with a broadly pitched gable. That house was from an earlier time, of a simple dignity in its echo of classic derivation. That gabled double story with its sketched columns was so typical of a period, a culture gone forever, that it touched me as no human could have done at that time with the memory of a then incredible stability.

A tooting sounded in the distance, a motor horn insistently pressed, and was repeated closer by.

"That's their breakfast signal," said the boy. "But wait a minute, still, in case any of them are outside."

We waited but no uniformed figure appeared; they were all in the building.

"All right. Let's go," he said, the brisk order betraying his close acquaintance with the military. It was the copied tone of a sergeant mustering a squad.

The pile of rubbish was outside the burned out house so we were not likely to be noticed in the few moments spent collecting as much as we could carry before we made off under the shelter of the bushes bordering the little gardens. In one of them a man bent over the ground, taking the opportunity while the Russians were eating, but he did not even turn his head at our stealthy passage.

"He's got spuds buried there," the boy muttered. "Bet he curses the day he made his winter store in the middle of his garden."

"Probably there was a trench already dug there," suggested Ronni. She was bent over, the remnants of a chair balanced in her shawl on her shoulders as she moved herself quite quickly forward with the aid of her stick. She looked for a second, the second of seeing her from the outside and not as herself, like a witch in a fairy story. I caught the eyes of the boy on her and the mischievous glitter of his look held the same perception. The unspoken insight between us filled me with a recollection of gaiety that mysteriously drew me and repelled me at the same time; it was as if I had known that look before, or known the boy before. Somewhere the look of one who conveyed a wonderful joke understood only by himself and me with just such a sparkling, black flicker of the eyes, lived and moved in my soul. The near-memory, instantly rejected, was like broken glass grating agonizingly in my breast.

Instead I forced another thought, something nearer and safer for my driving purpose. The idea that came to me when talking to the old straggler, that what we needed was a sharp-witted boy. That boy was already then near us; I had divined him before he appeared. I accepted completely that everything would go as we planned. I did not *know* this, or feel confidence in our plan; nothing of that sort. It was already accomplished in reality and needed only to happen in the given span of time.

There was a small elderbush at one end of the timber stretch of wall and we dumped our burdens between that and the wall where it was almost invisible. The boy slipped away from us on his mission and we retreated separately so that the repeated sight of the two of us together should not remain in any chance onlooker's mind. I went around by the far path and up the stream to the willows.

When I arrived at our hiding place, the old man was there, scratching away with a handful of rusty wire at the remains of the army identification on the sloping hood of the Volkswagen. Where it was already gone Ronni was patiently rubbing the scarred surface with a handful of mud and dried grass to blur the scoured paintwork.

"Just the same," he was saying with that pedantic care of pronunciation, "this boy is not reliable. He is a thief, a real rascal."

"Of course he is, poor little soul. And that is just what we need."

"Poor little soul!" he muttered resentfully. "I could do it just as well. Better!"

"Yes, but they would instantly suspect a grown-up man. He can get away with it, perhaps."

"He'll get away with it," I said, beginning to work at the green and gray paintwork with Ronni. The man was breathing heavily, more to impress us with his efforts than from lack of air, and he produced a wheezing rustle with every breath. He neither answered nor looked at me. I was not worthy of his attention. For his kind I was only a breeding animal and a hindrance in the circumstances. He would have left me behind without a second thought.

"In any case," said Ronni, always quick to pacify, "you have a much more important job. You have to take care of the motor and drive it. Have you tried the engine lately? The starter?"

His self-importance at once soothed, the deserter unwrapped the rotor arm from inside his padded coat, fitted it into place and spent a long time checking and cleaning and testing the machine.

That day went on for unlimited time yet I was not impatient. I knew. Only one unforeseen thing happened. The boy materialized like a shadow and reported with laconic economy of words his success. He wheedled himself into the courtyard by lounging on the gate and watching the loaders. They called a greeting, he went nearer, they joked with him in a broken mixture of three tongues, they even gave him food and offered him vodka which some of them were already drinking. He larked about, acting the small child and even when a senior N.C.O. appeared and warned him off, it was with a rough joke and a sketched cuff not really meant to land on his quick-moving head. He noted that the warrant officer had been drinking. By evening they would all be roaring drunk. They talked of some girls they were looking forward to in the town. The boy knew of the house to which they referred.

"Harlots," muttered the old man.

"They do it to eat."

"Phaugh!"

"Some of them have kids. They have to eat too." The boy was defiant.

"Poor souls," sighed Ronni and made a sign to the boy not to annoy the other. The little fellow shrugged with humorous unconcern.

"What is your name?" asked Ronni. "What should we call you?"

"Sigi," he said simply. "I don't know my other name."

Presently he went off to be seen in his usual haunts and to beg as much food off his soldier friends as he could stuff into himself. When we had done as much as we could with the car we huddled ourselves into the loose straw to rest in preparation for a strenuous night.

"It's all a terrible risk," murmured Ronni as we settled ourselves.

"But it's made you forget your plan of leaving me," I answered slyly and she smiled at that.

"Why wouldn't Sigi tell us his name, do you think?"

"I wondered at that. He must know it."

"Oh certainly. Perhaps he hasn't yet decided which side we are supposed to be on."

"Sides!" I felt again that near-memory, the question of loyalties that was a threat to my balance, to my resolution. There was an almost physical sense of shoving something away, something menacing that leaned on me.

It was already agreed that I should light the fire. Clumsy and top-heavy as I was, I still moved more easily and quickly than poor Ronni. I was to wait about ten minutes after the tooting supper signal and then make my way directly there, coming back as soon as it was ablaze, by the circuitous route. I must slide along the warehouse wall to its end to avoid making a silhouette against the glow of flames from the fire and, for the short run of unsheltered field, make all the speed I could to the nearest bushes so that I was well away down the path to the river before any possible viewer could notice the conflagration. It was a thousand to one chance that the fire would be seen, being on the far and blank wall, by anyone either inside the courtyard or its buildings, or by anyone from the outer dwellings of the town. They would certainly not be out after dark. By the time it was visible inside the warehouse the roof beams would be alight, we hoped. I secreted Ronni's precious matches inside my clothes. Meanwhile the old man fixed back the rotor arm in the Volkswagen motor and opened the gas tank cover in readiness.

We waited, holding our breath so that when the sound of the tooting came it was a shock of delayed expectation. Everything happened exactly as we had foreseen. By the time I reached the river path, high flames were leaping up the roof; the timber wall went up, not like paper which often burns reluctantly, but like dried twigs that burst into instant fire as if exploded. Sigi was waiting on the corner of the square building. As soon as the fire showed a clear grip of its prey he slipped along the wall, the opposite one from my shelter, which I was already leaving, and ran bent double to the main gates. He knew there was a pile of used crates on the inside just by the gate. He used the hinges of the gates, sturdy old chunks of metal, to climb by and was over and down the other side behind the boxes before he had time to draw breath. There he waited for someone to see or smell the fire, now leaping with splendid beauty to the top of the wall.

Breathless with effort and excitement alike, I topped the riverbank by one of the willows and saw a sight of wonder. Used as I recently was to the terrible and consuming glory of fire I never saw anything so marvelously lovely as that tremendous blaze. I wanted to sing and shout with joy and triumph, but prudently I saved my breath.

When I breathed easily again I gathered myself together and

made a dash for the hayrick. There I found Ronni, pressed back against its shelter and gazing in wonder at the sight. We fell on each other, clutching and kissing in a transport of pride. Then I looked around me.

"Where's the old man?" I was instantly suspicious.

"He was here—" She spun. "He's gone!"

For an instant I thought I saw a shadowy shape pass the quivering play of great, leaping flames and knew at once what had happened. Jealous of Sigi's role, he was off to the warehouse.

We both made a movement as if to follow him and then caught ourselves and drew back. The fire would draw us into madness as it did the old man, if we allowed it to.

Now there was a rumor of noise above the crackle and boom of the blaze. Then yells, shots, a crashing noise repeated.

"The roof," I said with awe.

We were waiting for the bells or sirens of fire engines, but of course there was no telephone working. No outside intervention would arrive until the disaster was seen from another unit or until a messenger reached the town.

We clutched at each other for support as a great bang announced an explosion and a column of towering sparks and flares burst up into the black velvet of the night. A harsh gasp of torn breath and Sigi's lean little form almost fell at our feet, while a thud and a muffled splash announced the booty, a twenty-liter can of gasoline.

"God, it's heavy," he gasped, and struggled to his feet, open mouth seen in the glow pulsing around us, as he dragged in air.

We clasped him wildly but he struggled out of our arms.

"Let me go," he shrieked. "I've got another one."

"Sigi, they'll see you!" cried Ronni but he was already gone.

She tried to run after him but I dragged her back and we waited, biting our lips and praying. An eternity of increasing babel filled the dark behind the blaze. We could see distant figures skulking, as here and there people ventured out to watch the breathtaking show. Now from the main road on the far side came the thunder of trucks but we could see from our vantage point that little could be saved. One great boom and puff after another was interspersed with extended crackling of ammunition exploding. It was a success beyond our wildest hopes, so overwhelming that we were frightened by its extravagance.

The second time Sigi crawled the last part of his perilous passage, dragging the heavy container after him. He was so exhausted now that for a little while he could not speak. I laid him on his side and pulled up his thin knees, and when I slid a hand inside his thin jacket his heart sprang and thudded there as if it must burst.

"Poor lambkin," I murmured, hardly knowing I spoke, "poor baby."

"Brave boy," said Ronni.

Tears of joy and pride slid over his dirty cheeks and I smeared them away quickly to save him from shame when he came to himself.

After a few moments he struggled and then got to his feet.

"Let's get out of here. We haven't got much time."

"But the old man?"

"Ha! We won't see him again. They got *him*! I told you he was nuts! Came racing in through the gates as if the place belonged to him. They blew him in pieces! Spattered him all over the courtyard!"

"Oh, God," mourned Ronni.

"Come on!" he cried passionately. "Let's get that damned car started and get away from here!"

"Help me with this, then," she said, already struggling with one of the cans. It took us minutes to find the trick of opening the cap. The reek of gasoline, together with the excitement, made me retch emptily and I had to turn away while they clumsily splashed the liquid into the tank.

Then we were tossing out the bales of straw and in a few minutes I pulled myself up into the driver's seat and felt for the ignition key. It was in place. I pushed down the clutch and moved the gear. The first time the starter whirred. Then it caught and the little vehicle moved out from its hiding place. I turned it as slowly as I could and in first gear we ground away, parallel to the stream and away from the town. The main road ran in a loop about a mile away and we would join it there. We bumped and lurched across the fields. As pandemonium faded behind us the noise of the Volkswagen engine gradually became appallingly noisy.

We did not know it then but that little spa was the outermost point in Poland of the Russian forward march. Their left flank lay there, which it was forbidden to cross. For Czechoslovakia they already planned a quite different treatment from the merciless redestruction of Polish territory and it was not to be invaded until the troops were again under control. Their reasoning was exactly the same as that of the German General Staff; the Czechs would conform to their rulers but with the intransigent and martial Poles only the utmost savagery could be expected to reduce courage to impotence. Thus, without knowing it, we moved in about half an hour out of immediate danger. In fact we crawled along the rising road at a snail's pace, ready at every bend to tumble out and take shelter if any offered. The caution was a nightmare after our euphoric elevation. The road trailed through rolling hills, not high but steep enough to form a clear barrier. Without our knowing why, the emptiness of the road and the lack of signs of warlike activity gradually gave us confidence. Even in the dark and without lights it was clear that there were no wrecks in the ditches, no burned-out houses showing gaping holes to the sky.

The reaction from high excitement came over me after about an hour and Ronni and Sigi were obliged to talk or sing to me to keep me alert. At one point Sigi even suggested that he should drive for a time but it was more difficult than he could know and I pulled myself together in a fog of weariness, grinding my teeth and tensing my muscles to force attention. When the east was clearly flecked with livid streaks we, or rather they, began to look for a place to stop and hide during the daylight. A low timber hut in a wired enclosure offered itself and in a last effort I maneuvered the car over the bumpy heath. The other two climbed down stiffly to pull down a length of the fence so that I could turn in it behind the hut but I did not dare move from behind the wheel. Ronni came back to me; she could now see my face fairly clearly and she called softly to Sigi who was engaged in forcing open the hut door. They half lifted, half dragged me from my position, clamped to the driving instruments with frozen hands and feet and crying with the pain from cramp as soon as I tried to move.

The hut, it seemed, was not weather-proof but there was old straw inside and its grudging hospitality would do for the moment. I could not eat the remaining piece of bread and could hardly even manage to drink from Sigi's vodka bottle filled with water. As I passed this bottle to Ronni I felt myself keeling over and they told me later that as I spoke in giving her the drink, I rolled on my side and was asleep. They slept for an hour or so and then Sigi went to spy out the land. An uncanny peace surrounded us, as if the war were on another continent. When I woke at last the day was going.

It had all happened just as I knew it would. The only event not already known in essence was the death of the old deserter.

Sigi had found water and brought me enough to splash on my face.

"Yes, all right," he said briskly, watching me blink and yawn myself back into life. "But where are the Germans? I don't quite like the look of it. There wasn't a soul on that road. They must have been withdrawn, or cleared off without orders. So what happens now? Who's in charge around here?"

"What about the local people?" asked Ronni.

"There's a village farther down the valley. But I don't speak their stupid lingo."

"We passed an abandoned frontier post somewhere on the road, or did I dream it?" I mumbled, and succumbed to a jaw-cracking yawn.

"That was miles back," he said impatiently. "We're at least twenty kilometers inside Czechoslovakia here."

"How clever of you to think of the language," said Ronni wonderingly. "That is going to be a problem we haven't thought of."

"The country isn't big enough for it to matter much," I said and yawned again, the water coming into my eyes. The example was too much for them and they both yawned in imitation. We all began to laugh foolishly.

CHAPTER 18

Now that we had someone quick and resourceful with us we were assured of enough primitive food to stay alive, for Sigi could and did steal for us all. The weather was cold and bleak with damp, raw winds but it neither rained nor snowed so we stayed where we were. I rested with the grateful lassitude of achievement. It was something like the feeling of going off duty, of having been relieved by another team in the operating room. Once when things were very bad and we were working twenty-four hours a day in shifts of four-hour alternating periods, I had felt like that after a delayed fresh team arrived and we, the old team, were granted a whole day to sleep.

Several days passed. Ronni was looking at me with a quite unusual expression of some new anxiety, but the impression faded again; I was sleepy once more and lay back in the nest of straw.

It seemed a moment later that I was half awake and heard her talking to Sigi.

"It's coming any moment now. We have to get her somewhere where we can get help."

"How d'you know?" he asked, curious.

"I can tell by her face. Her look has changed. It always does, just before."

"Looks the same to me," he grumbled.

"Well, there are things you don't know yet, clever though you are. Just take my word for it, will you!"

I felt no difference in my physical state. The weight and imbalance were neither worse nor better. I was inclined to agree with Sigi. They moved away and I could no longer hear more than a murmur; I dozed off again. I was used by now to the physical discomfort of my own body as if it had always been like that. And, for all I could see, it would go on like that.

"I could go and ask them in that old hunting lodge, the French prisoners? There is room there and they seem all right."

"Not in the village?"

"They would know. And I've heard some funny rumors."

He meant that the villagers would know we were Germans and the vague news Sigi referred to were the first circulating reports of the way the Czechs were behaving to their German fellow citizens farther to the south. For these least oppressed and most complaisant of all the occupied peoples were taking revenge for their own lack of courage during the war on neighbors who had lived cheek by jowl with them for hundreds of years. Not on the occupiers, or the soldiers; they were safely gone.

"But you must keep up the story that she is Polish. I wouldn't trust them, if they knew."

"Oh, surely," he began and then stopped speaking. Even at Sigi's age he felt on the one hand the primitive duty to take care of me and on the other the doubt as to the sanity of anyone at that time.

"I'll see," he then said and a little later was off again, this time on a foraging trip of a different kind from the search for food.

Ronni and I heard him return, talking in an unintelligible mixture of language which in some unfathomable way was understood. There were other voices, strange and male voices. The opening of the hut darkened and I struggled to my feet. I could see them dipping their heads at the low entrance and they spoke that language that filled me with a flood of dark unhappiness and pain.

"No! I don't want to . . ." I gasped, clutching at Ronni for help.

"But they are Frenchmen, darling. They won't hurt you!"

At this fearsome irony I cried out, in animal terror and rejection.

At that moment it happened. I felt the unspeakable release and collapse of my containing guts and instantaneously a straining drive and pressure. I clasped my lower stomach and groaned aloud.

"Go away! Leave me alone!"

They jostled around me, lifting me between them. Some spoke French and some other languages as I was carried out, struggling feebly, and laid at Sigi's instruction in the back of the Volkswagen. Ronni held my head, I could hear their voices and in a fading grip on the outer world could not understand why their language was not entirely French. They were, in fact, Belgians and Dutchmen but how they got there and why we never knew. No one knew better than I the ingenuity of prisoners of war. They just were there.

There was no doctor among them. But one of them was a priest. He held my hands and prayed aloud, sweating more with fear of my straining, struggling and gasping than I did myself. They laid me on a bed but I pushed myself off again. I must keep moving. Then I rested, then moved about again. Heads looked in at the door. Ronni shouted instructions. Water was brought, I saw great white sheets, pure white, and brown muscular hands ripped them in strips. Everyone was talking. It should have been a shambles. If I had been able to see it as a nurse I would have given up in despair. As it was, I think now all the forced use of my muscles in the last months stood me in good stead, and Ronni had much experience of childbirth. It was over in two hours, they told me afterward.

"A boy," crooned Ronni, and her tears of joy fell on my fevered and sweat-soaked forehead. "A great big beautiful boy with black eyes."

"His son," I heard myself whispering through bruised and cracked lips bitten almost through. "His son, with black eyes." Instantly I was deep asleep.

It was a big room, wood-lined and smelling of wood, light with windows, almost bare. They tiptoed in to look at me and to bring me food. I never consciously let the baby out of my hands. They looked down from high up, as pleased and proud as if they had done it themselves. I was hardly aware of them. There was the child and there was, on the periphery of the child's being, Ronni, who did everything but suckle him. That I did. All was a swimming, swaying peace and calm.

Presently I felt I must get up, so I did, still holding the baby. I moved about, testing myself out. I breathed right down into my pelvis as I had not done for months. *That* was a pleasure. The child's head was covered with a dark fluff, his tiny face was crumpled and ugly, and he clutched with little monkey paws so lovely they made me weep. The cracking sinews and muscles, the all-over bruising and stiffness, slackened, relaxed and faded.

Then the prisoners came, I never did distinguish their faces, and explained that we must move. A commission of the International Red Cross was sending a transport and we were to go with them. They had refused to go without us, but I must not speak. Did I understand? No, I did not understand. But I would do as I was told. What I did now understand was that they meant well with us. That I grasped. The transport was a big truck with a canvas cover. They lifted a small sofa into it for Ronni and me. There was an argument which had something to do with the sofa, but it stayed in the truck. They all sat or crouched on their haunches, on the floor.

Several times on the journey they hissed at me to keep quiet: not a sound! Once they jostled and gesticulated in a group outside the truck, shouting and protesting. Then they all got back in and we set off again.

Sigi clung to us now, as intimidated by this new hazard of officialdom as we were. When they stopped they brought us food in shining metal plates with deep rims; pappy, mild messes and paper holders of milk or liquids that tasted something like almost forgotten fruit. I held the child in my lap, wrapped in a shawl worn by Ronni for months over her head. Whenever he wailed I fed him. When I fed him the others looked away.

The truck tarpaulin smelled of some scented antiseptic, or I thought it did. That rather sickened me.

Hours, hours. Now we stopped again, a long time and I heard, among other speech, German spoken with a strange inflection. A short time after we started again came the hollow rumbling of a major bridge. In my dazed state I did not grasp that we were out of Czechoslovakia until I heard the prisoners of war talking of the Danube as we crossed it.

The bustle of the next stop was quite different. The sun was shining outside the dark canopy of our transport. I must have been asleep! I felt for the child's warm weight. To my weak astonishment there were nurses wearing familiar uniforms. Hands under my arms. Where was Ronni?

"Ronni!"

"I'm here, love."

"Don't go away."

"She doesn't need a stretcher."

"I can walk perfectly well."

Just the same, the ground shifted and swayed under my feet.

"Sigi is going on with us," explained the Dutch priest.

"Oh, but—"

"He'll be better off with us, right now."

Little bullet-head pressed into me, thin arms hugged me, the sharp eyes laughed with excitement at the prospect of journeying across Europe. Yes, he would be better off . . . I was supported by hands and was walking slowly, there was a chorus of cries, some-one said, "Wave" and I raised my hand, the one not holding the child in the crook of my arm. A thundering roar of engines and then a fading whine. Walking. I could smell fresh, clean air. There was a scent in the air that was familiar, a smell of hospital, its powerful cleanness made me dizzy.

"Gently, now, take it easy," someone said.

"You mustn't speak German," I muttered. "They'll hear you!"

"It's all right now. We are in Austria now. Just one more step. There we are!"

"Ronni! Where are you?"

"I'm here, love."

"There may be a hormonal upset," said a businesslike voice after a gap of nothing. "But I think it is just exhaustion. Let's give her a little time."

"Where's Ronni! Where's my baby!"

"Here is the baby. Find Frau Lonski. At once, don't stand there gaping!"

"Ronni! Ronni!" I could hear myself wailing and reproved my-self of making such a fuss. "Ronni!"

"I'm here, love. Here I am, Anna."

I sighed and gripped her worn hand. The child began to wail. All was well.

Act Three

MOTHER AND SON

CHAPTER 19

Coming out of the public park to go back to our room, I met the senior doctor of the local hospital.

"Good afternoon, Anna," he said. "You don't mind me still calling you Anna? You are young enough to be my daughter, after all. How is the baby? And how are you? I was thinking of you today, oddly enough."

He looked around at the dusty park trees and the roadway where trams now rattled again.

"It's hot, isn't it?" I said, for something to say. "We are all well, thank you."

I had to look up to see into his face, for he was a very tall man with a high, bald head and drooping fleshy features drawn down into length so that he somewhat resembled a bloodhound when he frowned as he did now, against the afternoon light of August. He took his shabby hat off to wipe his head which gleamed.

"Let's see if we can get what we'll agree to call coffee over there, shall we?" Over there was a once smart café on the far side of the street.

"You haven't been to see us for some weeks," he went on when we were seated. "I hope that means you are feeling splendid. The boy certainly looks healthy."

"Yes, he's wonderful," I agreed, pleased at this. It was one of the advantages of the lack of available clothing that his little body got plenty of sun and air and Rolf was brown and sturdy, a laughing baby.

We both watched the single waiter, slow, old and unsteady, on the other side of the terrace, but he did not see us yet. We were not impatient, it was pleasant to sit there in the shade of the café wall.

"What is Frau Lonski doing now—I suppose we should say Lonska, really."

"She always says Lonski," I said. "Now. She has a job, you know, thank goodness. I shall have to think about getting work, too."

"You are going to wean him?" he asked, looking down at the child waving his fists on my lap.

"I must work."

"Speaking of work. I was thinking of you, today. Oh, I've said that already, haven't I?" I wondered, not for the first time, why he was embarrassed. "I heard from a colleague today whom I haven't seen for years. He is with an Allied medical unit now, or rather a surgical unit. They have taken over the big military hospital up at Hollenberg, I expect you've heard. They are looking for experienced nurses. Especially surgical sisters."

"I haven't any papers," I said dimly.

"That is not irreparable. Fortunately the central medical register was moved to Marburg in 1943, so it survived. You can get copies of your qualifications from there. They are, you know, valid for Austria too."

"Still?" I said.

"Yes, in practice. Of course, you would have to register here with the nursing association and so on. But that you will know."

The waiter was now standing by our table, greeting the doctor as an old acquaintance and giving me sharp little glances under his shaggy eyebrows. He had eyes like a lizard, embedded in deep, hard-looking wrinkles. He was at least seventy. Yes, they had some coffee, or at least an imitation. He tottered off, flicking idly at the fallen flower petals and leaves on the empty tables, bare of table-cloths. There were small acacia trees around the edge of the ter-race to shield those sitting there from the dust and noise of the street and from the powerful sun. They smelled good, although like everything else they looked tattered and shabby. Strange how even the trees looked ragged after the catastrophe.

"I don't see how . . ." I began.

He interrupted, showing his embarrassment again.

"Has it ever occurred to you that it might be better for the boy as well as for you if you adopted him?"

"Adopt him?" Without meaning to I clutched the child fast. "Why should I do that? He's mine!"

"Yes, that's just it, don't you see. I don't know how things are in Germany now, but here you would not be accepted into the official register unless the child is accounted for in some—way."

"I know. I was thinking of some other kind of work."

"But nursing is what you were trained to do. It's your profes-sion. And skilled sisters are always needed. That's a commodity there is a permanent shortage of; not like coffee."

I stared sullenly at the rough table top. I knew I was behaving rudely and stupidly, but was unable to do anything about it.

He said gently in his rumbling voice, "I could get the papers through for you quickly."

"I don't . . ."

"Don't try, if you can't talk about it. I only want you to know. Because for both of you it's better if you can return to a reputable framework of living. I know what life has been like for you. For young people. But what you decide now is important for his life too. It's better for him to be a foundling with an adopted mother and grandmother, than to be exposed . . . People are not kind al-ways. And when they are it is often worse than their unkindness." He removed the burden of his wise eyes from my lowered face and looked out into the baking street where a tram clanged past. "Tact is so dreadful, I often think."

I could feel that I was going to cry and made a move to get to my feet, lifting Rolf up into my arm.

"Here's the waiter with the coffee," said his voice insistently. I sank back again into the barred wooden chair. The "coffee" was almost undrinkable and in making a joke of that we passed over what had been said.

When we were going, he returned to the subject.

"Talk to Frau Lonski about what I said. I must warn you that *I* mean to speak to her."

I nodded and managed to thank him for the coffee. He raised his hat again and watched me go away. I looked back as I stepped down into the street and he was still watching me and raised his hand to wave.

What he said was true, of course.

Veronika was working as bookkeeper for a man with a big grocery store. He was now a black marketeer and because she did not have any papers yet he paid her even less than he would have been obliged to pay anybody else. Ronni's job was really to falsify his books and her experience in the Polish occupation made her very good at that. As she said jokingly, he would much rather do that work himself, the old devil, but had never learned book-keeping and was afraid to make mistakes in his swindling that could be obvious to any competent inspector. Not that he feared them much then; he bribed them but old habit made him respect them still, and therefore fear a return to probity on their part.

When she came back to our room in the evening she would make a tale out of the events of her day. But neither of us wanted to live like that. And we didn't want Rolf to grow up like that. That was the lever.

Because Rolf was there, alive, there must be a future. And a future in which he could become a decent and happy man. Things must be so arranged for *his* life that he would take decency, dignity, straightforwardness, for granted. His life was not to be the moral sewer that Ronni and I both knew. I didn't want him to have to know even that people like Ronni's employer existed. Nor devious, inwardly dishonest men like my father, either. Nor men who put abstract loyalties before human beings. But there my thoughts came up against a black pall and stopped. It is clear now that I was making the usual mistake; trying to protect the young against reality. But although I know that now, I still think Ronni and I were right. What we knew of real life was no place for a child.

He was bathed and I rocked him on my knee, holding the dear, wobbling weight of his head in one cupped hand. His life was going to be different. For that to be possible, if it were possible, my own life must be clear of secrets, vulnerable unknowns. The doctor's talk made me see how vital my own background was going to be for Rolf. It didn't matter if we were poor, but we had to be "in order." There must be no shadows to touch him later.

As my own son he would be a by-blow of chaos, a result of disaster. The whisper of a raped mother would follow him; I knew human beings. "Russky-kid" they said now and would continue to say. It was not true but no denial could convince. I could not and would not produce a real father for Rolf, but we, Veronika and I, would make a seamless story of his parentage and stick to it. By the time Ronni came home my mind was made up.

So I went to the Allied hospital on the mountain and the little country town became our home. I stayed there for several years, until I was asked to take over first the nursing staff and then the entire supervision of this clinic which has been my life for the last twenty years. My life except for its center, that is.

I have been very fortunate.

The matron of the hospital was taken over with its other equipment from one army to another. I met her several times during the preliminaries but our real interview took place when I arrived to take up my appointment.

"Well, my dear, sit down. You have seen your room?"

She was a big and loose-fleshed elderly woman never seen out of uniform. Some circulatory disorder caused her to have constantly swollen feet and ankles and the discomfort of this state made her more sedentary than the matrons of large hospitals usually are. She had the suety look we all showed at that time from the poor diet, but there was no mistaking the force and competence inside her unimpressive physical envelope. I knew from experience that, always seated at her desk as she was, she must maintain a well-oiled information system. All positions of authority in the medical world are held by power people, from the senior consultants down to the ward nurse just appointed sister. That is not always true of some professions in which power is more obviously in evidence; but it is always the case with medicine that it attracts those who need and can exercise power over others.

"I understand you have requested permission to live out? That, of course, will not be possible at once, but we shall see, we shall see."

"Yes, ma'am." She had gone immediately to the center of the question mark posed by a new colleague. She pursed her wide, rather thick-lipped mouth and studied the papers in front of her, waiting for me in turn to declare myself.

"Dr. von Dettmarstein was very good to use his influence on my behalf."

"You have known him long?"

"Only since the spring, ma'am."

"Difficult for him, having his entire staff dismissed from under him! But that district commandant is no longer in the town, I hear?"

"They seem to change their units every few weeks."

"No doubt they have their little problems too." This with an indulgent smile for the Allied forces.

"I heard in the town that they were the last of the active

troops. The new district commandant is really a civilian in uniform and will stay."

"Yes. Yes. You have a home down there. It's rather a long way to go off duty."

"I hope to move my adopted son and Frau Lonski up to Hollenberg, ma'am."

"Ah! Your companion is not a relative, then? I somehow thought . . ."

"No, no relation, either of them. We all met on the journey, as it were."

"From Insterburg. Terrible, terrible."

"Not directly. I got separated and joined some others. I don't even know the name of the village. There was a young couple who remained behind because the baby was about to be born. Then there was an attack. A miracle we weren't *all* killed! Veronika, that is Frau Lonski, was washing the newborn infant. I was out in the court pumping water. The young man was trying to help his wife. They were blown to pieces, nothing left. We simply took the child with us and fled."

"Terrible, terrible."

"We managed to stay together until we reached here. Of course, there is no question of abandoning them now."

"Certainly not. You mean to adopt the child formally? You and Frau Lonski?"

"I have to. Formally, you understand. Frau Lonski is in her fifties, too old for the regulations. And partly crippled, too."

"Very noble of you," she said briskly. Having been told what she wished to know, she was putting papers together, forms she had been consulting and shuffling. Then her hands, plump, dry, large hands, stopped moving.

"But how did you feed the infant?"

"Ah!" The wide desk seemed to shift and the window light behind her dazzled me for a moment. "That was his little miracle.

We sheltered in the forest and there was a goat, a nanny goat. Providence meant him to live."

I thanked that poor dead creature once more in my heart for its usefulness.

"Providence, indeed." She was satisfied. "I see, I see. That was why you did not try to move fast. Of course, you stayed there as long as you could."

"Exactly. Until we fell in with the prisoners of war and they took care of us."

So Rolf's seamless story was woven, as near the truth as it could be kept. Even the goat really existed and really did nourish him. Only his shadowy parents were invented and there were too many thousand decaying bodies between Moscow and the Alps for it ever to occur to anyone either to identify or doubt them.

In other ways, naturally, I was much more questioned, by the foreign doctors. With them the effect was of staring across a tremendous crevasse, perhaps the path of an avalanche or the cleared rubble of a devastated city once weighty and extensive but now a pulverized heap of rubbish. These images come naturally from that time. I saw huge mountains for the first time then, glaciers, peaks of unchanging snow, the strange lifting and floating of wispy cloud above the world, pure distillation in pure air. I saw too the town and its attendant villages whole, undamaged. They made the wreckage behind me more real than memory. One broken wall on the snaky road into which a tank slid by mistake was still a topic of conversation there, seven months later. One unbroken wall might have provided remark where I had come from if there were anyone with surprise enough left in him to find anything strange. And there was another image stamped fresh into my mind, for I tried about that time to trace my mother and found that it was impossible for relatives to be provided with lists, whether of survivors or of the dead in Dresden. And when I appealed to my own professional association for any details they might have, someone sent me photographs, including some of the clearing operations. One of these made a particular impression, of long pyres like the orderly piles of split logs in autumn outside the houses in towns where, in my childhood, stoves were still fired with wood. The fuel was bought and stacked by the square meter, as these bodies were stacked in the picture.

I was very fond of my mother and sorry for her; she suffered more than I did from my father's final demonstration of self-righteousness. I mean final as far as we were concerned. I have no doubt it was far from final for his capricious conscience.

Possibly because it was the day following the arrival of these mementos, possibly because it was the first of a long series that became confused from their sameness, I recall clearly a conversation during the post-operation work. I was putting away the instruments in their appointed places. These were still slightly strange to me, not very different from what I was used to but just enough for me to need to concentrate on what I was doing. The heavy equipment was left from its former users but the foreign surgeons brought their own instruments with them. I say "former users" and not owners because, of course, it did not belong to the German Army either.

"D'you know what this hospital was before?" The junior assistant surgeon, like me, was in his first week there.

"It was a Wehrmacht base hospital."

"I really meant before the war."

"I believe it was a tuberculosis sanatorium."

"That accounts for those great wide terraces, then."

"I suppose so."

"You weren't here then?"

"Oh no. I'm not from here."

"Yes, somebody said you came from Prussia. So you're Prussian, are you?"

"No, I'm a Saxon. I was born just outside Bautzen."

"Oh." He sounded disappointed. Prussia, of course, was the

great, dark and distant land of the ogres. I already knew that. "But you came here from somewhere near Königsberg?"

"Yes. From Insterburg."

"I've never heard of it."

"Where did you come from, Captain?"

"Before here, you mean? I was at a base hospital in Stirling."

"I've never heard of Stirling, either."

He stared at me, resenting the comparison between a place in the infamous territory of Prussia with any link of his own.

"The Russians have got Bautzen now."

"There isn't much left of it for them to have."

I moved from the cabinet to the next room and began to load the sterilizers. The others were gone, I was a little behind with the work.

"These things are not the colonel's," I said half to myself. Someone in a hurry to get off had left half her own work for me to do. Being a stranger and younger than most of the others, this did happen to me at first.

"And of course, you're not supposed to do anything except for the colonel's operations!"

I glanced up, surprised at such an unprofessional remark and saw he was being sarcastic, with a look between dislike and the tentative beginning of flirtatiousness in his rather square face. His black hair was cropped like a fitting cap on his head, which was also squarish. All his bones seemed to be broad and wide-fitting, rather than the long-headed angularities of the northerners I was used to in recent years.

"The colonel would not be very pleased if his equipment was muddled up," I said, primly, I suppose.

"Your English is awfully funny sometimes."

"I dare say it is. No doubt it will improve. Do you speak German?"

"Only a few words."

"Well, you see?" But he did not see. I already regretted saying it, having no wish to get near enough to any of these people to quarrel with them. But, annoyingly, he persisted.

"What d'you mean—I see?"

Fastening a clip carefully, I said, "I mean that I am speaking your language, perhaps badly. But you cannot speak my language at all."

"Well! That's entirely different!"

"That's exactly what we Germans used to say to the Poles."

"*What!*"

I did not continue. This had gone too far already. I retreated to the operating room and this time he did not follow me there. But, stupidly, I had made an enemy. I should have to be very much more diplomatic and careful than this.

In spite of my care such conversations, often much more explicit than the first one, became an endless chain of repetition of which I can no longer separate the speakers and the occasions. This is quite unlike the events of the journey which could be brought back to mind with a painful wrench of deep reluctance from under the rubble of the past.

The propositions were always the same ones; that my people were the sole cause of the chaos the whole world was in and that every individual German was personally guilty of all the actions of government and organizations during the Nazi tyranny. This irrational concept was sometimes taken so far that it was once said to me, I do not recall by whom, that the two atomic bombs dropped on Japan were the fault of the Germans because "you began it all." If one remained silent under these accusations it was accepted as acquiescence in guilt and if one argued—for instance, that millions of the casualties in Poland and Russia were the responsibility of the Soviet authorities who had allied themselves with the Nazis when it suited them—then one was making impermissible excuses. There seemed to be no way out of this dilemma and I often wondered during those years what solution my former chief surgeon found, supposing that he survived the end of the war. The statements were always advanced as certainties, almost as absolutes, although they were really not even fact because where there was truth in them it was falsified by being spread over a millionfold variety of people and circumstances.

I recognized these propaganda stereotypes for I had myself been put through the machine of steady indoctrination and come out on the other side of it cured by the shock of brutal reality. That was my only advantage over the Allied officers, that I knew they were ignorant—and most of them remained ignorant—of the unreality of their cliché concepts. Every few weeks when a new doctor or administrator arrived at the hospital, the process of assertion, argument and occasionally the gradual recognition of complexity was repeated.

A few days after that first talk I was walking down to the town on my way to our room and was joined by the same doctor and a companion whom he introduced as Major Eastgrove.

I said "Good afternoon" to the major and then Captain Fraser asked me where I was going. Fraser, I now knew, was the name of the junior assistant surgeon while Major Eastgrove, it appeared, was in charge of the pathology laboratory.

"Fraser tells me you come from near Dresden," he began. "I was there for a month or so just before the war."

"Yes, she's a German," said Fraser. "Very much so."

I did not know what he meant with this, so I said nothing.

"You are not going back home, then?" Major Eastgrove was bent on making conversation.

"Not for the time being, anyway. I shall stay here, in Austria."

"I should have thought you'd want to go home," said Captain Fraser in a falsely teasing tone. "Haven't you got a family there?"

"I don't know," I said truthfully. "But it is hardly the time to travel far with a sick woman and a four-month-old baby."

"You have a child?"

"No, he is a foundling, from the trek." I was glad of the opportunity to say that.

"What is this word 'trek' I keep hearing?"

"Have I made a mistake? I thought it was the same word in English?"

"Well, there is a word trek in English, yes. Or it may be Dutch. I think it comes from South Africa, it means a journey by covered wagon I think, originally."

"Ah. Then I wasn't mistaken. Only we did not have a wagon."

"What did you have then?"

"Nothing," I was surprised. "We came on our flat feet." I had heard a soldier use that expression and it made them both laugh.

"From Dresden, here?" He sounded astonished.

"Oh no. Much farther. From East Prussia."

He was staring and I thought he did not believe me.

"So you can see that I don't feel like any more traveling."

"Indeed."

We walked together along the curve of the hill where the tank had slipped and demolished a wall. The day was hot with that oppression of accumulated heat that is characteristic of September; it was a dry summer and leaves were already coloring and falling from exposed trees.

"Summer is almost gone. It seems only a moment ago that spring came."

"Time passes fast when so much is happening." I suppose I did sound sententious, although for me the remark seemed like the most noncommittal platitude. In any case, they laughed again. I wondered what they would have said if I had told them the story of that journey.

"What were you doing in East Prussia?"

"Working."

"In a hospital?"

"Of course. Where else?"

"I thought you might have been in a camp," said Fraser.

"There weren't any nursing sisters at the front," I said, misunderstanding him. "Not, at least, until the front overtook us all."

"I meant another sort of camp. But of course, you have never even heard of concentration camps."

"You mean like Buchenwald? Of course I have heard of that camp. But there were no German nurses in places like that, you know."

"I love the way you simply admit it!" cried Fraser, pleased now that he had turned the talk in the direction he wanted.

"Admit what?"

"Leave her alone, Fraser," said Eastgrove quietly.

"Who, me?" with a finger pointed at his own chest. "She said it herself."

"Said what?" I asked. "I don't understand you. I've heard about Buchenwald because I knew someone who escaped from there."

"I suppose you helped him to get away?" He spoke with heavy sarcasm.

"Me? Oh no. I wasn't at home, I was in my first year at the University in Leipzig. But I remembered it well because afterward I had to leave medical school. That's why I became a nurse instead of a doctor."

"What are you talking about?" asked Fraser.

"Well, don't you know? I thought from the way you spoke that you knew the story."

"How should I know anything about your past life?"

"I thought you might have seen my nursing records."

"What did happen, then?" asked Eastgrove.

"My father hid this man, it was a former colleague of his. The police were just behind him when he got away. He'd been in the house for several days while they were getting him forged identity papers. So then we were all in trouble. I was barred from studying and my mother was arrested."

"And your father?"

"Oh, *he* got away. He could always get away with everything. He went to Stockholm."

"And you wouldn't have helped this fugitive, yourself?"

"I don't know. I don't think so. In any case, I wasn't there. But no, if I'm truthful no, I would not have sheltered him. I didn't know him. And I wanted to be a doctor. And then, there was Mother."

"What became of your mother?"

"I think she's dead. She was in Dresden, you see."

"Was she sent to prison?"

"She got two years for not reporting an escaped prisoner."

"When *was* all this?" Fraser sounded discontented. I was fated to do and say the wrong thing with Captain Fraser.

"That was—hm—1936."

"You don't seem very sure."

"It seems a long time ago, now."

"You must have been a child still," said Eastgrove thoughtfully.

"I was eighteen."

"That's very young. You probably would have helped this refugee, if you'd been at home at the time."

"No, I don't think so. I should have thought—I hope I should have thought—of my mother."

"But your father felt a responsibility to this unfortunate man?"

"Rather than to us. Yes. My father was a man who made gestures."

"Was? Is he dead, then?"

"Oh no, he's in Sweden still, he's the editor of a German-language newspaper."

"You could go to Sweden yourself, couldn't you?"

"Sweden? But how could I do that? I should have to leave Rolf and Veronika."

"They matter more to you than your real family, do they?" Once again I was trapped in a hopeless explanation. For I knew that even if Captain Fraser wished to understand me, he lacked the knowledge to do so. I should not have answered, perhaps, but by now I was annoyed and also upset by the familiarity and persistence of his questions, which would have been impertinent and insulting if it were possible for them to see me as a human being. But of course they did not; I was simply the defeated enemy.

"They *are* my family," I said and I could hear my voice trembling for I was by no means recovered from the journey and everything that happened during it. And the things before the journey, which I was hiding even from myself, made me deeply anxious and apprehensive with a new fear. I dreaded this questioning, which I could see would not stop no matter how many times I evaded some parts of it, for it might uncover the untouchable place and time. This dread was somewhere just under consciousness in my mind; I don't quite know how to describe this state but it was near enough to being admitted for me to feel its upward pressure as threatening to my balance. It was rather as if a plant were trying to extend its roots beneath a pavement which was cracking but still stiffly resisting.

The road came now to a fork and I could take an indirect way into the town from here which would bring me near where we lived. It was circuitous and I felt that weariness of the body and spirit that attends unhappiness even more than long privation; but better a longer and dustier walk than Captain Fraser and his nagging questions.

"I go this way," I said. "Goodbye." And was gone before there could be any suggestion made of their coming with me.

"You were rather beastly to the poor girl." I heard Major Eastgrove's light, casual tones behind me. If I had known the British better I should have recognized a rebuke in his apparently joking remark.

"My dear fellow, that's just what she wants you to think. Can't you see she's hiding something? There's something very fishy about her story."

"I dare say. But is it our business?" The voices were too faint to hear more, which was a relief. But when I reached home and took the sleeping baby from our landlady's kitchen I could do nothing for a little while, nothing more than sit still and hold him while weary tears ran over my face. Presently I pulled myself together and Rolf awoke when I moved him, so I began to talk to him while I washed his clothing. I called him "little traveler" and told him about my work and he stuffed his little fist into his mouth and waved his feet. Presently Ronni returned from her work and completed my comfort so that I forgot about Captain Fraser and his determination to blame me for the war.

Ronni could always provide that embracing goodness for me and for Rolf that arose out of her saintly nature. Her own griefs and worries she never spoke of, as I never mentioned mine. We talked only of the events of every day, and the people we saw. A deliberate but not artificial superficiality dictated our converse and we laughed a good deal in our trivial gossip; we were now, compared with the immediate past, happy and provided for. We talked all the time with the child and it was already a rule that one of us always held him or carried him when we were there. When neither of us was at home our landlady kept an eye on his welfare; we were fortunate in her.

That day Ronni was telling me of her employer and his commercial complications. We were laughing and Ronni was just explaining to Rolf as if he were an adult person how "her" black marketeer worried about his useful but ill-gotten goods, constantly fearing thieves, when we heard a knock at the outside door and a moment later the housewife put her kerchiefed head round the door and gave Ronni a special-delivery letter. It seemed almost miraculous to us to find the posts working again, our meager mail usually being one of the official forms needed to regulate our and Rolf's status in our new community. Both of us took it for granted that this letter must be connected with these processes and Ronni, who was engaged in cooking, dropped the envelope face downward on the table to be opened later at leisure.

I should perhaps explain that my assimilation into Austria took a different form from Ronni's. There was then a more or less tacit agreement by the Austrian authorities, which still existed or rather existed again, that any German left in Austria could elect to stay there and become Austrian. This was not completely formalized until some years later but the practice already existed. By this process both Rolf and myself separately became Austrian citizens. The case for Ronni was somewhat different. Her mother originally came from the Eger and was therefore an Austrian citizen by birth. She married a German from Teschen and Ronni in her turn married a Polish citizen from the Krakov district. Teschen like Eger and Krakov were part of Austria-Hungary until 1919, so that Ronni in two ways could establish a right to Austrian citizenship. The matter for her was a case of research; for me of naturalization. It was easiest for Rolf since he possessed no identity, no name and no parentage. His birth was registered in Bad Ischl and he was christened there as if—by one of the many empirical decisions of the time with which the curiously humane and devious Austrians quietly overcame chaos—he really had been born there. I was for some time rather suspicious of this somewhat casual acceptance, fearing that it might prove in the future to be unsound, but I need not have allowed my stricter German notion of officialdom to disturb my peace of mind.

With so many complicated arrangements being carried on simultaneously we spent a good deal of our leisure at that time answering official inquiries or waiting upon one or another local dignitary to obtain signatures, swear affidavits and eventually, to swear allegiance. Neither of us received any communication unconnected with these matters. Even the additional burden of my mother's unknown fate was, at the time I heard of it, not an uncomplicated grief but a setback in a labyrinthine journey back to respectability. Thus any letter was not personal news but yet another official document to be laid aside until we had time to puzzle it out in peace.

We ate our oatmeal, a major part of rations then, and Ronni picked up her letter. I was busy with Rolf and for a time I did not notice her stillness. But when I spoke and she did not answer I glanced up at her. She turned the sheet of paper and I saw that this time the communication was not a bureaucrat's form but a private letter written in a cramped hand closely and without margins on a crumpled sheet of what was originally packing paper. Paper of any kind was then unobtainable. As Ronni read her letter the tracks of her weeping shone in the wrinkles of her skin. She cried soundlessly and without distorting her features; the tears just ran down in a stream through the seams and furrows and dripped into a colorless apron. Her right hand lay on her lap inertly, the thumb twitching slightly and irregularly from rheumatism and with her left she held the letter up, the crumpled coarse paper shivering between her fingers. I have never forgotten the look of her hands at that moment; somewhere inside the puffy, veined dry usefulness of those hands was a lost grace left from the lines of youth. She laid the letter down tenderly on the bare board of our table and stroked it with her left hand, sensing the far distant reality of the writer, while her head remained erect and her faded eyes gazed straight before her unseeing, blind with the welling tears. I could see now that the writing was in Polish; Ronni had heard from her family. I remembered Iva's blank eyes, but was not frightened by the thought for that meager room, furnished only with the few sticks and scraps to be spared from the household of the very poor, was filled with a living beauty.

Presently the outer door of the cottage was opened and closed and the sounds roused Ronni, who shook her shoulders and sniffed. She felt for the torn rag in her apron pocket to blow her nose, and then got up stiffly and began to clear the used bowls and spoons off the table to wash them up. There was a shuffling tap at our door. I opened it and there stood Major Eastgrove with a cardboard carton in his hands. There may have been some affront in my expression, which certainly lacked the accepting kindness he would have received from Veronika. At any rate he ducked his tall head and muttered some apology, pushing the box into my hands, and backed away hastily, almost paralyzed by shyness.

The carton was half full of tins of various foods.

By the time I understood what was happening he was back at the house door, silhouetted in the mellow evening light. He smoothed a hand over his extremely light-colored hair so as to settle his forage cap neatly and half turned his head to send the sketch of an embarrassed smile toward our room. Then he dipped his head to go out and was gone, the sturdy old door closing behind him.

The round little landlady bounced at once out of her kitchen, her eyes popping out of her head with curiosity at the uniform.

"Who was that?" she asked in a hoarse whisper as if it were forbidden to ask.

"One of the doctors from the hospital."

"Oh. He didn't stay long, did he?"

I did not answer that, being occupied with the sight of the cylindrical tins in the carton to the exclusion of any other concern. When her look focused on the same target the landlady's eyes stretched wide and her curiosity changed to unbelief while her mouth slowly opened, showing her false teeth.

"Holy Mary," she whispered and came closer to make sure she saw aright. "It's food."

"Canned meat," I said, and found I was whispering too.

"You'd better lock it up!"

I took out one of the tins with its foreign inscription and held it out toward her. For a moment she just stared at it, and then wiped her hand reverently on her skirt before reaching out for it.

"You mean it?"

"Of course." There was nothing of course about it, needless to say. The tin was worth its weight in gold. But so was our landlady.

Under the meat tins was baby food. We were stunned with joy. There was enough for a whole week for Rolf. We could hardly believe it and kept passing the packets to and fro between us, laughing and crying at our incredible luck. A whole week without worry. That was a priceless gift.

"Oh, I say!" Major Eastgrove protested laughing, when I tried to thank him. "Don't exaggerate! It cost nothing. It's really nothing."

"Cost," I said. I shook my head. "You don't understand. You don't understand at all."

That was several days later. Major Eastgrove may not have understood but what he called the fuss I made told him something, and as long as he remained at the hospital Rolf did not need to go short of nourishment. This generosity was entirely altruistic, for a few days later something happened that dispersed any hopes he may have cherished that the usual reward for kindness by the occupiers toward the defeated would be forthcoming.

A group of younger doctors stood gossiping while I did something in the background, unnoticed by them, or at any rate unheeded.

"She was quite sweet. But, of course . . ."

"Wouldn't she, George?" Loud laughter.

"Oh yes. She did, all right. Only it sort of spoiled it, you know what I mean? To think she'd do it the first time of asking just for the price of an evening out? And greedy!"

"Did she take money?"

"No, said she'd rather have food from the shop. She had it all worked out, a list of things she wanted. It sort of depressed me."

"She doesn't look like a tart," objected a boy with red hair whom I saw then for the first time.

"They're all tarts." That was Captain Fraser. "Their morals are non-existent."

"Don't they ever say 'no'?" The red-haired youngster sounded wistful.

"Not to me!" said George and there was more laughter.

"I wish the military nurses hadn't been sent home. Now, with them you had to work for it."

"If you got it at all."

"Prettier, too."

"None of the girls here are pretty. Have you noticed that?"

"They have such pasty complexions. As if they never went out."

"And hygiene! Don't know the meaning of the word!"

"They say it's the lack of soap."

"Oh, any excuse!"

"Well, they all stink, anyway. Puts me off completely."

Major Eastgrove came in and I moved behind a screen so that he should not greet me. If I could have left the room, I would have gone but I was preparing for an emergency operation for the colonel himself.

"Who stinks?" he asked.

"The girls here."

"They haven't any soap and they can't change their clothes."

"They've been getting at you, old boy. They all say that. And *why* don't they change their clothes? Sordid lot."

"They haven't got anything to change into, most of them."

"Yes, they're all pathetic enough, now. I wonder what they were all doing a year or so ago!"

"*Kinder, Küche, Kirche,* that's what they were doing."

"If they weren't beating up concentration-camp inmates."

"If you dislike them so much," said Major Eastgrove, "why do you take them out? You could always ignore them."

"We're not all happy celibates like you, Major. Got to get a bit of frat occasionally."

"Specially as it's forbidden. That adds to the fun, of course."

"Forbidden fruit."

"Figs for preference."

"Why figs?" The red-headed boy.

"Ah, you weren't in Italy!"

"Look out," said Eastgrove suddenly. "Sister Anna is there."

I cursed him under my breath.

"Oh, is someone there?" George asked, without turning his head.

"Have you been there long, Sister?" asked Eastgrove, coming toward the screen.

"Yes."

The man who mentioned Italy now made a joke in broken Italian on the word *fegato*, and I felt my pasty complexion go even paler than it usually was. I looked at the clock. We were nearly two minutes late. There was no help for it now, and I came forward into the room, passing between the group.

"Sister doesn't like our joke," said George.

"It was only about fruit. Figs," said the man who had come from Italy.

"Your Italian is not very good," I said, neglecting to mention that my own knowledge was confined to the minimum picked up on a few weeks' holiday. "*Fegato* does not mean figs, it means liver."

At this moment the colonel entered, fully dressed, but without his mask and gloves. I held out the tray to him.

"Good morning, Sister. Good morning, gentlemen." His outstretched hands stayed where they were as he took in the atmosphere. "You're not ready, Eastgrove?"

"Coming, sir," said Eastgrove in a rather muffled voice as he scrubbed at his hands.

"What's going on in here?" The colonel's voice sounded the beginning of annoyance. He was, naturally, not used to being kept waiting.

"Nothing, sir," said George with emphasized surprise.

Someone mumbled that it was only a joke, we didn't mean anything. I saw George and the man who had been in Italy fix the culprit with frantic glares, but it was too late.

"Ah, a joke. I can imagine." The colonel's voice grated like broken ice.

"Sister has no sense of humor, I fear, sir," said Fraser, slyly.

"I wish to make a formal complaint, sir," I said.

There was a murmur of horror.

"But, really, Sister, we didn't even know you were there . . ."

"I do not mean your dirty sex jokes in bad Italian." I looked up at the colonel, whose eyes were on me. "And you did know I was there. But for you I do not exist. No, it is not that. But I will not allow it to be said that I have no sense of humor."

I was concentrating on what I said, having trouble getting it out correctly in my funny accent.

"Sir?" I said without waiting for an answer. "Your gloves, sir. The anesthetist's light is on, sir."

Fortunately many of the hardest medical words to say are basically Latin so that I knew them. I adjusted my mask and moved past the colonel into the main operating theater.

"Phew!" said a hushed voice. "Remember not to take *her* on again, chaps."

We were over two hours in the theater, patching together the mangled body of an officer who had crashed his jeep into a ten-ton truck on a mountain road. But the colonel did not forget the incident. As I helped him off with his gown and gave him his cigarettes, he was just going to say something and changed his mind. Instead he walked into the next room, bending his head to light his much-needed cigarette.

"Eastgrove. Barrett. You—what's your name?"

"Fraser, sir."

"Don't lounge about like that when I speak to you, Fraser." Captain Fraser was, needless to say, standing at attention.

"No, sir."

"If Sister is agreeable, I shall take this matter no further. At least, not for the moment. But I should be grateful to you, Eastgrove, if you would see to it that my opinion is known among those gentlemen not now present."

"Yes, sir."

"My view is that Sister possesses a marked, a very marked sense of humor. Good day to you."

As the door closed behind the colonel's stiff back, I was relieved to see that two of the three officers in the room were openly laughing. I laughed too. It struck me as genuinely funny, what the colonel had said. My sense of humor was only impaired by the thought that Major Eastgrove would not now continue his gifts of baby food for Rolf. But I was wrong. The little scene only prevented him from any attempt to profit from his generosity; which, when one thinks of it, was rather unfair.

CHAPTER 20

It appeared to me, unschooled as my social and personal reactions still were, that it was my own initiative in going over to the attack which procured a noticeable change of attitude in the junior officers toward me.

When the captain they called George invited me to show him the old imperial villa and drink coffee with him, he spoke with such courtesy that I replied equally civilly.

"I cannot tell you much about such places, Captain," I said. "As you know, I am not from here. A local young lady would make a better guide."

"But you will come out for a cup of coffee, won't you?"

"You are very kind. Thank you, but it is not allowed and I do not want to break the rules."

"Oh, but I'm sure that doesn't apply to you, Sister Anna," he urged. They were beginning to use the custom of adding the Christian name to the formal address, I noticed. "That really doesn't matter."

"It does to me," I said, and was pleased with this answer.

"Well, another time, then." He was visibly embarrassed at the ill success of his peace offering and I was sorry because he was really a nice boy and, like many young men, bragged about his sexual prowess more than he put it to the test.

Captain Fraser and he went off down the corridor together and after a moment I followed them, but they did not hear me.

"Leave her alone, you fool," said Fraser. "Just to have the fun of teasing her a bit isn't worth it. You'll be in real trouble with the colonel next time. You don't want to get transferred."

"I just didn't want her to think she's got it all her own way, under the old man's wing."

"He made it pretty plain, I should have thought."

Up to that moment I thought the colonel's statement a few days before was simply a joke, a method of easing an awkwardness among the staff. He sounded so quiet, after that one frigid comment on the subject of their jokes, that I had evidently misunderstood the incident.

Major Eastgrove's voice called from the door of the surgeons' dressing room and I went over to him.

"Do you know if any of the Austrian staff speak French well, Sister?"

"French, Major?"

"No need to look like that. It's the chap we operated on, you remember, the one who smashed his jeep up. Didn't you know he's French? He's not so hot today and nobody seems to understand what he's trying to say."

"I didn't know." I was trying to gain time, to decide whether I should admit to speaking that language well myself.

"He seemed to stand the operation rather well, but after his wife came yesterday he's all over the place. Temp. up, pulse fluttering, vomited twice, ward sister says."

"He shouldn't have had a visitor so soon," said Fraser.

"Well, what's one to do? She's his wife, and she made quite a scene. She'd come all this way with special passes and God knows what for priorities."

They used these idioms and slang phrases all the time and sometimes I found it difficult to understand, not only what they meant, but how serious they were. This uncertainty of mine was deepened by the realization that I had failed to understand the colonel three days before.

"And what's more, you don't appear to know, Eastgrove, she's still here."

"She's not in his room now, damn it, is she?"

"I don't know, but I saw her a few minutes ago in the main hall."

"I'd better go and have a look," said Eastgrove quickly.

"I'll come with you, Major," I offered. "I speak French." From his look I saw that the matter was serious. He certainly was not joking now, and I spoke out of the habit of putting the welfare of the patient before personal feeling. I knew, of course, that the foreign officer's life was by no means certain, having been present when his injuries were patched up. From loss of blood alone he was in danger, in spite of transfusions.

"Yes, come along, Sister. Fraser, alert the intensive team at once. The oxygen's been taken out of his room."

The injured officer was in a private room, the shutters closed and with a screen between the door and his bed. Even as the door was opened I could hear a feminine voice raised almost hysterically. The shock of hearing the language for the first time in a year without the merciful dimness of parturitional trauma was so great that for an instant I stopped dead and Eastgrove, a step behind, collided with me.

"I'm sorry," I stammered, and heard my own voice speaking French, so instantly and finally did the sound of an authentic Paris voice transfer me into the past.

Eastgrove moved past me and as he saw my face his look changed to astonishment and fear.

"What's the matter, Sister?"

"Nothing, sir. You must get the lady out of here at once."

"What's she saying? Though the tone is enough!"

"She seems to be reproaching him for something. But that doesn't matter."

I advanced around the screen, my nerves not completely under control so that I brushed against its frame and it swayed dangerously.

"Who on earth pulled that screen . . ." I did not hear the rest of Eastgrove's complaint for professional horror filled me with energy at the sight of the woman half lying across the bed. She was gesticulating, weeping with anger, her voice rising shrilly as she took in that she was interrupted. As always with hysterics, it was essential to act fast.

I pulled her upward off the injured patient with one powerful tug at the arm nearest me. I was standing over her and could apply a lifting action which, added to surprise, removed her from the bed altogether.

She screamed wildly, beside herself with egotistic fury.

"Outside, madame. Instantly. Nurse!"

"Yes, Sister."

"Take the lady outside. See that she is looked after. Get her off the corridor, at once."

Eastgrove already had the patient uncovered and the oxygen apparatus was being wheeled in. The room was now full of people moving swiftly in well-trained purposefulness.

"Swabs," he said through his teeth. "Sister, fix the saline drip quickly. She's pulled it right off. Hurry. What are you playing with that oxygen mask for? D'you think you've got all day? Hurry! He'll bleed to death. The chest wound is wide open."

This was a deep and long laceration from the jeep windshield. The pressure of the woman's body had undone half the work of the colonel's skill, the rib strapping was of course disturbed, and from the red foam now appearing at the patient's mouth his lung injury was bleeding heavily.

"Wouldn't it be better to get him into the theater?" Fraser was stuttering with anger and distress.

"Too late. Sister, get the emergency trolley down here. Go yourself. These fools will forget something."

I ran. Unheard-of breach of discipline, but I ran.

"Anesthetist, Fraser!"

Bells rang, the anesthetist on duty passed me, struggling with his gown, the orderly with his equipment almost knocked me down. I knew the trolleys were in order for I checked them myself, every shift at least once.

Two more orderlies appeared from nowhere and we had the apparatus down the corridor before anyone could have counted fifty. To an unskilled eye all would have looked like routine and order. To me the whole movement showed the adrenalin exertion of a disaster. And it was touch and go. We nearly lost him. At one moment I thought he was gone and so did the anesthetist, I could tell from his eyes.

Somehow we pulled him through for the moment and a nurse was stationed inside his room again, as for the first days, while an orderly took up guard outside to prevent any further disturbance. I stayed on duty myself in order to watch over the patient for an hour or so, in case of a relapse on his recovering consciousness when he might try to move and start the lung hemorrhage once more. I could tell him in something like his own tone and accent that he must remain absolutely still and quiet if he wished to live. For this purpose I sat down with some weariness in the ward sister's room and waited for the nurse on duty to press the bell to warn us.

In the moment that I was seated and doing nothing, waiting for the coffee promised by an orderly, I felt my own strange inertness, as if I were no longer of flesh and blood and nerves, but of some heavy, densely solid matter, perhaps a weighty kind of wood or even lead. I did not feel tired in any ordinary sense, nor faint, neither did I tremble. I just felt so heavy and dull that it might well be I should never move again but just sit there forever with my forearms lying straight out on the table before me and my dim eyes half closed.

"Come on, Sister, ducks. Drink it up, now," said the orderly in his strange accent. I heard myself answer his kindness automatically, and so as not to hurt his feelings drank down the coffee without tasting it.

"Poor kid," I heard him say outside, "I think meself they're half starved, sir."

"Well, they started it, didn't they?" answered Fraser's voice.

"I doubt if she did, sir," replied the man pertly. "Stands to reason, don't it—she can't be more than twenty-five or so now. Must have been a kid when that Hitler got started."

"It's not Hitler, Barnes, it's the Germans, all of them!"

"Ah, I expect you're right, sir," said the man, conciliatory. "Poor kid."

It was not for the first time nor the last that I noticed how much more humane sometimes uneducated people are than their "superiors." But at that moment it did not interest me. I only remembered it afterward.

It must have been a long time before the bell in the ward sister's room gave two sharp burrs to signal me. I pushed myself to my feet without my will telling me to. As Captain Fraser might have said, German devotion to orders without thinking or reasoning. I was quite stiff from my long, motionless wait.

The screen was now in its proper position. I saw as I came around it that the officer's head was unbandaged. He was visible for the first time. The black hair against the immaculate linen, the dark skin, the cranial structure, forehead, eye sockets, cheekbones, were a family likeness.

I knew even as I felt the inward blow of shock that it was not really Jean-Martin who lay there. It was another Frenchman of similar stock, of the same physical type. I knew that. But I could not move for a moment; again that weight rooted me where I was. I was a stock, a stone, with a black hollow inside it where something felt pain. The pain of broken glass grating its sharp edges together. The smudged dark eyelids fluttered, sunk unnaturally deep in bone hollows. The upturned pupils rolled down for a second and up again. A moment later the eyelids fluttered again, unwillingly, as if stuck together.

I touched the sunburnt languid hand on the surface of the bed-cover. It is always essential to give comfort with physical contact in such cases. Sometimes a hardly palpable pressure of the hand gives a patient courage to live, for the surrender to near-death, the pull of the grave, must be penetrated. I leaned closer, but not directly over the head, and the eyes now saw me. I forced my own look into his, willing his will, demanding some spiritual response to life.

"You must keep perfectly still," I said, very quietly but in the tone of an order. "Do not try to move. I am putting the bell-push under your hand here. The only movement you may make is to press it with one finger. Do you understand? Only with one finger."

I waited until he could give me the feel of his response. The indrawn lips moved minimally, a tiny puff and fall. The eyes were no longer totally blank; he knew and accepted my message. Those eyes so like the other eyes, were half-dead here and now, but somewhere else in another time they were filled with a snapping, crackling vitality, a dark glitter of liveliness that laughed into mine. Yet this man before me in the bed was no more of a likeness to Jean-Martin than, perhaps, a cousin might have been.

In the whirl of memory I vaguely felt I must have conjured up the scent that came through the hospital smells in his room, a moist sweet scent of wild violets in wet grass. The ghost of that perfume made me aware of aberration and therefore of the need to pull myself together because this man was a patient and might well die. Very carefully, so that I did not jerk his hand, I lifted my own and left the bell-push in place. There was a faint, faint motion in the slack muscles of his fingers.

"It's all right," I said softly. "Don't worry, there is someone here and I shall come back. We shall not leave you alone." The dark eyes opened again and I knew what he wanted. "I shall come back. You must believe that. Don't fret. Just keep quite still. Now you will sleep. Gently, now, you will sleep."

In a few moments the sedatives had taken their effect and he was unconscious again. I moved noiselessly away. Beyond the screen I asked the nurse on duty for strapping plaster, cut off a length and returned to fix the cord of the bell-push so that it should not shift under his hand.

"The lady left her scarf, Sister, when you threw her out. Will you take it down to the office, or shall I?"

"You will not leave this room. I'm going downstairs, so I'll take it."

I put out a hand, my head still turned to the patient, and she put into it the special scrunchy soft crispness of real silk which was the source of the sweet smell of violets. I lifted it to smell the wild wet odor and was back more than eighteen months in Insterburg in the sunny spring wind, standing on the concrete path by the wall of the nurses' quarters, and Jean-Martin stood before me with a few hedge violets in his brown, muscular hand and his eyes laughed with confident challenge into mine.

I heard myself saying in another world, "You'll be in trouble if anyone sees you here." He shrugged, laughing aloud. I said, "Who are you? I haven't seen you about." And he said, "But I've seen you. I'm one of the prisoners working in the gardens, we volunteered to have something to do." And he put into my hand, which had raised itself without my volition, the violets. I glanced at the badges on his faded summer tunic which looked as if it had been in the sea for some time but I only did that because I was abashed by the glinting conspiracy of his eyes. I was not a shy girl, but neither was his look the nervously flirtatious grin I was used to and that might have assured me of my own mastery over the situation. It was he who was sure, he had the smiling eagerness of a man who had never been refused.

From that day on I saw him everywhere, all the time. With the inevitability, the certainty, which is the hallmark of the authentic love affair, he and I were constantly meeting by the sweet dispensation that either makes or is made by lovers. In all true love affairs it happens in the early stages. Long before either plans for meetings, the drive toward each other so arranges matters even in the most unpromising circumstances that the magical and yet confidently expected encounters take place. What seems simply to occur of itself is, we know, the rising intention of the man and the woman to go where each knows the awaited being is likely to be, and every time the intention is realized the certainty grows and the atmosphere becomes so charged with desire and longing that it is felt by everyone around. We know this afterward but when it happens in youth we are ravished by an unknown and mysterious expectation that wipes out any previous experience or transmitted knowledge.

Difficulties, barriers, opposition, they heighten and strengthen the intensity of feeling. Ours was a love surrounded by lethal hazards, penal threats, and inspired by the loom of the approaching catastrophe. Such words are devalued nowadays. In the spring of 1944 they were real and immanent presences and the sounds of their repetition now are inadequate to express the menace, the danger of our situation. They were foreknowledge of a cataclysm it was forbidden to speak or to think of, which when it came in its turn to us surpassed in horror anything that has ever happened in Europe. To say that Jean-Martin and I were doomed is meaningless this year; in those days it was the most obvious fact.

There were many about us who from cowardice or envy or from the insane unreality that gripped millions, would denounce us, he to execution and me to ten years' hard labor. Jean-Martin was a prisoner of war, not only an enemy but one of the defeated who had refused to admit a craven peace with the conqueror and therefore to his captors a breaker of their armistice with his country. And I was a pure-blooded German, the blond vessel of the master race and its future. For rabid party men and their police our crime was the despoiling of a vestal virgin with all the lubricious hatred of sexual jealousy added to the orgy of fear and violence that raged all over the world.

Not for an instant did I forget this, not from that first meeting outside the nurses' home in the blowy April sun. It was always there, another presence with us. I had lived with it for years, since my father took it into our home with the escaped camp inmate. It cost me my profession then, decided upon since I was able to read. Only by the acquiescence of friends and the need of the régime for nurses was I allowed to train even for that secondary, subaltern position in medicine. It cost my mother two years in prison and a laboring existence in a factory after her release; indirectly it caused her death in the holocaust of Dresden. It cost me my home; after my father's defection our house went to a party functionary. It followed me until I left Insterburg with Jean-Martin and even more after that day when we became hunted fugitives at any rate in theory, of the Gestapo and the military security police although in fact there were too many desertions for all the culprits to be followed up. It was in my record still, after the war ended, converted by defeat into an advantage. Yes, I knew what I was doing. The knowledge intensified my passion for Jean-Martin to madness.

Fear heightened desire when I knew that I would come around *this* corner and he would be there, that I would pass through *this* door and his head would turn, his eyes glitter at me. I knew before I went off duty that he was moving *then* toward the turning off the roadway into the lane where I should chance upon him by no chance. When I went into the town I could feel him there in front of me and there he quite illicitly, but unchallenged, was. And one day he said, "You must arrange it so that we can talk," and I said, terrified, "I daren't," and he said, "Of course you dare."

It took a week of quiet intrigue and then I changed rooms with another nurse at the end of the lower corridor. The end room was separated from the others by a shaft built after the building was finished, for a food lift. And just outside it was the passage window into which Jean-Martin could easily climb.

CHAPTER 21

It was a small room, for one nurse only, uncoveted in spite of privacy because of the rattling of the food lift and by its narrowness. I invented insomnia to make my claim good and got heavy curtains as an unasked concession as well. After that I suffered from lack of sleep in heavenly reality, although reality is not quite the word since the world about me and myself were veiled in a dazing dream. Nothing in past encounters prepared me for love as Jean-Martin taught it to me. The precariousness of each day and night, the constant danger, raised our amorous passion to a piercing brilliance; we were consumed with our own insatiable desire until of me at any rate there was nothing left except Jean-Martin. He took possession of me in the biblical sense; I was mad and lost in love as the insane are possessed by devils.

Moments of peril arose and were dealt with by a boldness and wit that were not mine at all, but inspired in me from the unquenchable drive to be with and to enjoy Jean-Martin. One morning in June when even the windows wide open to the summer air and light had not dispersed his presence from me, the administrative sister came into my room for some reason.

"I should have thought that lift would cause insomnia, not otherwise," she said as the cage bumped to a stop.

"After two nights I didn't even hear it," I said. "Like any regular sound."

"Yes, it's quite true," she agreed, nodding so that her glasses gleamed. "I don't hear the trams on the other side, either. You remember when that accident happened in the road? I was absolutely unable to tell the board of inquiry whether a tram had just gone past or not."

She looked past me to where, as it appeared to me, two quite clear hollows showed in my pillow. I knew that she was not quite satisfied. She could feel something strange and penetrating in the air of my room.

"There he goes, on duty," I said and pointed out of the window.

"Who?" She craned.

"Why Major Schneider!" I said, "but you knew, of course!" And I giggled with that slight nervousness proper to such a remark in front of a woman so much older and responsible too, for discipline.

She shook her tight gray head at me indulgently.

"Ah, you girls!"

Poor Schneider. He was killed the next day in the first bombing of the hospital. It may have been at that exact moment when I was standing at my window, fastening my stiff cuffs to go back on duty while Jean-Martin lay behind me on the bed. That was the moment when the wall opposite, fifteen meters away, simply disappeared. Every closed window was splintered, but mine was open and I was blown back and flung against the far wall but otherwise unharmed. Like everything else outside our two selves, the bombing was quite unreal; my only concern was the problem of getting Jean-Martin out while the nurses' home was in uproar. I was not even afraid then of the bombs or of fire; only of being discovered and losing my joy that had taken over my whole life.

"Just lock your door when you go out," he said. "I'll stay here until I can drop out of the window."

312

"But if anything happens?"

"In the disorder nobody would be surprised to see me." He meant if the building were hit.

"What if they inspect the rooms for damage?"

"They'll come and ask you for the key," he pointed out, knowing the German exactness in keeping rules so precisely that we both laughed, holding our hands over our mouths in case we were audible outside. Later that day I suddenly thought clearly of the danger of discovery and began to shake with terror so that I was obliged to put down the instrument I was holding. The other theater personnel took it for granted that my "shakes" were caused by delayed shock after the air raid. God knows, in those days there was always a good cause for fear.

And the next day I did begin to fear the bombs, in real earnest. Jean-Martin reported that one of the prisoners working in the garden had been decapitated by a huge metal splinter. He expressed this event with a graphic sideways slice of his hand, palm upward. I can still see that movement now, neat, brutal, humorous, accompanied by a lift of his chin.

"So!" he said softly, "like a guillotine, and he's gone!" He put out that sinewy brown hand and slid it behind my neck, grasping my short back hair, and pulling my mouth against his, laughing secretly the while. I have seen Rolf make just such gestures, the image of his father whom he never saw. The taut, sprung vitality of his physical make-up is exactly his father's; he even holds his chin with that inimitable tilt while his dark eyes narrow and spark with enjoyment. The sheer animal happiness of a man who knows how to live is in him.

But after he told me of the fate of that unknown Frenchman in the air raid I lived in fear that one of the manifold accidents of war would take Jean-Martin from me and I should be left alone. And several prisoners injured on that day were operated on, one of them dying on the operating table to point the warning.

All about us during that summer, the world about us, slowly

built and taken for granted for a thousand years, was breaking apart under the tremendous blows that split buildings, trees, men, institutions, the brown earth itself, into fragments. We took these great and terrible events into our consciousness only gradually, at first as added hindrances and then as dangers that might rob one of us of the other; finally as what they were, the end of the world from which we must escape.

We could hear the guns, grumbling distantly to begin with and then thundering. Almost every night was made hideous by aircraft. The town and everything in it was being pulverized as if a giant pestle crushed it to its elements in a mortar. Every day and night familiar faces disappeared. Dead, mutilated or fled they were found or not found, their smashed bodies were recovered or remained under the ever-growing piles of rubble so that no one, not even the authorities, knew what might have happened to the missing. People went out of their minds from the incessant thunderous noise. People hanged themselves from the dressing-gown hooks behind their doors out of the fear of death or of the horror worse than death that threatened us. People avoided the eyes of their fellows and then were gone and were railed at as traitors if their going was known of. That madness too continued until in the late summer it gradually stopped, even among party members, except when they knew themselves overheard. Not that the cessation of idiotic slogans, empty phrases of the party and the Führer meant the end of danger from those quarters. Like scorpions biting their own extremities they were enraged by the inexorable movement of despair and revenge that threw its shadows and its great storms of noise and ruin before it as if all the oceans of the world were turned into molten white-hot lava and a tidal wave were about to engulf us all.

Their prophecies of victory could now be heard in every mind almost audibly echoing from the past years, with the denial that even much lesser defeats than this total destruction could ever happen. Now those loud claims of victory could be heard in retrospect to have had from the start a sound of protestation; but the unbelief that was always in them and in the voices that shouted them was now all they contained. What was now upon us was from the beginning in September 1939 always there, looming behind everything that happened, threatening constantly to become visible. Since Stalingrad it stood in the dark distance of every mind, a great cliff or block of warning, and now it advanced with earth-shaking bounds upon us; the reality of a mythological doom seemed now to have been known for years as the punishment for hubris.

This approach sent its reek of sulphur before it, penetrating into our dream state of privacy, and the day came when in a momentary pause of the interminable strain of the racket we turned to each other as if we had been discussing the question for weeks, and said in the same breath that it was time to go.

"I know where and I know how. I can arrange transport most of the way whenever I need it."

"You can?" I had been worrying about that.

"There are plenty of the boys asking for letters from us that we've been well treated. That's no problem. But you have to get some sort of pass, permission, or what have you."

"Permission?"

"To go away, darling! Think of road blocks."

It proved simpler than could have been expected. Six months before it would have been unthinkable, but other people besides myself were changed during that summer and in my withdrawal from my surroundings I had egotistically overlooked that obvious fact.

I was really feeling wretched, physically. It was not entirely a trick. A sensation quite new to me, like that of having overeaten, and a queer lurching of balance that made me dizzy and uncertain reminded me of sailing excursions made in the last year or so in the Haff. Once or twice we took our small vessel out into the Baltic swell outside the Mehring and now I felt again that sense of my element having been changed from sheltered waters to the swing and drive of open seas. This was internal, but I thought it part of my hyperstimulation combined with lack of sleep, tension from work, from constant bombing and from love. I was wrong; of course I was pregnant.

I reported to our doctor, who was a physician hardly known to me, my health being so stable. Even before he made any examination he made his diagnosis.

"But you are pregnant, Sister Anna!"

I stared with unbelief, although nothing could be more likely. I just had not thought of it.

"But what makes you think that, Doctor?"

"I can tell by looking at you, of course," he said irritably. "But we'll soon make sure."

I knew he was a party man. No need to fear moral lectures. And I knew that various hints dropped by me were believed and the Major Schneider killed by a bomb was "known" to have been my lover. Somehow I could never have actually said that this was so; as with the administration sister, I just allowed it to be the case. This made it quite natural for me to burst into tears caused in fact by the startling news and by the tense excitement of our plot.

"A few days' leave and you'll be perfectly all right," he said after examining me. "You've had a bad time lately. The terror-bombing too doesn't make life easier. But your general condition is excellent. All you need is a couple of nights of undisturbed sleep. I will telephone your chief. Don't worry about anything, the child is the important thing."

He meant, of course, a future soldier for the Führer and I did not disabuse him.

The senior surgeon was a different matter. His concurrence was not only necessary for a leave pass; it was also important to me that he should not think ill of me. And he knew me through and through from over two years of constant work together. He was also a somewhat stern believer; not in the Nazi jargon which meant some kind of pantheism or alternatively an imprecise hint that could cover Christian belief for use when speaking to party members. The kind of dishonest hint I used over the identity of my lover. No, my chief was an old-fashioned Christian and an uncompromising one. I was a little afraid of him for he had the kind of piercing knowledge which seems to be a part of a strongly held faith and which I later knew in Ronni. The party view of an illegitimate child was not likely to be his. And I knew I could not lie to him, either directly or by the method so much used at that time by me and millions of others. He would know at once that I lied.

So I was frightened as I went into his room, and kept my eyes down so that he should not see through them into me. But he was not at his desk. He stood staring out of the window with his tall back toward the door, hands folded behind him and his head bent. What he looked at I could not see, perhaps at nothing.

He knew who it was and said quietly, "I'm sorry about this, Anna."

I did not answer but fidgeted with uncontrollably restless fingers at the edge of his table.

"Is there anything I can do?"

"I don't think so, Chief." I whispered without meaning to, and then cleared my throat.

"The papers are on my desk. I've signed them. You can take them with you."

"Thank you. I . . ."

He turned now so that I was faced with the full power of his character, just as I feared.

"Don't say you're sorry, Anna. Because you're not. We both know that."

"But I am sorry. To have let you down."

"There is not much more to be done here," he said, understanding what I meant. "We too will be leaving here quite soon, I hear."

"Is the base to be moved back, then?"

"Not moved back," he corrected and smiled at my slip. "You know we don't move back."

I was forced to look at him then. We were too familiar with each other for me to insult him now by pretending not to understand him. I felt a deep and painful love and respect for him at that moment.

"Yes, that's better," he said quietly. "That's more like you. Listen to me. What matters now is only that a few people should survive who can carry over into the future what we once were, what we have stopped being in the last few years. That's all."

I said nothing.

"Do you know what I mean? I can't use the old words any longer. I can't even use the word 'German.' That has been smothered in filth by people like . . . I won't name anyone. Not *that*, either. Silence is the only dignity left to us. Remember that, Anna."

"Yes."

"I shall pray for you. Perhaps we shall meet again. Afterward. Somewhere."

He was saying something that he would not and could not put into words. Not out of fear but out of the dignity he had spoken of. I stared at him, we searched each other's eyes in silence. I knew that he was aware of everything and that he was telling me to escape. What I had so much feared in this meeting was happening, only I was no longer afraid of him. Or do I mean something more difficult to put into words? I was no longer trying to hide anything; I did not need to and all was understood. I shall never know whether he could identify Jean-Martin by name and person; but he knew essentially and accepted it as true love, the absolute feeling that it was. He knew I was given forever and no priest or parson could have made that state anything but what it was. He knew it better than I did myself. I have learned since then by my own observation of human nature that such overpowering emotions cannot be disguised from anyone who has himself once been enthralled in their enchantment.

Now we offered each other our hands and no more was said. He looked down at my practical little paw and I saw it too as from outside, half the size of his long-fingered, muscular hand, the hand of an artist. I put my left hand into his as well and he gripped me hard for a moment with all his energy. That was the only blessing on my marriage that was given and the only confirmation by authority I needed.

I did not know at that time that I needed anything of the sort; that is hindsight. But later it was of the utmost meaning to me, because of what happened. On the day it took place my only thought was to get back to my room and open the windows wide as our usual signal. Jean-Martin could look up from his gardening and see that I expected him. I could not wait for his appearance. The order for my leave charged me with a joyous energy of such power that I could not keep still for a moment and my whole body quivered in every nerve.

The news that one of us had been granted official leave for ten days spread within minutes; nobody had gone on holiday for months. The daily disappearances by death, injury or desertion were of a wholly different order from this event, which belonged to the legitimate convention of our service and was therefore comfortingly ordinary in its insane implication that all was under normal control. Nurses came in and out of my room in the next hour or so in a stream to take part in this reassurance, than which nothing in all the crazy duplicity of that time could have been more typically false. Chatter and laughter filled the corridor outside as if a coffee party were going on and made it impossible for me to speak to Jean-Martin, who came up the stairs carrying flowers for Matron on the next floor. Nobody but myself noticed his passage. Like me later in the Allied hospital at Hollenberg, the foreign prisoner went unregistered, practically invisible. There may well have been one among the nurses, orderlies and cleaners who came to congratulate me who was capable of divining that my state of mind was not that of a girl who had lost a lover only a few weeks before. But the febrile atmosphere of disaster, the clinging to the remnants of normality in the midst of threat and death, made the hysterical sociability unnoticeable, even commonplace. Precisely what no one present could allow was the recognition of the real.

A convoy of ambulances was to join a hospital train at an outlying station that night. The main-line railway station in Insterburg was in a condition of wreckage, like those of all large German towns and cities by then. Sometimes trains came and went through them, but we were quite used to detours after serious attacks and to catch trains at suburban halts was as unremarkable as the bombing itself. Life had restricted itself for months now to interminable hours in the operating theater alternating with hastily arranged outings into the surrounding country for an hour of quiet by whatever transport offered itself. I doubt if anyone would have thought it strange to see me leave the once rural railway buildings; a change of time and place was so frequent in any journey. In the bustle of loading the wounded for evacuation after dark a nurse in military clothing was just a part of the scene. As I walked quickly away and turned the street corner off the station square an orderly saluted and I returned his salute and called a greeting as I went. I felt no duty then. I was simply going on leave and did not even need to face the thought of desertion.

CHAPTER 22

I made my way through the streets straggling into the countryside to where a shabby tavern had once or twice offered myself and other nurses undisturbed sleep in the rare night off-duty. There were hours of waiting to be got through and in order to remain unremarkable I asked for a room to sleep in although I was so tensely excited that the thought of inactivity was unbearable. It was a shelter I had used before, at the back of the house, away from the little terrace where people sat in the sun. On that side I might meet someone else from the base hospital among the mainly uniformed customers. My small square of privacy faced northeast and was chill from sunlessness; it was a cool day with a westerly breeze sharper than usual for September. I pushed open the single window and the worn lace curtain flipped against the casement. In one side of the glass I could see the reflections of trees shaking their foliage, dusty now with late summer and shimmering in the uneven pane. The other side moved to and fro as the wind caught it, sometimes showing a corner of the courtyard below and sometimes a small meadow where scattered figures slept outstretched. But after a few minutes a dull, far distant thudding began and I closed the windows again, to shut it out. At once the stuffy, unused air of the room rose around me, the smell of the bare board floor, dust from the rag mats, the whitewashed plaster faintly sour, and an indescribably muggy warm odor of the feather quilt folded back to the foot of the high bed. Its cotton cover was a faded red and white check and the undersheet and pillows were of thin worn but clean white calico. Inside the whole house an afternoon quiet reigned, a stillness.

The bed with its thin mattress and thick, formlessly plump quilt drew me. My fingers were already unbuttoning my tunic, catching sideways at the placket of my skirt and fumbling open the buttons of my blouse while I gazed at the prospect of that bed in a dream. Neither the anticipation of my escape nor the immanent being of Jean-Martin faded; they were within me but saturated in the sensuous promise of sleep. In the same instant as pulling off my slips my body slid onto the unyielding surface of the bed and I drew the soft warmth of the feather quilt up and around me with a deep sigh of relaxation and a slight shiver at the chill cotton, first stretching out in a wonderful sensation of physical yearning and then rolling myself up in the downy depth that enclosed me. The transition to sleep was almost instantaneous and I did not hear the rustling tap at the door or the cautious move of the latch which must have been audible. I did not awake at all, sliding in sleep from the inner consciousness of Jean-Martin to the actual sensation of his body at once tough and soft, smooth and furred, the scent of his skin and breath as his mouth opened against mine and the sinewy hardness of his weight pressed on me. My slumbering body slipped into its natural state as part of him. The intense pleasure with its dual quality of urgency that was stillness, a piercing calm, flooded the combined being formed by the two of us and sank into deeper sleep.

It was quite dark. I woke as Jean-Martin turned my wrist to see the glimmering figures on my watch.

"Time we went," he murmured, his lips against my ear. "The truck will pass the end of this road—you know, where the main road crosses?—at eleven." I pulled on slacks so that the driver could at least pretend not to know I was a woman, and a dark blue sailing cap to push my hair into. With my loose pullover I saw in the half dark of the room a boy of fourteen when I looked at myself in the small, half-obliterated mirror.

"I've never before felt the charm of pederasty," he said. "But suddenly I see the point! What delicious thin flanks you have. Come along, quickly, before I start treating you like a schoolboy!"

As I ran down the stairs I realized with only a faint shock that he did not yet know my news. But that like all else but himself was unimportant. Even the horrifying risks we were running were stimulating instead of frightening as long as he was there.

There is a wideness about that country, it gives the impression more than anywhere else I remember that it lies under the sky, and the open horizons give the cloud formations piling up from over the sea a massive depth and breadth; there is altogether more sky than earth there. In fair weather a great clear globe is inverted over the land, rarely free from clouds for the Baltic is no tame inland lake but wild seas that storm against the dunes of the flat coast, raging against confinement between land masses into which they have wandered by mistake from the great ocean wastes. Jean-Martin, whose family came from the Atlantic coast of France, was always conscious of the sea and talked often of the great spaces of that ocean to which one day, as he said, he would take me. I had never seen the open sea, and never have since, but I imagined it from him.

That night there was a strong western breeze and you could smell the sea where we were. That I knew well, the Baltic, for we often made up parties to go sailing from the hospital in the first summer I was there when life was easy and our privileged position meant something.

Now "we" had changed its identity and the new "we" were fugitives. The recollection carried by the sea air, of former times before I knew Jean-Martin, brought that state sharply into focus. I suppose the growing disorder, the increasingly makeshift and improvised state of our work in the last month or so, had obscured reality for me even more than the coming of Jean-Martin, whose appearance in my own life was only possible because our world was falling into pieces. In the clearly regulated conditions of hospital life before the summer our irregularities would have been impossible.

But in a disorder where no train of patients arriving or departing came from the direction or at the time announced, where the duty rota was changed every day and night, where familiar faces disappeared without warning and new faces arrived or, more often, gaps were left vacant without explanation; in this confusion nothing was either possible or impossible. Things just happened, unrelated to each other or the past, and the future shrank to minutes, or rather to an unknown dimension, for time itself was unregulated and no measure used formerly had any validity. All habit was disrupted, both in time and space. Mealtimes, rising and going to bed, off duty and on; the very presence and shape of solid buildings was no longer certain. Our dining room as well as the operating rooms had been moved; the end of the nurses' home farthest from my own room was evacuated into a nearby school after bomb damage. Water and electricity went off and on for hours so that every kind of treatment for our patients must be carried out as it could be, or not, and all planned and authorized programs ceased to exist.

A bewilderment crept up into the consciousness in such circumstances that took in nothing, accepted everything, with equal dumb indifference. If men one day appeared with two heads, as they sometimes did with none at all, nobody could have expressed surprise.

The decision to go and the management of my leaving were still part of the confused meaninglessness. The quiet stuffy hours in the hotel room, especially the bottomless depth of sleep, were palpably an interim. Now we waited for the transport that would move us to an as yet—for me—unknown destination.

And during the silent wait standing together behind a broad

willow tree near the crossroads, a new state took its shape. Our own silence, imposed by caution, was the last influence on us of existential chaos and by means of it we passed into a state that was, in fact, peace. I remember us being picked up and the clumping thud with which my suitcase was heaved without a word into the truck; the journey has disappeared into a wheeling dream of dispersed moonlit darkness in which dim light was reflected off or from behind cloud masses. There was other traffic; long convoys of heavy trucks and many military automobiles. The convoys all rumbled northeast, the cars and motor bicycles veering their ways, sped in both directions. Other trucks occasionally passed us going in our direction which was almost due south, but like our own, these transports were all single vehicles. What our empty truck was officially doing on that road I had no idea. The driver wore S.S. flashes on his collar and spoke with the hard and clear accent of Berlin, answering the occasional remark of Jean-Martin in his comical German with gruff and cynical briefness, every second word being *Scheisse*. He obviously knew that Jean-Martin was French and therefore a wandering prisoner of war; it was myself who was disguised and neither spoken to nor mentioned by them. They spoke of Paris which the driver had last seen in July and Jean-Martin in the summer of 1940. Neither made any attempt to keep up the conventions of their supposed positions toward each other; I suppose this is more common than I thought. They were simply two men in the same *Scheisse* and they used this word with all its many variations and combinations in both German and French, the S.S. man saying *merde* at least as often as Jean-Martin did. It became a kind of refrain from which I was not so much excluded as simply agreed to be not there at all. This silence of mine was a part of the night and the drive, and penetrated into my mind as the quality of the change in my existence from an order degenerating into chaos—worse, that is, than disorder—over some unseen frontier into no man's land.

At last when the moon had set and dawn not yet come, the

driver stopped. Our bags and my case, together with two or three bulky parcels, were dumped at the edge of the road, now a winding country lane. Jean-Martin stood by the driving cab exchanging last greetings with his friend, who drove off with a stinking cloud of exhaust gas and a roar of motor. At once and without speaking, Jean-Martin took the strap of my case and dragged it into the nearby thicket. I realized that he knew just where he was and what he was doing.

"It will be all right until tomorrow," he murmured, keeping his voice to an undertone. "Come, let's go."

There was a pathway into and through the woods. We walked for about half an hour while the sky paled over the trees, and came then to a clearing and a forester's cottage. Once or twice Jean-Martin stopped to listen; but all that was audible was the night sound of the forest, and the wind.

"They are not here," he said, now speaking in a normal voice. He did not seem troubled or surprised by that absence. It was part of his knowledge, evidently, that "they" might or might not be present when we came.

"Just a minute. Stay there," he instructed me and went forward from the overhang of the trees into the clearing where his steps made a dark path in the gray of the heavily dewed grass. He walked without hesitation or caution up to the little house, skirted around it to the back and reappeared a moment later when he went to the door and I could hear the metal scrape of a big key in an old-fashioned lock as he opened it. I could even hear the creak of hinges as the door swung open onto a deeper dark. At a gesture of his arm I too went forward and entered the house.

There was a feeling of people in the house; men lived here as in an army hut, without domestic arrangements and without women. It was a smell of wood ash, food remains with an emphasis on bacon, thick clothing not often changed and the muggy heaviness of a place where a number of men sleep with closed shutters. It reeked of a sordidness that I found comforting and homely.

Through everything else penetrated the timber smell of its construction and the tarry preservative used to weather-proof the logs.

"There should be a lamp." We waited until we could see a bit in the gloom and then made out an oil lamp with no glass chimney and a wire handle. Once I put my hand on it Jean-Martin at once closed and locked the outer door. He clearly knew that the shutters were fast. He produced matches from his breeches pocket and light expanded to show a room that filled the whole ground floor of the house. In the far corner from the door rose a ladder-stair with no uprights between the treads that disappeared through a black hole to the upper floor. There were three small windows, with outer shutters and rough curtains of some frieze stretched across them inside. The door too had a curtain of sacks cobbled together and this, which hung down at one side, Jean-Martin now hooked across the door to prevent any threat of light showing from the outside.

"There are sheets in that bundle," he said, jerking his chin at one of the parcels we had carried with us. "They sleep in their blankets but you wouldn't care for that."

Still speaking he went to the combined cooking and heating stove and put out a finger to test it.

"*Merde*," he commented and flicked his fingers in the air. "They were here a few hours ago!" From a basket beside the stove he pulled split wood and shoved some twigs into the ashes. I took the bellows from their hook and made a draft and a little cloud of soft ash arose.

"They've got the chimney closed," I muttered and looked about for the flue lever. It was above the stove, a position I had never seen before. It moved awkwardly and rustily as I opened it a little. Then the ash subsided and after a few moments the fresh sticks smoldered and glowed, then crackled into thin flame. Through a latched door was the pump and behind it the shape of a flat sink-stone and several wooden water buckets.

I had brought ersatz coffee with me and we brewed some and

ate bread and raw ham with it. As I carved slices off the bacon I wondered how it came to be there; we never got it for meals in the hospital and it was generally assumed to be unobtainable. But, of course, I was now in no man's land where the rumored Polish black market operated.

We sat across from each other at the raw wood table, the lamp to one side, and ate and drank in peace.

"Are we going to stay here?" I asked.

"Sure," he said, his mouth full, and his dark eyes laughed into mine like a naughty boy's. "We'll get a bit of peace and quiet here."

"Won't 'they' come back, then?"

"Only now and then, to visit so to speak. They've moved on."

"And who are 'they'?"

"Better if you don't know, my darling. They won't bother us, that's all that concerns us for the moment."

Of course, it was madness, but I looked for nothing further. It did not concern me. Nothing mattered except that we were there and alone. Coming from a world gone mad, this was sanity and calm. Everything made sense in its own context.

Jean-Martin, to my unsurprise, was quite at home in the forest. At some time he must have been a hunter and although he could not have used a gun here even if there had been one, he very efficiently trapped hares and rabbits and a little deer which were all dispatched by his broad sharp hunting knife without my assistance and which I first dealt with as foodstuffs. There was a little garden in a picket fence with apple trees and a plum and Jean-Martin brought green herbs with him from his hunting forays, so we even ate salads, a forgotten delight. One day he came with a small sack of coarse flour. Another with a long strip of fat pork which I hung up in the top of the chimney where, through a trap door in the shingled roof, there was a widened space for smoking. If he was surprised at my knowing of such rural skills, he did not comment for everything here simply happened and was so because it was so. We even had salt. When my packets of hoarded coffee ran out Jean-Martin produced from one of his excursions a box of tea and it was real tea of high quality such as I had not tasted for several years.

Every few days we had visitors. They came in the night or at dusk, sat talking with Jean-Martin for a while and then went again. When their whistle of announcement was heard I went upstairs, and this too just happened, as if it were quite natural. They always carried weapons, whoever they were. I could hear the clank which sounds like nothing else, of small arms stood down by the door. I suppose I must have known that the visitors were outlaws, the bandits of the "Polish Home Army" which I knew was what they called themselves. But that I did not admit into my surface mind.

When they went Jean-Martin recounted to me their news. So I heard of Warsaw, the end of the uprising there and of other terrible events, all of which he spoke of with that extraordinary lapidary coolness that belonged to his mastery of living. Just as he trapped animals whose beauty made them precious, because we needed food, so he assimilated, and made me assimilate, happenings that if thought about could not be taken in.

When great squadrons of aircraft thundered over the forest on their deadly path I shook with terror recalled. Then Jean-Martin would hold me in a firm hold so that I knew that danger no longer existed; a danger I discovered at Insterburg only for his sake. No tremor of fearful nerves in him interrupted his organic assurance for my female fears; he was steady and calm always.

Somewhere my carrying of his child was known and was the subject of small endearments, little jokes and an extension of erotic pleasures.

"Now we are three," he said, "we have an audience. We are our own voyeurs."

Another time, on an afternoon of misty sun, he said, "How can

329

he fail to be marvelous, our son! He will be born as he has grown, in paradise."

It was a working paradise, but the work too was a source of happiness. Nothing after all is pleasanter than to gather the autumn fruits of someone else's hard winter and spring work. Whoever that forester was and wherever he had gone, we were grateful to him. I thought he lived there alone and pictured an old man who had never lived in a town and preferred his own company to any other for there was no sign that a woman ever managed that household; it was a male house in and out. Jean-Martin told me that it was found empty by "them" and that even when people still made excursions from the sparsely scattered villages round about, no neighbor came here. I think there must have been some local tale about it or its former occupant because not even the owners of the whole district, who also owned the land where it stood and presumably the cottage itself, ever showed any interest in it. Not surprising in normal times. But at that time, when a refuge from the Gestapo, the Army, the bombs and half a dozen other murderous enemies was worth its weight in gold, it was strange that a hideout so perfect should not have been remembered by someone. I knew that at least one member of the old Prussian family that owned this land ended on the gallows recently; that meant that his whole family down to remote connections was at least suspect. All that I knew from the newspapers and the radio in the hospital.

The house itself was in rough but sturdy order. Once or twice when it rained with heavy autumn storms the damp came through in the pumphouse, but no more than damp patches, and elsewhere all was as snug as constant care could make it. It had not been long uninhabited.

Of the outside world we got little news, only what "they" brought with them and that was concerned with their own doings or those of their friends. Most of it I hardly believed, and yet did not disbelieve; it was nothing to do with us, I thought. As his guards had often said to Jean-Martin in camp before he came to the hospital, for us the war was over. We were waiting for its end and then we should go, not to Paris, but to the west coast of France and live there almost as we lived here.

It was a long, still, golden autumn and only gradually did the weather get colder and the days shorter and darker. Leaf trees slowly turned color and formed splashes of brilliance among the near black of the needle trees. The busy squirrels ran about and they and the over-winter birds took no notice of us. Late one afternoon it turned very cloudy and a steady wind from the north howled and moaned all about in the great trees. I knew that wind from three years in those parts. Winter was coming. I was lifting potatoes planted by the forester, the last of our outdoor jobs. The storm rose and whipped the kerchief from my head so that my hair blew over my eyes. I stood upright and stretched, pushing my hip-bones down with my hands and drawing in great breaths of the rioting air. I could feel the change in my figure now and was beginning to feel differences internally. My stomach was a curve so that I had begun to lean back slightly when standing and I noticed that I stood in a new way and moved in a new way.

A long whistle announced Jean-Martin's return from an absence since the early morning and I called back, imitating a bird call. He emerged quickly from the thick forest and from his movements I could tell that he was excited. He glanced about him, saw me and changed direction, coming over to me instead of going to the house. Every line and movement of his trim and lean body filled me with joy as I watched him. He was not particularly tall nor broad, having a slender quick-moving toughness about him. Every movement was neat, graceful, co-ordinated and he never wasted energy nor did he ever move or speak just for effect as most people do all the time. I never saw any human being who so confidently lived in his own body.

As he came up to me and was just about to tell me something, there was a renewed burst of wind stronger than ever that rattled

331

the branches of the trees and blew a shower of brilliant brown leaves between us. He raised his hand to lift back the strand of hair, now quite long, blown over my mouth and as he did so we heard the long-drawn, melancholy hooting of a wedge of geese very high up and streaming steadily due south. We stood there, his hand on my face, and watched their strange passage, which brought pricking tears into my eyes.

Jean-Martin's look had changed to eagerness of another kind.

"Come," he said sharply. "Into the house!"

"What, now?" I cried, laughing at him. "But I haven't finished." And to tease him I gestured at the last row of potatoes waiting to be gathered into my box.

"Yes, now. Quickly. If not in the house, then here." Even as the idea occurred to him he caught my earthy hand and drew me with him to the nearest apple tree where we sank together to the grass. It was not in the least less urgent for me than for him. It was as if the southward drive of the birds had entered us. The great wind blustered through the little tree over us, scattering the last leaves and apples while we sheltered underneath it. I felt myself shuddering in every nerve, shaken in a transport of love as the apple tree by the gale. And yet there was that strange stillness of totality and certainty, a perfect center of calm.

CHAPTER 23

In the night the outlaws came. It was just after midnight, early for them. Twice I looked at the illuminated dial of my duty watch, the only means we had of telling the time. I could hear them talking below and could easily pick out Jean-Martin's voice when he spoke. They were talking a long time tonight. Usually it was a matter of a few minutes and I assumed that they came really not to talk to Jean-Martin but to collect a message or stores of some kind, from the stuff in the cellar which I was careful never to examine. But this time it sounded as if there were a conference going on in the room beneath. I decided that they must be eating and would perhaps even sleep in the house for the rest of the night. They did that once, in the outer of the two upper rooms. Jean-Martin suggested on our own arrival that we should use the inner room, only to be reached through the one into which the stairway rose, for that very reason: that "they" might sometimes want to sleep here.

I envisaged these people as moving constantly to and fro and my imaginary picture of them was heavily colored by the constant and fearsome warnings against the brigands, the terrorists, the bandits, on the official radio. There was some perverted justice in that picture, for whatever they were before they took to the woods, as the saying was, their life since then had turned them into savages.

Presently I got up and went to the window. By opening the shutter a little outside with a wedge of wood, we ensured some air in our own sleeping room and I could see through the space that it was snowing heavily. Since it was by now the first week of December this was natural, but perhaps because the autumn lasted so long, the advent of winter in real earnest filled me with dread. Without thinking what I was doing I pulled on my regulation nurse's dressing gown of thick woolen cloth and went through into the farther room to listen at the head of the stairs.

There were several voices, two or three that interjected remarks or questions in Polish and two, that of Jean-Martin and another man whose voice I had heard before, in French. This man's voice answered the others in Polish and spoke to Jean-Martin in French. He was obviously translating for those who could not understand both languages. I crouched down to hear better what was being discussed.

They were talking about prisoners of war. A question of their needing to be vouched for, and talk of their then being picked up and transported out of Poland. Eventually I made out that these men were now free and there was some difficulty about their being accepted by "the London Poles." Jean-Martin was arguing that the group should wait for the Russian Army to arrive and liberate them officially. This contention caused harsh and scornful anger and one man spoke for several minutes with fierce passion in Polish. The French speaker—I could hear his chair scrape as he turned—urged Jean-Martin not to stick to his attitude. He did not understand the Russians, he could not judge. There was something in the tone of his voice, although not in the actual words he used, that condemned Jean-Martin. He, unlike at least one of the others, was not yet angry but he disagreed completely with Jean-Martin's views. The freed prisoners wanted nothing more than to get away so that they could participate in the end of the war; if they waited for the Russians they would either be sent to Moscow or would have to remain in Poland. This puzzled me because we were, in fact, in Germany, in Prussia. Jean-Martin argued that the men should wait, if not for the Russians, at least with the Polish Home Army, until they could go direct to France and not to England. Slowly the reason for his obstinacy penetrated my understanding. He himself could not go anywhere but to his own home without leaving me behind. The other men, I now understood, knew of my existence. And they knew therefore Jean-Martin's reason for wanting to stay where he was.

The argument went round and round, getting nowhere. At last the interpreter, who was now impatient and scornful, suggested a fresh idea.

"If you have no more stomach for fighting yourself," he said, "at least make it possible for your comrades to fight. You cannot refuse them that. Come and clear up the position for them with our commander. Then if you still want to, you can come back to . . ."

"Be careful," said Jean-Martin coldly. "Do not say what you will regret."

"I doubt if I should regret saying it," replied the other. "For my part you are no longer a comrade."

There was silence downstairs. I found that I had been holding my breath and as I moved to release it I grasped the handrail. There was a loud creak from the wood. The men below all moved but no one spoke at once.

"German whore," said someone at last in German, clearly wanting me to hear.

Jean-Martin moved quickly.

"You take that back," said his voice.

"No." That word I knew in Polish.

There was a sharp movement and a quick babel of angry words. Then Jean-Martin shouted, "She has risked her life for me. Do you expect me to abandon her?"

There was an angry retort that I did not catch.

"Let go of me, damn you," said Jean-Martin.

"You swear not to hit him?"

"Very well."

"If you prefer this woman to your fellow soldiers, there is nothing more to be said."

"She saved my life, I tell you. The security police in Insterburg were on to me. You know that. I should have been shot or hanged if it were not for her."

"All right. So she was useful. Many have been useful and have been much worse treated. You needed her, you made use of her. That is all."

"I cannot simply leave her here," said Jean-Martin through his teeth.

"Very well. Then you abandon your comrades. It is your choice."

One of them said something in Polish and the French speaker translated.

"He says there is no reason why you should not come back for her or make some arrangement to meet her later."

"After all you've said about the Russians? Don't make me laugh!"

"Christ, do we have to talk all night about his bit of cunt! Leave the bastard here and let's get about our business!" That too was in German.

"Yes, leave him here! Come on, it's getting late!"

"If these men come to any harm, on your head be it. And if any of us survive, you will pay for it. We'll see to that!"

"Wait!" he said. "For God's sake . . ."

I found that I was going down the stairs. I was very cold and my knees shook so that I had to hold on to the rail, gripping it so convulsively that a long splinter entered my forefinger.

Everyone except Jean-Martin turned to watch me. All I knew

was what the interpreter had said. "You needed her. You made use of her. That is all."

"You will go with them," I managed to stammer at last, my teeth chattering. "But go now. Quickly."

"Anna!"

"Get him out of here!" I shouted.

I closed my eyes tightly and heard the bustle through a thundering noise in my head. When I opened my eyes the room was empty. Very slowly, like a sick old woman, I moved from the foot of the ladder and crept to the table where I let myself down into a chair. I did not believe it. He would return. I just sat there, leaning my arms on the table, staring before me, until the twittering of birds outside in the shelter of the roof told me it was day. But I still sat there, stunned.

CHAPTER 24

I do not know how long it was, but some days afterward I heard the whistle the outlaws used. I hid behind the door. A heavy tread approached and the door was pushed open toward me. As he advanced warily to the table I recognized the interpreter. He was alone. I moved and he whirled around, his weapon coming up. When he saw who it was, he lowered the machine-pistol and then laid it on the table, keeping his grip on it. I just stared at him, waiting.

He mustered me, saw the hunting knife in my hand behind my skirt and jerked his head, meaning he would not hurt me. I did not move, but watched him because I was not able to do anything else. His eyes searched my face; they were narrowed with caution, bare of any feeling.

"He will not come back," he said at last, stiffly.

"You mean he is . . . ?"

"No. He was all right when I last saw him. But he is not coming back."

"Did he send you?"

"I said that I would come when I was nearby," he answered carefully.

He waited but I could think of nothing to say.

He lifted his machine-pistol and made a practiced move to

check the safety catch before slinging it. At the door, with his hand on its edge, he turned, his head bent, not looking at me.

"We shall not be coming here again. And you'd better think of moving, too. There are no Germans left in this part of the country, and you'd better go if you want to get away safely."

The door thudded shut and his steps went away. The silence came back. I moved to the table and sat down, facing the door, and waited. Nothing happened. The knife lay on the table, where I put it on sitting down. I considered using it. That seemed the most reasonable of the various possibilities. My watch had stopped days before and I had no idea of what day it was nor of the time of day for the weather was now so lowering and overcast that the light of day was rather a lessening of dark into dusk than anything that could be called daylight. Or perhaps something was wrong with my eyes. My ears too, I seemed to hear nothing but the echoing silence in my own head. Steadily, out in the open, snow fell. The house was now cold right through, the chill of winter had come indoors. I moved my hand to touch the heavy wooden grip of the knife, smooth and pleasingly shaped, the rivets softly yellow with constant use, more like gold than brass. Tentatively, I folded my stiff hand around the handle. My hand was grimed with dirt. I had not washed since he left.

As I exerted a scrap of energy to lift the knife, which was an effort for it needed an active will even to breathe, the fetus moved in my belly. I felt a sensation in my head as if I had been hit with a heavy block of wood. The shifting in my stomach made me queasy; I leaned back in my chair and breathed deeply.

Quite calmly and practically I thought I ought to eat something.

I did not think that I could not even die. I just thought it was necessary to feed myself, that is, the child. The girl of before, who might have screamed with childish rage, howled with grief like a wounded dog, might have rushed out into the open and in among the trees of the forest tearing her hair or clothes, she was gone somewhere. She did not exist any more. She was dead; it was simply a question of disposing of the body. And apparently that was not possible, for some reason it was not allowed. The shell must continue to exist although the girl inhabiting it was gone. There was this thing inside that must be fed. It demanded its nourishment.

In the ensuing time something stealthily and silently happened. The body went about its minimum of affairs. But a webbed curtain came around it that thickened hourly until it was impermeable and toughly resistant to light. There was just the necessity to eat, drink water, defecate and sleep. It worked like a rather well-made machine for feeding a fetus. It thought of nothing, was inaccessible to memory, the curtain covered everything but the need, which was amputated and went on being by itself.

It would presumably go on being until the interloper had forced its way out into life. This animal being came from nowhere, was to go nowhere. It was just waiting to know that the thing growing inside it was separated from it. Everything else was increasingly shut out by a caul, by that web of intervention. Quite quickly it became impenetrable. An automaton fed a succubus.

One day I was among the trees, some way from the house. There was an approaching commotion along the path from the road. I was near a very big and old forest monster, I think it may have been one of the rare oaks for it branched heavily several ways only a few feet from earth. I climbed carefully up into the multiple fork and leaned against the widest branch. Unless some eye was actually focused on that sloping limb, I was invisible.

One man, shouting, came into view on the path, swinging his machine-pistol before him. Others followed. They staggered in the extremes of exhaustion, they were filthy, several were bandaged. They were German soldiers.

"Don't go near it," the leading man said on seeing the forester's house.

"Not even into the clearing," said another. "Here, this way looks fairly open."

"No, I think we might rest here," said the first man. They waited until the others came up to them and then collapsed in groaning heaps of weariness on the sparse snow under the trees. Some had cigarettes, some drank from their canteens.

"We seem to have shaken them off."

After some time I saw from my vantage point that other men approached. They wore a different uniform, something I had not seen before, or more precisely they, like the Germans, wore rags, the remnants of some other uniform. Quietly, they were much quieter than the Germans, about a dozen of these new soldiers assembled. Slowly, so as to be silent, they sank to their knees and waited until all were ready. One of them raised a hand and when he dropped it again a sustained bedlam of automatic weapons rattled and battered, there were cries and yells, and one by one the members of the first group keeled over, staggered up and fell with flailing arms, lurched with blood pouring from their mouths, at last lay still, all of them, although the fusillade went on long after there was no more movement. Then, quietly and purposefully, the members of the second group separated. Some went cautiously up to the dead and began to strip them of anything useful. Others spread out and encircled the house from the shelter of the trees. They encroached step by step and then entered the house. There were several more bursts of fire from inside the empty house as they searched it. Shutters crashed open, all kinds of objects flew through the windows, the clearing was filled and echoing with a confused noise, breaking wood and glass, shouts, shots in the air. One by one the men inside the house reappeared in the clearing, carrying things which they at once began to throw away. About five minutes later a long flame shot from the open front door and they all began to laugh and cheer, shouting to each other in strange tongue of short raucous monosyllables. Before the house was well in the grip of the flames, they were gone and by the time the roof collapsed in a great roar of fire there was nobody there to see but myself. As the fire died down I crept nearer and nearer to it, to keep warm. I stayed there through the night and for several nights after until the ashes were as cold as the surrounding woods. Then I left.

After that the road began.

The gaps in consciousness during my journey must have been caused as much by starvation as by shock, because those gaps have not been filled by memory. Everything else, or I think so, came back in that flood of recollection but the following time flickers in and out rather like the view of a village seen in the middle of the night by the flicker of vengeful flames. There are momentary visions that could be dreams, such as the child torn to shreds and the shattered group strewn over the *chaussée*. Sometimes I feel a flash of what must be memory but it is gone again before I can catch it long enough to fit it into a sequence. Then I feel that a single thread could perhaps suffice to pull back the first stages of my journey, but the thread eludes me.

It may be as well. For me and for others, it is enough of horrors. Only one circumstance I can deduce from objective evidence; I must have changed direction often and was at times just wandering, if not in circles then in purposeless trails and retracings of my path for there is a vague recurrence in the glimpses and the sensation of recognition now and then. I would not trust to that if it were not clear from the map and the time that elapsed between about the third week of December and the beginning of March when Ronni found me unconscious but still crawling. I think now, too, that I may have stayed for periods of days or weeks with other single people or groups; objectively it is clear that I should have starved to death alone in the totally ravaged countryside where both cattle and harvest were almost entirely destroyed and where anything that survived was denied to Germans and belonged now, such as it was, to the Poles already being driven forward from eastern Poland and Ruthenia into the former Prussian territories and as far south and west as the Pomeranian plain and Silesia. They were hardly better off than the outlawed former owners of that land for years afterward and in 1945 their only advantage over the handful of Germans who remained until their formal expulsion was that they possessed a theoretical right to be there. The rule of any kind of law, however unjust, was non-existent for several years and people, land and cities were entirely at the mercy of bands of armed men, struggling for and against the irreconcilable Polish resistance. That is all part of the unknown history of modern Europe which will never now be written. Even the victors in that long civil war have not written their version of what happened; according to their official history it did not happen.

I was told afterward that I fell to the floor of the French officer's room in a long fainting fit, still convulsively clutching the violet-scented silk left behind by his wife. I was off duty for eight days after that, the diagnosis being undernourishment. Except for the autumn of my desertion from duty that was the only occasion on which I have failed to arrive on duty at the correct time and place in all my professional life. On my return I found that the local staff now ate the main meal of their duty period in a dining room allocated to them and were fed from Allied rations. This turn of events made me extremely popular with the Austrian staff and I was quite forgiven for being one of the hated Germans. We were also allowed to draw medical prescriptions from that time on, and by a complicated swindle I could get penicillin for Veronika.

I was put to bed in vacant room for that night but the following day was taken back to our room at my urgent insistence by military ambulance.

There I lay for days, hardly able to speak, and for most of the time holding Rolf, sleeping and waking. Then I gradually began to talk to Ronni when she was there. It was that therapy that brought me back to something like normality.

So madame, monsieur, you wished to hear what I knew of the parentage and birth of the foundling who has, as you put it, abducted your only daughter. I hope I have satisfied your entirely legitimate curiosity on this subject, although I fear that Rolf's illegitimacy is only confirmed by my story. As far as that bend sinister is concerned you may wish that you had left the beginning of his life in obscurity. In a complete lack of information there was at least the chance of his having been born in wedlock to the mythical couple of no name in an unknown place in what is now Poland. But you wished it. I can only now admit that it is entirely my fault that a half-French and half-German bastard was born to seduce your daughter with his father's charm. The evening before last another telephone call came from Rolf, who wished to reassure me that Leona and he are well and happy. If you wish to see me again, I shall be happy to put my time at your disposal for as long as you desire. I ask only that you should come here to me because it would be difficult for me to arrange to go away for the next few weeks. I await your further suggestions as to what should be undertaken to bring back and discipline our naughty children. But I must warn you, as is only just, that when I talk to them they show no sign of penitence. Rather the contrary, they seem in the absurd fashion of the young to take their future for granted and to feel that they are doing something not even daring but something quite ordinary and normal. They appear to think that I should agree with this view, and apparently have already persuaded my son's superior officers that their betrothal, as they call it, should and will be followed by marriage as soon as Rolf's twenty-fifth birthday makes him eligible for promotion.

Act Four

SON AND
DAUGHTER

CHAPTER 25

She had not expected to be asked to identify herself when collecting *poste restante* letters, never having done it before, and for a long time after this Leona thought of the administrative detail as being peculiarly Austrian.

"They wanted to see my passport," she informed Rolf, coming back into the central hall of the General Post Office. "I say, how vast!" The place was so big that in spite of a number of people everything echoed; it smelled of dried ink and a century at least of dust and heavy boots wet with snow and mud.

"What a paralyzing girl," said an American voice coming from a group of three dwarfed by high traveling rucksacks. The speaker humped his load higher on his shoulders and pushed untidy hair out of his eyes. "Hey! We're looking for the American Express!"

"Well, you won't find it here," replied Leona disdainfully. "It's in the Kärntnerstrasse. And if I paralyze you, you sexist, you ought to fall down." And she aimed a deft and painful kick at the boy's booted ankle, making him stagger.

They were neither surprised nor abashed to find that she understood them. The one who got the kick hopped on one foot with exaggerated pain, unable to bend over to rub the sore spot because of his laden back.

"Ya wouldn't like to show us, would you?" suggested another of the trio.

"No, I wouldn't. You go down the street here to the end and turn left, past the cathedral and quite a way farther on and it's on your left."

"If there's many like that around here, we're going to have us a ball."

"Not if they all kick," replied the injured one gloomily.

"Never stops, not even in the winter," observed Rolf, referring to the continuous stream of tourists through the city. "I bet they have hash in those rucksacks."

"I expect the police search the youth hostels pretty regularly. Look, two letters." She showed him, turning the unexpected second letter over suspiciously. "It's Uncle Alain's writing. Shall I open it?"

"You'd better. Then we know what they're thinking."

She tore at the envelope, making the thick paper crackle imposingly. The letter was not long, which was just as well for Alain's handwriting might have been that of a doctor or a journalist, so nearly illegible was it.

"Hey Rolf, listen. I think we're going to get that money! He says Mamma thinks it ought to be given to me, and anyway that's what it says in Grandmother's will and can we meet to discuss it. Wait a minute, I can't read this word. Something, then realizing funds if I wish to or he will advance—something, better not to touch capital, he says. What are equities, Rolf?"

"No idea. What else?"

"Mamma was so glad and relieved to hear from us—yes, us—but to remember how hurt she gets to be left out of things and try to include her. And will I speak to him when I call this evening . . . Oh. Papa is better but has been persuaded to go to—that I just *can't* read—for a few days to recuperate."

Leona pushed the letter into her already overfilled shoulder bag and took a step as if to go.

"Aren't you going to read the other letter?" Rolf reminded her.

"Oh, of course. I was so excited at the news I forgot it. Look, it's in Mamma's own writing. Wasn't that sweet of her, to write herself with the money!" She scanned the brief note and again pushed money and letter into her bag.

"But who else would have written it?" asked Rolf, puzzled.

"Well, she said she'd ask the secretary to send me some money, just for now. But there's no news in it because I've been talking to her every evening. Except, she didn't tell me that Papa was away, we sort of agree not to discuss that. It would sound disloyal, wouldn't it?"

"I suppose your family is quite different . . . But I think, even after I've been gone from home for years, I'd be quite upset if my mother got a secretary to write to me for her."

"Oh, but it wasn't like that! It was only to enclose money, and that sort of thing is always done by Papa's staff. I mean, accounts at school and everything."

This was an aspect of her so different life perceived, not for the first time by Leona, as dangerous to dwell upon, and she now changed the subject.

"Let's get back to our pad. It's so much nicer there than anywhere else."

"We'll walk back. But let's get something to eat first. There's a butcher's shop just on the opposite corner."

"I just hope I can manage meat properly."

"Well, if you can't, I can. We'll get something easy. Pork chops?"

In the shop she sighed. "Heavenly *charcuterie*. If only I knew what to do with all these things. Look, black puddings. That's something I can do, *choucroute alsaçienne*."

"Takes too long for now," he pointed out. He asked the man behind the counter for cutlets and the butcher, as he chopped them off the piece, grinned across at Leona.

"We have them fresh on Tuesdays, too," he said, indicating

with his trimming knife the pile of dark sausages. "And you can get sauerkraut two doors down here. Real, in a barrel, not those packets. You like me to save you a pig's knuckle for Tuesday?"

"Gracious, do I need to order one?"

"Well, mostly we roast 'em. But I'll keep you one." The man nodded sententiously. "Other places, other customs," he quoted.

"I'll be in on Tuesday morning. Now we need some ham for ham and eggs. That's about all I can cook yet."

"You, a French girl, and can't cook?"

"How do you know I'm French? Do you think I'd better learn to cook?"

"Of course you're French. Any fool can see that. And you know what they say, love goes through the stomach." He raised his voice to a shout at the girl on the other side of the shop for the ham, and calculated quickly, only using his cash register when he already had the total.

"My turn to pay," said Leona. "Here, hold this, Rolf."

"Talking of learning," said Rolf as they went out, "I forgot to tell you. We shall have to get married, after all."

"Why? No, this way, we have to go to the baker's."

"I asked at the Flying Club and you can't learn unless you're an Austrian citizen. Something to do with neutrality. We don't train foreigners to fly."

There was a crowd in the large modern baker's shop, and a delicious hot smell. Leona was obliged to point at one of the things she wanted; such homely matters were included in none of her languages.

"You'd better tell your commandant that," she said over her shoulder, pushing her way with a scatter of apologies to the cash desk through the press of those expert enough to know that the third baking was just ready. "Then he'll give you your promotion."

"I don't see the argument there."

"Well, you said we couldn't get married until you're promoted.

And that's a more respectable argument than the usual one. For getting married, I mean."

A stout, elderly man gave her an outraged glare and she smiled sweetly back at him, slipping her money neatly under the glass of the desk before his. Her smile so increased the old man's annoyance that he passed some remark to the cashier about modern youth. This lady, however, although as old as himself, did not support him but replied a little tersely that they were all young once and wagged her gray head upon which she wore a black felt mountaineer's hat with a long pheasant's feather at the back. The combination of this unlikely headgear with the starched white coat worn by all the bakery staff was so comical that when the feather dipped at her movement, all the people waiting to pay broke into laughter, and Rolf was still laughing as they crossed the road again to the greengrocer reputed to sell real sauerkraut.

"Why does she wear that hilarious hat, d'you think?" asked Leona as soon as they were out of earshot in the narrow street.

"She has to sit all day near the door in a draft. And then, she's a cut above the girls who serve the bread. It's a badge of rank. *They* have to wear those hygienic little white caps—you see?"

"Oh, it's so funny!"

"What?"

"I don't know. The butcher. The baker. Everything." They held on to each other in pointless, ridiculous mirth.

But on the way across the bridge Rolf grew serious. "Just the same," he said slowly as they waited for lights to change, "I'm a bit scared you might get fed up with this place. It really is awfully provincial, so people keep telling me. And after Paris."

"We'll probably have to live in much more provincial places before we're done with the service. Military airfields must always be miles from anywhere. In fact, I think we're lucky to start off so near a real city."

"I hadn't thought of that. Lord, that makes it worse."

351

"Worse! But why?"

"Well, you must be so used to . . . it's beginning to worry me."

"When did you start to worry?" Astonished.

"Your letters reminded me, you said something ages ago about your father's secretaries always being around. Plural secretaries. I only know one person who has even one secretary. And another thing, you said he might go to the Foreign Office . . . !"

"But we fixed that, haven't we?"

"Yes, but just the thought of it. It's so terribly grand and important. And then I began to think. You know, about you and Kari being sort of half-engaged."

"We weren't half-engaged," she said sharply. They were by now crossing diagonally over the wide space of cobbles in front of the Augarten Palace and this reminded Rolf of his return to Kari's "hideout" in the morning after the Opera Ball. Leona stopped, still in the roadway, glowering at Rolf, who now really did look worried. She tried to trace his thoughts and as she did so apprehension gave her face an urchin grimace of fear which at any other moment would have made Rolf laugh again.

"Watch out," he said quickly, "there's a truck coming."

They hastened to the grass edge of the square and Leona set down the plastic bag containing half their purchases, the better to talk. Rolf still swung the second bag in one hand.

"Listen, Rolf, you mustn't take . . . I was exaggerating when I said . . ." She stopped. "No, I mean, I wasn't . . . But it's all . . . Oh hell, this is just what I was afraid of."

"What? The engagement?"

"There wasn't any engagement. And if Kari had asked me, which he didn't, I would have said no!"

"I didn't mean that quite. I only meant, Kari's father is about as important as you can get in Austria. That's what I was thinking, that your family must be at least as . . ."

"But it doesn't *matter*," she cried imploringly.

"But you'll *miss* all those things."

"What things? Dreary people, you mean? Being married off like an archduchess in the Middle Ages, you mean? Never having anything to myself, ever, like Mother? I told you about money, I told you! At the ball. You've forgotten. Or didn't you believe me? What do we want with all that? You've never had any money and don't lack for anything. Why shouldn't we go on living like you've always lived?"

"It's just . . . I thought of Paris suddenly."

"Paris! You've never been there, you don't know anything about it."

"But that's just it, don't you see?"

"No I don't see!" Her voice rose almost to a scream. "I've never lived in Paris either and I don't want to. People aren't nice in shops there. I don't care where I live. I'd rather live in the country anyway!"

Panic-stricken by Rolf's second thoughts, all her schooled self-assurance deserted her and with it her control. She stepped back from him on the uneven verge and knocked the soft plastic carrier which fell over, releasing a small package wrapped in waxed paper.

"The pork chops," she wailed and burst into terrified tears of self-pity.

Dismayed at her vehemence Rolf dropped the second bag, which instantly fell over in turn, and caught at her outstretched hands. It was exactly the same movement as after the missed step at the Opera Ball. They both felt it, and both caught breath and gazed into each other's dilated eyes. A bus stopped nearby and the people getting out and in stared in wonderment at the two of them, clutched in each other's arms as if a parting for life threatened them, around their booted feet various homely parcels strewn, and both laughing and crying at the same time.

Rolf released her after a moment. "Honestly, we're behaving like madmen."

"A good thing you're not in uniform," she said severely. "That will teach you to try and bully me." And shaking now with helpless laughter they scrambled about picking up their purchases, all of which seemed to have become nakedly unwrapped in their fall.

It was an old house with no lift and they climbed up three stories and around the glassed-in gallery of the courtyard to Kari's flat in the attics on the far side. The kitchen windows in these old-fashioned places faced out onto this wide entrance corridor on each floor, originally open to the court but in this house glazed in at a later date. The result of this arrangement was that the tenants enjoyed the vicarious pleasures of other families' meals and to judge from the smells most of these consisted of cabbage and garlic sausage. Kari was one of the few tenants prosperous enough to have installed a bathroom by cutting off the larder, the broom cupboard and a corner of the kitchen. This was considered in the house to make the occupants of Kari's flat superior to ordinary mortals and entitled them to be addressed civilly by the otherwise ill-tempered janitor. But they were also required to tip him regularly since they were sub-tenants, who were not allowed.

At this time in the early afternoon the house was almost empty; which accounted for nobody having heard the crash of broken glass. For as Leona carried the bags into the kitchen she saw at once that glass lay scattered on the stone floor and one window pane gaped jaggedly.

"Hey, Rolf," she called, "somebody's been here."

Rolf came out of the bathroom and stared with her at the damaged window. "I'd better look," he said and went into the only other room of the flat. As Leona bent for the dustpan she heard his startled exclamation.

"What is it?" she called, brush in hand at the door. "Why, it's Kari!"

He was lying on one of the two flat couches, fast asleep, and what Leona noticed with a sense of outrage was that he had neglected to remove his muddy boots, laced up to his knee breeches.

"Hi, Kari, you beast! I had that cover cleaned only yesterday at the laundromat!"

Kari turned over and groaned wearily at being disturbed.

"Now I know why that cover was so damned dirty," she scolded.

"What in the world are you doing here, Kari?" cried Rolf. "Aren't you on duty?"

Kari sat up on one elbow, still groaning.

"I'm absent without leave since the day before yesterday," he muttered. "And if that were all! Hell, Rolf, get that girl out of here. I have to sleep."

"Sleep! You'll get your lazy ass back to camp, but fast! You can sleep in the guardhouse, that's where you'll sleep!"

"I'm not going back," said Kari, now more or less awake and scrubbing at his thick blond hair. "I've quit. For good."

Rolf sat down on the other bed.

"You must be mad. Raving. You'd have been out in a few weeks. Don't you ever think what you're doing?"

"Yes. I did think. Is there anything to eat around here?"

"But Kari, I have to report you! You, even you, must know that."

"You can't do that."

"Oh, can't I? And get put on a charge myself? Grounded? Demoted?"

"But, man, this is serious. You can't turn me in."

"You're so right, it's serious. Kari, I always told you I drew the line at anything that would keep me from flying. You can't say you didn't know that, I've said it at least a dozen times."

"Yes, but this is different. Hey, haven't you seen the papers?" Now it had occurred to him, Kari looked across at the transistor radio on the bookshelf. "Of course, I'd forgotten, the batteries are out. And you haven't seen a paper?"

"Not for days. Why? What . . . Kari, what have you been up to?"

"We did a thing, last night," he mumbled through a yawn. "God, I could sleep forever."

"A thing?"

"An action. No, it was the night before last. And I haven't slept since. We crashed the car so we couldn't get away. We had to scatter."

"Car? Whose?"

"Not yours, don't worry. Yours isn't fast enough. I took Mother's."

"An action. So it *was* you, those burglaries, the night of the Ball?"

"Sure, but you knew that. I practically told you."

"I did not know it!" yelled Rolf and then was suddenly quiet again. "And the stuff you pinched, you used for this 'action'?"

"Right. Where you going, Leona?"

"To get the papers, of course. I'll be back in five minutes."

"But why did you come back here?" demanded Rolf. "You told me you couldn't use this place for a while."

"Nowhere else to go. But the police may know about this place."

"The police. Of course, the police."

"I can't stay. I just had to have an hour or so's sleep."

"Police." Rolf was stunned. "You couldn't use this place because of the police?"

"Well, what did you think I meant?"

"I thought you meant there might be somebody hanging around you didn't want to see. Like a girl or something."

"A girl! You sound as if you'd been hit by a truck. Pull yourself together, Rolf."

"That's what I feel like. And you let us come here, knowing all this?"

"Well, of course I didn't know it was going to go wrong. I thought we'd be in Italy before now."

"I suppose you think that would have caused less trouble than you being here? For us, I mean?"

"I didn't think of that. But you needn't be suspect."

"How d'you know the police know about this place?"

"I don't for certain. But I've lent it to one of the others from time to time. And he may have been picked up."

"May have been? What makes you think so?" When Kari did not answer, Rolf shouted again, making him jump. "Come on, you fool, make with the words. You're usually quick enough to open your big trap. Tell me the truth."

"He was hurt," Kari grumbled. "He couldn't run."

"And you left him to it? I see. What a swine you are, Kari."

"I . . . what's that?"

"Leona coming back, of course. Listen, why did you break the kitchen window?"

"I'd lost one of the keys. And I gave the other two sets to you."

"What you mean is—this fellow who used the place, he's got the third set?"

"Well, he could have. Yes, I think he has."

"So. He's got your keys and the police have got him? Fine."

Leona passed Rolf one of the newspapers, pointing to the lead story. Rolf read the headlines and the first paragraph, in heavy black type. Then he dropped the paper and put his head in his hands.

"But what possessed you to come back *here*?" cried Leona. "The police are bound to come. Perhaps any minute."

"No. He won't talk at once. Perhaps not at all. And we all emptied our pockets before we took off. So they have to search his last room first. I reckon they won't get around to this place for a day or so. And by then I'll be gone." He glanced quickly at Rolf's head, still bent in his hands. "I hope, anyway."

Leona moved her eyes from Rolf to Kari and back again.

"Just what do you have in mind, Kari?" Her voice was hushed.

"None of your business. Is there anything to drink?"

357

"Not for you," she answered, equally crisply. "You'd better stay sober."

"Have you seen it?" asked Rolf, lifting his head.

"I caught the headlines. You could hardly miss them, not even running." She picked up the sheets from the floor and began to scan the account. "It can't be true. Nobody could be so stupid! It says here a policeman was shot. That can't be right?"

"Where does it say?" cried Rolf.

"Here. The late message." She pushed the paper into his hand. Kari reached past her and picked up another of the three journals brought in by Leona.

"This is the afternoon edition . . . Yes. He's . . ."

Kari stared up at Leona. He swallowed and let out a long sigh. She said, gaping at him, "But to try to blow up the American Embassy! Didn't you even know it would be *guarded?* And you shot . . ."

"The pig only got a flesh wound in his arm."

"The . . . Oh, you mean the cop. No, I mean the night telex-operator. It says here . . ."

"Another man shot?" shouted Rolf. "Give it here." He scanned hastily down the page and then looked up helplessly at Leona. His lean features were changed, drawn and gray. "Shot dead. He killed him."

Kari crowed in a high, false voice, trying to laugh.

"The silly fellow, he's gone and died on me."

"'Massive Manhunt,'" intoned Leona, reading from the third paper. "'Roads and Airports Watched.' 'Public warned: Terrorists Armed and Desperate.'"

"He had two children," said Rolf. He crushed the paper in his fist and looked about the room, unbelieving. There was dead silence until something boiled over in the kitchen but none of them took any notice.

"But why?" asked Rolf at last, addressing no one. "What for?" He certainly was not questioning Kari and Kari acknowledged this by ignoring the questions. After a time Leona got up and went back into the kitchen to pour the water off the potatoes. She had seen Rolf peel them and picked one up but hastily dropped it again.

"Phoo, they will have to wait," she muttered, and pulled out the frying pan from the shelf behind a plastic curtain, yellow, with a pattern of idealized kitchen equipment.

"Awful," she said to herself, "dreadful. I must get a new one, it's all torn. What did I do with the dripping?"

"Anything else we need?" Rolf put his head in the doorway. "Funny how one talks to oneself in the kitchen. I'm going down to get batteries for the radio. There's news in half an hour."

"You could bring some cheese from the Yiddish delicatessen, perhaps. If Kari's hungry he'll need more than our spare chop."

"Good thing we bought one too many. I won't be long."

By the time Leona had managed to assemble the food and the implements for eating it on the table it was almost time for the news so Rolf brought the little Japanese set to the table. There was a talk about new agricultural machines, until their attention was sharpened by the news-reader's voice. Johannes Becker had died in the General Hospital of his wounds from a police revolver. From the way Kari's face sagged and turned a sickly gray color they knew that this was the name of his friend.

Leona said, "Will there be riots now?"

"Riots? Why should there be?"

"I was thinking of sixty-eight," she pointed out. "There probably would be in Paris."

"We don't have riots here. But then, we don't go in for terrorism either, so who knows. Anything is possible."

"What did they want to do, d'you think?" She spoke to Rolf as if Kari were not sitting there.

"I suppose, strike a blow against the imperialist-fascist . . . I don't know."

"It was the C.I.A. offices," interrupted Kari impatiently. "They

359

keep records there of all the militant groups, and we intended to destroy all their lists, dossiers."

"Dossiers," said Rolf. "What are they—something out of an old French Krimi. And two men dead."

"One of theirs and one of ours," agreed Kari, sticking to his point.

"I hope you are not now going to say that one can't make omelettes without breaking eggs?" Leona asked, hostility breaking through the unreality.

"I wasn't, no. I was going to say, the police won't know now where the keys belonged. Now that he's died."

"Ah." Her sigh spoke more than words.

"But they'll find you here anyway," said Rolf.

"It's not registered in my own name, this flat."

"Oh. Of course."

"You look quite shocked at that." Kari, recovering himself still more, contemplated the two faces. "What innocents you are, both of you. It's just because you look romantic, I suppose. That makes you seem extraordinary. But in fact, you are both perfectly ordinary people. Obviously not much is to be expected of a girl, and she's young. But you—I must say . . . You are so completely, with your background, the very man who ought to long for a revolution. I've always assumed that. I admired you for biding your time, knowing how to wait, never showing anything. Now I wonder if there was anything there, at all."

"Anything there?"

"Behind the impression you were being careful, sound, not letting yourself be carried away until you'd reached a position where you could really do something . . . You weren't thinking like that at all, were you?"

"Like what?"

"Of the future, with controlled anger, waiting to take your revenge."

"Revenge? For what?"

"For what happened to your parents, your own life."

"You need to get your logic polished up. Why should I even want revenge and on whom? There's nobody to revenge myself on. For all I know my parents were Nazis. What then? That would make them guilty of whatever happened to me, since their lot started the war and lost it. No—wait. You've been deceiving yourself about me as about other things. You wanted to believe that I must resent something, I can see that. If you feel immense dissatisfaction with no cause at all, how much more must I feel it, a landless and penniless foundling. Right? But I don't feel anything about myself. I just want to do the things I want to do. Live my life."

"A happy man, no less!"

"Why not? No need to sound so contemptuous. What's wrong with being happy?"

Kari shook his head to free it of something, his light blue eyes more blankly opaque than usual. "I just don't understand you. Happy! Is that all your ambition?"

"I haven't any ambition. What you seem to have taken for deep-laid thoughts of heaven knows what was just an empty skull. What would I be ambitious *for*? I want to fly, I want to ski, I want to climb mountains. And I do all those things and get paid for it. And now Leona is going to coach me so that I can compete in the service horse show next autumn. If I do have an ambition, that's it."

"Leona!"

"She knows horses, don't you, Leona?"

"Mmm," she nodded, still watching Kari.

"Then . . ." He stopped and thought, blurted out with an effect of violence, "then you won't want to fly me out to Italy?"

"*Fly* you?" Leona shrieked above the broadcaster's voice, droning on about Vietnam. "So that's it. I knew you had something in mind."

"I'm on duty tomorrow at eight o'clock," said Rolf steadily.

"And at the latest then, I have to report that I've seen you. Face it, Kari. I have to."

Kari made a hasty movement, pushing his chair backward and moving his arms so that both the others stiffened with a new, crazy, thought. But Kari was no longer armed. For the first time Leona understood that he was frightened. Up to that ungainly move of the arms she accepted his bluff as real, but now she saw with surprise at her own slowness that he sweated and could hardly control the shivering of his limbs.

"So there is no question of me flying you anywhere."

"You wouldn't just leave me to it? You can't, Rolf, you can't."

"You promised me, if I went to the Opera Ball for you, you'd cut all this out. Didn't you?"

Kari just glared wildly at the so harmonious features across the table littered with used plates and glasses, the remains of food. His eyes were unnaturally distended, his teeth clenched to conceal the trembling.

"Didn't you?" insisted Rolf, not looking at Kari. "You knew you had no intention of stopping. This was already planned. You were lying to me. Now you've killed a man. Somewhere this has to stop."

"I didn't kill him. It was he and Hannes, they shot it out between them. It was Hannes who wounded the polenta."

"And the telex-operator?"

"You can't blame me for that. There were a lot of shots. The police or the guards may have shot him by mistake."

"You know you killed him," said Leona, awed. "I can see it in your face that you remember exactly. Telex rooms are always brilliantly lighted. I've seen rooms like that. Underground because of 'security' and lit by neon tubes. That's how it was, wasn't it?"

"You've never been in the American Embassy in your life!"

"Well, I have. And the telex room in our Embassy too. They are almost the same only the Yanks have more machines clattering. That's the only difference you can see. And see is what you absolutely can, in there."

"You don't know what you're talking about." The cry was of desperation. "I tell you, Rolf, we could see nothing in the uproar. When did Leona ever go into the U.S. telex room?"

"When they had a diplomatic open house, it must be three years ago. They had some new installations and everybody was invited to see them. It's you who don't know. You call us innocents, but you're a bloody amateur, that's what you are. You play at armed bandits for fun like other people risk their necks on ski jumps. And now you want to ruin Rolf as well. That's what you're all about, Kari Lensky. You just want to destroy things."

"Shut *up*," he yelled.

"You shut up! If you really cared about the oppressed masses you'd be slaving away at some awful mission hospital in the wilds of Africa, not killing ordinary clerks at home. Poor fellow, what did he ever do to you!"

"Just the same," said Rolf wearily, "the thought of him getting life . . ."

"You could get leave, Rolf. You could hire a plane."

"I'm not due for any more leave, I've had too much as it is. And they would know."

"You could ask for sympathetic leave. Say your mother's ill."

"I tell you, they'd know."

"And if they did guess, so what? They would still let you. Think of the stink, man. The court-martial, the police. The Foreign Office. They would all be relieved to get rid of me quietly. You know it."

"Rolf, he's just trying to involve you, can't you see that? He's sick, he's not normal. He wants to wreck your life."

"You keep out of this!" shouted Kari.

"Shut up, both of you. We'll have the whole house down around our ears. Don't forget the window is open."

"Let's go in the other room then." Kari stumbled to his feet. "My God, I've got to have a drink."

"There's some wine here."

"Not wine. A drink." He turned about, bewildered, frowning. "I thought there was a bottle of brandy here somewhere."

"In the cupboard in the other room."

"This can't really be happening," said Leona as he disappeared. "We're dreaming."

"What *am* I going to do . . . ?"

"How long do you think he's got, before the police find him?"

"I can't even guess. They might discover something at once, or it might be days. We don't know what they know, after all."

"They could have a picture of him?"

"He's got to leave here, anyway. That's the most urgent thing."

"Look, I've got an idea," Leona said eagerly, "We could dye his hair. That would change his whole appearance, being so fair. He'd look entirely different."

"His eyes would give him away. And so would the hairdresser."

"Eyes. Eyes. Glasses? Not dark ones, just tinted. My own reading glasses are tinted, they change my eyes quite a bit."

"I didn't know you wore glasses."

"Well, I'm supposed to, to read. I don't, of course. I wonder if they'd fit him. As for his hair, I can do that. I did it several times for a girl at school. It was deadly secret, we did it after lights out."

"He would still need another passport, a new identity card, to get clear away."

"He may have them. Or know somebody. Ask him."

It was now wordlessly agreed that Rolf must deal directly with Kari, although how they knew that Leona only made matters worse was unclear to both of them.

"I doubt he has," said Rolf. "You're right there, he's a complete amateur."

When he came back into the kitchen, he shook his head. "Nothing. Not a notion. He's lying on his back, drinking schnapps. Staring at the window. He agrees the hair dyeing is a good idea, but doesn't like using your glasses. Says he couldn't see with them."

"Rubbish, they only magnify a bit. They aren't strong lenses. And if he changed the way he moved, not seeing the same as usual, that would be a good thing too." She stopped, and thought of a new factor. "How were they proposing to get away if the action succeeded? Did he say?"

"I'll ask him. That might be . . ."

Leona followed him to the door to listen.

"We booked on a winter tour to Venice, the airlines do all-in trips cheap, off season, to fill the payloads. You can go all over the place, even New York or Tunis, all over. We picked Venice because we have friends in Italy, another group of . . ." He cut off abruptly what he was about to say.

"But your passports?"

"That's just it. You give the tourist agent the passes, he books and registers the numbers, names, all that. Then you get your passports back. The group leaves all together, you see, it's much easier than for single passengers. Actually, both our passports are still at the travel agent's. Hannes' girl was to pick them up. But I expect she was too scared."

"When were you going?"

"Tomorrow. With rucksacks. Most of the time you use your student pass. Hannes had one and I'd kept my old one, never turned it in."

"Is that important, student passes?"

"Oh yes, you can go almost anywhere on them. Cheaper, too."

"So if somebody went and picked up your passports from the tourist office, you could still go?"

"They'll have been warned by the police, you dope."

"Why? Did anybody else know, besides the girl?"

"No, nobody else knew, just the three of us."

"The trouble is, your name. There's only one family with that name." Rolf came back to the door. "Go through the newspapers again, Leona. Perhaps they say somewhere that the police haven't got any names yet. See if you can find anything."

"Hannes did the bookings," said Kari slowly, "and his name is Becker. The girl's name is even more commonplace. Novak."

"You mean, if somebody just went in and asked for the three passports for Herr Becker?"

"It still wouldn't work. I'd have to use my own passport at Schwechat."

"Yes. But you'd have your passport back. In fact, you'd have three of them."

"If you're thinking of me using Hannes' passport, that's out. He was short and dark, very dark."

"Hell. And the girl?"

"The girl! She didn't have a proper passport. She was going to travel on her international student's pass. She's done a year at Bologna and still registered there."

"What does she look like? Come on, Kari, co-operate, will you!"

"But it's rubbish. Oh, all right. She's sort of mousy, light brown hair and eyes. And a giant, she topped Hannes by a head."

"She doesn't by any chance wear glasses?"

"She does, yes." Kari sat up. "Of course, her Italian's much better than mine, but I do speak it a bit. You don't think it's possible?"

"Is she pretty, or striking-looking?"

"God no. Face like a potato, always looks dirty."

"And this pass. It's not new, if she's been studying some time?"

"Can't be. She's done ten semesters, it must have been re-stamped several times."

"So it must be messy. And probably in one of those yellowish plastic covers as well. Or we could get one. Now look, if you wore an anorak and jeans, the hood up, your hair dyed and untidy over your face, close-shaved but dirty, glasses. Rucksack and perhaps a plastic bag with books, you'd just look like any traveling student, male or female. You'd have to keep the anorak on all the time or somebody might notice your crutch. That's the only way you can tell, sometimes."

"There's somebody at the door!"

There was, somebody who after some shuffling leaned on the old bell, forcing from it long, nerve-rending shrills.

"They can see Leona in the kitchen, through the window. We'll have to answer."

"Perhaps she's in the bathroom?"

"She isn't. She went to clear up. I could hear the clatter."

"My God, Rolf, what are we going to do? It's them."

He rose to his feet and they both turned toward the door. They heard Leona's voice, frightened, calling that she was coming. There were two of them, one very young in uniform, and an older man in ordinary clothes and a loden overcoat. There was something horribly banal and absurd about the formal way the older man took off his hat as he came in.

"May we come in?" he said, and produced his police credentials. He had eyes and skin and hair all the same dark dun color as his suit so that he appeared to be colorless and featureless.

"May I perhaps see your identity cards?" he said in a voice that matched his looks, being quiet and toneless. He was looking at Rolf but it was somehow clear that he knew Rolf was not the man he sought.

Leona leaned over to pick up her shoulder bag from where she had dropped it on a chair on coming in. Nervousness made her clumsy and she knocked a plastic bowl off the corner of the cupboard. Both she and the official bent down to pick this up, he stepping from the tiny hallway into the kitchen to do so. As he reached down an exclamation from the uniformed policeman made him jerk around, half bent over.

"No! Kari, no!" shouted Rolf.

For a tumultuous moment they were all in each other's way. A blast of wind filled the small room with winter, the casements swung, reflecting doubled and distorted flickers inward from the darkling sky. All this was endlessly drawn out, a reeling turmoil and noise.

A vision of Kari falling, crashing down into the basement court, hitting its paved, empty, clean surface, squashed like some great fruit, filled Leona's inward sight with a vision of such nauseating horror that she closed her eyes tightly to shut it out. She screamed wildly, one long-drawn protest of anguish, and fell back against the doorframe, clutching her surging stomach with crossed arms. For a moment she was half-conscious, seeing and hearing nothing but the roaring in her ears, the flashes against her shut eyelids from the bang of her head against the wood.

And when she opened her eyes again what she saw was as unreal as her horrifying vision. Kari, facing into the room, bent forward, his arms caught behind him by the three other men, his head down, gasping and retching. He was still there. He didn't jump, then. But surely, he would be facing the other way, they should be dragging him back? As her sight cleared she saw the middle-aged man in the brownish suit with a startling quick neatness move his grip from right shoulder to right wrist and pull Kari's back-stretched arm in toward the straining back so that Kari's right wrist was between his shoulder blades.

"All right," he said, not even breathing heavily. "I've got him now."

Both Rolf and the uniformed policeman at once let Kari go. The young constable pulled his leather belt straight, put up his hands and pushed back his disordered hair.

"Nearly knocked me off my feet, when he turned," he grunted, complaining.

"Couldn't face the fall," said the older man.

Rolf sank down on the flat couch, grasping its edge on either side of himself, his arms held rigid so that his shoulders hunched and his dark head bent forward, hiding his face. The helplessness of this movement pierced Leona's heart with a sharp pang of love and pity. Where everything else was confused to meaninglessness, she understood instantly that Rolf was filled with bewildered misery that Kari himself had forced Rolf to help capture him.

"On your way," said the older official brusquely. And then, "Where's his coat?"

Rolf did not answer. Leona, with a start of nervous haste, saw that she was expected to fetch the leather driving coat still lying where Kari must have flung it down on a chair when he first came in. She moved over, feeling curiously stiff, picked it up and held it out, bunched up, to Kari, who did not lift his lolling head. Stupidly, Leona looked down at the thing in her hand; he could not take it in any case, nor put it on, because his right arm was twisted up in that painful grip and his left held by the second man. Roughly this man in uniform pulled the coat out of Leona's uncertain grasp. Kari lurched slightly and then moaned aloud as the muscles of his arm pulled against his own movement. The younger man moved in, half-supporting Kari.

"He's almost out, looks like," he muttered.

"Shock. But don't rely on that. He's tried it once." He stopped almost before he moved and said to Leona, "Just a moment. I still haven't seen your identity card."

"But I haven't got . . . I'm not . . ."

"What d'you mean, you haven't got . . . ?" he sounded savagely angry suddenly and she felt fear of him. Taking her own innocence for granted, it had not occurred to Leona that simply by her proximity to Kari she was suspect, nor were the policeman's problems in dealing with three possible terrorists at once a consideration that could possibly enter her inexperienced thoughts. But she did realize that she must show him her passport and looked confusedly about for her shoulder bag, locating it after a moment on the top of the kitchen cupboard by the plastic bowl the official had put there on picking it up.

"There it is," she said to herself, and moved toward it with a new purposefulness.

"Don't touch that bag," he ordered her harshly and jerked his head at his junior. "I've got this one. You pick it up." And after a pause. "Well, search the thing, man. Christ, I'll have to breathe for you next. Is there a weapon in it?"

"No, Chief. Just a lot of papers and stuff. There's a passport here, though."

"Give it here." He took the little booklet with his left hand and opened it skillfully with his thumb. "That's all we needed. A foreigner." He glanced up under his brows, never slackening his grip on Kari's wrist, and compared the girl before him with the photograph in his hand. He looked at her with concentration, really seeing her as a separate person for the first time and recognizing as soon as he did see her that she had nothing in common with the various types of young women who move like satellites around juvenile revolutionaries. Instead, on this inspection, she presented a quite different complication; everything about her proclaimed the possibility of influence somewhere.

"You're not registered here, are you?"

"N-no. The hotel. My parents are there."

"I shall have to take this with me. Or you can come with us. One or the other. If it's all right, you can have it back tomorrow. And I shall leave a man on the stairs here, if you remain here. You understand?"

She looked involuntarily across at Rolf for help.

"Of course she stays here," said Rolf to the policeman. "She has nothing to do with it. We just borrowed this flat for a week or so. Until . . ." He stopped, some barrier forcing him to abandon any attempt to explain.

"Make sure he's clean," ordered the older man, and as the uniformed boy approached him Rolf jerked his head away with humiliation and anger. But although he knew himself entitled to refuse the attentions of the civil police, he did not resist the fumbling hands, waiting until the two were satisfied that he was not armed and then quietly producing his military identity card. This visibly annoyed the official as it was meant to do.

"How much d'you think that means, eh? *He*'s got one of them, as well." And he jerked at Kari's wrist, making him gasp, at which Leona and Rolf both winced.

"Not quite the same," said Rolf.

"Just the same, you come with me. You can report to your adjutant from my office, for what good that will do you."

"I must do that in any case," said Rolf. "Where are we going? To the *Revier*?"

"*Revier*?" said the official. "Revier nothing. This is a State Police matter."

Kari seemed to mumble something, lifting his head a little with a rolling motion as if its weight were too much for him.

"What was that you said?"

Kari made an effort and forced his voice to loudness, a thick, slurred stammer. "I said, what have you got against him? He helped you to take me, didn't he? He's on your side. Law-abiding citizen, all law-abiding citizens help the polenta. Ergo, he's practically a Gestapo snuffler, an eager agent of the State Police."

A vicious tug upward on his wrist reduced Kari to a moan and silence.

"I know your sort," said the policeman, almost good-humored now. "Nothing you'd like better than to have a nice yacking match over politics."

"I was trying to save you from jumping," cried Rolf. "And nothing more."

"Don't answer him," advised the older man. "What you haven't grasped yet is to be hated by his sort is a compliment. Now come on. Let's go. And no funny business or my boy here will use his gun. Like you used yours on an unarmed man, you fine hero."

As he passed her Rolf looked at Leona but he did not speak and she was left alone to be badgered by the thought that he wanted to pass some message to her that she was too slow to understand in the instant of his eyes on hers.

She wandered purposelessly into the little kitchen and sat down at the square table; cleared of its red and white checked cloth it looked rather dirty but she had no idea of how to clean it, nor the energy to do so. She sat there looking, still dazed, at her hands before her, feeling herself alone. She had never felt alone before, for unlike many only children she was neither shy nor introspective and from infancy there was always a nurse or a governess to arrange for companions until school removed even privacy. She was alone now because Rolf was gone, gone in a different way from his previous absences on duty in the last two weeks, when she was already waiting for his known and anticipated return, was dreaming his certain reappearance, almost as he went from her sight. There had always been other people; now there was only Rolf and when he was removed there was nothing.

The emptiness was absolute and threatening. She began to move about in the confined area of the little flat which only a few hours ago was a cozy husk about them and now was transformed into a prison. In the only other room she took in ugly sparse bits of furniture as if they advanced upon her. The high old-fashioned couch on one side and the much newer one opposite, lower but equally hard; the cheap and too shiny round table top between them with grazes and scratches all over its surface; the unpainted shelf piled with tattered paperbacks; the miniature Japanese radio set; the crude pattern of the flimsy unwashed curtains that were never drawn hanging slackly beside the window. The windows were now closed but looking at them she felt again that appalling vision of Kari falling and her stomach churned so that she hastily turned her back on the window and faced the brilliantly gleaming doors of the clothes cupboard.

"All this horrible varnished wood," she said aloud. "Why didn't I notice it before?"

Only this morning it was homely, now she knew she had liked

its difference from everything she was used to. It had been play. Now it was deadly earnest and she was alone with it. She or "they" had turned the furniture back into casual purchases from a junk shop collected without choosing by Kari, who never saw what things looked like. It was all in the abysmal taste of the twenties, and poverty-stricken like the twenties. The only new, clean, bright-colored things chosen by herself and Rolf were not at the moment visible, towels, feather quilts in striped cotton covers, new kitchen cloths; they had bought them in their housekeeping game because Kari's stock was meager, dirty and ragged. They all came from a linen shop nearby, where the girl who served them told them about her skiing holiday, ten days at Lech, and they congratulated her on her splendid tan that made her unpowdered face look like natural wood with its smooth sheen of health.

That was a nice girl; it now struck Leona hard that she was a working-class girl who spoke to them without servility as an equal, and who did the same things Leona did and could afford time and money to do them; she skied, she went to dancing classes and gymnastics after work, she wore gay, well-cut clothes and looked forward in the middle of winter to swimming and boats in the summer. Me and my boy, she had said. Was she, was her boy, the people Kari wanted to make a revolution for? Did Kari ever see the people around him any more than he saw things? His revolution had not only already happened, it was already taken for granted. Kari's graceless lumber crowding the small room belonged to the distant past. It occurred to Leona with force that he must have bought this stuff just because it was ugly and poor. It was all a game for him as for Leona, the game of playing truant, of playing grown-ups without having to be grown-up.

These were revelations to Leona at least as much as they could have been to Kari. She could not help knowing, now that she did know, that the one who never had been playing was Rolf. Her first impression in the anteroom at the Opera was that Rolf was grown-up. And he was. Rolf had something to lose; that is, he was

373

adult. Others playing at living were going to lose Rolf what he made for himself, his own life. There was no rich papa there behind the scenes, no mother from whom one might "borrow" a motor car and smash it up, no mother to send him packets of money for playing with. This was his own life and his only life. The money *he* had gone to the post office to get to pay for those feather quilts and their covers was almost all he possessed. And just two of the notes Leona did not even count before she pushed them into her overfilled bag were enough to replace Rolf's savings.

She longed to be able to tell him that she now understood. She knew she could not formulate it, but if only he would come back she would tell him somehow. He would not come back, he would be arrested, "they" would not believe him, they would think he was one of Kari's absurd conspirators. Terrified by these thoughts, unnerved by the quiet, she turned on the little radio and music poured out of it. A passionate and lovely soprano, a deep bass singing with authoritative magnificence against tumultuous music never heard before. The voices produced an intensely erotic cloud of meaning, demanding, possessive, almost savage. A yearning of boundless and terrifying dependence filled Leona from inside her body and she longed for Rolf with fear, doubt, anxiety, with a fierce longing to be possessed, to be part of him and inseparable. In the despairing sensuousness transmitted from the music as if it were within her and not outside, innocence disappeared forever and the child playing at love was initiated through fear into life and death.

Later, she did not measure how much later, the tempest of sound ended and she could not take in the announcer telling her that she had been listening to a performance of *Salome* by Richard Strauss, conducted by . . . But she suddenly did understand when his chatter was replaced by an already familiar news-reader. His flat neutral tone returned her to here and now with a slap like cold water as he announced that the police with admirable efficiency had already made two arrests of persons connected with the attack on a foreign embassy two days before. Two arrests. The shock sent a wave of heat all over Leona's body, followed at once by a trembling chill. Cold sweat broke out on her forehead, she leaned against the table, lamed and shaking. Then a repetition returned her to sanity and she grasped that the second arrest was that of a woman identified as Renate Novak. The friend of Johannes Becker, the girl with a face like a potato as Kari had said with his curious disdain for other people. Not Rolf. The words plunged vertiginously in a phrase from the music. Not Rolf, not Rolf; they hung singing in the air.

CHAPTER 26

"For the third time," said Chavanges with a dull-voiced, tenacious steadiness, "it is either a revolting fantasy or, as I am certain, a deliberate invention. She has taken stories heard from that time and concocted this pathetic chronicle from them in order to make any opposition appear discreditable. I cannot understand how you, with your mind, your wide experience of the world, how can you take this stuff seriously, and not the scheme that produced it?"

"Let us be logical," said Alain, leaning forward slightly to touch the wedge of typed paper lying open in a neat cover on the table between them. "First, a fantasy; if this is a product of daydreaming then the woman is not normal. That cannot be the case: she is a successful professional woman. So we may dismiss fantasy."

"I wanted to be charitable," put in Chavanges.

"Your judgment, then in fact, is that this account, purporting to be true, is a farrago of lies deliberately invented as part of a fortune-hunting marriage swindle. That, of course, would be a criminal offense, if proved."

"Certainly it would. But such intrigues rarely come before the courts anywhere. The protection of the young girl is usually the sole concern of her family, as in this case."

"But would a woman in Anna Forstmann's position take such a risk? Even without a lawsuit, supposing evidence could be ob-

376

tained, the story could hardly be kept secret. Her reputation would be ruined."

"You speak of her position. What is it? She has no position. She's a nurse, that's all. True, a nurse who has got herself, probably by other maneuvers, of this sort, into a job of some responsibility. But still, a nurse, almost a . . ."

"You didn't speak of nurses in that tone three weeks ago," said Solange. "When you insisted on the doctor bringing in a trained sister in place of the hotel woman."

"Now, now," Alain held up a warning hand. "Our views on the nursing sisterhood are for the moment immaterial. I want to put another point to you, my dear fellow. I understand from both of you and from others as well that this young man is notably handsome and attractive. The accomplished Madame Perriot described him as 'Apollo-like' and Madame Leclerc was hardly less complimentary, although she, I would say, is a good deal less of a judge of male beauty than the other lady. Solange, on the other hand, says he seems a perfectly ordinary, decent, unself-conscious young man, only very good-looking."

"Well, there you have it! All the women have their heads turned by a charming profile and a quick smile. His stock in trade."

"Possibly. But the point I want to make is this—if he can turn every feminine head by his looks alone, what does he need with plots and subterfuges?"

"Ah, but the plotting is his mother's or his guardian's, whatever she is. She knows the world well enough to know that looks are not enough for a nameless and penniless youngster."

"But he is not a youngster. He is nearly twenty-five, I gather, and in the midst of his career."

"Career! He's an airman, and in the Army at that."

"Surely that in itself indicates a lack of ambition for worldly goods?"

"Those he hopes—expects—to get by other means."

"And your evidence, indications of self-interest?"

"Ah, my dear Alain, you weren't there. You didn't see him."

"No. I wish now, deeply wish, I had come with you in the first place."

Solange from the window gave a smothered sigh of impatience. She continued to force herself to gaze as if abstractedly out at the leafless plane trees on the Ring where a group of workmen in shiny white overcoats slashed by broad red diagonals to make them visible shoveled frozen and dirty snow into a waiting truck. Everything was foggy with intense cold and where heavily clad people waited at the tram stop one could see how they stamped their feet and shifted about uneasily. She spoke to the window, not turning her head.

"You are still missing the main point, Alain. Supposing Anna Forstmann did form an elaborate plan, how could she have known beforehand that she would have to deal with French people and therefore invent a French prisoner of war? In any case, neither she nor anyone else knew that Rolf would be at the Opera Ball that night. Until this stranger appeared even Kari Lensky's family were expecting him to partner Leona. The change was completely unexpected by anyone present."

"By 'anyone present,'" Chavanges said to Alain, as if trying to help, "Solange means the little group of gossiping women she knows here. And you know how reliable the talk of idle women is."

"They may gossip but they certainly are not idle." Solange now sounded tart for she had been made to feel fairly useless in the last week or so by the ceaseless activity of the women in question. "Why, Angèle Leclerc even does her own cooking! In any case, gossip is useful. They all know, or know of, Madame Forstmann and they all admire her."

"*They* admire her!"

"When you meet her, Alain, you will agree with me, I'm sure, that she's not at all the type of woman who would or could invent

378

such a story. She just is not the imaginative sort, you know how I mean? She wouldn't have the fantasy for it, she's too—earthbound."

"From experience of writing reports," Alain grasped at this argument with relief, "I would say that even a professional writer would need a good deal more than fourteen days to dictate that and get it typed. Still longer if she wrote it out herself first. That is, if it were being composed anew; not reported."

"Exactly!" Both his companions spoke at once, each claiming his comment as confirmation of the opposite view.

"She had it whole in her mind beforehand, and probably in the form of notes, too," Chavanges asserted, and banged down his hand on the pile of papers.

"I don't really see . . . even to have a considerable report in memory is a very different matter from actually formulating it. It's hard work for professionals."

"She could have written most of it in the past. All that was needed at the last moment was the identity and nationality of the boy's father."

"You mean, in case the question of his paternity ever became important, just in general?" hazarded Alain. He was obscurely humiliated by the determination of his lifelong friend to stick to a theory so inherently unlikely and wished to offer him a more reasonable base for his conviction. "Because, you see, as to identity, there we come up against objective evidence."

"Evidence? What evidence? What do you mean?"

"Well, naturally you are not a lawyer. That's what I am there for. The first thing I did, before starting to read it, was to telex for confirmation of this . . ." And Alain held up Anna Forstmann's covering letter, which Chavanges stared at almost with bewilderment as if seeing it for the first time.

Solange, still facing the window, drew a long breath as this crucial point was reached. She knew she must not betray her knowledge that this obvious step had been taken, and still less that she

understood the implication of her husband's neglect of it. A gulp
of nervous strain almost choked her and she clutched at the rope
of pearls at her throat.

"You did? And what . . . ?" Chavanges spoke slowly, his tone
sullen.

"The family named here exists. Their elder son—the old people
are still alive—*was* named Jean-Martin, he *was* captured in 1943.
He was in the main POW camp at Thorn and was transferred
from there to a working party at Insterburg in March 1944. In the
late summer his mother heard from him for the last time. After
the war he was posted missing and has never been heard of since.
I checked too, of course, with the War Ministry."

"But does that prove . . . ?"

"I'm afraid the evidence is so strong that, speaking for myself, I
hardly needed to wait for the photograph I asked for."

"A picture," murmured Chavanges tonelessly. Alain slid an envelope out of his flat document case and from that he slid in turn
a piece of pasteboard. It was a snapshot of three young men in the
uniform of conscripts, two staring solemnly into the lens, the one
in the center smiling. He was not Rolf, that young man of about
Rolf's age photographed in 1939. But he might have been Rolf's
brother. The dark hair grew evenly in the same line from the
bland forehead. The eyes with their distinctive tilt glinted with vitality and enjoyment of some joke. The nose, long enough to give
the face character, showed the aquiline bump of the bridge, not
strongly marked but sufficient to convey an imperfection of symmetry that underlined the evenness of the features otherwise. The
mouth curled in a line rather sweet for so masculine a face, perhaps a little self-indulgent but full of energy and humor. More
than anything, the tiny pull from the corners of the nose could be
identified, since this man was smiling, as the precise echo of the
pull of Rolf's smile. His hair was cropped much shorter than
Rolf's and he seemed to be less tall so that his shoulders looked
wider. But the family likeness was unquestionable.

Chavanges could not even pretend not to recognize the face; he was not likely to forget what Rolf looked like. There was no need to ask his opinion; that would have been pointless cruelty.

"So he existed," he said at last, and very carefully he laid down the picture, face down, on the table and pushed it back toward Alain. What he thought was, he will never be faithful to her; she will suffer. The silence inside the warm room stretched out; it began to seem impossible that it should ever be broken until, at last, with scared artificiality Solange looked at her watch, gave a smothered exclamation and murmuring something about an appointment, made her escape.

Released from the ban, Alain pulled his case toward him and said he feared they must talk about money. The small matter of his mother-in-law's will would have to be settled.

Solange had not even mentioned what, to her, was the clinching argument for her own view of Anna Forstmann's narrative because she was sure that both those men of affairs would dismiss it as feminine and silly. That was the conviction almost from the start of her reading it, of its authentic ring of truth. She felt it not only as real twenty-five years ago but as if the journey in some way she could not analyze were still there and real now. A lawyer like Alain might search records and "prove," if he wished to do so, the falsity of the account by pointing out that the R.A.F. raid on the military hospital at Insterburg took place in September 1944 and not in June. That the only possible signal stop on a railway into Warsaw that could correspond with Anna's account was sixty-four and not less than forty kilometers from the city. That there was no assistant surgeon in any Allied hospital outside Bad Ischl in 1945 called Fraser, the nearest likeness being an administrative officer by the name of Franks who could hardly be the man described by Anna for he would not have been regularly present in the operating room. That the only spa near the Polish–Czech border near the confluence of Vistula, Oder and March into a major valley showed a sole tributary stream to the north of the town; that is, on the far side of it from where Anna claimed to have set fire to the police warehouse. That the only serious road accident involving a French vehicle on the Laufen pass in September 1945 was the crash of a twenty-ton truck which would, of course, not be driven by an officer. Solange knew very well how one might go about discrediting Anna's story. But she knew too that there is an incontestable sound and feel of what is real and true, just as the sound of a gold piece dropped on the floor is the sound of gold striking a hard surface and not that of copper alloy; but it is not easy to express how the ear knows the ring of gold from that of base metal.

Metals came into her drifting thoughts because the car was stopped for nearly ten minutes by some large confusion nearby and she sat back against the deep upholstery, almost inertly, resting from the tension of the discussion she had left, so quiet, so restrained and so deeply disturbing. The driver was not familiar with the city and found himself on the wrong side of the Belvedere gardens near a road-building operation invisible to them but involving the slow transport of a huge crane. There was little traffic for nobody who knew the district drove by this route if it were possible to avoid it. Simply, they must sit there and wait, in a haven of calm surrounded at some distance by the thump and trundle of excavation machinery. There was a small park open to the roadway, with trees and shrubs and floating above it an immense oval dome of green copper; standing among the low trees, half hidden were several anonymous monuments giving the place the air of a disused and well-kept graveyard, which it was not. Against the tearing clouds in rapid movement the great globe seemed to rise and swing as if it would float away into the stormy sky. Solange gazed at the green shape and wondered without much interest what it was; the curve, massive but light, had the coherence, the certainty of perfection. She knew little of architecture and it did not interest her. It was a shape and a color; she did not even perceive that its own excellence gave it the quality of movement rather than the hurrying bulks and rags of broken cumulus.

"I wonder what building that cupola is," said the driver idly. "Do you know, Madame?"

"I'm afraid I don't," Solange answered. "I should, I suppose, but I don't."

"It's obviously something and not just a railway station, anything of that sort."

"We could get a guidebook and look it up. I don't know, now I come to think of it, why we haven't done some sight-seeing these last days."

"But you know the city, Madame?" Phillippe's employment dated from after his employer's resignation from the diplomatic service, but he knew that they had lived in Vienna.

"Well, you know how it is, when you live in a place you always think there is plenty of time to look at things. And then, suddenly, you're leaving."

"Yes, I expect that's how it is. And we'll be leaving again now, now that Monsieur is well again." Phillippe did not mention that he had, in fact, been doing some exploring during the idle days while M. Chavanges was ill. Madame possessed a rare virtue, of which she was unaware; her voice and manner did not change for different kinds of people, she spoke to the chauffeur in just the same tone she used to an ambassador. It was one of the factors in her ignorance of the world and human nature, for strangers reacted by showing her a courtesy and consideration quite different from the veiled resentment with which the wealthy are frequently met. What she did notice was that the man's voice changed slightly on mentioning her husband, who was respected but not always liked; and as always when this happened Solange interpreted it as being an attribute of power, something that certainly did not attach to herself in her own view.

"It's beautiful, the city," he continued. "I wouldn't mind staying here a while if one could only eat here. But the food is really dreadful."

"I wonder why that is."

"They cook everything too long," he said decisively. "I'm sorry about this long wait, Madame."

"There's no hurry." And she smiled into his driving mirror because he was smiling at her indifference when she might well have blamed him for getting them into this backwater.

"Still, perhaps I'd better go and ask that policeman, shall I?"

"Yes, do that," she agreed to what he clearly wanted, to stretch his legs.

The uniform worn by the policeman standing some way ahead at the street corner reminded her of the remark, "an airman. And in the Army, at that." He can't admit the possibility, she thought, yet he knows he must. He is powerless here, the world of feeling is foreign to him and he has no means to deal with it. He is not used to being helpless. The alien idea that power, and the use of power, are pitiable was too much for her; she could not follow it. But neither did she doubt the validity of the insight or the deep pity it left her with. She frowned up, out of the car window, making an effort to get hold of her thought and failing. Like that great green dome that rode up into the hurrying clouds and was immovable, it was two entirely different things at the same moment.

Coming back, Phillippe once more let a gust of cold into the car, and explained that the obstruction was caused by the installation of a crane needed for excavations going on to tunnel a new subway. He showed her with a gesture where the monster could now be seen from the back window and she was astonished that he had discovered all this without speaking a word of the language. The policeman saluted them as they slid past the corner, pleased that anyone so clearly capable of making a fuss had not done so.

He was not the only one to be relieved at an awkward moment passing with surprising calm. Alain expected angry reproaches at his account of the decision to release to the runaway Leona her grandmother's inheritance. Certainly, the amount seemed to Chavanges modest enough to be neither negligible nor dangerous. All the same, such complaisance was unexpected; it was not like Chavanges to pass over much smaller derogations of his authority with scarcely a word. He asked one or two questions of detail without much interest, and the one question his friend dreaded and which had induced Solange to make an appointment to coincide with their discussion was not even asked. Did he refuse to admit to himself that Solange and Alain knew where to get in touch with Leona? Or did he not dare risk the humiliation of a lie or a denial?

They returned instead to the account of Rolf's birth.

"In a way you are right. Madame Forstmann must have been carrying this story with her, inside her mind, for years. Well—we know how long. A generation."

"But you are convinced by it?" Chavanges asked.

"Yes. Even before I showed the photograph to Solange. Of course, if it were possible to trace these events back, there would be discrepancies. It would be strange indeed if there weren't. But it is impossible to read some parts of this story and disbelieve them. As you know, you often joke about it, I do not care to use the word 'truth' lightly. But this story is true."

"At any rate, your advice would be that to attempt to attack it in the courts would be hopeless?"

"Quite hopeless. You would need evidence of collusion, of planning. And—think of Leona. For what would you sue? Leona cannot be made a ward of court except in France. And Forstmann cannot be constrained against his will by the courts of another country. All you could do is to ruin him."

"We could get an injunction. To return her to her parents."

"I dare say you could. But—you want her to be brought back by the police? And if she refuses to come? Or runs away again? And, as so often in family difficulties, it is necessary to think of the future."

There was another long silence, while Chavanges took up the position abandoned by Solange at the window.

"You mean she would never forgive me." He spoke to the reflections in the already darkening glass. "What would your advice be, then?"

"I don't know. I feel singularly helpless. In effect the only persuasive objection to Leona's marriage is its imprudent suddenness."

It was all so quiet, so blanketed by an almost fierce self-control, that it might be said that nothing was happening. Chavanges had almost the manner of one recapitulating something that belonged to the past, and Alain could not know that the defeat was indeed past, the inner defeat that robbed Chavanges of his confidence. Solange had said, tentatively, that her husband's illness could have been self-induced, that he had retired into fever and unconsciousness; but this was so little like what Alain knew of his friend that he thought it fanciful and expected some new maneuver, some objection in reverse that would put off an admission of impotence.

"You say nothing . . . ?" he said at last, afraid to force the issue.

Chavanges turned from the window, through which he had seen nothing at all.

"I'm trying to understand," he said slowly and his thick brows were indeed frowning, his eyes puzzled as well as wounded. "Trying to grasp where I went wrong."

"Perhaps *you* didn't go wrong at all," Alain tried to put it delicately. "Perhaps it just happened, nothing to do with you? These things do happen. And, you know I'm fond of Leona—I don't want to intrude but I can't help feeling thankful that it happened before she married this Lensky boy, instead of after. Since she evidently has it in her to feel so strongly . . . ?"

"But if it is only a passing fancy? She will suffer . . . I thought, I mean I would have thought if such a violent change in her had ever occurred to me . . . that she would have come to me. That she would have told me. I thought . . ."

This was shocking intimacy and Alain shrank from it but his instant thought that he must show nothing was unneeded; Chavanges did not see him, he looked about him at the pretty room searching for something that was not there. His friend could look at him without being caught. The puzzled eyes, the wide brow, the hard mouth and the whole visage, even the protective hunch of the shoulders expressed a depth of uncomprehended suffering. His look was the unbelieving pain of an animal brutally injured by its trusted master. Alain felt his own heart within his breast quail with pity and for the first time since he was a young boy a sharp pricking behind his eyes warned him of the nearness of tears. He was appalled by the anguish of love and pain in one who always took his own dominance for granted and who now had lost it decisively. The whole outer shell of this man's life had been torn off by the only creature who could have dealt him this flaying wound, the only human being he had ever loved. The frightening vulnerability of those who are not lovable, who do not know how to reach others, came home to Alain as the deepest of human miseries.

At this moment, something after four o'clock in the afternoon, a slight tap at the door announced the entry of a hotel servant, a middle-aged woman, small, thin and sallow as a gypsy. She carried a tray of coffee which she set down and arranged on a side table. Neither her appearance nor the chink of china and silver disturbed Alain's thoughts. He was too used to being waited upon even to notice her until he saw the twist of disgust that distorted Chavanges' mouth and heard astonished the savage tone, almost a growl in which he spoke. Alain spoke no German but he hardly needed to understand the words; the expression of features and voice conveyed hatred and rejection out of all proportion to the slight interruption. The woman replied civilly and quietly, evidently explaining why she and not the waiter had brought the tray. She then picked up an ashtray with cigarette and cigar stubs and went to the door, but with her hand on the door handle she said something further, no more than a phrase, but in a tone of joking familiarity.

With an ostentatious gesture Chavanges took out a thin wallet and almost threw a quite large banknote into her discreetly ready hand, and in a moment the two men were alone again. Nothing at all had happened except that Chavanges objected to being interrupted. Yet some thread of subterranean meaning issued from the exchange of foreign speech, a thin tendril of impropriety, a minute assertion from the servant to Chavanges for which Alain could find no reasonable explanation.

"But even if Leona should change her mind . . ." he began as the door was closing.

Chavanges lowered his broad head and clenched his hands. He looked at the door, now shut, the handle still moving.

"Don't . . . !" He caught himself up. He shuddered visibly, shook his head and stood there for a moment, rigidly watching the door.

To cover his astounded sense of some outrage having occurred, Alain crossed the carpet and began to pour out coffee that smelled aromatically strong and stimulating.

Behind his back Chavanges moved. "Have some cognac with it?" he suggested in a strained voice which tried to attain casualness. "You were saying?"

"Good idea, I will," agreed Alain. "Yes, what was I saying?"

Solange, on the other hand, having at last arrived at the Leclercs' apartment, replied to a similar question. No, she would love just tea; it was, she thought, too early to drink yet.

"I'm never sure when is the time to start," said Angela Leclerc. "Since I don't really drink at all except when I have to, in public."

"It seems to vary a lot," said the tall girl in jeans with loose brown hair who had brought in the tea tray and now gave its nearer handle a tentative shove to make sure it was properly set in its frame.

"That's just it," agreed Angie, and looked at the clock. "Listen, Susy, you can't have been in the park for two hours today with Angèle. You know you're supposed to walk her two hours."

"But it was snowing again."

"I know. But two hours, please, every day. Be a good girl and don't cheat, hm?"

"All right," agreed the girl laughing. "I admit I did cheat a bit today but I won't again." She loped to the door where a small girl stood waiting just out of sight, and took her by the hand. "Come and say good day to Madame, Angèle." The little girl advanced solemnly, bobbed to Solange and lisped a greeting.

"Mind you," said Susy in English, watching the child with affectionate approval, "I did think, coming to a French family, that life wouldn't be quite so Spartan. Might have stayed in England, almost."

"Bad luck!" said Angela, laughing as she bent to kiss her daughter.

"Isn't Madame pretty, Susy," they heard the little girl say as the two went away together. "She smells lovely too. Very expensive."

"Well, Madame is awfully rich," agreed Susy, and they disappeared, prattling happily.

"She behaves just like a brat in the films sometimes," said Angela, shaking her head. "I'd say it was nature copying art, like Oscar Wilde said, only Angèle never sees the T.V. ads and anyway they don't have children in them here. It must be original sin, I fear."

"All small girls flirt like that, Leona did, too. Is that your nanny?"

"Well, au pair. We can't afford a nanny."

"And she wears jeans in the house and her hair undone?"

"They all do," sighed Angela, "but then, so do I half the time. And, you see, it's different . . . Susy's the daughter of a country doctor and so was I. She came to learn German, but of course, has learned hardly a word. Although her French is now really quite good. I just don't know what I shall do when she goes to the L.S.E. next autumn."

"L.S.E.? No, don't tell me. It sounds like Elysée, but it can't be. The young, they are so different suddenly."

"Yes, you must be feeling that a good deal, things being what they are. I feel it's a bit unfair for you, you're still nearly young yourself."

"I don't feel it, I promise you."

"Have you heard anything?"

"Yes, I told you, Leona telephoned. Since then she has called every evening. But it may be awkward now that he's back."

"Oh, I didn't ask how your husband was! Better, I hope?"

"Yes, he's better, but . . . I don't know, he's so quiet, as if he were tired all the time. And of course, terribly cross."

"Yes, always after flu. Georges is a perfect brute if he has even a cold." Angie poured out tea. "And then, it must have been an awful shock to him, this business with Leona."

"You think, not for me?"

"Oh yes, but you're more—resilient is what I mean, I think."

"That's not all you mean, is it?"

"Well, I'm pretty curious to see Leona again. But you mean, about him? Look, don't repeat this, will you? But Georges did say, at the Ball, before it happened, that your husband was very intense about her. And I thought so too. So I suppose I just assumed it was worse for him, and besides, you're so much cleverer than he is."

"Cleverer! Me?"

"Well, about people . . . I thought it was so bright of you to send for his friend—Maître Who, is it? Your nice queer Alain."

"Oh that. That was hardly clever, more like habit. I don't know what I'd do without Alain, and not for the first time by any means!"

"But no, I think it really is worse for him. After all, he must know, even if he doesn't admit it . . ."

"What—know?"

"That she was really getting away from him. I'm sorry. Perhaps I shouldn't say that."

"No, I'm glad, because if you think that, if you see that from outside, that makes it better, more sensible, what Alain and I have done about that money." She stopped to draw a deep, nervous breath. "Poor Alain is telling him, now."

"Could you do it without his consent, then?"

"Yes, I was the trustee, with Alain. I did tell you how it was? No? Well, my mother left a bit direct to Leona, of course Leona doesn't remember her, she was just a baby. It was money that was tied up for her in Switzerland during the war and you know how things in France were, after the war; so it was left like that just in case. And she left it to Leona on her eighteenth birthday for whatever she wanted. It isn't much, but I felt it would give Leona a feeling of independence. I mean, if this thing turns out to be just . . . just as you said, getting away from her father. As a matter of fact, I don't believe it is, but one can't know, not for a time. But if she changes, or Rolf changes, she wouldn't have to come back, begging."

"You must be a bit scared, doing that."

"Horribly. That's why I decamped and left it to poor Alain."

"He's very formidable. Yet—I feel sorry for him."

"So do I. Yes, really, I was thinking so, coming here. But I felt Leona must be able to make up her own mind."

"I wonder—I do wonder, if your mother thought like that. When she made her will?"

Solange shot a startled glance at Angie. "That's clever of you. She may have. When I was married the idea was to make things safe. But she may have thought it all a bit too safe—more a fence than a settlement. Not that she ever said so, but . . . I rather think she wasn't consulted much. Any more than I've ever been."

"It's all rather old-fashioned, isn't it? As if the war had never happened for them. Yet the war must have changed everything."

"You don't remember, surely?"

"No, I was seven when it ended, but I remember my eldest brother coming home from the Far East. He was quite odd for a time and he used to complain that we didn't know anything. And I suppose in France, the changes were even greater. But after the Occupation, I think people wanted to go back to the past, somehow. I know with Georges' family, they might as well have been playing at being in the *belle époque*."

"How? Over you being English?"

"Hm. And—they didn't know about me until it was settled. Or hardly knew. You know, Georges picked me up?"

"Picked you up? Where?"

"In St. James's Park. Isn't it funny? Mother and I were in London shopping and we walked across the park and there was this young Frenchman watching the birds." She broke off to laugh at her own unintended joke. "In both senses, evidently. So he took us to tea at Fortnum's. We thought it was just an affair, really, and then suddenly we knew we would get married. Things do somehow seem to work themselves out, if you mean them to. I don't think one knows always when one is serious . . . I can't explain."

"But afterward, you understand, it is better to have been serious," said Marie Perriot's dry voice from the doorway. "Once, that is, one is married."

"Marie! Do come in. We were talking about youthful love affairs."

"Not surprising in the circumstances. How is Monsieur Chavanges now? Yes, yes. The little Leona, figuratively speaking little, anyway, had a lucky escape there."

Solange lifted questioning eyebrows at this remark and Marie, thinking herself to have been tactless, changed the subject back again to past love affairs.

"Not only youthful, either. I was twenty-seven in 1944 . . . but it began in 1940, really. Well, you know how stuffy Paul is, so it will surprise you to hear. You see, I was in Bordeaux and I had a hotel room. All to myself. He was to wait for a ship, or to be told where to go to get a ship, and I was determined to go to de Gaulle, too. But the important thing was my room. There was ab-so-lutely nowhere to go in Bordeaux then. They said even the ex-King of England could find no place to lay his tiny, disloyal head but that isn't true, he was never in Bordeaux at all. So Paul seduced me in order to have a comfortable bed and somewhere to bathe. It's the sacred truth. And he'd only arrived that very day."

"The same day!" cried Solange.

"Even that is too much to say. It was evening when he arrived in the town on his last breath of gasoline. It took him two hours and not a minute more. Then we were separated for years, I didn't even know where he was. So one evening in 1944 I walked into the Ritz Bar, downstairs of course, and there he was looking very dashing and propping up the bar as one does in London. He walked over and said, 'Darling, it's been an age, where have you been and what are you doing this evening?' And I said, 'If you don't want to run into my fiancé, we had better go upstairs.' Men were much handsomer in the war than they are now."

"So? And then?"

"So he said all right, let's go up to the other bar. So we went upstairs and never looked back."

"My husband was in the Foreign Service right through the war," said Solange. "But we weren't married until years after that."

"Oh dear, I'd forgotten that! How tactless of me."

"It's only envy that makes me mention it," replied Solange. "It's very nice of you both to cheer me up over Leona."

"If you need to be cheered, good. But you know, it may simply be sex and just blow over."

"Then I *would* need cheering up. But somehow I don't think it's just that. When I watched them that evening, it didn't seem to me to be sex at all."

"I agree," said Angie thoughtfully.

"They seemed, you know, solemn. As if something serious, magically serious, were happening. Not excited. As if they'd discovered something mysterious and wonderful. They looked almost awed, in fact."

"But even if it is just an affair, is that so terrible?" asked Marie. "I'm not, you understand, saying, not for a moment, that promiscuity is anything but nasty. But an enchantment like this, so young and beautiful, like a fairy tale?"

"Perhaps it might not have been. But after such a fuss has been made, it has all become so public."

"Oh I do agree. It's the fuss." Angela sighed. "Things are so much easier if nothing has been said."

"You don't need to persuade me," Solange disclaimed. "It should never have been taken so disastrously seriously. But then, if Leona hadn't known it would be, she wouldn't have run away."

"You know, you seem to be so much on their side," Marie risked candor, "that I don't quite understand how you ever agreed to the arrangement—suggestion—with the Lenskys about their son with Leona."

"I don't understand the Lenskys, either," said Angela. "They are so modern."

"Oh yes, *their* position is quite clear. They wanted to get Kari under control. But . . ."

"But I didn't agree," protested Solange. "I wasn't consulted."

"Wha-at?"

Solange shook her head. "It began to be mentioned, gradually, to Leona, generally spoken of. There never was any discussion. That, I supposed, would come after this visit, when the two young

394

people had met again. And I don't think Leona took it in as a definite future that would be permanent. It was not being allowed to go to the University that she rebelled over. She wanted to do that first."

"It seems incredible!"

"She was so used to her father arranging everything. And so was I. Even to get her a few days at St. Anton—as I thought—was a struggle. I never have been able to manage him," Solange wailed, half laughing at herself but aware that she could never explain. "Either I give in or I lose my temper. Because, he does keep *on* so."

"I suppose, if you never did take a hand it was hard to start, and you couldn't know there would be a crisis until it was there."

"But I feel now that I ought to have known. Leona has her father's will in fact. Only it was never used, not for years, although she always dominated other children as a child. You see, she never needed to use it. He gave her everything before she wanted it."

"It seems so strange not to talk about things. We seem to discuss everything endlessly."

"It just didn't occur to me that I could. Until I saw her with a boy that she matched with, saw them together. Then it struck me, as something . . ."

"Something absolute?" suggested Angie.

"Yes, absolute. You noticed it too, then? When I watched them, they didn't see me, they stood by the wall out of the way of the dancers. And it was already real, then, settled, unchangeable. I couldn't hear what they said and I wasn't listening anyway. It was enough just to see them. Enclosed in their own—what? In their own wonder. You could feel it. And, of course, he felt it too. It wasn't what *I* said to him that caused the shock; any other time he would hardly have heard, just shrugged it off. But he knew."

"And what did you say to him?"

"I said he was in love with her."

"Oh. Oh dear," said Marie.

"Yes, it wasn't very nice of me. But sometimes he just drives me mad and I have to get back at him. But that night at the Ball, when he looked down and saw them dancing together—he knew then that he'd lost her."

"Did he say anything?"

"No. I just saw it in his face, lost love."

"Then why . . . ? Oh yes, I see. He wanted to arrange her marriage himself, to prevent anything like this happening. But, I must say, the part the Lenskys played . . . ! Not that one doesn't understand them, too. But it wouldn't have worked, not nowadays. Those arranged marriages are practically a prescription for adultery and nowadays that means divorce. But, surely, now that this other scandal has broken, he must be just a little reconciled to Rolf Forstmann?"

"Other scandal?"

"But you know about Kari Lensky?" cried Angela.

"Mind you, it's still only rumor, or was last night. But Madame Lensky was so frantic that it's obviously true. He's on the run from the police. He had something to do with that attack on the U.S. offices."

"But it can't be true! You mean, what I heard on the News-in-French this morning? With two dead? *Kari?*" She laughed with shock. "It's a black joke!"

"It's true all right," said Marie.

"But how terrible for his mother. Oh, my God! I didn't think of that! Leona is staying at Kari Lensky's flat. The hideout, they call it . . . Hideout."

"Hideout!" echoed Angie and they all stared at each other in horror.

"You don't think Rolf had anything to do with it?" implored Solange.

"Or even knew about it?" cried Angie, clasping her hands.

"Oh, surely not. No, they couldn't. They would never have gone there if they'd known."

"Of course," Solange sank back for a moment in her chair with a gasp of relief.

"But being there, they are bound to be involved, I'm afraid."

"With the police?"

"And the military."

"But for heaven's sake, I must do something. I must—Angèle, where is the telephone? I must tell her father. I must do something. I mean he must . . ."

"Wait a moment," said Marie firmly. "Let's think. 'In a crisis, do nothing.' That's always good advice."

"But why didn't you tell me at once?" cried poor Solange.

"I thought you knew and didn't want it discussed. From what you said—before, I've forgotten. I was trying to be *tactful*."

"Heavens, I couldn't have helped discussing it! But I can't do nothing. I must get Leona away from there . . . Only I don't know where it is, the hideout."

"You don't know the address?"

Solange shook her head, near tears. "I was afraid to ask too many questions. I thought it would destroy her confidence in me. Besides—if he asked me I wanted to be able to say I didn't know. He would know at once if I told a downright lie."

"You have to wait, then, until she telephones?"

"I could ask 'Inquiries' to find out the number?" suggested Angela.

"There isn't a telephone there. Leona said so." Solange almost ran to the door and came back. "Should I get in touch with the police? Or the Embassy?"

"I'd wait, until we've worked it out. If you start asking for help somebody may think you know more than you do, and that wouldn't be good for Leona or Rolf."

"What do you think the Army will do?"

"To Kari?"

"No, to Rolf, of course."

"Transfer him." Marie was prompt and certain. "That's the

first thing that comes into any military mind at the least hint of a scrape. They'll think Rolf knew Kari well enough to have known something. That means he ought to have reported it. So they'll have just one idea. To get him away on to the responsibility of another command, quickly."

"Oh dear, oh dear, my poor Leona. And all those terrible investigations!"

"Is it bad, being transferred?" asked Angela.

"It's terrible. Poor boy, what a shame. Dragged into such a mess and by a no-good like Kari Lensky!"

"You're sure they will transfer him?"

"Positive. I know the soldierly mind," said Marie somewhat grimly. "I had four years of them. In fact, the best thing Rolf can do, the moment his part in the inquiries is over, is to volunteer for a year to fly famine relief for The Samaritans. They are always looking for pilots and he could be seconded."

"What a strange idea."

"Not really. I'm on their International Committee, you know. The army authorities here and elsewhere quite like the idea. It gives the pilots a lot of experience."

"So you could fix it?" asked Angela, slowly.

"If I were asked," said Marie carefully, "I could certainly put a word in."

"Volunteer, you say?" Solange said thoughtfully. "For The Samaritans?"

"Probably other things too, I just happen to know about The Samaritans. So, by the way, does Madame Forstmann."

"Is she on the committee too?"

"Madame Forstmann is on everything."

"Anna Forstmann . . . I . . ." Solange frowned and was silent.

"She'd do anything for her boy. Of course, he *is* her son. I see you have heard something."

"You know that?"

"Oh, one hears things, gradually. Nobody ever says, but I've assumed it for some years, almost since I've known her."

"I thought it was a deadly secret," said Solange humbly.

"Well, it is, for strangers. But there aren't any secrets here, you ought to know that."

"And it wouldn't harm his future, if he volunteered?"

"On the contrary, I should think. It would save him from being transferred, which is always bad. They'd probably be so grateful that they'd decorate him. And certainly, they'd promote him. I believe that always happens on secondment."

"But it would mean Africa, or somewhere."

"Only for a year. Two at most. Leona would probably adore it."

"No worse than for a diplomat, after all," said Angie.

"And Madame Forstmann, have you thought, may know how to get hold of them. Rolf, anyway."

"But of course, why didn't I think of that? May I telephone her, Angela?"

"You see," said Marie complacently. "So much better to talk it over before doing anything."

CHAPTER 27

Somehow the familiar route seemed different, and not because Rolf took the train; he often used a rail pass when funds were short. But the reason he was going into the city and the reasons for his agreeing to go, as well as all the other strange circumstances of the last few days, had changed the outward look even of things seen so many times that they were hardly visible. A whole lot of things were visible now as insecure or altered that before had been taken for granted as being just what they seemed. Gullible, the adjutant had called him; and "I would somehow have expected you to have more sense." Rolf would have expected that of himself too; it was his mother who sighed and said that everyone was gullible where personal feeling was involved. That was on the telephone; he hadn't seen her or anyone else or been off the station until this afternoon. A pass was granted smartly enough for this outing and the most astonishing thing about the whole queer business was his own instant acceptance. Not that he wanted to be seconded to fly wheat to anybody, let alone dried milk, but that it was the only way he could get into the town to see Leona.

If the adjutant was surprised at the ease with which Rolf was persuaded that secondment was from everyone's point of view preferable to transfer, he did not show it. The trouble with a transfer, and just before he was due for promotion at that, was that "it stayed on the papers" as, at the very mildest, a permanent question mark, a "why?" that accompanied its subject during and after his service career. Whereas to volunteer, the adjutant urged, was perfectly respectable, even admirable; the most rigid selection board or the most grumpy civilian bureaucrat could find in it nothing worse than a taste for adventure. Where the devil they got the whole idea from was a minor mystery. As if that mattered. Probably some bit of official jargon from the Ministry—Rolf remembered those circulars of information well from his short and exquisitely boring spell in the adjutant's office—praising an opportunity for junior officers to widen their experience by taking a Red Cross course or by proposing themselves for the examination board for the staff college. At least this queer assignment would be flying. There was one terrible thing that absolutely useless types got sent to, a factory course for which the volunteers needed to be practically press-ganged; at any rate this was not as bad as that.

The truly horrifying thing about it all was the way Kari's nonsense, interpreted always, as it were, by its being just Kari and made harmless without anyone actually thinking about it, by Kari's father being able to fix anything, was now public and official. From one day to the next everybody Kari had ever joked with seemed to be in trouble, most of all Kari himself. Men Rolf hardly knew were being questioned far longer than he was himself by a couple of much older officers who had always been somewhere on the periphery as chair-warmers and were now only too identifiable as "Field Security" and someone in civilian clothes from the Ministry whose title was not mentioned. This person spoke hardly at all but was not the less sinister for that. He was old and his look was gloomy and withdrawn, he gave the impression of only half listening to question and answer, occasionally murmuring something to a questioner but otherwise just sitting there slumped in his chair. He did speak once, not directly to Rolf but including Rolf in a remark made to himself. The half-colonel from Security was nagging about the little flat; not about what Rolf had been doing there—he had been allowed to put in a statement about that so that no other name was openly mentioned in order for it not to be recorded in the protocol—but about what Rolf thought Kari did there. After some time, when Rolf had still not formulated something never quite faced in his own mind, the old man produced his undertone, head turned half to the interrogator and eyes nearly closed.

"No need to bully the boy. It's obvious he took Lensky for a homosexual. Without 'taking' anything at all. Right?" And shortly after that Rolf was dismissed, still without having put into words his answer to that "Right?" It only half penetrated his despondent bafflement that the three men watching him—he supposed the old one watched although he did not seem to do so—picked up his unspoken answer out of the air. And indeed the sudden, wincing frown with which he greeted that word was reply enough for any witness.

Was it true that he ought to have known that the pranks of Karl Henri Rilla-Lensky would issue in murder? It had been said so often now that he accepted it. But if that were the case, then it was equally so for Kari's parents and for a dozen brother officers, not to mention their seniors. Nobody had taken Kari seriously for the good reason that he was not serious, he was playing. But loaded guns and explosives go off and perhaps the more easily if one is playing with them and not applying all those routines, those regulations designed to fence in the sanctioned use of lethal weapons with ifs and buts. And the result was two dead men and it was due only to the fact that the fashionable "enemy" of the moment was a civilized country and having its own troubles with embattled juveniles that they could be assured the escapade would not endanger the entire community. Rolf Forstmann was, for his age and for the place he lived in, almost criminally unconcerned about politics, but he knew enough to know that there were other

kinds of countries and among them neighbors, who would not
have reacted with pained protests and the opening of an Embassy
fund to help the widow and two orphaned children of their mur-
dered employee. If he had not known all this before, it had been
rubbed in enough in the last few days for him to be unlikely ever
to forget it again. That was the public aspect of the disaster and
bad enough.

Its personal aspects seemed naturally infinitely worse to Rolf
and his mind had been so much concentrated on them that he actually thought in such concrete terms as he sat gloomily staring
out of the carriage window of the slow train. Was it really his own
fault, his own neglect, that now brought his pleasant life to the
very brink of ruin, only to be rescued by changing it, or rather by
transferring it bodily, to another continent and another authority?
Surely those security fellows, the civil police who said they were
watching Hannes Becker for over a year, Kari's mother and father,
were more culpable? Why him? Simply because he happened to
have been there. Because Kari had singled him out as stand-in not
out of an exclusive friendship for he had many friends, all unconscious of what had been going on under their noses. No, because
he recognized in Rolf this stupid sense of responsibility that
would not let Kari down, but which did not apparently impose
any corresponding duty on Kari. That was the start of the whole
unrolling chain that now fettered him.

And because he had gone to the Opera Ball and left Kari free
to carry out his stupid schemes, *it* all began, and because *it* began
and took over his life and being, he was blinder even than normally. Everything was changed in the last few weeks, and from
being a member of a commune Rolf was turned into a private person. Everything changed, was transformed, intensified, so that he
himself was changed. And not only himself, he saw now. The
jokes and hints of his companions, carried on from former days,
had ceased abruptly, at once, in the first few hours on duty after
the Ball. They recognized the change and knew as he did that

remarks and laughter that would have been flattering as well as embarrassing *before* would now be mortal insults attacking his male pride at its deepest instinctive root. The dimension Rolf lived in now was a new world not even to be thought of clearly by himself, let alone others, and must be protected by ceremonious and unspoken barriers which were recognized and respected by everyone.

Everyone, that was, except Kari. Not because Kari used Rolf in the first place, but because he lied and went on lying, that secret world was menaced by the creeping outgoing rings of discovery, by the groping of inquiry and publicity. It was within reaching distance of exposure, of being handled, discussed, to being public property. Even the obscurely recognized scrupulousness, the almost feminine delicacy, with which he had been treated in every detail that touched this subject served only to exacerbate his touchiness. The very need for care, for others knowing they should be careful, was an outrage.

And the outrage had been committed by Kari. His original fault of not wanting to go to the Opera Ball—only seen as a slight by Rolf after it turned to Rolf's immeasurable advantage—had been spoken of to strangers. He had been forced to admit that there could exist a man who did not attach overriding importance to that being who was now Rolf's inmost and most intensely real self; that was an affront that could never be wiped out even if dueling were still possible. That rankled like a poison dart. It made an enemy of Kari and Rolf felt the fierce animosity that filled him when he thought of it, with disgust and rejection. It was primitive, one should not feel such things but such things go deeper than education and survive in all their archaic force in spite of being rooted out in each generation. Hatred was wicked but it was undeniably there and when he thought of those first moments when he saw her anxious childish eyes in the anteroom at the Opera, Rolf could hardly contain his rage. He deserves to be shot, he thought savagely and clenched his fists, shifting in his seat with fury so that the timid-looking elderly man who shared the compartment with him got up and went out into the corridor away from the young man who scowled like an anarchist. And in uniform too. It would never have done in his young days when an army officer was expected to be a gentleman, *that* he would swear.

It took nearly two hours at the intimidatingly modern offices of the international Catholic charity organization to which Rolf was directed. Church organizations are expected to be housed in Gothic or, in Austria, in Baroque edifices but this place had been designed for its purpose by an advanced young architect and was peopled not by the imagined bumbling priests and bead-clutching sisters but by brisk and competent young men and women of Rolf's age who were much more efficient than anybody Rolf knew in the service. God's purpose was never mentioned once, everybody concentrated on carrying it out instead, and Rolf found himself pressed into their company with a thoroughness and neatness that robbed him while he was there of his raging impatience to get it over. There was no point in impatience for they were almost as fast as he could have wished with their questions and their forms and their "sign here, please" and their snatching up telephones to check with the adjutant and not brooking any delay there either: it was understood that the papers would be sent on afterward, was it not? Even Rolf's coldly unforthcoming statement that he was about to be married failed to ruffle them; they got out of him in three minutes that his fiancée spoke perfect French and English and no, she had no business experience, no, no nursing experience either. Yes, he was sure she would be willing to submit to their mild discipline during his period of duty and he understood that she was required to be poisoned as he would be with a dozen different inoculations and let us make an appointment now for her to be inducted and injected and no doubt inspected too.

When he landed—he felt as if from a catapult—in the roaring thoroughfare outside it occurred to Rolf that he had not yet asked

405

Leona if she objected to going to some place just south of the
Sahara Desert, see, here it is on the map. A very large and very
empty-looking map. He would do well to get over there and put it
to her. He took the underground, it was faster than trams. There
was a long walk from the local station, the same way they had
gone that day. He ran the last stretch.

You'd never dream they were a bunch of holies, he rehearsed
telling her. If they are all that breed it won't be too bad. At least
from the people point of view, although from the look of that
map the rest of it might not be much fun, apart from actually
flying. And they would have nearly two months to do everything.
He no longer questioned that it was all going to happen.

He took the shallow, curving stairs two at a time, all three
flights of them, but slowed to a stroll as he reached the gallery.
No light from the kitchen window, she was catching frugality
from the neighbors. There was no light inside, either, and no blue
flicker from the gas heater. It was not cold in there, coming from
the street, but it was bleak and smelled dusty, hollow. It thudded
sickly in him that Leona was not there.

She was gone, he assumed it at once. Of course, she could not
stand the loneliness, the poverty of this miserable hole by herself.
She had gone back to the splendid hotel with the effulgence of
light in its entrance which was all he had ever seen of it. Her parents were there, safety, plenty, the protection of the imagined father. She was gone and gone finally where he could never follow.
She was gone. The word boomed in his hollow mind, echoed
deeply like an artillery shot against a fortress wall, tolled like the
great bell of the cathedral, too deep and heavy to be rung but
once a year. He did not even look to see that her few garments
were not there for he could see the telegram lying inside the door
that would have told her of his arrival; he stepped on it, not noticing, as he entered.

He did nothing, just stood there. There was nothing to do,
there was nothing at all anywhere, not inside and not outside. Just

nothing. He saw that she went only yesterday or today. Or there would have been a letter lying there as well as the wire, a letter from him with the scarlet "express" stamp on it. The thought of a letter made him look around but there was nothing on the table or anywhere else, no message. He turned his head without moving otherwise and looked past the doorway into the kitchen. But nothing lay on the scrubbed table there, nor on the cupboard, the places hallowed by generations for leaving messages saying the woman who should be there has gone shopping, will be back at tea time, suppertime, some time. He wondered, now that it was so, how he could have missed the lurking possibility, so clear and echoing, of her going, of her being simply lost in not knowing what to do, in being alone. How could he have been so sure? A subdued clatter from the other attic flat came through the connecting wall over there. Then people talking, pop music, a voice declaiming some huckster's slogan. The woman there had come in from work and at once, as she always did, turned on her television set, her constant and only companion. How could anybody be so crudely unfeeling as to go about their ordinary affairs? Did she not know? The thought of anyone at all knowing *this* gripped him like a fist in his stomach, a grip that twisted. Under the dark blank that must be misery swelled a fearful humiliation.

CHAPTER 28

"What isn't landscape is architecture in this part of the world," decided Alain.

"What! That little church? There's one like that in every village."

"That's what I mean," he agreed indulgently.

"If *they* impress you, you should see Melk."

"I hope you aren't developing local patriotism, Leona, my child." He deliberately made it sound like measles. "You are very quiet, Solange."

"Are you all right, Mamma?"

"Yes, darlings, of course. I'm just relaxing, that's all."

"Melk," Alain turned the name over in his mouth. "Odd word. Where is it and what is it?"

"You're teasing me," she said haughtily and they all laughed a little.

"I recognize this," Solange sat up. "This is the spa. The clinic is on the other side of it." She leaned forward so that Phillippe could hear her through the open glass shutter. "You remember the way, Phillippe?"

"Oh yes, I've done it twice now. I won't land you in an excavation site again, Madame."

"I didn't mean that," she protested, and the driver chuckled to himself.

"I saw that church again this morning, across the square from the other side where you go up to the airport. The cupola, that is, not near to. It's called the Karlskirche."

He had taken Monsieur Chavanges to the airport that morning.

"I'm sorry I didn't even see Papa before he went back." She sounded false but in fact she meant it as well as not meaning it.

"Well, he's been away almost a month," Alain pointed out. "And with me away, now—we can't both be away for more than a day or so."

They all knew that Chavanges had made up his mind to return without arranging a meeting with Leona because he could not face the actual admission of his capitulation. It would come to that, but not just yet. The resounding explosion of Kari Lensky's reputation as a possible bridegroom effected a cantankerous uprush of masculine pride in him; that he would not and could not admit to. He would wait until Leona came home in a few days' time and both his wife and his friend discreetly agreed to the importance of business affairs that called him home.

"The one good thing about that appalling Lensky boy," as Alain had said quietly to Solange. "It did revive his pride, poor fellow."

"You will be terribly nice to your father when we do get home, won't you?" said Solange now. "Yes, all right, I know you understand. You don't have to say anything."

The long car slid through tall and elaborately decorative iron gates standing open for their passage, described a graceful curve and slid to a stop before the shallow, curved steps of the clinic entrance.

"Don't wait out here in the freezing cold, Phillippe," said Solange as they all descended. "Come along."

Alain paused to look up at the exterior of the building, a high frontage of pale gray stucco picked out with white, elegantly wrought balcony railings, it was all swing and lightness in the matching snow. As the door swung open on one side the long, attenuated lilies of the tiled hall flowered dimly through the flash of glass.

"Entrancing! Pure *art nouveau!*" he cried. "Phillippe, that's your task for the afternoon. Find out who built it and when, while we're talking to Madame Forstmann. We shall be quite a time, so go to it."

The porter ushered them through an outer office with two desks and a whole guard of filing cabinets, where they were greeted in stumbling French by a young nurse. A small crisis had arisen, as so often, but Madame would be only a few minutes and could she bring them coffee.

"You ought to take more interest in your surroundings, Solange," scolded Alain. "Life must be so dull for you if you don't look at things."

"At the moment I'm more interested in coffee," replied Solange, who was used to this exhortation. She went through the open doors on the far side of the office into Anna Forstmann's privacy, followed closely by Alain and more slowly by her daughter.

It was obviously a workroom but equally a place of other interests. The lights were on to welcome them as if it were already evening, a big center lamp of Lalique glass which flooded everything with dispersed and shadowless brilliance and the reading lamp on the wide writing table, yet nothing affronted the eye with points of glare. There were books in rich bindings behind glass and others still in their colored jackets in an open white bookshelf. In a satinwood cabinet stood pieces of china, some of which looked as if they might be choice, but Alain was not interested in porcelain. The cloudy white curtains were looped generously over the typically wide window from side to side and the almost white carpet on which Chavanges had once shed clumps of snow was as unmarked as if it had been laid yesterday. The azalea bush, still in full crimson flower, reigned as the only unsubdued color, on its round pedestal table. All the woods were pale, the upholstery was pale, the papers on the desk were laid in orderly series. The quiet was pervasive as music. There was no one but themselves in the room so Alain could survey it in peace.

He crossed the silent carpet to where two drawings hung side by side. They were at once recognizable as the work of Klimt, which, in that apartment, was surprising. Each showed the clothed figure of a woman, the same woman. Possibly because Klimt shows an obsessive concern with one aspect of the nude—that is, the body as disrobed rather than as not yet clothed, as stripped rather than simply naked—clothed figures by this artist acquire from some unresearched source a hint of pornography. They carry a promise of a lewd uncovering which is powerfully suggestive, improper and decadent with a quality of distaste as if the painter felt some unadmitted disgust for the sitter, or perhaps for women altogether. This woman lounged standing, against a decorated pillar, angular in pose but exaggeratedly sinuous and long-necked, staring disdainfully and emptily at the viewer as if at a customer for her long-dead pleasures. It was the same pose in both pictures, taken from right and left so that the pair half-faced each other. The pairing of the two who were one was obviously intentional so that their doubling was also disturbing. On the right the model held her hand half raised to her uncovered throat; in the other the hand hung slackly by her side and in spite of the insolence and stupidity of the face both the hands and her eyes conveyed a profound unhappiness and impotence.

"Look at these marvelous Klimts," he said at last, "Leona, come and look."

"Mmm? Yes, I've seen them. They're horrid, aren't they, give me the shivers."

"They're marvelous. I'd give anything for them."

"You like this period, don't you, Alain?" said Solange as the two women came up behind him. "Can't stand the things myself. The colors are so nasty, especially the skin, like a corpse."

"They are a bit leprous," agreed Alain. "That's what is so splendid. Though not leprous, more likely . . . Hm."

"She looks as if she knows she's about to cop out," said Leona. "Die, I mean."

"There! You see, you *can* see things, if you look!" he was delighted. "Now how does he get that effect, that one knows she died young?"

"Poor thing," said Leona, "she's obviously hungry."

"Ah, Madame," Solange greeted an unheard entrant. Alain turned from the pictures with a jolt of recalled curiosity to meet the writer of that desolate narrative which had inflicted him with its hunger and cold so that he hunched in his room after reading it once more through the day before—just to be sure of his judgment—as if the luxurious hotel room were an unheated barrack and he as half-starved as he was in January twenty-five years ago in Slovenia before he was wounded. Absurdly, he felt shock and recognized that so powerful was the effect of her memories, together with his own forced recall of that time from the other side of Europe, that he had actually expected to find a young woman in her twenties, filthy, spent and desperate. Before him stood a woman who looked to be in the latish forties but was older than that, smaller than either Solange or Leona, and not so much thin as spare and, as it were, naturally abstemious. She created without any dynamism, any intention, a sensation of calm and control which declined to advance anything except a neutral civility; having hidden for many years a large part of his own nature Alain recognized this as one who habitually disguised herself, not as a deception but as a shield. If he had not known the story Alain would still, he was sure, have known that important fact. Except for the impression of neatness and of evenness in her person, she produced no presence, making Solange and Leona appear startlingly, even blatantly, physical. He was so astonished by his apprehension of a different woman, not that young woman of the past grown up and growing old but another, an entirely other human being, that he quite gaped and could only make conventional replies to introductions and greetings with a considerable effort.

"I see you were looking at the Klimts, Monsieur," she then at once said. She spoke with a slight, a very slight, foreign intonation which was not enough to be an accent; just enough to convey to one accustomed to self-discipline how much of a perfectionist she must be. "You admire his work, I see."

"Indeed. And these are exceptionally good ones. In fact, they are marvelously expressive. I envy you them."

"I was fortunate. They were given by a patient who could not afford his bill. Yes, it is odd, isn't it? Professor Smolka was very much annoyed. *His* bill was paid in money, you see, but the nursing account was settled by barter."

"So they are the property of the clinic?" asked Leona with the frankness of youth, dragging against the carefully threading pattern of civilized discovery. "I thought they were yours."

"They were the property of the clinic. But I made haste to pay the patient's bill and took the Klimts off the clinic's hands. In fact, I acquired them very reasonably indeed, as you can imagine. And Professor Smolka as good as told me so."

She did not quite smile at this, yet conveyed a satisfaction at this perfectly licit but cunning procedure which made them all smile in congratulation.

"Is that the only time such a lucky misfortune occurred?" asked Alain enviously.

"Unfortunately, yes. Either our patients are prosperous or penniless as a rule. Imagine if someone happened to possess a Breughel and couldn't pay his bill! But I can hardly see the Professor agreeing to that. He would be lying in wait if it happened again."

During this exchange coffee was being laid on a side table and they all moved toward it.

"I'm sorry Monsieur Chavanges had to leave before you came," said Anna Forstmann, as she indicated a chair to Solange and they seated themselves. "But he wrote to me, as you will know."

"We thought in about a month's time," said Solange. "You will come, of course, Madame?"

Anna looked at her, considering. "I can't quite make up my mind. I've never been to France, you know."

"Surely then, this is the perfect moment?"

"It seems to me, if I may say so, to be almost predestined," ventured Alain.

"But of course you'll come," Leona was almost offended. "Rolf would be upset if you didn't." For her, that settled the matter. "May I cut the *savarin?*"

"Oh, please. You may trust it, Monsieur," she said to Alain. "It was made by the Professor's cook. But it isn't quite a savarin, having no brandy in it."

"It's called *Gugelhupf* here," said Leona laughing and cutting up the fluted structure rather unevenly. "Heavens, I've made a mess of it!"

"*Gugelhupf!* Another splendid word. I really think I must learn German," said Alain.

"I don't think you'd find that in the grammar books." Leona was dubious. "It's very local."

"More local patriotism?" said Alain slyly.

"*That* came up because I mentioned Melk," Leona explained to Anna. "But tell me, what's happening about the Samaritans? Rolf mentioned it in his letter but it wasn't settled, he said."

"Oh, it is now," Solange cut off a piece of cake with the side of her little fork and popped it into her mouth. "Those gossiping *idle* women, when they get their teeth into something . . . !"

"Who? Madame Perriot?"

"It's what my husband called her," explained Solange.

"Women just have an entirely different way of getting things done," Alain picked up his cup. "Help! You don't *use* these cups, Madame?"

"Only on very special occasions. You like porcelain, too?"

"I don't know much about it, but any fool could see . . . I am really fascinated by pictures."

"He spends half his time here glaring jealously. I think he's planning an art robbery. But he can't make up his mind which to concentrate on, the Albertina, all those scratches, or the Kokoschkas."

"He was a patient of ours a few years ago."

"Pity *he* didn't pay with a painting."

"He did give me a sketch, I'll show it to you presently."

"Obviously I've made a terrible mistake in my profession," Alain grumbled. He cheered up as he thought of something. "I shall enjoy showing you the few things I have myself."

"He's got a Braque," said Leona, eating. "But listen. Do tell me. *What* has been settled?"

"Well, Marie Perriot asked somebody and he asked somebody else, I think including poor Madame Lensky who is on one of the committees, and still somebody else telephoned the commanding officer's wife and it was suggested to Rolf that he should volunteer and he agreed and then they all telephoned each other back again and that's that."

"I'm sure it wasn't as simple as that sounds," said Alain.

"Not much more than that," replied Anna. "In such a small place, where people know each other, one just knows whom to go to."

"I must say, as a rescue operation in a potentially catastrophic situation, it could hardly be bettered."

"And speed!" admired Solange. "One must grant it to the Catholic Church. When they want something done, they really get moving. You know, he's gone into Vienna this very day to start the enrolling process?"

"He? You mean Rolf?" A sharp rise in her daughter's voice made Solange first glance and then gaze at her. She thought with a sensation of shock and guilt that she ought to have noticed before how tired the poor child looked. Her poor little face was quite pinched, and her eyes looked smudgy. "D'you mean he's gone into the city *today*?"

"Yes. Yes, but what . . . ? Is something wrong, darling?"

"Wrong?" she almost whispered. "But I'm not there. He won't know where I am." She could not believe it. It was too dreadful to be real. "You mean, you let me come all this way to talk about pictures when Rolf may be standing there in that cold little flat and thinking where is she?"

"But we didn't come to talk about pictures, my lamb," protested Alain, dismayed at the uncivilized precipitancy of the young. "We came to talk about your future, about weddings and settlements and . . ."

"Settlements?" cried Leona, her eyes starting out of her suddenly gaunt head. She shook her shoulders and pulled back her hair with a rough gesture, making herself positively ugly. "Future?" As if stung, she jumped to her feet, shaking the table on which a thin tinkle infuriated her with its sociability. "My future is probably standing there at this very minute, thinking I've been run over or something!" She turned on poor Alain like a fury, the tears of rage bursting into her wide eyes, making them instantly red. "Settlements! That's what you think of. I bet that was Daddy's idea! He wants to get his hands on us. I know. He wants to get back in control. God, I must get back. At once! A bus, is there a bus?"

"Darling! Please!" Solange began to protest about manners and in the same moment saw how heartless that was. She turned, uncertain, and fell into Anna Forstmann's calm eyes. "The car!" she cried. "Where is Phillippe?"

Leona ran to the door, and turned, wringing her hands. "What's the time? Do you know what time he was going to this place, these people?"

"I'm not sure. Two o'clock I think, yes I think it was," her mother stammered. "Let's go and find Phillippe."

Before they were well into the hall Phillippe appeared, literally towed by their hostess and still wiping his lips from coffee.

"I'm so sorry, Phillippe, but we must go at once," said Solange.

"No, not us," Alain laid a hand on her arm. "Phillippe, if you will, drive Mademoiselle Leona back into Vienna as fast as you can. Then return for us, and there's no hurry about that. Don't get into any trouble with the traffic, though, will you?"

"At once, Monsieur," agreed Phillippe, pleased with the air of crisis, and snapped up his uniform cap from the hatstand as if it were a weapon.

"Come on," cried Leona. "Come *on*, Phillippe!"

"Oh dear," murmured Alain, "like the proverbial whirlwind. I feel suddenly quite old."

"Let us go and finish our coffee," said Anna, shaking her head and laughing to herself with an odd little shaking. "I think we might even take a cognac with it. I mean," she was leading the way, "we may as well have the compensations of age since we have the disadvantages."

"I'm quite upset," muttered Solange, still dithering slightly as if that whirlwind were shaking her.

"Don't worry too much," Anna laid a light hand on Solange for an instant. "It won't do them any harm. He can't be finished before half-past four, I should think, and then he has to get to the other side of Vienna."

"But she was so upset," wailed poor Solange. "I've never seen her like it."

"And even that, they enjoy at that age. The anguish is all part of the excitement, the passion. And, of course, the newness. The once-ness of it."

Solange sighed, "The truth is, I think, you know, that I envy them."

"Who wouldn't?" said Alain. "That splendid rage of self-centered glory. She's a perfect Valkyrie, the little one. For two pins she'd have scratched my eyes out, I do believe."

"Fortunately Rolf is just as wild." And already Anna was putting glasses and a promising-looking bottle onto the table with the coffee cups. "They will have a wonderful time in Africa."

"God help the Dark Continent is all I can say." Alain accepted a stout shot of brandy with relief. "Is he like his father? You must remember, I haven't seen him yet."

"As like as two pins," said Anna. "I hope the cognac is to your liking?"

"It's excellent, many thanks. And *most* welcome. There's nothing like a drink at the wrong time of day to set one up from the toils of living."

He looked across at Rolf's mother, hesitated and then plunged.

"We won't, of course, discuss it. But I should like you to know that I was in Slovenia that winter."

"Ah." And nothing more was said. Solange looked from one companion to the other and felt a pang of something like jealousy.

"The trouble with words," she reflected, lifting her glass, "is that if you *know*, you don't need them. And if you don't know, they don't help."

"They are useful for some things," said Anna. "Though they so often, and how fortunate that is, don't mean quite what they say."

"You mean," agreed Alain, "that we should make some arrangements?"

"Well, I don't really see those two madcaps arranging their own wedding, do you?" Solange laughed aloud at this notion and Anna laughed with her and then went on. "À *propos* arrangements. I think I ought to tell you. I don't know, you understand. We have not discussed it. In fact, I think Rolf has no idea of the extent of property he is marrying into. But I really don't see him accepting any settlements. He is too serious in a sense to be unwary of the threats of responsibilities."

"Pride is all very fine and large," replied Alain soothingly. "But a little money never hurt anybody. He'll get used to the idea."

"I rather doubt it. But we shall see."

"It's going to be interesting," said Solange. "And to start with I am going to leave all the wedding arrangements to her father."

Alain, about to make a startled objection, was forestalled by Anna, who spoke first.

"How *very* wise of you," she agreed. "That will show him. And that they will have to go through, but since they know they are escaping to Africa—as they think—they won't mind it."

"As they think?" queried Alain.

"Oh, they will go, yes, but it will hardly be the picnic they look forward to, don't you agree?"

"A picnic is just what they don't want. They want tremendous difficulties to overcome. And anyway, they have to pay somewhere for their enormous good fortune."

"We may thank God that they need to discover difficulties."

"Above all, that they didn't seek them in the way of the Lensky boy and his friends."

"The astounding thing about that story, to me," said Anna, shaking her neat gray head, "is that a girl was involved. Imagine any woman wanting revolution!"

CHAPTER 29

All was steely once again in the deepening twilight and the mysterious dispersion of that atmospheric quality that was not light
brought back with a swelling longing to Leona the great sweeps of
lonely snow in the north. The street lights came on in a hamlet as
the long motor slid curving up its only street. They made the late
afternoon suddenly dark but the air paled again as soon as the
frost-tinged yellow blobs were gone. On a hillock so that it was
distantly visible a bulbous church spire, ghostly with snow, floated
in mist. Leona sat in front with Phillippe and constantly twisted
her hands together.

"Fortunately the traffic is all the other way at this time," he
said. There was a good deal of traffic for they were within the attraction orbit of the city by now although still well outside the
city limits.

"Can't we go faster?" she begged.

"We're going much too fast as it is. That's the thing about
driving the Rolls. If I were pushing a Renault along like this we'd
be in jail by now."

She knew it was true but reminded of the bumping and rattling
of Rolf's old Fiat she clenched her teeth with raging impatience,
narrowing her eyes against the continuous flashing stream of lights

420

dazzling up and flooding past, scattering splinters over the wet surface of the road.

"We won't go straight in on the main road," she said, trying to keep her voice level. "It's the airport feed and crammed with every sort of junk. I'll tell you when and we'll take the side road and go along the canal."

"Are you sure?"

"Of course. It's much quicker. It's the 'in' way to go to Schwechat. I'm surprised you don't know it." He did not reply to this, not because she was the daughter of his employer but because he was slipping between a tractor which should not have been on the road and a large bus. On the down side one delivery van was passing another and if she had had any sense at all she would have gasped, at least gasped, with fear. She seemed not even to notice either his cutthroat panache or his beautiful skill. Instead she leaned forward to examine the roadside where a local rail line ran unfenced. "Slow down now. It's about a couple of hundred meters. This side. There. You see the sign?"

"This really is better," he said after a while, showing surprise at her having known what she was about. "Hardly anything here."

"When we turn onto the canal road there will be trucks, but not yet. There's a roundabout up here. Not yet though."

She could not remember just how many of the exits from the circle they must pass to come due north for the new bridge and this so worried her that she bit her lip fiercely. But all was well, Phillippe seemed to know by instinct so quickly did he follow her directions.

"Is this the Danube?" he asked as they swept up over the bridge.

"The canal. We don't cross the river. Hell!"

A monstrous double truck maneuvered across the roadway, backing into a gateway hardly wider than itself.

"Now, now," cautioned Phillippe, but he opened his window

and shouted at the harassed driver up in the cabin, who shouted back.

"Oh God," she muttered. "This is taking forever. Why did I ever go out! I'll never leave the house again as long as I live without leaving a note for him."

It never even occurred to her that Rolf might not have time to go to the flat. She knew he would be there. As if on purpose the truck inched forward again, unsure of the angle to the gateposts. The second time he got it right, the driver, and twisting his long-haired head to see the obstacle he trundled his vast mechanism back off the road with a deep rumble. The instant there was room Phillippe put a finger on the horn and slipped past with a hand's breadth to spare.

"What your father will say to me if I scratch his enamel," he said, thoroughly enjoying himself.

"To hell with the enamel. Just don't let's get arrested. We'll have to slow down in a minute."

The last few minutes were of a tension, flicking in and out of narrow turnings with cars and people swarming everywhere as if the road belonged to them, that she thought the pressure in her midriff would actually make her sick. She was, too, ashamed of her bullying tone to Phillippe that issued in that hoydenish slanginess, that attitude to every other road user which would have condemned anyone else if she had overheard it. He could not know, Phillippe or anyone else for that matter, what a dreadful time the last few days had been for Rolf and the last thing in the world she could have done at that moment was to say anything, even by implication, that might indicate a real and sufficient ground for her harsh irritation.

Knowing nothing of the processes of the law and still less of military law, she imagined Rolf to have been brutally interrogated, even incarcerated, an expression she had been using to herself. The cinema and sensational fiction were bad preceptors of such events and she imagined something in the nature of jackboots and blinding lights. That the chief object of those shadowy figures might be, above all, to avoid any further scandal while still discovering any offshoots of the activities of Lensky and his friends was something too inverted for her to consider. Neither was it within her small experience to weight against Rolf's ill-fated friendship his otherwise unexceptionable career, his known stable character, his popularity or, more than any other factor, the knowledge of human nature that grows in men who spend their lives dealing with it. The civil policeman who so frightened her knew within minutes that Rolf was quite simply not the kind of young man who becomes involved in conspiracy. And the military men who had lived with him for three years knew it even better. They thought of him perhaps as somewhat of a simpleton but in the circumstances that not unjust opinion was all to Rolf's advantage.

Leona thought of Rolf as returning distraught, exhausted, battered morally if not physically. As possibly under duress of some kind, of snatching a narrow opportunity from surveillance in order to see her. These shifting doubts were dispersed during the time she was with her mother and Alain and the presence of Anna Forstmann must have exposed their crudeness if she had thought to examine them with reference to Rolf's mother. But she did not think of it; her imaginings existed compartmentalized by her lack of experience.

"Here we are," she cried, coming out of her abstraction. "The next turning. The third doorway."

As the great car silently ceased moving she jumped out and leaned forward at the door in the act of being about to slam it.

"Listen, Phillippe, I'll thank you properly tomorrow. I have to fly now."

"How do I get back to civilization, before you rush off?"

"Oh. Turn right in the next street here, where we came. It's the main street to a bridge. From the bridge you can see a flickering light on a tall building, and that's the Ring. All right?"

She was gone, running, and disappeared into the house door.

What a tartar, thought the driver. He could see traffic lights and lit a cigarette, waiting for them to change so that he could illegally turn in the connecting roadway. I feel sorry for the man. She's got her father's temper, that one.

She raced up the stairs at such a pace that she was obliged to pause on the third flight. She could feel her heart thudding like a dynamo as she hurried to the corner of the corridor.

No light, she screamed inside her head, he's had to go back already. And her feet dragged with the disappointment and the sensation of letting Rolf down. The rickety old door was on the latch but in the cloud of reaction she did not notice that. It was dark inside but she felt immediately the presence of Rolf's being, before she took in the bulk of his back, turned toward her. She put out her hand, still quivering, to search for the light switch which, as usual, did not work at once. He heard that and swung around. As the meager light came on she saw his face before it changed. She saw loss and bitter humiliation, yes, she saw, or perhaps the perception of his feeling went into her direct from him. And in that instant, with a holy fear, she felt her whole responsibility. Without the sureness of her being there, of her being turned toward him and entirely concentrated on him, he was destroyed. He was now as dependent as she was herself, resisting it but in the moment of not finding her being forced to admit it. He knew now what she had taken for granted from the first, from the moment in the snow-reflected dim bedroom of their first night together when he came from the window toward her.

They did not speak, there was nothing to be said and they were not able to speak. After a while they moved forward into the living room and sat down, exhausted, on the couch. Rolf leaned back and she with him. They rolled over and lay there, clutched together, silent and motionless, their arms around each other under their heavy coats and their heads pressed convulsively together. In the next flat a jaunty little tune signaled the children's program and the prattling voices of puppets made an enclosure for their quiet.